PRIMAL
FURY

BOOKS BY JACK SILKSTONE

PRIMAL Origin
PRIMAL Unleashed
PRIMAL Vengeance
PRIMAL Fury

P R I M A L
FURY

JACK SILKSTONE

THOMAS & MERCER

Published by Thomas & Mercer, Seattle

www.apub.com

Amazon, the Amazon logo, and Thomas & Mercer are trademarks of Amazon.com, Inc., or its affiliates.

ISBN-13: 9781477818176
ISBN-10: 1477818170

Cover design by Cyanotype Book Architects

Library of Congress Control Number: 2013919399

Printed in the United States of America

PROLOGUE

OSAKA, JAPAN

The girl was delivered at 1949 hours, exactly one minute early. A curt knock at the apartment door signaled her arrival. The client, short and Japanese, was dressed in a Western-style pinstriped suit. He put his whiskey down on a side table, strolled deliberately to the door, glanced through the peephole, and opened it.

She was everything the website had promised: barely eighteen, beautiful, and Caucasian. Her classic Eastern European features were perfect—blonde hair, high cheekbones, and crystal-blue eyes.

"Make yourself comfortable," he said, gesturing toward the king-size bed.

She smiled nervously and stepped into the room.

"Sit." He pointed to the bed as he took off his jacket and tie, draping them over the back of the sofa.

She sat down, folded her hands, and looked around the apartment. Clearly she was new to this. That excited him even more.

He removed his shirt as he watched her. "You speak English?" he asked, dropping his pants and removing the belt.

"A little." Her accent was thick. Her voice trembled.

"Good." He crossed the room and stood in front of her in his underwear, the belt in his hands. "Now show me."

She rose nervously and dropped the brown coat she was wearing onto the floor, revealing a lacy black bra, matching French-cut underwear, and sheer black stockings.

He ran his eyes over her firm body, a buyer assessing horseflesh. She shuffled nervously when his gaze lingered on her breasts. The lace bra was a size too small and flesh strained against the sheer fabric.

"Take it all off," he ordered.

She reached around behind her back and unclipped the bra. It dropped to the floor. She placed her fingers under the elastic of her underwear and paused nervously, giving him a pleading look.

A loud crack pierced the silence of the room as his open hand made contact with her face. He'd thrown his entire weight behind the blow and it sent her sprawling across the room. She screamed as he dragged her onto the bed by her hair and threw her face down. The scream stopped abruptly as he looped the belt around her neck and pulled it tight. With his other hand he tore her underwear off and proceeded to rape her from behind.

Less than fifty meters away, in another room of the apartment block, two Japanese men watched the encounter. A bank of screens showed the digital feed from the apartment and five other places like it. Racks of hard drives stored the video being captured by the hidden cameras. The men responsible for monitoring the equipment sat with their feet on the desk, drinking cans of soda and eating prawn crackers, watching a game of local baseball, and occasionally glancing at the screens.

"Room five is getting a little rough," observed the younger of the men.

His companion leaned forward to look. "He's banging that blonde bitch hard."

On the screen the client was continuing to rape the girl, pulling on the belt with both hands as she clawed at it with her fingers.

"Lucky son of a bitch," the younger man said as he looked back to the baseball game. "Do you think the Tigers will get up?"

"No chance."

For another five minutes the two men watched the baseball game without glancing at the monitors. Finally the older man looked across to see that the client was finished. He reached across for the phone to call up the girl's minder.

"She's not moving," his partner said. The client was dressing but the girl lay sprawled on the bed, motionless.

"You sure?"

"You'd better call Masateru."

The other man nodded, punched a speed dial on the phone, and studied the screen again. "Hello, *waka-gashira*, one of the girls looks like she is dead." He listened for a moment before replying. "Yes of course, we will see you in a few minutes." He placed the phone down and turned to his colleague. "He's coming up. You stay here and stop the video when we enter the room."

He opened a drawer in the desk and pulled out a chrome snub-nosed revolver. Stuffing the pistol into the back of his pants, he left the room. It was a short walk down the plush carpeted corridor to the elevators. He only needed to wait a few seconds before the elevator chimed and the doors slid open to reveal Masateru. He was a handsome man in his thirties, medium build, and dressed in an impeccable light-gray suit, crisp white shirt, and dark tie. He wore his jet-black hair slicked back in the style of 1930s gangsters.

"Which room?" he asked.

"Number five." The Yakuza henchman gave a sharp bow.

Masateru led them down the corridor, pausing outside the room before rapping his knuckles against the door. He reached into his jacket, retrieved a swipe card, slapped it against the receiver, and pushed the door open.

The client was fully clothed and standing in the center of the room. Masateru stepped forward and stood in silence, slowly turning his head to take in the situation. His eyes paused on the girl on the bed. She was on her back, naked, her head turned toward them. Her once pretty face was distorted in death, her tongue poking out through blue lips, her eyes wide open and bulging.

He reached into his jacket, took out a pack of slim cigarettes, and extracted one. He turned to the now pale client and offered him one as well. The man declined and Masateru lit his with the snap of a silver lighter. "It would seem that we have a situation." He sucked heavily on the cigarette.

"I didn't mean to kill her . . . She, it was—"

"Yes, you did." Masateru let the cigarette bounce in the corner of his mouth as he spoke. "And why shouldn't you? She is, was, a *gaijin* and you are Japanese. Just like it is your right to violate her body, it is your right to take her life should you choose to." He inhaled deeply and walked across to a small table to ash his cigarette in a vase. "The problem here is not your right to kill this bitch. The problem is you have destroyed something that does not belong to you."

"Of course, of course." The man nodded in agreement. "I would be happy to pay for your property." He pulled a thick wallet out of his jacket. "How much extra do I need to pay?"

Masateru reached into his pocket for his phone and punched numbers into the keypad. He looked up and showed the man the screen. "You owe seven million yen."

The client's jaw dropped. "That's crazy. How can an uneducated foreign whore be worth that?"

"She was young, my friend. Think of all the years of fucking we won't get out of her now." He shrugged. "I tell you what, for that price I'll let you keep the body. You can have another go."

The older man turned on Masateru in anger. "You little shit! Do you know who I am?" He puffed out his chest and flashed his police badge. "I could end your little operation here with one phone call. You could spend the rest of your time in prison as a plaything for the Africans. Do not think for one second that you can intimidate me, you Yakuza lapdog!"

Masateru wiped the man's spittle from the lapels of his jacket and calmly stubbed out his cigarette on the table. "There seems to be a misunderstanding. If you cannot pay then I am sure another arrangement can be made. We are not unreasonable people. I mean, it's not like we need to release the video of tonight's activities to the media . . . Do we?"

The police officer opened his mouth to reply but thought better of it.

Masateru nodded. "No, I think it would be in everyone's best interest that you reach an agreement with the *oyabun*." Masateru dialed a number on his phone, waited for it to ring, and passed it across. "I think you will find him very reasonable."

"Superintendent Supervisor Tanaka . . ." The voice on the other end of the phone was as smooth as velvet, the voice of an experienced statesman. "It's a pleasure to talk to you. I hope that you enjoyed your evening?"

"Very much, thank you, although there was one minor problem." Tanaka turned his back on Masateru and walked over to the windows that looked out over the city of Osaka.

"Yes, I am aware of the situation, Superintendent. Rest assured that you can count on me to make the problem disappear. Consider this a one-time gift from me to you. In the future if you want to kill *gaijin* you will have to pay for the privilege like everyone else. However, I would recommend that you attend one of our other facilities for this pleasure. You will find the price more appealing."

"Thank you, *oyabun*." The senior police officer bobbed his head. "What about the tapes, the video footage. Will it be destroyed?"

"I will excuse the death of a whore and I will wipe your slate clean."

Tanaka glanced at the girl lying lifeless on the bed. "What do you want from me?"

"Please, Superintendent. I do not want anything from you other than to call you a friend."

"That's all?"

"Yes, you will find that being a friend of the Mori-Kai Yakuza comes with great benefits, the least of which you have experienced tonight. We are honored to call you a friend."

"No, *oyabun*, the honor is mine."

The head of the Osaka Regional Police Bureau handed the phone back to Masateru. "What happens now?" he asked.

"There is a car waiting for you downstairs. It will drop you back at your office. Or perhaps you would like some more entertainment?"

He glanced at the girl's body. "No, I think I've had enough for tonight. Perhaps I'll try one of your other offerings later in the week."

"Very good." Masateru followed the policeman out of the room and into the corridor. He spoke to the henchman waiting outside the door. "Call the cleaners and have the whore dumped at sea."

CHAPTER 1

CROATIA TO HUNGARY

The minibus nosed its way onto the car ferry that was tethered against the concrete wharf. Two men swung the gates shut behind it and the boat chugged its way out onto the Drava River. It was late at night and most of the twelve girls on the bus were sleeping. Only Kalista peered out of a window, watching the men guide the craft across the slow-moving river that cut the border between Croatia and Hungary.

She was the elder of two sisters, her seventeen-year-old sibling Karla snuggled next to her in a thick jacket to protect her from the cold. Tall, beautiful, and blonde, both girls had won a local beauty contest to earn their place on the bus. Men from Hungary had come to the village and run selections before awarding the girls the opportunity to leave their families and head for the bright lights of Budapest. There, they were told, they would learn the skills of modeling before gracing the catwalks of Paris and Milan.

It had been young Karla's idea to enter the competition. She was by far the bolder of the pair. Some would have even called her reckless, always the first to throw herself into any adventure, forever trying to escape the drudgery of village life. Physically, the sisters were almost identical—the same high cheekbones, blue eyes, and full lips. They had long been the most popular girls in the village. Boys would whistle as they rode past on bikes, long tanned legs flashing as they pedaled furiously, Karla always racing to be first.

The bus shuddered as the ferry nudged up against the wharf on the Hungarian side of the river. Karla murmured and nuzzled her head against her sister's shoulder. The other girls on the bus did not stir; like the sisters, they were all aspiring models, plucked from obscurity by the Hungarians. The bus drove off the ferry and up the bank to a border security post. There, the driver and a modeling agency representative got off, the second man carrying a large envelope.

"What's going on?" Karla mumbled.

"Nothing, just the border crossing. We'll need to show our passports." Kalista rummaged around in her backpack but stopped when the two men got back on the bus. The driver jumped behind the wheel, the bus started off again, and they drove through the glaring lights of the security checkpoint into Hungary.

✫✫✫

"Wake up, wake up!" A man's voice jolted the girls from their slumber.

Kalista's head snapped to the front of the bus, where a rough-looking man with a heavy beard was standing. He glared at them with the intensity of a wild animal.

"Get up and get off the bus!" he screamed in English.

All the passengers were stirring and one of the younger girls burst into tears. Kalista grabbed her sister's arm and backpack and jostled into the aisle. They were the first off the bus and into the floodlit courtyard that greeted them. More bearded men stood at the edges of the open area. Karla rubbed the sleep from her eyes and they grew wide as she noticed the large guns the men carried. A dog could be heard barking in the background.

All the girls spilled off the bus gathering in a huddle on the cobblestones, under the watchful eye of the heavily bearded brute

8

and the guards. Once they were all off the bus he yelled at them again. "Get into line, whores."

The girls stared at him in shock.

"I said get in line, bitches. Are you fucking deaf?"

Kalista stood defiantly. The guard moved forward and grabbed her by the arm. She lashed out, driving her foot into the man's crotch. He grunted, doubling over, and she hit him in the back of the head with her backpack.

"Karla, run!" she screamed, grabbing her sister by the arm. They sprinted around the bus and down the driveway toward the estate's gates. The metal gates were closed, flanked by tall stone walls.

The girls were fast, used to physical exertion on their father's farm. They covered the distance in seconds. Spurred on by the sound of a barking dog, they leaped onto the gate and started climbing.

Kalista felt a searing pain in the back of her leg as she was torn from the wrought iron. She screamed in agony as the Alsatian attack dog savaged her leg, pulling her down. She hit the ground with a thump and the dog bit her arm, its fangs tearing into her flesh and meeting bone.

Karla leaped from the gate and landed on the dog. It yelped in pain, released Kalista's arm, and backed away snarling. As it launched forward to attack again, strong hands pulled it up short. The handler wrestled the dog away, disappearing into the darkness.

"You fucking idiots. Look at her, she's worthless now." The bearded thug yanked Karla off her sister and bent over the wounded girl. The dog had mauled her arm and leg, leaving deep wounds that wept blood. The girl moaned, concussed from falling off the gate and in shock. "Together they would have been worth a fortune. Now this one is worthless. May as well put the bitch down." He turned away in disgust, heading back up the driveway to the stone manor and the other girls.

One of the guards scooped the wounded girl off the ground and carried her toward the manor. Another grasped Karla by the arm, dragging her sobbing to an adjacent building. The wooden barn once housed horses but now it was a basic dormitory. He pushed her through the double doors into a large room filled with beds. The doors slammed shut behind her, and a bolt slid across, locking them in. All the girls from the bus were in the room, huddled in twos and threes on the metal frame beds.

"Where are we?" one of them asked.

"What's going to happen to us?"

"Where's Kalista?"

The chorus of questions continued until the lights were turned off. The girls wept in their beds, terrified of what the next day would bring. Karla sobbed uncontrollably. It had been her idea to try this modeling contest and now her older sister was badly hurt.

At precisely seven o'clock the next morning, the doors opened and a woman entered. She was a brunette, petite and pretty, with the body of a dancer. The woman gathered the girls onto two of the beds and spoke to them in English, a language most of them understood. Karla interpreted for the few who didn't.

"I know most of you are very scared. You don't understand what is happening." She paused for Karla to translate. "My name is Aurelia, and if you follow my instructions and do as you are told things here will not be so bad. These men will not harm you. You will be taken from here to another place where you will be given to other men. If you listen to me and learn, then these men will also treat you well. They will lavish you with gifts and you will live like princesses. If you try to escape, you will die. It is that simple. Now we will eat breakfast and then we will start with your lessons."

She led them out of the dormitory and across to the manor, where the girls would be fed and trained. They glanced at the high stone wall that surrounded the estate and at the heavily armed guards patrolling the grounds.

As they filed in through the door to the dining hall, Aurelia pulled Karla to one side. "Your sister will live," she whispered, "but she won't be coming with you. I will look after her but you need to focus on yourself now."

Karla nodded and followed the other girls to the line for food. Tears welled in her eyes as she picked up a bowl of watery gruel and took her place on the long wooden table. They ate in silence.

CHAPTER 2

THE MANOR, SOMOGY COUNTY, HUNGARY

Over the next week, Aurelia prepared the girls for their new lives. She taught them how to apply makeup and how to dress, walk, and entertain powerful men. She provided them with a wealth of advice, all of the tricks she had learned in her days as a professional dancer, including pieces of information that would help make their life in sexual slavery a little more bearable.

"Are they ready?" the thickly bearded Gusztáv asked. He was responsible for ensuring the girls were prepared before they were shipped off to the crime syndicate's headquarters for auction. He regularly summoned Aurelia to his rooms to update him, and occasionally for her to service his more personal needs.

Aurelia was dressing in the corner of his bedroom. "Are they ever ready? What woman could ever be ready for this?"

Gusztáv lay sprawled on his bed, naked except for a pair of shorts. His muscular frame was covered in tattoos; dragons and other mythical creatures wound their way around his arms and over his shoulders onto his hairy chest. "Deep down inside, every woman is a whore. These girls were born ready; you just polish them up a little—and we are smart enough to make money from it."

Aurelia watched him with barely concealed hatred as he hunted in the drawer of an antique bedside table for a cigar. The bruises on her neck would be visible for days. She took her only solace in knowing that as long as he found pleasure in abusing her, the girls would be less likely to feel his rage. She might not be able to protect them once they left the manor, but at least here they were safe.

"Their photos are done." She took a USB drive from her handbag and threw it onto the bed.

"Good, we can ship them off early. Maybe András will give me a bonus." He found a cigar and fumbled on his side table for a cutter.

"What about Kalista? What will happen to her?" She walked across to the table on the other side of the bed and picked up the cigar cutter.

"Kalista? Who the fuck is Kalista?" He snatched the implement from her hands and snipped the end of his cigar.

She handed him a lighter from the same table. "The girl who was injured."

"Oh yes, dog-food girl." He lit the cigar and puffed a foul-smelling cloud of smoke into the room. "If she lives, I will sell her. If she dies, then the dogs can finish what they started."

Aurelia's eyes fell on the handgun that occupied the same table as the cigar cutter and the lighter. How easy it would be to take it and shoot this devil dead in his bed.

She sat down on the bed. "Where do the girls go from here?"

He took the cigar from his mouth and gave her a look. "I've told you before, Aurelia, ask questions like that and you will find out. You might be a little long in the tooth, but some Arab with an anal fetish will still pay good money for you. Then what would happen to your sick mother, hey? You should be thankful that I'm so generous. Now get the hell out of my sight."

Aurelia nodded and made for the door. She opened it, then turned back to face him. "My mother . . . do I still have your permission to visit her this afternoon?"

He puffed another cloud of smoke into the air. "Only because you still fuck like you enjoy it. Now go!"

After she left the room, Gusztáv picked up the phone by the bed. "Aurelia is allowed to go to the village but have someone keep an eye on her. That bitch is asking too many questions."

He slammed the phone into its cradle and turned his attention back to his cigar. He puffed another cloud and stared at the door, deep in thought. After a few moments, he picked up the phone again. "Load up the bitches. I want them on the road to the castle in an hour."

CHAPTER 3

SOMOGY COUNTY, HUNGARY

Aurelia rode the four miles from the manor to the village on her bicycle. Despite the crisp afternoon air the journey was pleasant and improved her dark mood. With every turn of the pedals the feeling of despair lifted ever so slightly. She was riding toward hope, not just for her but for the twelve girls she had left behind.

She continued down the tree-lined road as it entered the village of Hencse, passing between the houses that lined it on both sides. This was as far as she usually went. Her hometown was the longest distance the syndicate let her travel these days. As she passed the last house of the village she stood up, pushing harder on the pedals of the old bike.

Two miles north of her home village was the township of Kadarkút. Five times the size of Hencse, it was a bustling rural town of nearly three thousand. It was less likely she would be recognized here.

She rode to the city center, where a stone lion stood guard in a traffic circle. She passed a row of flagpoles and a memorial before turning into the parking lot of a tourist information center. She leaned her bike against a picket fence and walked quickly into the gardens adjoining the tourist building.

She spotted Kurtz immediately, a tall blond man sitting on a garden bench with a smile on his face like the Cheshire cat's.

"Wilhelm, I was scared you wouldn't be here." She wrapped her arms around him and buried her face into his chest.

"I gave you my word; why wouldn't I be here?" He spoke English with a heavy German accent.

Aurelia pulled away from him, tears running down her cheeks as they sat together on the bench.

"He did this to you, didn't he?" Kurtz pulled back her hair to reveal the bruises on her neck.

She shrugged his hand away and brushed her hair forward to cover the marks. "They're all brutes. They treat the girls no better than animals."

"How many girls are there?"

"Twelve. I have their photos like you asked." She reached into her pocket and pulled out a USB stick identical to the one she had given Gusztáv. "There are photos on there of all the girls except one. She was attacked by a dog and won't be sold."

"They set a dog on her? Is she going to be OK?" The PRIMAL operative made a mental note to expect guard dogs at the manor.

"I'm not sure. She's getting sicker. I've done everything I can but they won't let a doctor see her. I'm worried she's going to die."

"We won't let that happen, OK?" Kurtz reached into his jacket and pulled out a plastic blush container. "But first I need you to do something that's very important. Put this on the vehicle that they load the girls in. It has a magnet in it. All you need to do is slip it underneath and it will stick."

She nodded and took the device from him, slipping it into her bag. "When are you going to come for us?"

"As soon as the girls are gone, I'll come for you. Once they've reached their destination, another team will free them. In forty-eight hours it will all be over."

"And I'll be with you." She leaned in and kissed him. He wrapped his arms around her.

"Hey, lover boy, we've got a problem, *da*." A tiny speaker in the German's ear interrupted with a Russian-accented voice. "Not completely sure but I think someone followed your girl."

Kurtz pulled away from Aurelia and quickly scanned the park. "Where? Who?"

"There is a man with hoodie looking at her bike," said Aleks.

"*Scheisse.* Maybe he's just a cyclist. Can you check it out?"

"*Da*, you move to the other side of the park. I will deal with it and then pick you both up in the Audi."

"Moving now." Kurtz took Aurelia by the hand and led her swiftly away from the bench, toward the other side of the park.

★★★

On the opposite side of the street, Aleks started an Audi station wagon and pulled into the parking lot. As he got out, the man who had been looking at Aurelia's bike started walking away, heading to the tourist center.

"Hey, you," the big Russian called out in English. With his beard and bald head, Aleks knew he was an intimidating sight.

The young man kept walking.

"Yes, you! Hey, you want to buy bike?" He caught up to the startled youth, who reached into the pocket of his jacket.

Aleks moved fast, clamping one hand around the teenager's neck and the other around his wrist. "Nice and slow, yes?"

The young man struggled, trying to pull a phone from his pocket. Aleks slammed his forehead into the youth's face, knocking him unconscious. He laid the limp body gently on the gravel and examined the phone.

At that moment a black four-wheel drive screamed into the

parking lot and skidded to a halt. Through the windshield Aleks could make out an assault rifle in the hands of the front-seat passenger. At least two other men rode in the back.

"We've got company," he transmitted over his communications interface as he drew his pistol.

The HK45 barked twice, shattering the front window of the four-wheel drive. An AK appeared in a side window, thrust in the Russian's direction. Aleks sprinted into the tourist center as a barrage of 7.62mm slugs slammed into it. He ran through the flimsy structure and out the back door as more gunfire tore through the building. The sole occupant, the attendant, did not need to be prompted. He took cover behind the counter.

"I've got one vehicle with multiple shooters," Aleks radioed Kurtz as he ran through the memorial gardens at the back of the building.

"Good to hear you're making so many friends, Aleks. We're near the church across the gardens. Can you get to us with the car?"

"*Nyet*, the car is not an option. Coming to you now," he said, breathing heavily. For his size he moved swiftly, leaping over the waist-high fence that separated the gardens from the cemetery and church.

Bullets whistled through the air and smacked into the side of the church. Aleks hunkered down behind a headstone and fired off a magazine in the direction of the shooters. He reloaded the HK, pulled a distraction grenade from inside his jacket, yanked the pin, and lobbed it into the gardens.

It exploded with a loud boom, sending a cloud of smoke and sparks into the air. Using the blast for cover, he sprinted to the steps of the church.

Kurtz was waiting in the doorway, his own pistol drawn. He provided covering fire as Aleks entered, then pulled the doors shut and slid a solid wooden beam across to lock it.

"Little early in the relationship for a wedding, hey, lover boy?" Aleks quipped.

Aurelia was standing deeper in the church, her eyes wide with fear.

"Shut up and get me something to barricade this, *Dummkopf*."

"What brings you to house of God?" The church's Orthodox priest approached them with his hands up, speaking calmly in Hungarian-accented English.

"We seek refuge from evil men, father," Aleks replied, flashing an Interpol identification card before hefting one of the heavy pews toward the door. Kurtz helped him wedge it against the wood.

The priest disappeared through a side door into the vestibule and returned moments later with an ancient-looking double-barreled shotgun and bandolier of shells.

As he moved to secure the other doors in the church, Kurtz gave the priest a quizzical look.

"Someone must defend the church," the priest said as he cracked open the weapon and dropped a pair of cartridges into the chambers. He stood protectively over Aurelia. "I spent a little time in the army when I was a younger man."

"There's a door at the back, down the stairs. It's locked," Kurtz yelled, now at the rear of the building.

There was a heavy thump on the front door and Aleks fired two shots from his pistol into the wood. They failed to penetrate. "GET DOWN!" he screamed as an AK barked and rounds punched through the wood, tearing it into splinters.

The doors shuddered as a heavy weight slammed into them.

There was yelling from the other side. Aleks crouched against the thick stone wall, listening intently as the criminals debated how to gain entry into the church. He leaped to his feet, shouting, "Grenade, GO, GO!"

Kurtz grabbed Aurelia and with the priest they ran to the back and continued down a flight of stairs that led to a metal door.

The gangsters at the front had wedged a hand grenade up against the door. It detonated and the blast shattered the heavy beam and drove the bench backward, creating a gap almost two feet wide. One of the men fired an AK through the gap before ducking into the church.

Aleks squatted near the top of the stairs. Cautiously he raised his head and spotted the man. He pulled the trigger of his pistol. The big slug caught its target just above the ear and the man's head exploded, spraying a stained glass window with brain matter. Another assailant fired through the entrance, blasting chunks out of the pulpit.

"Where does this go?" Kurtz asked the priest, indicating the back door.

"Outside, over the bridge to my house." The priest had an arm around Aurelia.

More gunfire smashed into the walls above them. Aleks was forced to fire blindly over the top of the stairs. "One dead, two shooting."

Kurtz slid back the metal bolt of the door and peered out. It was all clear. "Get her to your house. I'll cover my partner and we'll follow you."

The priest nodded and grabbed Aurelia by the hand. As the two of them dashed from the doorway to the bridge, a gunman appeared at the corner of the church. He fired from the hip and hit the priest, knocking him to the ground. Aurelia screamed and kept running.

Time stood still for a second as the sights of Kurtz's pistol lined up with the gunman's head. He could make out the color of the man's eyes as they blinked in slow motion. The HK roared, and a round tore through the criminal's face.

Aleks came outside and stepped past Kurtz, kicking the door closed as he changed the magazine on his pistol. He spotted the wounded priest and ran to his side. Kurtz sprinted toward the bridge, following the terrified Aurelia.

The scream of a high-revving engine announced the four-wheel drive as it burst through a hedge and sped toward Aurelia.

Kurtz was caught in the open. He dived for cover as a burst of gunfire stitched the ground next to him. The car barely slowed as Aurelia was grabbed and forced into the backseat. With a roar it punched back through the hedge and disappeared.

Kurtz fired off a few rounds but it was too late. Aurelia was gone.

Aleks was kneeling beside the priest, checking his wounds, when the last gunman stepped out of the back door of the church. The man took aim with his AK before an ear-splitting boom cut him in half, the priest discharging both barrels of his twelve-gauge.

Kurtz barely registered the threat, focused only on the direction the vehicle had taken Aurelia. "Fuck, fuck, fuck!" he fumed. "Aleks, we need to get to the car now." He started off toward the tourist center.

The priest was sitting up with the smoking twelve-gauge held in his hands. Aleks held a field dressing against the older man's hip.

"Your friend needs you," said the priest. "I will be fine."

The sound of police sirens could be heard in the distance.

Aleks grasped the priest's hand. "Thank you, father."

"No need," said the priest, grimacing in pain. "But come see me again later. For confession."

CHAPTER 4

They had parked the Audi in a thicket of trees a few miles out of town. Sunlight was fading and outside the car Aleks lit a gas burner to brew a pot of coffee. Kurtz had a laptop and a small collapsible satellite dish set up on the hood of the station wagon.

He activated a program to establish a satellite uplink to his organization's headquarters, located on an island in the southwest Pacific. A bar showed the progress of the connection, which crawled along slowly, then halted.

Unable to establish a connection

"*Scheisse!*" He slammed the lid of the laptop shut and punched the hood of the Audi. He needed to talk to PRIMAL's head of operations and he wanted it to be face-to-face.

"Here." Aleks handed him a cup of coffee and reopened the laptop, studying it intently. He frowned, pressed a few keys, moved the dish slightly, and grinned. "See, you laugh at big stupid Russian with hands like bear, but now we have a secure connection."

Kurtz slapped his partner on the shoulder and took his place in front of the screen. He activated a secure video-conference dial-in and waited.

"Kurtz, how ya doing, bud?"

Vance, PRIMAL's director of operations, was an imposing African American with a shaved head. Kurtz thought he bore a striking resemblance to the actor Laurence Fishburne.

"The girl was compromised. The syndicate captured her," Kurtz said, his voice flat and emotionless.

"How?"

"Not sure. She had a tail; they suspected her of something."

"What about you and Aleks?"

"They saw us, we killed three, but at least two got away."

"Shit!" There was a pause. "Did you get the information we needed?"

"No, she didn't know where the girls were being taken. I gave her a tracker but there's no chance of her planting that now. The girls are probably being moved as we speak."

"So are you OK?"

"We're fine. But they're going to kill her."

"We don't know that yet."

"Yes, we do, Vance. They'll think she's talked to the police. She could already be dead."

"Yep, and you've been compromised. So the best course of action is to get you as far away from that location as possible. Go to the safe house in Budapest. This phase of the mission is dead."

"But the girl . . ."

"There's no argument here, Kurtz. You're to exfil now. I'm not risking your lives for one source. I need every asset I have to take down this network and that includes you two. Do you understand?"

"*Ja,* I understand." Kurtz fought to keep the anger from his voice.

"Good. Now Bishop and Saneh are inbound to a staging location in the Ukraine. One of Chua's Blades has infiltrated the sales component of the network. He's vouched for Bishop and it looks like we might be able to get an invite to the next auction. If we're lucky that's where they'll have taken the girls."

Chua, PRIMAL's chief of intelligence, ran a global network of deep-cover agents, or Blades. He had been working leads on a highly secretive sex-trafficking group for almost six months now. His Russian Blade Ivan had started doing business with the Hungarian trafficking syndicate. It was Ivan's work that had led Aleks and Kurtz to rural Hungary and subsequently to contact Aurelia, their first inside link to the syndicate. He had also been the first to identify the potential link to Japan and a possible source in the Japanese police.

"What happens then?" Kurtz asked. "Are we going to pick up the girls or are we going to abandon them like Aurelia?"

"Jesus, Kurtz. This is bigger than a handful of girls. We're trying to take down an entire operation. We're not playing around here. We're going to find the head and chop it off. Now get your ass on the road. I'll check in with you tomorrow."

Kurtz nodded.

"Aleks, you there?"

"*Da*. I mean, yes."

"Make sure this crazy son of a bitch gets to Hungary ASAP, you got me?"

"Yes, I got you."

"Good. Bunker out." PRIMAL headquarters closed down the video link.

Kurtz stared silently at the screen with clenched fists. Aleks watched him without saying anything.

"You heard what he said, Aleks. We need to go." Kurtz folded the satellite dish up and slid it in a bag with the laptop. He opened the passenger door to the Audi and climbed in.

Aleks put away the gas stove and coffeepot, placing them in the back of the station wagon, which was already piled high with luggage. An onlooker may have assumed that it was ready for a holiday. However, the ordinary-looking suitcases were packed with state-of-the-art weapons and equipment. Aleks contemplated the arsenal for a few seconds before shutting the trunk and getting into the driver's seat.

The Audi's V8 rumbled to life and they started up the dirt track that led them back to the main highway. Aleks turned on the headlights and leaned across to activate the GPS. He tapped the screen a few times until a blinking dot appeared on the screen.

"The tracker looks like it's stationary. Maybe we could pick her up on the way?"

Kurtz looked across at Aleks. "You mean it? You'd do that for me? Even after Vance ordered us not to?"

"I know she means a lot to you. Vance will not know." He paused for a second. "Plus, you are my best friend. How could I not do this?"

CHAPTER 5

CASTLE LORAN, EASTERN HUNGARY

"Look, it's a castle!" one of the girls on the bus cried out, startling the others.

Karla peered out through the window as the bus slowed. Sure enough, looming above them was the hulking shape of a medieval fortress, complete with a moat and battlements.

As they approached the stone structure, she tipped back her head, trying to get a better look. It was far more intimidating than the manor they had just come from. She had never seen anything like it; the huge walls were lit up by floodlights, making it look more like a sinister prison than the home of a charming prince from a fairy tale. A shiver ran up her spine as they drove through the gateway and into the bastion.

"It's not a castle," she murmured. "It's a prison."

"Off the bus." The assault rifle–wielding thug who issued the order looked like the type of man who would beat them if they failed to comply.

Karla grabbed her backpack and followed the others off the bus. They waited for a few seconds in a courtyard before being marched past a stable filled with expensive cars. She followed the girl in front of her through an archway and up spiraling stairs.

She reached out and touched the stone walls as they climbed. They felt cold and smooth. How many other girls had walked these stairs? With every step it became clearer that escape was not possible.

After at least six flights of stairs they reached a landing. To the side a guard stood in front of a set of heavy doors with a huge dog. It reminded Karla of her older sister. Images of the horrendous wounds on Kalista's arms and legs flashed through her mind and she started to cry. Sobbing, she followed the girl in front as they climbed up another few flights of stairs and headed down a corridor. Another guard directed them in through a heavy wooden door.

There was a clunk as the door was pushed shut behind them, followed by the click of a heavy lock. They were in yet another prison.

The room was large, about the size of a squash court. On each side there were eight wooden beds, each matched to a tall wooden wardrobe.

Karla dropped onto one of the beds and buried her head in her arms, weeping uncontrollably. Many girls did the same, lying on their beds and crying while others wandered around the room, exploring their new surroundings. First, they opened the room's doors and found a bathroom and rudimentary kitchen. Moments later, one of them opened her wardrobe.

"Oh!" the young woman exclaimed as she examined the contents. The other girls gathered around.

The wardrobe was filled with beautiful dresses, hanger after hanger of long, expensive-looking gowns. She pulled open the drawers to reveal lacy underwear, makeup, and an assortment of accessories. At the bottom of the wardrobe was a collection of high-heeled shoes.

Their plight was momentarily forgotten as the girls pulled items from other wardrobes. Even Karla stopped crying and was drawn into the moment. None of them had ever owned clothing like this; in their villages women wore flat shoes and plain clothes.

Before long a few of the girls had discarded their old garments and were laughing and giggling as they pranced around in the new outfits.

None noticed that they were being watched from a corner of the high ceiling, where a camera recorded everything.

CHAPTER 6

THE MANOR, SOMOGY COUNTY, HUNGARY

"Who the fuck are they?" Gusztáv screamed into Aurelia's face. She was tied naked to a chair in the cellar of the manor. Blood pooled on the cobblestones under her, running down her thighs. He had raped her savagely when they first brought her into the makeshift dungeon. "They come into my territory, they kill my men, they turn my woman into a spy, who the fuck are they?"

Aurelia whimpered. Her face was already battered where he had punched her repeatedly, her once beautiful features a bloodied, swollen mess.

"If you don't want to talk, that's up to you." He leaned forward to whisper in her ear. "But if you don't, I'm going to feed you and that Croatian bitch to the dogs."

Tears ran down her cheeks and onto her bare flesh. Her body convulsed in sobs, straining against the ropes holding her to the chair, but still she said nothing.

"Fine, have it your way."

He nodded to the guard in the corner, who handed him a pair of pliers.

"I didn't want to have to do this." Gusztáv locked her hand down with his vicelike grip, trying to force her fingers straight. She struggled, scrunching up her fist. He forced it flat and clamped the pliers onto one of her long fingernails. She screamed in agony as he tore it from her finger, thrashing against the ropes like a woman possessed. Eventually her head slumped forward and she hyperventilated as she wept.

"Tell me who they are and it all stops." Gusztáv caressed her hair as he spoke softly.

She looked up at him with eyes filled with hatred and tears. "They will come for me, you know. It doesn't matter if you kill me because they will still come for me. Then they will kill you all and burn this place to the ground."

"Who are they, Aurelia?"

"Wilhelm is from Interpol. He loves me."

"Interpol?" He took a phone from his pocket and dialed a number. "András, Interpol is sniffing around. We've got to shut down the manor." He paused. "How the hell would I know how they found us? Why don't you ask your friend . . . No, the girls are already on their way to you." He paced the cellar floor. "No, only eleven, one of the blondes was bitten by a dog." He paused as the voice on the other end of the phone became agitated. "The bitch tried to escape. This is not a problem; I will close up here and move to another location, then I will find you more blondes." He put the phone back in his pocket.

"Tell everyone to pack," he told one of his men. "We're leaving."

"What about her?"

"Give her a hit."

The man took a syringe and a length of rubber tube from the wooden table in the corner of the room. He wound the rubber around her upper arm until the veins bulged, then he plunged the needle into her flesh.

Her eyes flew open as the heroin rush hit her.

"It feels good, doesn't it?" whispered Gusztáv as he stroked her hair. "You're lucky, most girls don't get to experience such pleasures." He paused, allowing the drug to take more effect. "You betrayed me, but I forgive you."

She spat in his face, then turned away, already feeling the effects of the drug.

"Stupid whore!" Gusztáv lifted a boot and pushed her chair over. Her head flopped backward, hitting the stone floor with a thud. "Finish the bitch off!"

The mafia henchman had another two syringes filled with heroin ready. He leaned down next to Aurelia and injected them one after the other into her arm.

Gusztáv squatted next to her. "You were a faithful dog for a while at least," he said as her petite frame started to convulse and her breathing grew shallow. "There are far worse ways to die."

As he strode away, his big form growing smaller through Aurelia's slitted eyelids, the building suddenly shuddered, dust falling from the exposed beams on the roof.

"WHAT THE HELL WAS THAT?" he screamed. "Get up there and find out what the hell is going on!"

Aurelia managed to smile despite the heroin's assault on her nervous system. Wilhelm was coming.

CHAPTER 7

Aleks's distraction worked exactly as planned. The two five-gallon gas cans exploded, turning night into day and drawing every set of eyes in the compound to the ball of fire rolling into the sky.

He touched another icon on his iPRIMAL smartphone, setting off two demolition charges. One, prepositioned on the power lines, knocked out the electricity to the building, plunging it into darkness. The other was a frame charge he had placed across the stone wall that surrounded the compound. An avalanche of rock and dust was thrown inward by the violent blast, leaving a door-size gap in the barrier.

As soon as the debris hit the ground Kurtz hefted a MATADOR breaching weapon onto his shoulder and thumbed the trigger. The rocket shot through the newly made gap, across thirty meters of lawn, and slammed into the ancient manor. Its detonation blew a gaping hole in the building.

Kurtz moved through the breach first, his suppressed KRISS submachine gun firmly at his shoulder. He wore jeans and a shirt, his chest covered by an armor plate carrier. His head was encased in a ballistic helmet and attached to it was a pair of the latest-generation multispectral night vision goggles.

Aleks followed in similar attire but carrying a short-barreled version of the heavier-hitting HK417 assault rifle. They moved swiftly through the darkness to the manor. At the front of the compound they could hear men yelling.

The fuel fire at the front gate continued to burn, blowing a thick, acrid smoke across the entire estate. The syndicate's gunmen were going to struggle to see in the dark, let alone through the thick smoke. No such problem for the two PRIMAL operatives: Their goggles displayed a thermal image unhindered by smoke or dust.

Three heat signatures rounded the corner of the manor, two armed men and a dog. The two men moved cautiously, blind without night vision equipment. Aleks lined up his laser and dropped them with a series of suppressed shots from his 417.

The dog was on them a split second later. Snarling, it leaped, fangs bared. Kurtz lifted his arm to protect his throat and the animal clamped onto it. There was a loud snap followed by a bright-blue spark, and the canine dropped to the ground, turned tail, and ran into the darkness yelping hysterically.

"What do you know, it worked!" Having been warned about the dogs by Aurelia, Kurtz had donned a carbon-fiber arm guard with an integrated Taser circuit designed and built by PRIMAL's resident scientist. Tonight had been its first field test.

As they closed in on the two-story manor, Aleks threw a stun grenade through the hole Kurtz had blasted with the rocket launcher. It detonated with an ear-bleeding bang.

Kurtz ducked through the entry point. As he stepped over a body, bright muzzle flashes confronted him and rounds sparked off the walls. Kurtz triggered his laser designator and the KRISS submachine gun sent a stream of heavy slugs down the corridor. The torrent of lead shredded the gunman, smearing his blood across the hall.

Kurtz covered the corridor as his partner came through the breach. Moving in practiced unison they worked their way to the first doorway. It was open and Kurtz led, his more compact submachine gun easier to maneuver in the tight space. He identified three unarmed people in the room as well as the heat signature from a cooktop and ovens. It was the kitchen.

"Three nonhostiles," he whispered into his throat mike.

Aleks was already approaching them. "Get down on the floor; we will not hurt you," he said in English.

It was pitch black in the room and his voice startled the three people. Two dropped to the ground but one of them lunged toward him with a knife. Aleks blocked the blow with his weapon and kicked the assailant across the kitchen. Kurtz finished him off by smashing his KRISS into the side of the man's head, knocking him unconscious. He zip-tied his hands and left him on the floor.

The two remaining staff were terrified. They could see nothing in the darkness, although the noises told the story clear enough.

"Ask them where she is," Kurtz whispered.

Aleks asked in English, then in Russian.

A terrified kitchen hand answered: "In the cellar, end of the hall next to the stairs."

As Kurtz was leaving the room he saw the beam of a flashlight flickering down the corridor. He jumped backward into the kitchen as a hail of gunfire blew shards of stone across the doorway. Calmly he pulled a high-explosive grenade from his vest and flicked it down the hall, sending it skidding along the wooden floorboards.

Terrified yells filled the air.

The grenade detonated with an explosion that shook the walls. Kurtz waited a moment before surveying the damage. It was carnage; two bodies lay crumpled on the floor and a third man was dragging himself away, legs shattered and bleeding. Kurtz put a single shot through the back of the wounded man's head.

They reached the staircase at the end of the hall. Aleks covered the stairs to the next floor. An AK fired blindly from the upper landing and Aleks responded with a burst of his own.

"I'll hold them off, you go get the girl."

Kurtz pushed open the cellar door with his boot. A volley of fire greeted him. He waited as the rounds thudded into the heavy wood. One of the bullets struck the side of his helmet, snapping his head back.

"Son of a bitch!"

"You all good?" asked Aleks as he unleashed another burst of fire into the landing above.

The answer came as Kurtz lobbed a distraction grenade into the cellar. The gunmen fired blindly for a moment, then Kurtz stormed down the stairs, firing his KRISS as he went. A torrent of 230-grain projectiles tore through an upturned table, leaving the two gunmen crouched behind it ripped to shreds.

When Kurtz reached the bottom of the staircase a flash of white light overwhelmed his goggles. Something smashed into his weapon, sending it flying across the room. Another blow slammed his NVGs into his eye sockets.

Kurtz desperately raised an arm to protect himself as his master hand reached for the pistol on his hip.

It was too late. Gusztáv was already on top of him. The Hungarian used the heavy metal flashlight like a club, swinging it wildly in the darkness. He smashed it into the PRIMAL operative's shoulder and Kurtz roared in pain, his hand numbed by the blow. Encouraged by his opponent's anguish, Gusztáv swung again, hitting the other arm.

That was his undoing. The built-in Taser activated, sending a high-voltage blast through the metal flashlight and into his body. Kurtz reeled as a residual charge grounded through him.

"Kurtz, you OK?" called Aleks, still covering the stairs to the upper level.

"No," Kurtz moaned. "I Tasered myself!" He pushed Gusztáv's

limp body onto the floor of the cellar and secured his hands with a set of plasticuffs.

"And they call me the clumsy one. Is the girl there?"

Kurtz tilted his NVGs up, activated the light on the side of his helmet, and scanned the room. The beam fell on the naked flesh of a woman lying on the ground, tied to a chair that had been tipped over. Kurtz dashed across the room. She appeared unconscious and barely recognizable.

"Aurelia!" He pulled out a pair of medical shears, sliced through the rope on the chair, and laid her naked body gently on the side. Aurelia's face was a bloodied mess. A rubber tie remained wrapped around her arm and a syringe lay next to her. He shone the helmet light directly into her eyes: The pupils were fixed and dilated. Her breathing was almost nonexistent, a flutter, her heartbeat the same. He ripped his medical kit from the pouch on his belt. "Stay with me, Aurelia, stay with me." He stuck a miniature heart rate sensor to her chest, synching it with the iPRIMAL on his wrist.

It started beeping angrily. She was flatlining. He pulled an auto-injector from the med pouch and punched it directly into her chest.

The sensor didn't change.

He waited, hoping for a beat as the life-saving chemical stimulated her heart muscles.

Five seconds passed—nothing.

Then ten.

It was too late; the flatline on his combat interface never even flickered. She died on the cold stone floor, clearly a victim of a forced overdose.

Kurtz reacted calmly, taking off his glove and closing her eyes with a gentle hand. He picked his gun off the ground, inserted a new magazine, and slung it on his vest.

Gusztáv regained consciousness when Kurtz's helmet light shone directly into his face. Blood ran down his face into his beard.

"Where are the girls?" Kurtz demanded as he forced the Hungarian up onto his knees.

"Who the fuck are you?" Gusztáv responded in accented English as he squinted into the bright light.

"Where are the girls?" Kurtz repeated himself, his voice devoid of emotion.

"Gone. There's no one here."

Kurtz lifted Gusztáv up and slammed him into the cellar wall. "You're fucking lying. Where's the wounded girl?"

"Dog-food girl?" He grunted. "She's as good as dead." He squinted into the bright helmet light. "Look, if you're police, you're going to get into shit for this. My boss is a big deal around here."

"I'm going to ask you one last time, where are the girls?" Kurtz's voice was hoarse.

"You're already dead, pig. You don't know it yet, but you've fucked with the wrong people. You're going to end up deader than that bitch over there." He spat in the direction of Aurelia's corpse.

Kurtz stared directly into the man's face for a long moment. Then he snapped.

His forefinger went through the handle loop of his Benchmade dagger and he drew it from its sheath behind the pouches on his chest. His other hand reached out and grabbed the flesh-trader by the face.

He punched the knife into Gusztáv's throat, stabbing furiously, driving the blade in and out again and again. The cold steel severed all his major arteries, the point hacking into his spinal cord. Kurtz rammed the blade home one last time, all the way through his spine and out the back of his neck. He wrenched it free and let the body collapse onto the floor.

Gusztáv flopped around on his side like a dying fish. Blood gurgled from his mouth as his legs spasmed. Kurtz left him there in the darkness, dying alongside Aurelia's body.

"Did you find her?" Aleks asked when he returned to the top of the stairs. "Where is she?"

Kurtz continued up the stairs to the second floor. "They killed her," was all he said.

Working as a pair, it took them another ten minutes to clear the upper floor. Kurtz moved like a machine. Devoid of emotion, he executed a wounded man and shot another down as he ran. It was clear he had no intention of leaving any of them alive.

A small group of gunmen had holed up in the barn behind the manor. They were firing randomly, peppering the building with gunfire. The PRIMAL operatives had surveyed them from the top floor, standing well back in the rooms to avoid any chance of being spotted. Exiting through the front door of the residence, they hugged the building, working around to the flank.

"We could set fire to the barn . . . that would sort them out," suggested Aleks as they crouched in the darkness.

"No," Kurtz snapped. "There's probably a girl in there. Aurelia had been looking after one who was bitten by a dog."

"Then we need to get her out. We could use one of those cars . . ."

A line of vehicles was parked alongside the manor, a battered old Mercedes and two four-wheel drives. They snuck up to a four-wheel drive, its shot-out windows confirming it was the one used to abduct Aurelia. Aleks tried the door. Locked. He reached in through the shattered window and unlocked it. A single suppressed pistol round ensured the interior light wouldn't come on as he opened it.

Another burst of AK fire slammed into the upper story of the manor as the remaining criminals fired at shadows. Kurtz lobbed a distraction onto the roof. It bounced on the slate tiles and exploded, drawing even more fire.

Aleks tore the wiring out of the Toyota SUV and jury-rigged an ignition circuit. It started with a cough, the diesel engine running rough in the cold air. He reached in, placed one hand on the brake, and dropped it into reverse. Then he gave the accelerator a jab and jumped back from the vehicle. The truck reversed slowly toward the barn, gaining more speed on the slight decline. Aleks and Kurtz jogged behind it, using the car as cover.

One of the criminals spotted the vehicle and shouted a warning to his comrades. They opened up with their guns, punching the rear of the car full of holes as it rolled toward them. It crunched through the double doors and smashed into a row of dormitory-style beds, finally grinding to a stop in the debris pile it created.

The PRIMAL operatives peeled out from either side of the vehicle and unleashed a savage volley of suppressed gunfire on the remaining hostiles.

Alert for any others, they cleared the main dormitory room.

"Lots of beds here, Kurtz. At least twenty girls at a time." Aleks strode deeper into the barn.

"Imagine how many girls these *Schweine* have sold into slavery." Kurtz moved through a door at the back into a short hallway with small rooms on either side. It was the remnants of the stalls where the horses had once lived, the spaces still containing discarded equestrian equipment. Kurtz checked them one by one.

"We need to get out of here. If we stay longer, the police will be on us." Aleks was waiting in the dorm, alert for any more of Gusztáv's men.

"*Ja*, one more room." Kurtz swung the door inward and found a small stretcher covered in tattered blankets. He had turned to leave when he heard a faint moan coming from the pile of rags. He pulled back a blanket and exposed the deathly white face of a beautiful young woman.

"Aleks, I've found her."

She moaned in pain as he checked the bandages on her arm and leg. Aurelia had done a good job dressing the wounds but the smell of dead flesh told him they were infected.

"It's going to be OK," Kurtz whispered. The girl moaned as Kurtz wrapped her in a blanket and picked her up.

"Aleks, we need transport and we need it yesterday."

"We'll take her with us, *da?*"

Kurtz carried her into the dormitory, where Aleks was waiting. "She needs antibiotics badly. I need to clean and close her wounds."

"Then let's go. We should be able to use that old Merc." Aleks took the lead, his 417 in his shoulder, protecting Kurtz, who carried the girl in his arms. Once they reached the battered old Mercedes, he checked the door. Unlocked. Kurtz laid the girl on the backseat and hopped in next to her. In the front Aleks used a knife to lever off the dash. He was about to rip out the wiring when he thought better of it. He flipped down the sun visor and the keys dropped onto his lap. He turned to see if Kurtz was watching but he was busy with the girl.

The diesel sedan started up with a clatter and Aleks drove it down the gravel driveway toward the front gates. Using his goggles to guide him in the darkness, he gunned the engine and hit the front gates at speed. They sprang open as the bumper smashed into them, and he spun the wheel sideways, sending the car sliding onto the asphalt road.

Within minutes they were back to where they had hidden their Audi. Quickly, Kurtz transferred the wounded girl from the Mercedes. Aleks rigged an IV bag to the back of the passenger seat and pulled a sleeping bag from the trunk. Kurtz had already laid out the medical kit and quickly rebandaged her wounds. They hooked her up to the IV drip, made her as comfortable as they could in the backseat, and started off on the road toward Budapest.

They drove in silence, the rescue of the girl doing nothing to dampen the sense of failure that both men felt. Aurelia was dead and no amount of criminal blood would change that.

Kurtz had been driving for half an hour when his phone rang through on the hands-free. It was PRIMAL headquarters.

"Kurtz, it's Vance. How're you guys tracking?"

Kurtz gave Aleks a sidelong look. "We had a slight holdup but we are on the move now." His voice was flat, emotionless.

"Holdup?"

"*Ja,* a problem with the car. We ran over some nails. This *scheisse* Audi doesn't even have a spare."

There was a pause. "But everything's OK now?"

"*Ja, ja,* Aleks fixed it. We're almost in Budapest. We'll go straight to the safe house."

"All right. I just wanted to give you a heads-up on movements from this end. Chua's Blade has come through. He's hooked Bishop and Saneh into the network. They're airborne as we speak and heading for the Ukraine. They'll hang there till they get the invite and then run a covert op in Hungary to find out who's in charge of these sex-trafficking scumbags."

"What about us?"

"You guys are backup for Saneh and Bishop. Once they confirm the target we'll push you forward. I'll give you a full brief when you hit the safe house."

"Understood."

"Safe driving, and try to stay away from the 'nails' this time." Vance terminated the call.

"I think he knows." Aleks looked concerned.

"Without a doubt."

"You think we're going to be in trouble?"

"*Nein*, but we would be if one of us got killed. Vance isn't stupid. He knows we joined PRIMAL to help people, and if he has a problem with it, then he's not the man I thought he was."

Aleks nodded and they drove in silence for a minute before he spoke again. "I am sorry you lost her."

Kurtz stared at the road, then glanced at the girl on the backseat. She was asleep. "I just hope this hasn't ruined any chance to rescue the others."

CHAPTER 8

UKRAINIAN AIRSPACE, EASTERN EUROPE

"Lady and gentleman, we're about thirty minutes from wheels down." The pilot's British accent filled the aircraft's luxurious cabin.

Bishop keyed the intercom built into his armrest. "No worries, Mitch. We're going to check in with the Bunker. Let us know when we're five out."

"Wilco, mate."

Bishop and his companion were the only passengers on the business jet. The pair of covert operatives made quite the couple. Bishop was medium height with an athletic build. The former Australian Army officer looked like the type of rugged, mischievous, good-looking man that women often fell for but seldom dated.

Saneh, a former Iranian intelligence officer, was as deadly as she was beautiful. From her Persian ancestors she had inherited movie-star looks: long brown hair, high cheekbones, green eyes, and a figure that caught the eye of every man she encountered. Where Bishop was more of a sledgehammer, perfect for demolishing targets, Saneh was a scalpel, a deadly mix of subterfuge and manipulation.

Bishop activated a button that lowered an LED screen from the ceiling of the aircraft. He took a tablet from the pocket on the side of his chair and used it to establish a communications link with PRIMAL headquarters, the aircraft's point of departure.

Saneh adjusted her chair, returning it to the upright position. Like Bishop, she was dressed in comfortable pants and a T-shirt. Clothing more suited to their mission was packed in their luggage.

"Bishop, Saneh, how's the flight?" Chen Chua, PRIMAL's American head of intelligence, appeared on the flat-screen.

"Luxurious and smooth as a baby's bottom," replied Saneh. "Mitch may love his warbirds but he flies this jet like a dream."

The pilot, Mitch Freeman, also captained PRIMAL's combat aircraft.

"I'm glad you got some rest because things are going to get hectic once you hit the ground."

"Wouldn't have it any other way," Bishop said.

"You're going to love this one. While you were in Sudan, Aleks and Kurtz did some great fieldwork on a sex-trafficking network based in Hungary. For now we're calling it 'the Syndicate.'"

"Creative," Saneh deadpanned.

"Your job is to penetrate that organization and gather more intel."

"What's the cover?"

"Ivan spun them a story regarding Yuri wanting to branch out to selling commodities other than weapons in the Middle East." Yuri was an arms dealer who worked for PRIMAL, less by choice and more out of a healthy respect for an organization he didn't want to cross.

"It's the old team again." Bishop had been working with Ivan on the mission that had resulted in Yuri's boss being killed and also led to Saneh's recruitment into PRIMAL. Ivan was Chua's top undercover intelligence operative. He worked behind the scenes on PRIMAL operations, recruiting agents and gaining access to organizations and individuals.

"Yuri's still under our control?" Saneh asked.

"Very much so; we're his best customer. He also still thinks he's working for the CIA. The man is ruthless, but he's got morals. Jumped at the opportunity to take down a bunch of sex traffickers."

"So what's the plan?" Bishop asked.

"We're waiting for a call back from the Syndicate with the time and location of the auction. Mitch will organize transport; Mirza and the CAT are already on the ground and will provide a ready reaction force if required. Aleks and Kurtz are in Budapest and will support with ground surveillance if you need it."

"Do we know exactly where the meet will occur?" asked Saneh.

"Not at this stage but it will be somewhere in Hungary. Now, are you both clear on the cover story?"

"Of course," Saneh replied curtly.

"I think I've got it." Bishop grinned. "If I remember right, I'm the arms dealer and Saneh is my assistant."

"That's correct. We've built you up to be a bit of an entrepreneur of the illegal markets. Filthy rich from selling arms to the Middle East, you've decided to branch out into the flesh trade. Saneh is your assistant, mistress, and madam. She's coming along to confirm the quality of the product."

"All right, all right." Saneh sighed. "Now what about the leads in Japan?"

"Nothing as yet. We're not even sure that's where the pipeline leads. My informant in their police force thinks this might even have a Korean link."

"A tangled web of networks. It's never straightforward, is it?" said Saneh.

"No it's not, and as Aleks and Kurtz have already found out, these people are well armed and capable."

The aircraft's intercom interrupted the call. "Touching down in five minutes, chap and chapette!"

"That's my cue, team." Chua wrapped up the conversation. "Good luck. Oh, and Saneh, try to keep Bishop out of trouble." He terminated the call.

Saneh got up and put her backpack away into a storage compartment, preparing for landing. Bishop watched her with a grin. "Already getting into the role, I see."

"You can be such a child, Aden."

"C'mon, it's not that bad." He sat back in his chair and strapped himself in.

"It's demeaning." She pulled her own seat belt tight across her hips.

"It's cover, that's all. We'll operate the same way Mirza and I always do."

She raised an eyebrow.

"OK, so not exactly the same." Bishop gave her another smile.

"Oh, it'll be the same. You getting us into trouble and me getting us out."

The whine of hydraulics announced the final approach to the isolated airstrip near the Hungary-Ukraine border. The single strip of tarmac and the rusted hangars were used once a year for military exercises, which would not coincide with the PRIMAL operation.

They hit the runway with a thump and Mitch reversed the engines; with a roar they decelerated and angled toward the hangars.

"Time to go to work," Bishop said to himself as he grabbed his equipment bag and headed for the door.

CHAPTER 9

MAGLÓD, BUDAPEST, HUNGARY

The safe house was in the middle-class suburb of Maglód, near Budapest. A PRIMAL Blade had chosen the rental property due to its close proximity to the airport and good access to the main highways leading out of the Hungarian capital.

The two-bedroom, single-story residence could only be described as quaint. Shrouded in trees on all sides, it offered privacy from the neighbors and was unlikely to draw any unwanted attention.

Aleks parked the Audi in the single garage and turned off the headlights. He glanced at his watch. It was four in the morning; they had made good time.

In the glow of the car's interior lighting Kurtz checked on the girl while Aleks lowered the garage door and started rummaging around, searching for the key to the house.

"The lights, *Dummkopf*," Kurtz said, flicking the switch. The bright fluorescent lights came on with a flicker.

"Found the key." Aleks unlocked the interior door and Kurtz pushed past him, carrying the girl.

"Bring the med kit."

The house was small, neat, and tidy. The bathroom and kitchen simple and serviceable. The wallpaper looked like the inside of a doll's house; floral designs graced every wall.

Kurtz placed the girl on a bed in one of the rooms. She moaned as he covered her with a blanket.

"It's OK, it's OK, you're safe now," Kurtz whispered.

Aleks placed the medical kit from the car next to the bed and unzipped it. Kurtz selected a syringe and injected a mild sedative into the girl's arm. Giving it a few minutes to take effect, he laid out the other equipment he would need to treat her wounds.

The bites on her arm were deep gashes that exposed the muscles of her forearm. Kurtz injected a local anesthetic and went to work, trimming away the rotten flesh, removing debris, and closing the wounds with neat stitches. They worked for three hours, cleaning and stitching, Aleks attending as Kurtz performed the intricate work. Finally, once he had tied off the last stitch and injected her with a dose of antibiotics, they withdrew to the living room.

Aleks opened the seventies-style refrigerator to reveal a dozen of the locally brewed Borsodi Bivaly. "I think I love Ivan." He popped the top off a couple of beers with a multitool and passed one to Kurtz. They both sat on the sagging sofa and stared at the wall, exhausted.

"We should probably set up comms and check in with Vance," said Kurtz.

"*Da . . .*"

Neither man moved. They drank in silence.

A minute passed . . . then two.

Finally Kurtz broke the silence. "We did the right thing?"

"We did, comrade."

"I had to try. I couldn't leave Aurelia to die because of us. First Jess, then her . . . I just couldn't."

Kurtz had been in Sudan with Bishop and Aleks when they had lost Jess, a female doctor who was working with them. She had died in Kurtz's arms and it had affected him profoundly.

Aleks nodded sympathetically. After a moment, he sighed, took a big swig of beer, and stood. "Let's get the rest of the equipment out of the car and then sleep. You take the bed. I will take the couch. Vance can wait until we're rested."

CHAPTER 10

CASTLE LORAN, EASTERN HUNGARY

"Come on, pick up, you lazy French fuck." The phone continued to ring despite the man's protests.

Finally it picked up. "*Bonjour . . .*"

"Rémi, it's András."

"*. . . vous êtes sur la messagerie de Rémi Marcen. Veuillez laisser un message. Je vous rappellerai plus tard.*" The machine answered in its owner's lilting French accent.

"For fuck's sake, Rémi, call me!" András dropped the phone on his desk. Turning to his computer, he opened his e-mail account. There was no reply to the message he had sent. "Retarded frog bastard." He slammed the desk with his fist, sending the phone flying.

The head of the Hungarian crime syndicate was not known for his patience. A short, barrel-chested man with a jet-black mop of hair and thick eyebrows, he charged into problems like an angry bull, without wasting much time on thought.

His office was a contrasting mix of technology and medieval architecture. Behind him the rough stone walls were covered in rows of flat-screens displaying the feeds of a dozen different cameras. Some showed heavy wooden doorways, others long stone corridors or the inside of lavishly furnished rooms, and still more showed night vision images looking down on a roadway and the edge of a forest. One of the screens showed the inside of a large room filled with wardrobes and beds. Young girls sat on the beds talking, oblivious to the camera watching them. From his office András could monitor almost every inch of the castle.

He stared at the phone for a few seconds and then scooped it off the timber floor and into his duffle coat. Then he stomped across a handwoven rug and out into the frigid corridors. He walked the battlements whenever he wanted to clear his head.

He passed a pair of armed guards patrolling the hall with a guard dog. They greeted him in Hungarian and he gave them a curt nod in response. Climbing a flight of stairs, he exited onto the battlements. He fumbled in his coat for a cigarette, then fought the icy wind to light it. Achieving his goal, he stared out into the darkness.

The castle was a recent acquisition; their previous facility had been a decrepit factory on the outskirts of Budapest. But changing clients had brought a need for a more upmarket location, or so his partners had insisted. The castle was expensive but suited their needs perfectly. A former boutique hotel that had catered to Hungary's wealthy elite, it was isolated, impenetrable yet remarkably luxurious.

He took a deep drag of the cigarette and started pacing the battlements. He walked around the keep, the inner sanctum of the castle that was built adjacent to the southern wall. Historically it was designed as a final bastion should the outer wall be breached. Now it housed his office, luxurious guest suites, a restaurant, a ballroom, even a gym.

He flicked the ash from his cigarette and it drifted in the wind, down into the courtyard in front of the keep. Beyond the courtyard were thick outer walls and a moat, important defenses from an era when helicopters and high explosives did not exist. Perched over the front gates was a hulking square gatehouse. It was in this prison where the girls were kept, on the top floor that served as their quarters.

He smoked as he walked, making his way along the outer battlements to the gatehouse, where he unlocked a pair of heavy doors and entered. He walked up a few flights of stairs to the top floor and headed down a corridor until he could hear girls giggling.

He took a moment to listen through the locked door, smiling. So many pretty girls in this batch, he thought. Their photos had already been e-mailed to his investor and he anticipated a high level of interest, especially for the blonde. She would fetch well over a million US dollars.

He frowned as he remembered what had driven him to walk the battlements. He left the girls and gatehouse, locking the heavy doors behind him. Standing on the battlements, he took out his phone and dialed Rémi again.

Finally his call was answered. "Who is this? Do you know what time it is?" The accent was French and heavily laced with sleep.

"Get out of bed, you lazy dog, we've got problems."

"Keep your pants on. I was asleep."

"Then wake the fuck up."

"What's wrong? Did the girls arrive?"

"It's not the girls; it's the talent-spotting gang."

"Gusztáv and his men?"

"Yes, they're all dead. Someone blew up half the manor and killed them all."

"*Merde*! Do you know who did it?"

"He called me right before it happened. Said that Interpol was onto them."

"That's not possible. I'd know about it. We don't have any operations running in that area. It has to be local police or another gang."

"I own the fucking police, Rémi. They're the ones who confirmed the hit. It was brutal. Almost everyone was killed and none of my people have any idea who did this. That's why I called you."

"I don't know who it was, but I'm telling you, it wasn't Interpol."
András exhaled deeply. "You've really got no fucking idea?
You're my Interpol agent! Why do I even pay you?"

"András, be reasonable."

"No, you be reasonable. What do you think our investors will
do when they find out about this? Those insane bastards will chop
off my fingers and feed them to me. Shit, we'll be lucky if they don't
chop off our heads."

"Calm down, calm down. I'll put some feelers out. We'll find
out who's responsible and you can hit them back. There's no need
to involve the investors. You can find another gang to source the
product; there are plenty out there to choose from."

"Find me the bastards who did this, Rémi. I'm going to tighten
security but I can't have some invisible threat jeopardizing my operations."

"OK, I'll look into it. Is there anything else?"

"Yes, hurry up and confirm the names I sent you."

"Already under way. I'll contact you in the morning."

The Hungarian syndicate boss ended the call and headed back
to his office. He needed to have this problem well in hand before
his guests started arriving.

CHAPTER 11

RESIDENCE OF THE MORI-KAI OYABUN, HIMEJI, HYOGO PREFECTURE, JAPAN

Masateru sat in his master's waiting room and reread the two documents. Information regarding Mori-Kai business was never e-mailed to the *oyabun*. He insisted on hard copies, kept in a safe or immediately destroyed. Masateru memorized the photos on one of the documents, placed them back into the manila folder, and knocked on the door to his master's office.

"Enter!"

Masateru stepped into the office of one of the most powerful men in the district. The room was impressive, a modern renovation fusing traditional Japanese architecture with cutting-edge building materials and technology. Visitors were immediately confronted by the view overlooking the estate's manicured gardens and a lush green valley. The layered roofs of Himeji Castle were visible in the distance. Like an ancient sentinel, it watched over the sprawling city, a stark reminder of a bygone era.

The *oyabun* sat at his desk, working on a laptop. Dressed in a silk robe and slippers, he was a physically unimposing man: short with shoulder-length gray hair and a small, neatly trimmed moustache. To the casual observer he looked more like an artist than a crime boss.

Masateru walked quickly across the room and offered the folder. "A report from Rémi and photos of the latest acquisitions."

The *oyabun* was distracted by his laptop for a moment, leaving Masateru standing with his arm extended. Once finished, the *oyabun* closed the screen and took the folder. He looked at the photos first, scrutinizing each of the eleven faces. Then he read the documents. A frown formed on his features as he finished them.

"This is most concerning." He paused, taking a sip from a cup of black coffee. "If Interpol does not know who conducted the raid then what hope does that fool András have of working it out?"

Masateru nodded. "I also question why this has come from Rémi and not András himself."

"I want you to take care of this. Go to Hungary and find out what's going on. Make sure there won't be any future problems with the delivery of product . . . and take two of the Kissaki." He referred to their paramilitary wing, an elite group of operators named after the razor-sharp tip of a samurai sword.

"Yes, *oyabun*."

"One more thing." He handed the manila folder back. "Number nine, the young blonde. Bring her to me."

"Yes, *oyabun*." The Yakuza lieutenant walked backward out of the room and pulled the doors closed. He turned and walked swiftly down the polished hardwood floor to the front door, pulling his phone from his pocket. It took a single call to organize transport arrangements. His driver would take him to the airport, where two Kissaki and a private jet would be waiting. Within twelve hours he would be at Loran Castle.

CHAPTER 12

PRIMAL HQ, LASCAR ISLAND

"Someone at Interpol just ran a check on Bishop's alter ego." Chen Chua ambushed his operations counterpart as he crossed the floor of the Bunker.

Director of operations was Vance's official title. With Chua's help, he ran their missions from within the facility known as "the Bunker." Hidden on PRIMAL's private island, the headquarters supported the small teams of operatives deployed in the field. Independently financed, accountable only to itself, PRIMAL was an organization hell-bent on bringing justice to those who evaded it. Vance and Chua were the men at the helm of this tight-knit team of high-tech, heavy-hitting vigilantes.

"That's good, right?" The powerfully built African American was not a man for subtle messages. He insisted on the facts up front.

"Very good," Chua said. "It tells us the Syndicate is very well connected and they've checked him against the fake profile that the team inserted into the system."

"So they've bought his identity?"

"They'll cross-reference it with some other sources but I'm all over those as well. It's likely that Bishop will receive an invite to the next auction."

"Good stuff, let me know when the call comes in." Vance made for his office.

"There's another thing."

Vance stopped.

"Have a look at this." Chua pointed at his monitor.

"Can you bring it up on a big screen?" Vance gestured to the bank of monitors bolted to the bare stone walls of the PRIMAL operations center.

One of the screens flickered and a satellite image popped up. It showed a compound consisting of two buildings, a large primary dwelling and a smaller structure behind it. There were a number of vehicles around the buildings.

"The tracker that Kurtz gave his agent popped up here yesterday." Chua used a laser pointer to highlight the main building.

"This is the interim processing facility that Kurtz and Aleks were checking out?" Vance dropped into his command chair.

"It would seem so. This shot was taken from a commercial satellite just over a week ago. Note the bus parked next to the barn aligns with their contact's report on a new batch of girls recently arriving."

Chua hit a button and replaced the image with a number of screenshots captured from a local news broadcast showing a burning building surrounded by fire trucks and police cars.

"These are only a few hours old. It's the same facility."

"You're sure?" asked Vance.

"We've been through all of the footage and compared it to our imagery. It's definitely the same."

"The front gate has been breached," Vance observed from one of the images. "Looks like someone busted out."

"Look at the number of body bags." Chua pointed to another image showing firefighters lining up casualties.

"Looks like they got hit hard." Vance got up with a smile and started heading back to his office.

"Don't you think it's likely that Kurtz and Aleks did this?"

The big man stopped and turned to Chua. "I'd be disappointed if they didn't."

"It could affect Bishop's op. The Syndicate will surely increase the level of security at all their facilities."

Vance shrugged. "It is what it is. Let's just see if he gets an invite."

CHAPTER 13

CASTLE LORAN, EASTERN HUNGARY

The two BMW X5s powered along the narrow gravel road that led through the Loran Forest to the castle. They swept out of the tree line and across the clearing that surrounded the ancient walls. The convoy slowed as it reached the bridge over the moat and passed through the stone arch that held the gatehouse aloft. In the cobblestoned courtyard they turned in a tight circle until they stopped in front of the keep.

Masateru and his two Kissaki bodyguards alighted from the vehicles and started up the stairs. The two former Japanese Special Forces operators were a direct contrast to their boss. Heavily built, with short military-style haircuts, they wore black suits and white shirts open at the neck. The cut of their jackets was loose, designed to hide the B&T MP9 machine pistols they carried.

"Welcome to Castle Loran, Masateru," András greeted the Yakuza lieutenant at the steps to the keep. "Your visit is a welcome surprise. What brings you to Hungary?"

"I think we both know that already." He used both hands to smooth out the creases in his light-gray woolen suit and slick back his hair.

"Yes, of course, everything is in place for the auction. Already the girls—"

"Take me to your office. We have business to discuss."

The Yakuza lieutenant led the way up the stairs and into the foyer of the mafia headquarters. Seemingly immune to the lavishness of the former boutique hotel, he passed through the main hall, guards in tow. He headed directly to the bank of elevators that had been installed in the ancient building. András followed with his own men.

When they reached the office they left their men in the hallway. Masateru took a seat to one side of András's desk, allowing the Hungarian to sit behind it.

"So tell me about how you have fixed this problem." Masateru reached into his coat and extracted his cigarettes.

"What problem is that?" András feigned surprise, his thick eyebrows raised.

"You know better than to think there will ever be secrets between us."

"It is only a small problem. My men are dealing with it." András reached for his own pack of cigarettes, hand shaking.

"A small problem? I would hardly call the loss of your entire supply network a small problem." Masateru lit his cigarette and tossed the gold Dunhill lighter to András.

"They can be easily replaced." András lit his own cigarette and handed back the lighter.

"That is not what concerns me. What concerns me is you have no idea who did this. What's to stop them from doing it again?"

"I have some leads. My men—"

"No you don't," Masateru cut him off. "You have no more idea who did this than I do. That is why I am here. I will find out who did this and then you will kill them."

"Thank you." András nodded respectfully. "Do you want me to cancel the auction? Some of the guests have already arrived and we have a new client who has the potential to significantly increase our market."

Masateru took a long drag from his cigarette as he considered the information. "Is there anything linking the manor to this location?"

András shook his head. "No."

"Delay the auction. I don't want any clients to leave until I complete my investigation. In the meantime, ensure security is increased."

"Very good."

Masateru inhaled deeply from his cigarette, sending a stream of smoke into the air. "Tell me about this new client."

András nodded. "My contact in Interpol has confirmed that Mr. Martin is a well-known arms dealer. He's former SAS gone mercenary, sells weapons to most of the Middle East. Rebels, Al-Qaeda, he doesn't care."

"Hmm . . . British Special Forces would have been perfect for assaulting the manor."

"You think he could still be involved with the British government?"

Masateru continued to stare into space, his mind running through a range of possibilities. "Unlikely." He ashed his cigarette into the tray on the desk. "If the British were after us, Interpol would know. But keep a close eye on him."

"I've brought in more men. I can hire others if you think it is necessary."

"No, we use only men you trust. We don't know if this is a rival gang yet or a government agency."

"Or the family of one of the girls we've kidnapped."

Masateru laughed. "Do you expect Liam Neeson to leap through the window and start blasting away? No, this will be either the law or a rival. Either way, I will find out who they are and they will be dealt with."

András stubbed out his cigarette and rose out of his chair. "Would you like to see the girls?"

Masateru shook his head. "No, I will wait until the auction." He reached into his jacket and put the photos he had shown his *oyabun* on András's desk. "All of them will be sold except this one; she's coming back to Japan with me."

The mafia boss picked up the photos. Masateru had circled one of them with a thick red pen. It was the prettiest one, the blonde they called Karla.

"She has a sister, yes?" Masateru continued.

"That's correct; she was bitten by a dog."

"Where is she now?"

"I don't know. She had been at the manor—rather bad injuries, you see. But the local police didn't mention finding a girl, just the bodies of our men."

"Then where is she?"

András wore a blank look for a few seconds. "They must have taken her."

"So get her photo to the police and find her. She will lead us to those responsible. Then we can take action of our own."

CHAPTER 14

ABANDONED AIR BASE, UKRAINE

The roof of the aircraft hangar was riddled with holes. Sunlight streamed down in thin shafts that cut through the dusty interior and cast a dappled pattern on the fuselage of the PRIMAL business jet and Mi-17 transport helicopter parked inside.

In the back corner of the hangar, the PRIMAL team had set up their equipment. A pair of laptops on folding tables provided the network link back to the Bunker and PRIMAL's databases. Other tables held a range of weapons, ammunition, and technical kit.

With the arrival of Mitch, Bishop, and Saneh, the PRIMAL team in Ukraine had reached seven, a significant commitment for an organization that usually fielded teams of two or three.

The first team on the ground was a four-man squad led by Mirza Mansoor. The former Indian Special Forces operative usually partnered with Bishop but had recently been placed in charge of the fledgling Critical Assault Team. The CAT was an in extremis reaction force and would be responsible for backing up Bishop and Saneh with heavy firepower. Mirza and his men had flown in on a Lascar Logistics flight with all their kit. Yuri, PRIMAL's arms dealer, had leased the Mi-17 helicopter.

"The old crew back together again." Bishop smiled at the team gathered around the makeshift operations desk. "Mirza, it's good to have you and your boys along. Thanks for setting up shop for us."

Mirza gave him a curt nod. The two of them formed one of PRIMAL's most effective teams, and this was the first mission in over a year where they would be working separately.

"Don't mind him," said Mitch. "He's just a bit sad at being replaced by a beautiful woman." The pilot laughed. "But can you really blame Bishop? He gets rid of his sidekick and ends up with our glamorous Persian here." He gave Saneh a cheeky wink.

Two of the CAT operatives started laughing. Pavel and Miklos had been with them the last time they were in Ukraine and knew the history behind the group. It was only the new team member, a South African named Kruger, who had not been on that mission.

"It's OK, Mirza," Saneh said. "I'll keep your man crush out of trouble."

Everyone burst into laughter except Bishop.

Mirza gave a slight smile. "Just don't let him near anything that flies, drives, shoots, sails, or moves, for that matter."

The laughs continued and Bishop shrugged. "OK, OK, very funny. Everyone's a bloody comedian today. This is a big one, yeah? We need to focus."

The team fell silent.

"We've got a lot of moving parts and although the Bunker is taking care of most of the coordination, the buck is going to stop here with us."

Bishop looked over the team; now they had their game faces on.

"As you all know we've already got guys out on the ground. Aleks and Kurtz have been following up on a lead in Hungary. Their contact was blown yesterday and subsequently killed. We're not dealing with amateurs here, people."

"Where are Aleks and Kurtz now?" Pavel was a close friend of both men. When the swarthy Russian had been wounded on a previous mission, it was Aleks who had dragged him to safety.

"They've relocated to a safe house in Budapest. Once Saneh and I get an invite to the Syndicate's auction, they'll insert to provide overwatch."

"Do you know anything else about the location?" Mitch clearly wanted to get ahead on his flight planning. He would be tasked with flying Saneh and Bishop in on the Mi-17, then using it as an insertion platform for the CAT, if necessary.

"Negative. Chua thinks it's in eastern Hungry, just over the border, but they're not a hundred percent. Once we get the invite we'll know for sure."

"What about us?" Miklos had a concerned look. "Looks like everyone else is in the job except us."

Saneh smiled at the handsome Czech. "You're here to help me pull Bishop from the fire when he falls out of the pan."

"Ah, it would be my pleasure." Miklos gave her a dashing grin of his own.

"OK, keep your pants on, Micky," Bishop said. "She's right, you're our ace in the hole. Once Mitch has flown us in he's going to come back here, bolt on the weapons pods, load up the CAT, and get ready to rock if the shit hits the fan."

"As no doubt it will," Mitch added.

"Give me a break, not everything I touch explodes. This should be a perfectly smooth intel collection job. In and out, no dramas."

The entire team stared at him with raised eyebrows.

"Oh, bugger off and prep your kit, already," said Bishop. "Once the auction coords come through we'll start detailed planning."

They all moved back to their kit and Bishop started to go through his luggage. He opened a small plastic case and removed a pair of what looked to be standard Ray-Ban aviator sunglasses. This particular pair was far from normal. One of the lenses contained a microscopic sensor capable of capturing an image and storing it on a tiny solid-state drive buried inside the spectacles' frame. Although it lacked the resolution of a handheld camera, its capabilities were hidden to all but the closest scrutiny. Both Bishop and Saneh would be going in clean with no weapons or equipment that would arouse suspicion; the only mission-specific gear would be the glasses and a modified iPod that had tracking and messaging capabilities.

Interrupted by the incoming e-mail sound from one of the laptops, he rose to check it. The Gmail account had been set up for him by the Syndicate and passed to him through Ivan. There was a message in the inbox. It contained a brief invitation:

0900 hours tomorrow. You and the woman only. Auction next day.
47°37'28.23"N 21°54'16.84"E

Bishop dropped the coordinates into their mapping database. They landed on what looked like a field situated next to an isolated farmhouse. As a rendezvous point, it made sense: The Syndicate would want to keep their operations as discreet as possible.

"Anything yet?" Saneh leaned over his shoulder to look at the screen. Her breasts pushed gently against his back, causing his mind to wander.

"Huh?"

"Is that the auction location?" she asked.

"It's a pickup point, twenty miles over the border in Hungary." He reopened the e-mail for her to read.

"So the iPod tracker is going to be vital?"

"Yeah, although the auction shouldn't be too far from the rendezvous." Bishop zoomed out, showing a rural region of farms, small villages, and a medieval castle dispersed among the forested landscape.

"Heads up, team!" Bishop yelled so everyone in the hangar could hear. "Location just came through. We're in business."

CHAPTER 15

WEST OF THE UKRAINIAN BORDER, HUNGARY

The Mi-17 utility helicopter roared in over the trees, circled the landing area once, and touched down in a vibrant green field. The front door opened and a crew member kicked out a set of stairs. A few seconds later a figure disembarked from the aircraft and strode across the grass to a pair of waiting BMW SUVs.

Bishop was wearing a pair of chinos, a white shirt, a dark-blue blazer, and the high-tech Ray-Bans. "We in the right place, lads?" he asked the two men standing with the vehicle.

"Your name?" one of them grunted.

"Nigel, Nigel Martin." Bishop extended his hand.

"You are in right place." His own hand remained by his side.

"Right, OK then." Bishop turned and waved to the crewman standing in the doorway of the helicopter. "Friendly fuckers," he muttered.

A minute later another figure appeared. The mafia thugs turned their heads as Saneh's long brown legs descended the aircraft's stairs. She wore a floral dress that hugged her curves. A large sun hat and pair of sunglasses completed her outfit.

Pavel played the role of crewman and carried their luggage to one of the BMW X5s, deposited it in the trunk, and returned to the helicopter.

Bishop and Saneh climbed into the backseat and the driver raced them down a single-lane road as the helicopter climbed away. Bishop gave Saneh a sidelong glance, and she smiled back.

So far, so good.

They drove for another ten minutes into a thick forest, climbing over small rises and dropping down to cross a shallow stream. They rounded a corner and slowed. Through the windshield Bishop could see a heavy chain-link fence with an access control point. They stopped in front of the gate and the driver lowered his window to converse with the armed guards manning the security post.

Just past the checkpoint, they pulled off the road and parked behind the guardhouse.

"You get out here for security check."

Saneh raised an eyebrow as their escorts alighted from the vehicle and pulled open their doors.

"What's all this about?" Bishop asked one of the guards, who directed him into the run-down building.

Inside, it was dusty and decrepit. The guards led them into a room where another burly Hungarian sat on a chair behind a solid wooden table. On the table were a plastic container and a wand-style metal detector.

"You put phones in here." He pointed at the bucket. "No phones or weapons allowed."

"Look, champ, I need my phone. I've got a business to run," said Bishop.

"NO PHONES!" the man yelled, thumping the table with his fist and sending the plastic container an inch into the air.

"Fine, fine, keep your alans on." Bishop dropped a phone in the container. He gestured for Saneh to do the same.

Once they had surrendered the cell phones, one of the guards ran the detector wand over them both. Confident they had no weapons he gestured for the third man to enter the room.

He brought in their luggage and placed it on the table next to the plastic container.

"Hang on a second." Bishop made as if to complain. In response, the head guard gave him the kind of threatening look he expected. He shrugged and feigned changing his mind. "Fine, go ahead. I've got no guns."

They opened his bag and started looking through his belongings, using the wand to check for metal. Inside his toiletries bag they found a pair of handcuffs complete with fluffy pink covers. The guard held them up, giving Bishop a questioning look.

"What's this for?"

"Do I have to spell it out?"

The guard's face didn't change.

"Clearly I fucking do." He nodded toward Saneh. "Little bit of rough and tickle, yeah? Sometimes my assistant gets out of line."

The guard's blank look turned to a grin and he translated into Hungarian for the other guards. They all laughed and one of them slapped Bishop on the shoulder. Saneh shot him a withering look. The guard dropped the handcuffs into the container.

Happy with Bishop's luggage, they moved on to Saneh's. Despite their enjoyment of the handcuff joke they searched her belongings quickly and without comment. The only thing they scrutinized was her pink iPod; the guard inspected the small device and dropped it back into her bag.

The plastic container with their phones and the fluffy handcuffs was secured in a cabinet alongside other similar containers.

"Back to the car!" With the security procedures over the guards led them back to the BMW, loading their luggage into the trunk. With a roar they accelerated down the road and resumed their journey through the forest.

Minutes later they climbed a gentle rise and reached the edge of the forest. They slowed as the dense trees and undergrowth were replaced with a freshly mowed field.

"Wow!" Bishop looked out through the windshield at the castle. "You're kidding me," whispered Saneh. "Who are these people?" The BMW drove into the shadow of the high walls and slowed as it passed through the open gates, under the ancient stone arch, and into the courtyard. It pulled in front of the high-walled keep.

"We're here," grunted the driver.

A doorman dressed in traditional livery opened the car door and Bishop stepped out. He looked around, taking in the high walls and gatehouse that sat over the entrance.

"This way, sir." The doorman had taken their bags and climbed the short staircase to the entrance of the stone fortress.

Inside, the castle had been tastefully renovated. Entire walls had been removed and the ceilings reinforced by steel girders, opening up what was once a confined space. There was a reception party waiting for them in the foyer of the now modern hotel.

"Mr. Martin, welcome to the Castle Loran." A stocky brute of a man with dark hair, thick eyebrows, and no discernible neck extended his hand. The move almost burst the shoulder seams of his ill-fitting suit. "My name is András and I will be your host for the next twenty-four hours." His English was heavily accented, his voice deep and authoritative.

Bishop took his hand and shook it. "Please call me Nigel." He glanced over his shoulder at Saneh. "This is my assistant, Miss Dominique."

"Excellent, I was very happy to hear that you would be joining us. I'm excited about discussing the business opportunities." András ignored Saneh.

"As am I."

"In the meantime I would ask that you follow this gentleman to your room." He gestured to the doorman, who was waiting with their bags. "I have some pressing commitments but I look forward to seeing you at dinner in the main hall at six." With that András walked off with a couple of his heavies in tow.

"Charming fellow," Bishop commented as the doorman led them to the elevators.

Their room was on the fourth floor. Tastefully decorated and remarkably comfortable, the room had been spared no cost. Four-poster bed, marble-tiled bathroom, even a huge spa nestled in the corner.

The doorman placed their bags in the room and departed with a nod. Once he was gone Bishop walked across to Saneh and wrapped his arms around her.

Saneh stiffened. "Handcuffs! What the hell . . . ?"

Bishop cut her off, whispering in her ear. "I'm almost certain they're watching and listening to us. Try to keep up appearances, OK, Dominique?" He stroked her hair and gave her a kiss on the cheek. "The handcuffs had a built-in skeleton key," he whispered. "Mitch's gift, not my idea."

With that he gave her a slap on the bottom.

"Unpack your bags. Dinner's at six. I'm going to make full use of that tub," he announced loudly. "Lay out our clothes and then you can join me."

CHAPTER 16

PRIMAL SAFE HOUSE, BUDAPEST

"What is your name?" The girl was sitting up in bed, sipping from a carton of juice as Kurtz checked her bandages.

"My name is Kurtz."

She slurped at the juice. "That's a nice name. You're a policeman, aren't you?"

"*Ja*, I'm a policeman. I work for Interpol. What's your name?"

"Kalista."

When she had come to in the morning, Kalista had screamed for her sister. Kurtz had sat with her, holding her hand and consoling her as she sobbed. She had finally fallen into a deep sleep and he had checked on her regularly, monitoring her fever. It was only in the past few hours that her temperature had finally broken and she had started to recover.

"Your job is to find people, isn't it, Kurtz?"

"That's one of my jobs."

"Can you find my sister Karla? They took her with the other girls."

"I will try." He made to leave the room.

"Can you stay a little longer?"

She looked so fragile and scared, wrapped in bandages and attached to an IV bag. He sat down on the chair next to her bed.

"It's my fault, you know. I should have never let her go. I could have made her stay at home." Tears welled in Kalista's blue eyes.

Kurtz reached out and took her hand. "No, it is not your fault. The only people who can be blamed are the ones who took you. Those men cannot hurt you now and soon they will not be able to hurt your sister."

"I don't know what I will do without her. I feel so bad . . . My poor parents."

A tear formed in the corner of the combat veteran's eye. His hand shook and she held it tighter. "I will find her, I promise you."

There was a soft knock on the door and Aleks stuck his bearded face around it. "Hello," he smiled pleasantly. "Kurtz, we've got a call from HQ."

"I have to go, but will be back soon." Kurtz let go of her hand and joined Aleks in the living room. Two sets of earphones were plugged into an iPRIMAL smartphone that sat on the coffee table.

The pair donned the earphones and Aleks activated the call.

"Vance, Kurtz is here."

"Team, I'm gonna keep this real short. Forty minutes ago Bishop and Saneh inserted into Hungary. They RV'd with the crims running the next level up in the Syndicate."

"Where?" asked Kurtz.

"Ease up, tiger. I know you wanna hit these fuckers and you'll get your chance. We tracked them north from the RV point to an estate known as Castle Loran. Chua will flick you an intel pack once he's finished working it up."

"A castle?"

"That's right. I'm not shitting you. It is an actual castle. Their phones were taken off them at a security post but Saneh kept her tracker and it's pinging somewhere from the castle."

"No comms?" questioned Kurtz. "Do you think they've been found out? Are they in trouble?"

"There's nothing to suggest they are. Their duress procedures weren't activated."

"So what's the plan?"

"I need you to infil to the area around the castle and confirm their exact location. Mitch tells me that if you can get within a thousand yards with the kit you've got, you should be able to pick up their transponder."

"*Ja*, we have a receiver. Not a problem. What about kinetic options?"

"We all want these fuckers KIA, Kurtz. But this is just one more link in the chain, and we're looking for the next level. In saying that, I want you to be prepared to reach out and touch these dirtbags if Bishop and Saneh are in trouble."

"Understood," said Kurtz.

"Be aware that these guys are also hooked in with the local police. They used an Interpol database to check Bishop's cover story."

"Don't trust the police, got it. Is there anything else? We're ready to move once we get the intel from Chua."

"Nope, that's it. What about you, Aleks? Everything good?"

"Everything is fine, no problems here." Aleks didn't sound convincing.

"All right then, stay out of trouble."

Kurtz terminated the call.

"He knows about her," Aleks whispered once he had removed his headphones.

"How?" snapped Kurtz. "He might know about the job but he doesn't know about Kalista."

"And what are we going to do with her? She needs to see a doctor."

"We can't take her to a doctor. They'll call the police. You heard what Vance said, that could compromise the entire mission."

"Maybe we could take her with us?"

"Take her with us? Are you serious? What happened the last time we got a woman involved?" He referred to the team's previous mission, in which they had flown to Sudan to help rescue Bishop and a woman he was working with. The PRIMAL operative had been recovered safely but the female doctor had been gunned down as Kurtz tried to save her.

"You're right, she will be safer here."

"I'll talk to her. You pack the car; make sure the sniper equipment is on top."

"How long do you think we will be gone?" Aleks asked.

"No more than forty-eight hours."

CHAPTER 17

CASTLE LORAN, EASTERN HUNGARY

When Castle Loran had been converted into a hotel, the architects had taken great pains to maintain the nostalgia but improve the level of comfort. The dining hall was a tribute to their success. A thousand years ago it would have been a dark, damp space filled with wooden benches, the floors covered with straw and refuse. Today the stone floors had been polished to a marble-like finish, the rough-hewn benches replaced with fine antique furniture. At the back of the hall a bar filled the entire space; shelf upon shelf of spirits reached up the high stone walls, serviced by a ladder mounted on runners. Around the bar a group of men sat on stools, chatting quietly. Another three men were sitting at the dining table engaged in a lively discussion.

Conversation stopped as Bishop and Saneh entered through the double glass doors at the front of the hall. Bishop cut a dashing figure in a tailored tuxedo. However, he was not what drew the eye.

The split in Saneh's dress rode up to midthigh as she navigated her stiletto heels across the polished floor. The black silk hugged her body, accenting every curve and well-toned muscle. A deep V neckline revealed the edges of her breasts, framing cleavage that took a man's breath away. Her dark hair cascaded over her shoulders, and her lips were painted a rich shade of red that contrasted with her dark complexion. The overall effect was the undivided attention of every man in the room.

Bishop scrutinized the occupants while they remained distracted. Their host András sat at the head of the long table. To his immediate right sat a gentleman in a well-tailored suit. He had long hair and a designer stubble. Bishop thought him probably Italian or French. Next was an overweight, swarthy man in a tuxedo. He looked Arabic, with a large hooked nose and thick black eyebrows. Bishop noted the absence of a glass of wine in front of him. At the bar to the rear of the dining room, another three men were watching Saneh walk the floor, two of them Japanese. Bishop made a mental note to engage them in conversation after dinner.

"Mr. Martin, good of you to join us." András gestured to the place on his left. His dinner suit struggled to contain his barrel chest and broad shoulders.

"I apologize for my tardiness, I was a little preoccupied." Bishop lowered himself into the seat. A waiter appeared to assist Saneh. She sat next to Bishop, lowering her eyes to avoid the stares of the Frenchman and the Arab.

"I bet you were." András chuckled. "First things first, though, I would also like to extend an apology." He picked up his glass of wine and took a swig. "Due to unforeseen circumstances the merchandise will not be auctioned tonight."

"Why the delay?" the Frenchman asked sharply.

"We've had a minor security issue, nothing to be concerned about," András replied.

"What kind of security issue?" the Arab asked.

"A minor problem with a local provider, nothing to concern you or your clients. My men have it well in hand."

"Anything I could assist you with?" Bishop asked.

"No," András responded coldly.

"When will the auction happen?" the Frenchman asked. "My clients will be expecting delivery sooner rather than later."

"The delay will be no longer than forty-eight hours."

"What about my phone, then?" the Frenchman continued. "I need to contact my people."

"No phones, no contact with the outside world. You will stay here in the castle."

"But—" the Frenchman exclaimed.

"Perhaps you would prefer that we terminate our business?" András cut him off.

The Frenchman looked angry but said nothing. The margins he made selling sex slaves to powerful men were too high to jeopardize by protesting further.

"No?" András asked. "What about you?" He gestured to the Arab.

The Middle Eastern flesh-trader shook his head.

"Very well, now we eat. Then we drink. Tomorrow I will arrange some entertainment and then we will auction the produce."

The food was disappointing in comparison to the surroundings, only made palatable by the expensive wine being served. They made small talk over the mediocre dinner, Bishop keeping his answers short and simple, avoiding any long-winded dialogues involving his background. No one spoke to Saneh; she ate in silence as the men discussed topics ranging from cars and guns to global politics. Once dinner had concluded, András invited them across to the bar. Saneh took the opportunity to excuse herself and return to her room.

"She is truly a beauty." The Arab cornered Bishop before he could make his way over to approach the Japanese men. "What's her name?"

"Dominique."

"She is Persian, yes?"

"She is indeed. You have a very good eye."

"Of course, it's something you develop in this business." He offered his hand. "My name is Shedir."

Bishop's skin crawled as he forced a smile and shook the man's soft hand. "Name's Nigel. Your clients in the Middle East would lean more to blondes, though."

"Yes, this is true. Although I have always preferred darker women myself."

"Same here." Bishop signaled for the bartender and ordered a drink.

"Perhaps you would be willing to part with her? For the right price, of course."

Bishop couldn't help but smile. He imagined what Saneh would do to the rotund Arab if she heard this conversation. He would not even see the elbow that would rob him of his consciousness and probably his life. "I'm sorry, she's not for sale."

"Come now, my friend, everything is for sale for the right price. In your business you know that better than most."

Bishop took a sip from the gin and tonic that had been placed on the polished hardwood bar. "Let me think about it. I mean it's not like either of us is going anywhere soon."

"That's all I can ask."

With that, Bishop left the Arab and made his way over to the two Japanese men standing at the other end of the bar. One of them had ex-military written all over him: short hair, muscular build, an alert stance, a rugged watch, and a suit jacket cut to hide a firearm. The other man was more interesting; he wore an Italian-cut light-gray suit and a two-tone shirt, white collar and cuffs with a maroon front. His hair was slicked back in the style of an old-school gangster. Bishop put his age at midthirties.

He gave them a nod as he sidled up next to them at the bar.

Both men continued their conversation in Japanese. From his tone Bishop identified Mr. Slick as the boss and guessed he was issuing an order to his security guy. The bodyguard bowed his head. "*Hai*, Masateru." Then he left the bar.

"You must be Mr. Martin," said Masateru to Bishop.

"That's correct. So how do you fit into all of this, Mr. . . . Masateru?"

The Japanese man frowned. "I am a friend of András."

"Ah, I see. What sort of business are you in?"

"Private business." Masateru turned his back and left the bar.

Bishop took the man's cue and ordered another drink. Masateru seemed an enigma. He sported none of the indicators of a Yakuza member. He had all his fingers, no visible tattoos, and none of the lapel pins that the Japanese mafia favored.

"Gentlemen." András interrupted the conversations. "For those of you who haven't brought your own . . ."—he glanced at Bishop—"I have arranged entertainment." He snapped his fingers and a side door opened.

Four women dressed in slinky outfits and high heels strutted into the hall. They were heavily made up, picked for their ample curves. They were not the women that Bishop was here to rescue; they were professionals, paid for their time.

The women approached the bar and a voluptuous blonde targeted Bishop as soon as she spotted him. There was clearly a hierarchy among the women. The blonde was a little older, more practiced, and as such she got what she wanted, and apparently she wanted Bishop.

She looked desirable, in a trashy way. Fake breasts, long legs, and angular features, overly made up with an outfit that showed more skin than a Brazilian swimsuit. But compared to Saneh, thought Bishop, she looked like a tramp.

"Hello." She gave him a seductive smile. Her local accent was soft and refined compared to András's.

"Evening," he responded pleasantly.

"Oh, you're English." She smiled. "I like English, you make the best lovers."

"Really?" Bishop was not sure where she got that assessment from. As far as he could remember, the English were always renowned for the exact opposite. "Do you get a lot of Englishmen here?"

"A few, not many. Mostly Arabs and Russians." She leaned in close to Bishop's ear. "They're a bit strange."

"Yes, they are." Bishop signaled for the bartender, who poured her a glass of champagne. "What about the Japanese, do you get many of them?"

"No, not that I have seen. They're new."

"Interesting."

"Not really, I hear they're a little . . . how you say? Lacking." She held up her little finger and wiggled it suggestively.

Bishop laughed. "Don't let them hear you say that. They look nasty."

She took a sip of the champagne. "So are you in the same business as our host, Mr. . . . ?"

"Martin, Nigel Martin." He offered her a hand and she shook it with a smile. "And it depends what sort of business that is, exactly."

"Oh you know, exports and the like."

"In that case I'm in a similar line of work. I tend to export the type of things that people need to solve problems."

"What type of problems?"

"All types, but mostly ones that require extra . . . persuasion."

The comment was lost on the woman, who simply nodded. Bishop had a feeling that he had gotten all the information she had to offer.

"Well, lovely to meet you," Bishop said as he finished his drink and turned away. He excused himself to András and made his way back to the room.

Saneh was already in bed when he arrived, her black silk dress hanging over the back of a chair, heels tossed on the floor. Bishop knew she was angry. She was normally fastidious in putting away her things. He undressed, threw his own clothes over the other chair, and approached the bed.

"Don't even think about it." She turned away as he switched off the lamp and slid into the bed.

"We need to at least pretend," he whispered. "They'll be listening and probably watching."

"Fine." She rolled over to face him and pulled the duvet over their heads. "Sorry, I'm just annoyed. That bunch of misogynist bastards wouldn't give me the time of day."

"Oh, I'm sure they'd give you much more than that. You looked stunning at dinner."

"You noticed, eh?" She smiled but looked away. "Smooth talking isn't going to get you laid, Aden."

"No?" He wrapped his arms around her and placed a kiss gently on her neck. "What else do I need to do?"

"That's a good start, but I'm still not in the mood." She rolled over and he nuzzled in behind her, continuing to kiss her neck. He caressed her body and she moaned softly.

"I know that, just keeping up our cover." He unsnapped her bra and slid his hand around to her breast.

Saneh placed her hand on top of his and arched her back, turning her head back to kiss him. "The things we do for PRIMAL."

CHAPTER 18

OVERWATCH POSITION, CASTLE LORAN

"I bet Bishop and Saneh are cuddled up in a big four-poster bed while I lie in the mud," Aleks whispered.

"They'll be doing more than cuddling," Kurtz replied.

Both men were lying behind Windrunner sniper rifles. The ultra long-range rifles were a versatile and potent weapon system. Heavy .408 CheyTac rounds would enable them to precisely engage both personnel and vehicles out to two thousand meters, and the takedown design of the long rifles allowed them to easily fit in the trunk of their car, perfect for covert operations.

Overnight they had driven the Audi into the forest, using night vision goggles instead of headlights, and parked it off a remote track. Now it was just after dawn, the rain had stopped, and the castle was barely visible through the morning fog. They had chosen an observation post on the forward slope of a densely forested hill eight hundred meters from Castle Loran. Both were dressed in ghillie suits: jumpsuits covered in layers of shaggy camouflage material that made them almost invisible to the naked eye.

"I don't think so," Aleks said. "Saneh is always funny in the field. All game face, no touchy-feely."

Kurtz nodded slowly. "She's a professional, unlike Bishop. He's always thinking with his dick." He smiled, flashing white teeth between the heavy layers of camouflage cream.

Aleks laughed softly. "This is true. He is like a teenage boy, running around with dick in hand."

"Good man to have in a gunfight, though." Kurtz reached forward and made a slight adjustment to the sight on top of his Windrunner. The high-tech sniper rifle sat on its bipod legs with a short spigot under the butt that kept it snug in his shoulder. Like the two men it was wrapped in now soggy camouflage material. "Damn the rain, it makes this stuff smell like wet *Hund*."

Aleks was focusing his attention on his forearm-mounted iPRIMAL. It was synced with a digital scanner hidden a few meters away, the laptop-size scanner aimed at the castle.

"Any sign of them?" Kurtz asked.

"*Nyet*, nothing . . ."

"They'll be fine; Bishop won't let anything happen. If they need us they'll activate the beacon."

"Another patrol." Kurtz lowered his face to the scope of his weapon. Through the powerful optic he could make out the number on the plate of the BMW as it drove out of the castle walls. It followed a dirt road across the open fields before disappearing into the forest. The castle's guard force conducted regular vehicle patrols along the numerous tracks that crisscrossed the estate.

"Why do they not send out foot patrols?" asked Aleks.

"Because they're lazy criminals, not professional soldiers."

"So stupid . . . If they brought out some of those dogs they could probably find us."

"If they thought someone was watching them, that's probably what they would do." Kurtz was still scoping the castle. "Another vehicle." He watched a white van drive out through the castle gates and follow the same route as the BMW. When it reached the edge of the forest it turned off the main drive onto a cart track that curved back around and into the cleared field that lay between the

PRIMAL snipers' position and the castle. Halfway across the field the van stopped and two men alighted.

"They're setting something up."

The men pulled out a number of folding tables and set them up on the grass. Wooden boxes, chairs, an ice chest, and a variety of other items were placed on and around the tables.

"I think they might be having a picnic," said Kurtz. "Maybe breakfast." He glanced at his watch. "It's about that time."

"Not a picnic," Aleks said as he shouldered his own weapon. "They are going to shoot clay pigeons."

The men got back into the van and drove another twenty meters. They stopped in front of a depression cut into the ground and started setting up a mechanical device in the hole.

"Do you think we should move?" Aleks asked. "They are pointing right at us."

"*Nein*, too risky. We should be OK here. Shotgun pellets don't go very far . . ."

CHAPTER 19

CASTLE LORAN

"PULL!"

With a loud clack, the trap machine catapulted a small disk made of clay into the air. A shotgun boomed and the clay pigeon shattered into a cloud of dust.

"You see, it's just a matter of leading the target." Shedir lowered the shotgun and glanced sideways to where Bishop was standing, his own weapon held in the crook of his arm.

"Just can't seem to get the bloody hang of it."

"You are improving," Shedir said.

"PULL!" Bishop tracked the target and blew it from the sky with a single cartridge.

Shedir nodded approvingly. "See, soon you will be ready for a wager."

"Yes, I am getting better, aren't I?" Bishop knew that the Arab was goading him into a bet and he had a good idea what the terms would be.

András and the Frenchman were seated at one of the tables talking, eating, and drinking. They had lost interest in the shooting after half an hour. Only the Arab had wanted to continue; he displayed a level of skill that suggested he had been professionally coached.

Saneh was sitting in a chaise listening to her iPod, her long brown legs exposed to the sun. The clouds had cleared by midmorning, allowing her to wear a short summer dress and tortoise shell–rimmed sunglasses. She appeared completely disinterested in either the shooting or the drinking. When the Frenchman had approached her she had smiled politely and used short answers to end any attempt at conversation.

A short distance from the tables the four-wheel drives were parked side by side. Three Japanese men, including the two from the previous night, waited with the cars, watching the shooters intently. During the drive out Bishop had once again tried to strike up a conversation but to no avail. On the upside, he had been successful in capturing images of their faces with his Ray-Bans.

"What's with our friends?" Bishop nodded toward the men by the vehicles as he and Shedir drank from bottles of mineral water.

"The Japanese?"

"Yeah, strange chaps. Tried to chat with the John Dillinger lookalike but he was a bit cold."

"I think they're the money behind the operation. András doesn't talk about them and they're not very friendly."

"Yes, I picked up on that."

"How about we make this interesting?" Shedir dropped his empty bottle on the grass and picked up his shotgun. "Three targets, lowest number of cartridges wins."

"Wins what?"

"Let me see. If you win I'll give you a hundred thousand dollars."

"And if you win?"

"If I win . . . then you give me one night with that beautiful woman of yours."

"Excuse me?" Saneh had left her chair and was standing behind the pair.

Bishop turned and gave her a smile. "Hardly seems like a fair deal."

"OK, then two hundred. I have the cash in my room."

Saneh scowled.

"Deal."

"Excellent, I insist you shoot first."

As Bishop readied his stance Shedir moved back to stand next to Saneh.

"PULL!" The shotgun roared as the clay disk spun out of the trap. Bishop missed.

He fired again. This time the disk disintegrated into a cloud of bright-pink dust.

"I'm looking forward to tonight." Shedir murmured just loud enough for Saneh to hear. He took his own stance and Bishop stepped back.

"PULL!" The Arab's barrel tracked the disk as he fired, blowing it from the sky. He turned to face Bishop and Saneh. "A lucky shot."

Bishop stepped up again. This time he hit the clay pigeon with the first shot.

"Very good shooting, my friend." The Arab was enjoying himself. "Although secretly I think you are going easy on me."

"He better not be," Saneh muttered under her breath.

After his next shot, Shedir was still ahead by one. Bishop's only chance of winning was if his opponent bungled at least one of his two next shots.

"Let's make this really interesting," said Bishop as he reloaded. "Final round, two cartridges, two targets at once, winner takes all."

Shedir paused and stared at Saneh for a few seconds, his eyes tracing every curve of her body, highly visible through the tight summer dress. "All?"

"You win, you get the girl, no conditions."

"A good challenge, one I cannot resist."

Saneh had her hands on her hips, more irritated at being used as a betting chip than by the threat of actually being owned by the Arab.

"In that case, I insist you go first." Bishop moved forward to the trap and explained the situation to the assistant.

While he was away, Shedir turned to Saneh. "You have to know he is going to lose. Tonight you're going to be mine, and after that he's not going to want you anymore."

"Are you ready?" Bishop jogged back. Saneh glared at him.

"As ready as I will ever be." The Arab took his position holding the shotgun held tightly against his shoulder.

"PULL!" The targets came out of the trap together but spread apart as they flew higher. The shotgun roared twice in quick succession and the air was filled with pink dust.

"Well, that's a bit of bummer!" Bishop exclaimed. "Not much chance of me beating that."

"No, my friend. But perhaps you can draw. Then we will have a rematch." Shedir laughed as he smiled at Saneh.

Bishop prepared himself—unlike the Arab, who used a classic shooter's stance—by squaring off against the target, hunching forward as he would in a close-quarters-battle environment.

"Wait!" Saneh ran forward to kiss him. "For good luck." She leaned in and whispered in his ear. "You mess this up, and I'll kill you."

He winked and kissed her on the lips. "Trust me."

"PULL!"

The trap machine spat the two targets skyward; they had only climbed a few feet and just began to part when Bishop's shotgun roared. Once.

"Guess that's a wrap, old man." Bishop smiled.

Shedir's mouth was open in shock as he stared at the dust cloud that marked the demise of both targets.

Bishop placed the shotgun on a rubber mat and walked past Saneh over to the table.

"Who won?" András asked as the two men reached the table. Saneh had returned to her deck chair and iPod.

Bishop had already stuffed a handful of grapes into his mouth.

"Mr. Martin won," the Arab responded coolly. "I will have your money for you at dinner."

"No rush," said Bishop, reaching for another bunch of grapes.

"When is the auction, András?" Shedir demanded, directing the conversation away from his loss.

"Tomorrow. The security situation has stabilized so we will progress."

"Got it all under control, eh? Good stuff," said Bishop between mouthfuls. "I'm keen to see your girls in the flesh."

"You won't be disappointed," András promised. "We've got some excellent specimens in the next batch. Perhaps you can spend some of Shedir's money."

CHAPTER 20

PRIMAL SAFE HOUSE, BUDAPEST

Kalista gently touched the stitches in her arm. They did not hurt as much anymore, the swelling having subsided. She swung her legs out of bed and examined the wound on her leg. It was the same, tender but not as sore. Standing up she took a few tentative steps. Her leg was a little stiff, but she could walk.

On the chair at the end of the bed she found her clothes, washed and folded. She stripped off her gown and put on her jeans and sweater, realizing Kurtz and Aleks must have taken her clothes off and seen her naked. She blushed at the thought and then shook her head: She was being silly. They were police officers and professionals. They had saved her life.

She found her shoes under the bed and slipped them on. Feeling hungry, she wandered around the house, checking in all the rooms. The house was bare, except for the fridge, which was well stocked.

Kalista sat on the couch with a yogurt and a torrent of thoughts poured through her mind. The policemen had said that they would return within a couple of days but that seemed like a week ago. They had told her not to leave the house, but what if something had happened to them? What if they had gone after her younger sister and been killed by the kidnappers? What if they *never* came back?

Panic built in her chest and she forced herself to breathe. The room felt so stuffy and she felt she needed to get out. She limped stiffly to the front door, ignoring the pain. It was locked, a deadbolt. She struggled with it, hands shaking, then started sobbing, fumbling with the door as tears streamed down her face.

Finally she unlocked the door, wrenched it open, and stumbled through the garden and out onto the street. Wiping away tears, she looked up and down the leafy neighborhood in a panic. She spotted a black four-wheel drive on the opposite side of the street and started running. Panicked, she sprinted around the corner, checking over her shoulder every few meters to see if the car was following her.

"Help me!" she cried out to a woman walking along the street with her bicycle.

The woman stared at her blankly. She didn't speak English.

A dog barked in the distance and Kalista ran. Her heart raced as images of the dog attack filled her head. She ignored the pain in her wounds and ran as fast as she could.

A block away she finally stopped, collapsing onto the ground in a blubbering mess of hysteria.

Someone spoke to her in a language she did not understand. A hand grasped her shoulder and she looked up.

"Do you speak English?" a man in a police uniform asked.

"Yes . . . yes." Kalista's face was puffy from crying, her hair knotted and filthy. Her jumper and jeans were bloodied where the wounds had started to seep through.

"You will come with us." The police officer offered her a hand.

Kalista allowed the man to help her into his police car. She gave her details and told her story as they drove a short distance through the leafy suburb to the local station.

A female officer rebandaged Kalista's wounds as she sat in the waiting area wrapped in a blanket. The policeman who found her had disappeared into the office to run an identity check on the database. When it turned up a priority hit on the Interpol watch list he rung the number listed.

"Capitaine Marcen?" he asked in English once the call connected.

"Yes, who is this?"

"It's Sergeant Szalai here from the Budapest Police."

"How can I help you, Sergeant?"

"Well, sir, I have a woman here who I think is on your watch list. She says her name is Kalista. She looks exactly like the picture on the system and she's definitely Croatian. The woman says she was rescued by Interpol agents but they disappeared."

"Where did you say you were located?"

"Budapest, Maglód police station."

"Good, now listen to me. This is very important. You need to make sure that this girl goes nowhere. She is a key witness in the kidnapping and murder of a number of people, possibly including Interpol agents. She is not dangerous but the people after her are. I have men who are close by; they will come to get her but until then I need you to ensure she is safe, do you understand?"

"I understand."

"I am going to call my people and arrange for them to come and get her. OK?"

"Yes."

The Hungarian policeman placed the phone back on his desk and looked out through the plexiglass that separated the office from the waiting area. Kalista looked frail and scared, a young girl a long way from friends and family. Her story, if true, was harrowing. Kidnapped by sex traffickers, mauled by a dog, and left to die before being rescued by Interpol agents. At least she was safe here, and before long she would be back in the custody of Interpol and well outside the reach of anyone who could harm her.

CHAPTER 21

CASTLE LORAN

"I don't think Nigel Martin is who he claims to be." Masateru was sitting in one of the leather chairs in András's office, dressed in one of his trademark Italian suits. In his hand he held an apple, which he was slicing into thin pieces with a razor-sharp tanto blade. He had spent most of the day watching "Nigel Martin," studying him during the shooting, then at lunch and again at dinner. Twice the Englishman had attempted to engage him in conversation.

"He seems normal enough to me." The Hungarian syndicate boss was watching the bank of monitors behind his desk as he sipped a glass of scotch.

"A little too normal." Masateru finished the apple, dropped the core onto a side table, and began spinning the black knife on his palm.

"You're paranoid."

"Am I?" He pointed at the screen showing the camera feed from Bishop's room. On it was a grainy night vision shot that showed the rough outline of a woman straddling a man. "That woman of his, she acts submissive in public, but alone she is . . . different."

András laughed. "Just because he lets a beautiful woman lead him around by the nose does not make him a threat."

"In this industry it could make him a liability."

"His client base in the Middle East and Africa is all I care about. His organization sells weapons to half of the world's dictators. Men who want guns generally want girls and they have the money to pay for them."

"The men who wiped out your talent recruiters had guns, lots of them, no doubt."

András placed his glass down. "Getting guns is one thing. The men who attacked Gusztáv's gang were highly trained professionals, not gun runners."

The desk phone rang angrily, interrupting the conversation. András snatched it up, glancing at the caller ID.

"András here," was all he said. After thirty seconds he dropped the phone back into its cradle. "They've found the missing girl; she's in a police station in Budapest."

"Excellent." Masateru opened and closed his knife.

"I'll have my men bring her here." András was already making the call.

"Good." The Japanese gangster was staring intently at the blade spinning on his hand. "I would very much like to speak with her."

CHAPTER 22

PRIMAL HQ, LASCAR ISLAND

"Boss, we just got a sitrep from Aleks and Kurtz," announced the intercom on Vance's desk.

PRIMAL's director looked away from his monitor and reached out to hit the voice button. "Thanks, Frank."

"No dramas. We still on for this afternoon?"

"You looking for another ass-whipping?"

"Yeah, right, old man. See you then."

"Roger."

Vance took off his glasses and rubbed the bridge of his nose. The spectacles were a recent addition; PRIMAL's resident doctor had insisted on them following his last full medical. Apparently he was now shortsighted, another ailment to add to the long list. Twenty-plus years as a CIA field operative had not been kind. Fortunately he only needed the glasses when reading and shooting. He hated to admit it but his scores had significantly improved since donning the black-framed lenses. Something Frank, one of the watchkeepers, had found out firsthand. The former British para officer was a crack pistol shot, but he had gone down in three straight rounds. Vance was looking forward to the rematch.

He looked back to his monitor and pulled up the operations log. At the top of the list of inbound traffic was the report from Kurtz and Aleks. He opened it.

Have established an OP in vicinity of target (800m to NW). Confirmed Bishop and Saneh are in location, seem to be in good
health. Multiple armed pers in location, ten or more. Dogs spotted.
Scanner established link with the low-power transmitter. At least
2+ Japanese identified. No sign of girls. Nothing further to report.

He looked at the read receipt. Chua had read it only minutes
ago. The door flew open as if on cue and the Chinese American
powered into the office with a can of energy drink in one hand and
a tablet computer in the other.

"You read the latest from the boys?"

"Just finished it."

"Looks like we might be on the right trail in Japan." Chua
dropped into the comfortable leather couch that sat in the corner.
"If Aleks and Kurtz are right about them being Japanese, then it's
almost certain there's a Yakuza link." Chua cracked the energy drink
and chugged down a mouthful.

"How are things tracking in the land of Toyotas, panty-vending
machines, and raw fish?"

"For a well-traveled man you're particularly uncouth, Vance."
Chua smiled. "Things are coming along nicely. We've identified a
suitable contact in the Tokyo metro police. He's well positioned in
the organized-crime team and a bit of an altruist. With your
approval I'll get Ivan to pitch to him in the next twenty-four hours.
We'll lead with an FBI back story and see where it takes us."

"Consider it approved. Talk to me about the armed guards at
the castle. Anything to be worried about?"

"Nothing we can't handle. I assess we're looking at up to twenty
shooters in total. Nothing I can find suggests they would be more

than hired guns and thugs. Might be a sprinkling of ex-military types. Why? You expecting this to go kinetic?"

"I hope not, but if it does I want to make damn sure Bishop and Saneh aren't left hanging. I think we've got it covered. Aleks and Kurtz can provide surgical fire support while the CAT flies in from the Ukraine."

"What's their response time?"

"Forty-five minutes from blades turning to landing on target." Vance paused. "That's the bit I'm not real happy with. I'd like Mirza and his assaulters a little closer."

"I'll see if I can find them a staging base; going to be bare bones, though, no fuel."

"That's fine, I just want another option up my sleeve. If it looks like it's all going to hell I want them in the mix ASAP."

"I'll get on it." Chua made for the door. "Oh, and Vance."

"Yeah?"

"Love the glasses."

"Get the hell out of my office, you intel puke!"

CHAPTER 23

CASTLE LORAN

Bishop's watch buzzed gently, waking him at 0330 hours. He rolled out of bed and grabbed the dark tracksuit he had placed on a chair the night before.

"What are you doing?" Saneh's voice was drowsy with sleep.

"Don't get up, I'm going to the gym."

"Can't sleep?"

"Yeah, jet lag."

"Do you think it's a good idea to go out?" She sounded annoyed.

"It'll be fine."

"I don't think it's good for your health."

"You go back to sleep. I'll be back in an hour."

She rolled over and pulled the duvet over her head, pretending to go back to sleep. Hidden from the camera she switched on her iPod. The screen came to life and she thumbed through the menus, looking for a particular song. She fast-forwarded AC/DC's "Thunderstruck" to 1:47 and keyed the pause button three times. The little screen blinked for a few seconds and an entirely different menu appeared. She confirmed the miniature device was active and then slid it under her pillow. She now had a link with any other PRIMAL operatives outside. If anything happened to Bishop she could contact them immediately.

"I'll see you when I get back." Bishop shut the door gently behind him.

✮✮✮

The dialogue with Saneh had little to do with the gym. Instead, it had let her know that he was heading out to conduct a previously planned mission. She had argued against the risk but Bishop had insisted. It was a simple plan: He would locate the computer terminal he had identified earlier, use the USB key hidden under the sole of his running shoe, and plug it in. The Trojan horse it contained would do the rest.

The corridors of the castle were cold and empty. Soft lighting had been installed intermittently along the walls and it cast long, eerie shadows. Bishop almost expected to turn a corner and run into the ghost from *Hamlet*.

"Something is rotten in the state of Hungary," he whispered under his breath.

He moved through the upper stories of the keep, using a route he had previously observed to avoid the CCTV cameras. Finally he found the door he was looking for. A sign marked it as OFFICE. He stopped and listened, his ear pressed to the wood. There was no sound coming from inside so he tried the handle. It was unlocked. He cracked it open and peered in.

The room was unoccupied. He slipped inside and shut the door.

In the corner was a computer terminal. He inspected the desktop, removed the USB device from its hidden compartment in his shoe, and plugged it in.

As the PRIMAL virus worked its magic Bishop explored the rest of the room. It was large, about the same size as a double garage. Unlike the rest of the luxurious hotel, it was run-down and dirty. Along one wall were a couple of battered-looking couches, in the middle was a decrepit-looking coffee table festooned with girlie magazines, and in the corner stood a refrigerator that Bishop thought had to be full of beer. He opened it to check; yes, it was. The far wall housed another door.

He checked on the USB key; it was finished. Chua's team in the bunker would now be able to hack into the computer via its Internet connection. He pulled out the device and was putting it back in his shoe when he heard voices at the door.

Slipping on his shoe, he sprinted for the only other exit from the room, the narrow wooden door opposite the computer and desk. He pushed it open, stepped inside, and cautiously closed the door behind him.

It took his eyes a few seconds to adjust to the darkness and he noticed a distinct smell in the room. It reminded Bishop of football socks. Then it hit him—it was the smell of a number of men living in close proximity. As his eyes adjusted, the reality of his predicament became clear.

He was in a barracks-style dormitory with six beds, three of which were occupied.

"Holy shit!" he mouthed.

Behind him in the office at least two voices were talking softly. He had accidentally stumbled on the guards' quarters, and now he was trapped.

There was only one way to go, deeper into the room, between the sleeping guards. He tiptoed as softly as he could, reached the other end, and went through another door. It creaked, and he bit his lip. He slipped through the gap as the office door into the dorm opened.

From the smell Bishop could tell he was in the bathroom. He raced to the window, searching for a way out, aware that any guards coming off shift might want a shower. The single window had once been a narrow arrow slit that archers used to fire at castle assailants.

Fortunately for Bishop, the builders who had renovated the keep had enlarged the opening and installed a small sliding-glass window. He slid it back and pushed his head out through the hole.

The window overlooked the battlements—he was in luck. The wide stone walkway that capped the castle wall lay about twelve feet below. He slid out through the gap feet first, his toes scrabbling for a hold as he lowered himself from the window frame.

As he hung by his fingers, the door to the bathroom creaked and the light came on. Bishop let go of the window frame and pushed off into the darkness.

He hit the ground hard, the voice of his physical-training instructors at the Royal Military College blaring in his head: *Two-foot landing, Staff Cadet Bishop!*

He fell backward into a heels, ass, and head landing. Stunned, he rolled sideways into a dark shadow cast by the castle's security lighting.

A head appeared in the window, silhouetted by the inside light. The guard stood there for a second, then closed the window.

Bishop still felt dazed when he got to his feet and he ran his hand over the back of his head. There was already a lump forming. The cool early-morning air helped to clear his senses, and he moved across the battlements, sticking to the shadows.

The growl of a powerful engine caught his attention and he leaned over the edge of the stone wall, looking down into the courtyard.

A black four-wheel drive pulled up in front of the keep. The doors swung open and leather jacket–wearing thugs emerged from it. Two of them moved to the trunk and struggled with a large object.

Bishop moved back along the wall, toward the keep, trying to get a glimpse of what it was. As the men moved up the stairs into the light of the entrance he realized the bundle was a young woman. She was bound and gagged, her long blonde hair disheveled.

Bishop squatted below the edge of the wall. He had no idea who the girl was but had a feeling her arrival related directly to the security scare that had delayed the auction. His biggest concern at the moment, however, was how he was going to get back into the keep. If found, he would have a tough time explaining how he managed to get out of the fortress without passing through one of the guarded exits.

CHAPTER 24

"Put the bitch over there." András indicated the coffee table and chairs in the corner of his office.

Two men dumped Kalista into the chair and stood on either side of her.

"Untie her hands, you idiots."

They released her hands and feet. Instantly she recoiled into the fetal position, terrified eyes scanning the room.

"Look at me, Kalista." András sat on the coffee table in front of her. "I'm going to ask you some questions and if you answer them truthfully nothing is going to happen to you, OK?"

She nodded.

"Some men rescued you from the farm, yes?"

She nodded again.

"Can you tell me about those men?"

"One of them was a German, he was very tall," she spoke quietly. "The other was Russian, I think. They said they were with Interpol."

András stood up, walked over to his desk, and returned with a single piece of paper. On it were the faces of the invitees to the auction. "Are any of these men the ones who took you?"

Kalista leaned forward to look, then shook her head. "No, none of these men."

"Tell me what happened after they took you."

At that moment the heavy doors to András's office flew open and Masateru stormed in.

"Why wasn't I told she had arrived?"

András turned his head and to his surprise Masateru was still dressed in a suit, his hair slicked back. When did he actually sleep?

"I was just about to send one of my men to find you."

Masateru gave him a look that suggested he did not believe a word he was saying. "Has she told you anything yet?"

"Not really. She says the ones who took her said they were Interpol, but clearly we know that isn't true." András walked back to his desk and threw the paper down.

"What about the arms dealer? Did you ask her if she knows him?"

"I did. I showed her his face. She has no idea who any of the buyers are." András was looking at the screens behind his desk. A frown creased his bullish forehead.

Masateru sat down on the table next to the girl. He took his knife from inside his suit jacket and unfolded it. The tanto blade was jet black; only the razor's edge was silver, a thin line of cold steel. He spun it in one hand as he slicked back his hair with the other. "What's your name, pretty one?" he asked.

She stared at him with wide eyes. "Kalista." Her voice trembled.

"Kalista, what you need to understand is that you belong to us. You are not a person anymore, you're a thing. An item, a product to be used for whatever we want."

Tears rolled down Kalista's cheeks.

Masateru leaned forward until his face was only inches away. He grasped her face with one hand, continuing to spin the knife in the other. "I want you to tell us everything you know about the men who took you. If you don't, you're going to find out what happens to an item that is broken, a thing I don't want anymore."

Kalista shuddered, tears pouring now. "I don't—know—anything else." The words came in sobbing bursts.

Masateru squeezed her face harder, distorting her pretty features. He traced the back of the tanto blade down her cheek. "That's a lie, my little angel. How about we make you a little less pretty?"

"Where's the arms dealer?" András was staring at the screen that monitored Bishop and Saneh's room.

"What?" Masateru released the girl's face and whirled around.

"Look, she's alone." András pointed to the screen. The grainy infrared image showed one body in the bed. You could make out the woman's long dark hair flowing over the pillow.

"Where the hell is he?" Masateru asked, his eyes darting from one screen to another.

There was no sign of the "former SAS soldier"-cum-arms dealer on any of the other screens.

"I told you they were involved," snapped Masateru.

András turned to the guards standing on either side of Kalista. "Get everyone up. Search the entire castle. Check the cameras to see where he went. I want him alive!"

The Japanese mobster jabbed his knife in the direction of the screen that showed Saneh sleeping. "Bring that bitch to me."

CHAPTER 25

Saneh knew something was wrong when the boots echoing along the hallway stopped outside her door. She heard the key in the lock and was fully awake when the door opened and two armed guards strode in. From under the sheets she activated her iPod. The tiny device sent a low-power, short-burst signal out into the cold night air. Her hope: that a waiting sensor would receive it and relay the precoded message.

The guards waited for her to dress as she feigned the clumsiness of a sleep-jumbled mind and struggled with her tracksuit. As she pulled on her sneakers she could hear more boots on the cobblestones outside her room. They were searching for Bishop, she realized.

The guards ushered her from the room toward the elevators. The automatic weapons they carried emphasized the seriousness of the situation, this being the first time Saneh had seen weapons inside the keep. In her head she played out the moves that would transfer one of the guns into her control. An elbow to the throat of one, a savage kick to the side of the other's knee, then safety off and a short burst to finish the job. Despite the severity of the situation, she felt calm. In fact she almost smirked as the quote on a T-shirt Bishop had given her ran through her head: "I might seem calm, but in my head I've already killed you twice."

They took her up one level and pushed her into András's office.

"What do you want?" Saneh played the demanding, rich, spoiled woman to the hilt. "If you hurt me, Nigel will be very angry!"

"Where is he?" Masateru barked.

"Why? Has something happened? He went to the gym an hour ago . . ."

"He's not in the gym," András replied coldly. "Please, take a seat." He pointed to the chair next to the one Kalista occupied.

Saneh looked at the terrified blonde cowering in the chair, then back to András. "I'm not some whore you can treat like this."

"Sit down," snarled Masateru.

Saneh dropped into the chair.

"Who are you and Mr. Martin working for?" asked András.

"You already know that," she replied.

"Don't play games with me. We know you're involved."

"Involved in what? Your security issue? We came here to buy women we can sell to the Arabs. I'm as concerned about security as you are."

"Enough!" Masateru whipped his knife from his jacket and extended the blade with a flick of his wrist. "It is time to stop feeding us lies. Now you will tell us the truth."

"That is the truth," Saneh said, putting a slight waver in her voice. Tears formed in her eyes and she started to shake.

"Do you know this woman?" Masateru grabbed Kalista by the hair and dragged her from the chair. Kalista screamed in pain, reaching up to grab at his wrist. He held the tanto blade to her throat. "Do you?"

"No, no, no!" Saneh screamed hysterically.

"She is worthless to me then." He made to cut the girl's throat.

Saneh leaped up with lightning speed and kicked the knife from the Japanese gangster's hand. He reacted equally quickly, punching her in the face and knocking her to the floor.

She sprang to her feet, lip split and bleeding but ready to counterattack. The two guards unslung their weapons and cocked them, pointing their muzzles directly at the PRIMAL operative.

"Tie them both up," said Masateru, holding the wrist that Saneh had kicked. "And hurry up and bring me the fucking Englishman."

CHAPTER 26

TEN MINUTES EARLIER, OVERWATCH POSITION, CASTLE LORAN

Aleks was fighting the dreaded "nod monster." His eyes were tired and heavy; every few minutes his head would start to drop lower and lower until he awoke with a jerk. He pinched the inside of his hand, trying to break the cycle. He was amazed his body was so willing to sleep when he was damp, cold, and uncomfortable, not to mention that his ghillie suit smelled like a wet dog.

Bishop and Saneh's low-frequency signal had come through half an hour earlier. It did not mean they were in trouble but served as a warning that the situation could escalate rapidly. Aleks was paying particular attention to the gatehouse located above the castle's main entrance. It seemed to be the most heavily guarded of all the structures.

He gave the castle another scan with the thermal-imaging scope. No sign of Bishop or Saneh. Fatigue was quickly forgotten as he realized that the number of heat signatures on the walls had doubled. The guards were also using flashlights, clearly searching for someone.

His concentration was broken as his earpiece let off a shrill beep. He glanced at the screen of his iPRIMAL. The precoded message said:

Compromised. Request immediate extraction.

He hit a button on the iPRIMAL and the little device showed him the feed from the radio scanner. The low-frequency signal had originated in the keep.

Aleks gave Kurtz a nudge with his boot. The two of them had been lying side by side for nearly forty-eight hours, one sleeping, the other keeping watch. Kurtz woke in an instant and lifted the shaggy hood of his ghillie suit. "What is it?"

"Message. Saneh and Bishop want out."

Kurtz lifted the flap of camouflage material that covered his iPRIMAL and read the alert.

"*Scheisse.*" He powered up his own thermal scope and started scanning the castle. "Marked increase in guard activity. What's it all about?"

"Don't know. A car arrived fifteen minutes ago. Nothing else."

"That's not unusual." They had logged a number of vehicles coming and going during the night.

"That is what I thought, but in the last few minutes the number of guards has increased and they have been searching with flashlights. Then the message arrived."

"Guards are definitely looking for someone," Kurtz observed.

"Do you think the Bunker will have any extra info?" Aleks asked.

"We should know soon enough; the message will have relayed straight through to them." Kurtz continued to scan. "Did you see that?"

"What?" Aleks asked.

"Look where my laser is pointed. There's someone on the battlements trying to hide." The laser designator on their rifles could only be seen by another thermal scope dialed to the exact same wavelength.

"I've got it. Someone's crouched there. It could be Bishop."

"Looks the right size."

At that moment both of their headsets started beeping, indicating an incoming call.

Aleks accepted the call and it linked to both of them through the wireless headsets they wore under their camouflage hoods.

"Team, it's Vance. What's the situation?"

It was Aleks's shift so he responded. "About fifteen minutes ago at oh-four-thirty hours a vehicle drove into the castle. The emergency transmission came through just after and now the guards are going crazy."

"What about Bishop and Saneh?"

"We've got eyes on someone attempting to evade the guards on the battlements; it could be him. The transponder is still transmitting from the keep. They could be holding Saneh up there."

"Any indication of why they requested evac?"

"*Nyet*, just increased activity and the possible friendly on the wall."

"Roger." There was a pause. "We've activated the recovery plan. Mirza and the team are airborne and on their way. ETA to your loc is twelve minutes."

Aleks used his fingers to zoom out the map on his iPRIMAL. He could see the icon that represented the PRIMAL CAT. It was moving rapidly toward their location. They were a formidable force, four highly trained commandos delivered by a gunned-up helicopter. The Hungarians were in for a bad morning. "We have them on screen. I'm going to stream my feed so you can see the target." He married the data link on his scope to his iPRIMAL and added it to a shared menu.

"I'll take a look," said Vance. "You and Kurtz are to provide surgical fire support. Make sure nothing gets into the castle until our boys hit the ground. Once that happens, Mirza will have the conn."

"Affirmative," Aleks answered.

"OK," Kurtz confirmed.

"Bunker out."

CHAPTER 27

CASTLE LORAN

Bishop crouched precariously on the battlements, the increased guard activity having caught him halfway between the keep and the gatehouse. Armed guards were approaching as they patrolled the wall, using powerful flashlights. Bishop had no choice but to hang over the side again.

He held on by his fingers on the inside of the castle wall. The flashlights progressed above him and he could hear the guards' gruff voices. Below, another team was hunting, the barking of their dog sending shivers up his spine. Something had gone wrong, he knew. Somehow they were onto him.

Forearms burning, he waited for the searchers above him to pass. When they were nearly at the keep, he climbed back up onto the walkway. He sprinted to the gatehouse and crouched next to the heavy metal door. It was locked.

He looked up to see if there was another way in and spotted a camera pointing directly at him.

He squinted as he was illuminated by a powerful floodlight. Shielding his eyes from the beam, he glanced over the edge of the battlements and down into the courtyard. The guards with the dog were over by the entrance to the keep. He spotted an electrical cable on the wall of the gatehouse, fastened to the stone with steel clamps and running up to a CCTV camera. It looked like it could hold his weight; the only problem was how far it was from the wall.

"HALT!" one of the guards screamed.

Bishop leaped off and hit the stone wall of the gatehouse hard, his fingers scrabbling for the cable. As he fell he managed to hook his fingers under it. He had miscalculated, though—the cable was not strong enough.

The first bracket popped out of the stone, the one above it went, then the one above that. There was a horrendous wrenching noise and the CCTV camera ripped cleanly from the wall. Bishop hung on with both hands as he dropped. Another bracket a few inches below his hands caught him. It held for half a second and then gave, the one after it went as well, and Bishop slid down the wall, jerking as he reached each of the brackets. Within seconds they had all popped from the wall and he landed with a thump on top of the minibus parked in the courtyard. The steel roof buckled, slightly absorbing the force of his fall.

He rolled off the vehicle, checking his limbs for damage, then noticed the security camera sitting on a tangle of cable. The red light was still flashing. He gave it a smile and touched his head in a salute.

The bark of a dog brought him back to reality. The animal had been released and was tearing across the courtyard. Behind it, even more guards were pouring out of the keep, all heavily armed.

Bishop ducked into a stone arch and up a well-worn set of stairs. They spiraled upward inside the battlements and he sprinted as fast as he could, trying to keep ahead of the dog. Three flights up he burst out onto a landing, lungs heaving. In the middle of the corridor was a cleaning cart. Leaning against it, a cigarette hanging out of his mouth and a cell phone in his hand, was one of the hotel staff.

"Sorry!" Bishop grabbed the phone and the cigarette. He stuffed the phone in his pocket and grabbed an aerosol can from the cart.

The cleaner stood with his mouth open as he watched the tracksuit-clad guest aim the canister of air freshener back down the stairs.

Bishop could hear the clatter of the dog's claws on the stairs, the canine rapidly approaching.

He sucked hard on the cigarette to fuel the ember and squirted the aerosol. It belched a jet of flame into the corridor, blackening the sandstone stairs.

The smell of burnt fur filled the air, followed by a yelp and a series of high-pitched wails as the attack dog retreated down the stairs. Bishop dropped the flaming canister into the cleaning cart and pushed it into the stairs. It crashed downward, catching fire as it tumbled.

"Gives you cancer, saves my life," quipped Bishop, returning the cigarette to the startled cleaner. He ran down the corridor and up another flight of stairs, leaving the burning cart blocking the route behind him.

As he climbed he punched a number into the phone. It beeped: no reception. "Fuck!"

He went up another two flights of stairs. The next landing was as high as the castle walls, and he realized it was at the base of the gatehouse. There were doorways on each end to the battlements and a central stairway that led upward.

He checked his phone again; it had a single bar of reception. He hit redial and it connected to PRIMAL's emergency line.

"Hello, Rachel speaking."

"Rachel, it's Nigel, I was wondering if the old man's there."

"One moment." There was a slight pause.

"Nigel, good to hear from you, what's up?" Vance struggled to hide the tension in his voice.

"Just a small problem. I was wondering if you had anyone who could help."

"I've got some friends in the area; I'll put you through." There was another short pause.

While Bishop waited there a thump came on the door that led out to the battlements. The wood around the lock creaked, then came a loud thud, and it started to splinter. The guards on the other side were not waiting for someone with a key. He was running out of options and knew it was only a matter of time before he was cornered.

"Hello, Nigel, can I help?" Bishop could identify Aleks's voice anywhere. The Russian accent was like music to his ears.

"I'm at the base of the gatehouse. Someone's trying to get in from the battlements. I need help now."

"Acknowledged, special delivery on its way."

Another heavy blow to the door and the wood around the lock failed, splintering as it was forced inward. A split second later Bishop heard two wet-sounding slaps, followed by the distinctive cracks of supersonic bullets.

Thick red blood ran in from under the door. He jimmied his hands into the fractured wood and tore it open.

The two guards were crumpled on the walkway. Bishop ducked out and retrieved an AK-74 from one of the bodies.

"Thanks," he said into the phone. "I need you to keep the walls clear. If you haven't already, we need to invite the rest of our friends to join the party."

"No problem, backup is only a few minutes away. Are you with Saneh?"

"What? No, she was in our room. Why?"

"She triggered an alert. The transponder is still active in the keep."

"Fuck. I've got to hole up here. Pass my location to our friends. Once they get to me we'll go get Saneh."

"Will do."

Bishop heard noises below and dashed up the central staircase. Smoke from the flaming trolley hung in the air. He checked the phone; no coverage again.

He crouched to one side of the stairs and waited, AK held at the ready.

Moments later the barrel of an assault rifle heralded the arrival of the guards. Bishop stitched the first guard with a burst, sending him tumbling down the stairwell.

The return fire was heavy, bullets ricocheting up the staircase. Bishop was forced to move backward as the weight of fire increased. He returned fire to little effect; the amount of ammunition the guards were pouring up the stairs was overwhelming.

The hallway was rapidly becoming a death trap and he retreated from the staircase until he reached a locked door. He could hear voices on the other side, female voices. It made sense; this was where they were keeping the girls.

"GET AWAY FROM THE DOOR!" he yelled.

He fired two shots into the lock and kicked it open. The faces of eleven scared teenage girls greeted him.

"Does anyone speak English?" Half a dozen hands shot up.

"I'm here to help you, but first we need to stop the guards from getting in."

A tall, blue-eyed blonde ran forward and started pushing one of the beds toward the door. Other girls came forward to help her.

Bishop fired a burst from the AK down the corridor toward the stairs and then slammed the door shut. The girls helped him push beds up against it. They toppled a wardrobe on top of them. Most of the furniture in the room was quickly piled up in front of the entrance. It would be enough to buy a few precious minutes. He checked around the room; the only other door led to the bathroom.

"What's your name?" he asked the pretty blonde.

"Karla."

"Listen to me carefully, Karla. I need you to take all of the girls into the bathroom. You need to lock the door and hide behind anything solid."

"OK." She shepherded the girls out of the dorm.

Bishop turned over a heavy wardrobe and took cover behind it. Outside, guards banged at the door. Rounds ripped through the wood as they fired, tearing into the makeshift barricade.

He checked his watch: The CAT would not be far away. He just needed to hold off the guards for a few minutes more. He thumbed the magazine off his AK and checked it. It still had rounds but felt light, almost empty. He flinched as more bullets splintered through the door and wondered how long it would take until one of them found its mark.

CHAPTER 28

"The Englishman needs to be taken alive." András was focused on the television feed from the makeshift dormitory. It showed Bishop crouched behind an overturned wardrobe holding an AK.

"He's not going to give up," said Masateru. "See how he keeps looking at that mobile and his watch? He's been in contact with someone; you need to be ready for reinforcements."

András picked up the phone on his desk and dialed an internal number. "Bring more men up from the outer guardhouse. When they're inside, seal the castle." He turned to Masateru. "Once the gates are closed there's no getting in."

"Or getting out. Good, and what about the local police?"

"Of course! If the local cops are here, anyone else is going to think twice about attacking." András punched another number into his phone. "My cousin is married to the local police chief's sister. He will send everything he has, but this early in the morning it will take time."

Masateru left András to make the call and turned his attention back to Saneh and Kalista.

"I'm going to make this very simple." He took the tanto blade from his pocket and snapped it open. "You!" He pointed the knife at Saneh. "Tell me who you work for, or . . ." He grabbed Kalista by the hair, hauling her up off the chair. "This pretty little thing loses her face." He ran the blunt side of the knife down her cheek, leaving an angry red mark on her skin.

"What are you doing?" Saneh's arms were zip-tied behind her back. "She has nothing to do with this. Look at her, she's a scared little girl!"

"She is, isn't she, and so pretty." Masateru's eyes were emotionless as he turned to Saneh. "It would be a shame to damage such beauty. You wouldn't want to be responsible for that, would you?"

Kalista jerked her head away from the blade. "She's Interpol, they're all Interpol!"

"The bitch is lying." András had finished his call to the police. "If they were Interpol I'd know all about it."

Masateru yanked back Kalista's head, pulling her hair savagely. The razor-sharp blade of his knife cut effortlessly into the flesh of her cheek. He sliced downward, parting her peachlike flesh with a deft flick of his wrist.

The blade was so sharp that it took a few seconds for Kalista's body to register the trauma. Then she screamed in agony as a crimson line appeared on her face. Blood poured from the laceration, running down her neck and into her sweater.

"Now, who exactly are you?" he asked Saneh.

"You already know! I'm Nigel Martin's assistant. I work for the Dostiger arms syndicate. Now leave her alone, please!" Saneh's voice was hysterical.

"If I need to cut out her tongue to loosen yours, then I will."

"You're going to die badly for this," Saneh said softly.

"Really?" Masateru glanced up at the screens behind the desk. "And who's going to do that? Your boyfriend? He seems a little preoccupied."

Up on the screen, Bishop was still hunkered behind the wardrobe as bullets ricocheted off the walls around him. The door had been forced slightly ajar by the guards' attempt to breach. They were close to smashing through the makeshift barrier.

"So your choices are limited," said Masateru. "Either you tell me what you know or the next time my blade touches her skin it will be her throat." He let go of Kalista's hair and she slumped back into her chair. Her hands were clasped to her face in an attempt to stem the flow of blood. He turned and pointed the blade at Saneh. "And then, if need be, I'm more than happy to go to work on your flawless features."

"Fine." Saneh let out a deep sigh. "I'll tell you everything I know."

What Masateru and András did not know was that Saneh now controlled the situation. She knew she needed only to generate a few minutes of time. Enough for a faint thud of a helicopter's rotors to grow into a powerful roar.

CHAPTER 29

PRIMAL MI-17 EN ROUTE TO CASTLE LORAN

"Aleks, can you confirm the last known location of Bishop and Saneh?" Mirza Mansoor was strapped in the back of the Mi-17 helicopter as it thundered through the darkness. The commander of PRIMAL's Critical Assault Team studied a tablet with a satellite image of the castle displayed on it.

Two areas of interest were marked on the screen: one inside the large building on top of the castle's front gate, the other a broader area that covered the upper levels of the keep.

"Bishop phoned us fifteen minutes ago from the base of the gatehouse above the main entrance. He said he would stay there." Aleks's voice came through Mirza's headset. "Saneh is probably still in the keep with the transponder. We haven't been able to confirm her status."

"Acknowledged."

Aleks continued, "The door to the gatehouse has already been breached. That's the best way in."

Mirza shook his head in wonder. Aleks was still ten miles away and it sounded as if he were sitting in the chopper next to him. Mirza had been a PRIMAL operative for more than two years and still had not been exposed to all the gadgets. It didn't help that Mitch, the resident scientist and pilot of the chopper, kept introducing more gear.

"Got it," he confirmed. "We're going to fly a single pass and then rope in on the eastern wall. Can you provide fire support from your position?"

"*Da*, we just need to move a hundred meters."

"Roger, move now."

"Affirmative, Aleks out."

"Two minutes, lads," Mitch cut in from the cockpit of the helicopter.

"Gear up, team." Mirza slid the tablet into the purpose-built pouch on the front of his armor. "We're going to rope onto the battlements and gain entry to the gatehouse." He picked up his full-face helmet from where it was sitting on the floor between his boots. It fit snugly against his skull, the face mask hinging down to cover his eyes, nose, and mouth. Once it was in place he pressed a button on the iPRIMAL strapped to his wrist and activated the helmet's digital systems. From the outside it made him look almost alien, with bug-eyed reflective lenses and gill-like side vents. On the inside, tiny projectors took the feed from the multispectral sensors and overlayed an augmented reality of the world outside, feeding Mirza vital information as he led the team.

"One OK," Mirza announced when he was ready, his voice projecting over the helmet's integrated communications system.

"Two OK," Pavel announced.

"Three OK." Miklos was next.

"Fucking helmet, built for tiny hands." Kruger, the six-foot-five South African, was fiddling with his face mask. "OK, I got it, four OK."

Apart from the numbers they wore on their shoulders they were all dressed the same: black carbon-nanotube armor shielding most of their body, torsos covered with ammunition and grenades, and the full-faced combat helmets. Their assault rifles were integrally suppressed Tavors chambered in 7.62mm blackout and individually customized with a range of attachments.

All four had come from different backgrounds; Mirza and Miklos were sniper and surveillance specialists, Pavel a communications and hacking guru, and Kruger a heavy-weapons and demolitions man. Together, trained in urban combat, they made a formidable team.

"Aleks here. We are in position," he broadcast over the communications network.

"Start taking out the lights and make sure no one else gets in," ordered Mirza.

"Acknowledged. We have a four-wheel drive approaching the front gates. Engaging now."

Mitch's voice came over the airwaves. "Tower, this is Ghost Rider requesting a flyby."

"Let's get this show on the road," replied Mirza. "Kruger, you ready?"

"Ready to rock out with my fitty-cal out." The South African was manning a rapid-fire .50-caliber M3M machine gun at the front left door.

The Mi-17 came in low and fast, its turbines screaming as Mitch brought it into a sweeping turn. An AK barked from the castle wall and another two weapons joined it.

"Taking fire!" Mitch announced as he touched the tablet screen strapped to his thigh.

On the inside pylon of the helicopter, a dummy fuel tank split in half to reveal a gun pod. Using the heads-up display in his helmet Mitch focused on the muzzle flashes from the castle and returned fire.

The 12.7mm minigun rained fire down on the ancient walls, blowing the first gunman clean off the walkway. The chopper continued its route circling the castle, the minigun's rotating barrels spitting fire at anyone foolish enough to expose themselves.

Meanwhile Aleks and Kurtz made short work of the four-wheel drive that had raced up the road toward the castle. They engaged simultaneously with their Windrunner sniper rifles. Two .408 rounds smashed the engine block and sent the car careening into a ditch. Another two rounds into the cabin dispatched the driver and passenger. With that target neutralized they went to work on the castle's lights.

"We're all clear, bringing her in." Mitch flew the helicopter down over the castle walls. He jabbed another button and the rear clam-shell doors swung open with a hiss. Using the cameras positioned around the aircraft, Mitch held her steady over the wall.

With Mitch concentrating on hovering, Kruger opened up with the side-mounted machine gun. He blasted away at anything that resembled a threat, high-explosive rounds tearing chunks from the castle walls and turning gunmen into pink mist.

"Rope out," announced Miklos, kicking the coil of rope out the back of the aircraft. It uncoiled as it dropped, the thirty-foot length hitting the wall with a foot to spare. "On rope." He stepped out and slid down the thick rope like a fireman's pole. When he hit the ground he grabbed his weapon from where it hung across his back and snapped it into his shoulder, aiming back toward the keep.

Pavel was a split second behind and covered toward the gate-house. Mirza was next, then, with a thump, the big South African joined them. "All clear."

The rope dropped and there was a roar as the chopper slid sideways, lowered its nose, and powered away from the castle. "Tal-lyho, let me know if there's anything you need."

"Thanks, Mitch," said Mirza. "Team, let's get off this wall and into the gatehouse. Aleks and Kurtz, we're going to need your cover."

The two snipers had continued knocking out the lights. Now, as if on cue, another light shattered high on the keep, sending glass showering into the courtyard.

Pavel moved first, his weapon in his shoulder as he stalked along the battlements toward the gatehouse. "Contact front!" He let rip a burst from his Tavor, the weapon making a barely audible clicking sound, the subsonic blackout rounds hissing through the suppressor.

An AK barked from the shattered doors to the gatehouse. Simultaneously another AK fired from high up on the keep, sending bullets ricocheting between the PRIMAL operatives.

"Contact high, our six." Kruger fired up at the keep. His bullets ricocheted off the parapet, forcing the gunman to take cover.

"Target acquired," Kurtz's voice broadcast over the comms network.

A second later the man raised his head. Kurtz's high-velocity sniper round took another second to cover the nine hundred meters. It slammed into the top of the parapet, sending shards of stone slicing into the shooter's face and hands. He toppled backward out of sight.

Mirza fired the grenade launcher underslung on his Tavor. The 40mm round flew through the open doors of the gatehouse and detonated. Simultaneously Miklos lobbed a flash-bang over Pavel's head and into the smoking doorway. It detonated with a crump.

Pavel and Mirza led into the building, weapons held ready. They need not have bothered. Two dead bodies were sprawled on the cobblestones, AKs dropped beside them. The acoustic sensors on the CAT helmets picked up footsteps beating a hasty retreat down the internal staircase.

The heads-up display in Mirza's helmet directed him to Bishop's assessed location. "Next floor up and down the corridor," he transmitted as he led the team up the spiral staircase and into the corridor. A dead guard lying in front of a bullet-ridden doorway signposted the location they were looking for. There was little left of the once-heavy wooden door. Mirza gave it a thump with his gloved fist. It creaked ominously. "Anyone in there?"

"Why don't you come in and find out?" a voice called back.

"I know how this one goes," replied Mirza. "You're waiting on the other side with a fire extinguisher and a bag of flour."

"You're never going to let that go, are you?" Bishop asked from the other side. "You've got to admit, it was pretty funny."

"It's the last time I go on a holiday with you."

There was a loud crash as Kruger barged in, toppling the remains of the furniture out of the way. With a grunt he forced open what remained of the door, causing it to collapse in a heap.

"Kruger, we can't take you anywhere, can we?" said Bishop.

"What can I say? I like breaking things."

A burst of fire ricocheted up the staircase behind them.

"I'm being rude. Come in, all of you." Bishop stepped to one side, giving the team a sweeping bow as they filed in.

Miklos pitched a grenade back down the staircase and followed the rest of the team inside. It went off with a loud boom that shook dust from the walls. "I like what you've done with the place," he commented as he shook Bishop's hand.

Miklos guarded the door while the rest of them gathered around Mirza, who had pulled out his tablet.

"Do you know what Saneh's status is?" asked Mirza. "I'm getting a strong reading from her transponder."

"Haven't seen her since everything went to shit. My guess is they'll have taken her to the offices in the top floor of the keep."

"Many more tangos?" asked Kruger.

"Fair few, although with Aleks and Kurtz out there and now Mitch in the helo, at least there won't be any more coming in."

"We'll head back across the walls to the keep, breach our way in, and fight our way up into the keep. As we get closer we should be able to narrow down her location," said Mirza.

"Good plan," agreed Bishop. "Any chance you brought me some gear?"

"*Ja, ja.*" Kruger unslung the backpack he was wearing and dropped it on the bed. Inside were Bishop's lightweight combat vest, an MP7 submachine gun, his iPRIMAL, and a comms headset.

As Bishop donned the equipment over his tracksuit, the door that led into the bathroom creaked open.

Miklos's weapon snapped up, ready to fire.

"Whoa, check your fire!" Bishop took two steps and pushed the weapon down. "Friendlies." He turned to the door. "Karla, you can come out now."

Karla's face appeared around the door, and her eyes went wide with fear as she took in the four black-armored PRIMAL operatives in their buglike helmets.

"It's OK, they're with me."

One by one the girls appeared. They filed in and sat down on the beds, watching nervously, looking like children in their pajamas. Only Karla was brave enough to approach the operatives. "Are your friends here to take us home?"

"Yes," Bishop stated. "But I need you to stay here a little longer while we take care of the bad men."

"Watch out for their dogs," she said. "They used them on my sister."

Bishop studied the girl's face and tried to remember what the psychologist had told him about PTSD on his last medical. She seemed too calm, almost distant.

Mirza had already checked out the room and reassessed the situation. "Kruger, you stay here and protect the girls with Miklos. Pavel, you're with Bishop and me."

The South African nodded his head in acknowledgment, then opened the front of his helmet to reveal his strong angular features. "I'll look after them."

"Miklos, make sure you keep an eye on the door; anyone who tries to get in that isn't us gets slotted, OK?"

"Wilco."

Bishop actioned his submachine gun and led Mirza and Pavel out of the shattered doorway and into the cold, dark corridors of the castle.

CHAPTER 30

CASTLE LORAN

"Where the hell did that helicopter come from? My men are being taken apart." András was staring up at the CCTV screens at the back of his office, occasionally catching a glimpse of the black-clad assailants. More than half of the screens were now blank as the cameras were systematically destroyed by whoever was assaulting the castle. "Where the fuck are the police?"

"They won't arrive in time," Masateru replied calmly. He was now sitting opposite Saneh at the coffee table. Kalista remained huddled in her chair, bloodied hands clutched to her face.

Saneh had spun him an elaborate tale, explaining that she had been hired by the arms dealer Nigel Martin to help infiltrate the organization. The operation, she revealed, had been funded by a wealthy Russian whose daughter had been abducted and sold into slavery.

As she had told her story, the gunfire outside the castle and progression of blanking screens had made it obvious that Mirza and his men were on the way. Her story had bought precious minutes, but she doubted Masateru believed it.

"Whoever these people are, they're here for the girls," Masateru said. "They're also going to try and get this one back." He rose from the coffee table, pointing at Saneh with his knife. "She's coming with us." He waved his two heavies over to Saneh, put his jacket on, and ran a hand through his hair. "Tape up her mouth."

His men had come prepared; they taped her mouth shut and checked that the zip-ties on her wrists remained secure.

Another of the video feeds on the wall flickered and went blank. The amount of gunfire outside had petered off to nothing, a good indication that most of András's men were dead or cowering.

"Where does this lead?" asked Masateru, pointing to a door in the corner of the room.

"Down to the stables. We can go together."

Masateru shook his head. "You will destroy all your files and *then* follow." He waved his hand at the four AK-wielding guards. "You have enough firepower to hold them at bay. Trust me, if you get out and your bread crumbs lead these devils to the *oyabun*, then it would have been better for you that you died here today."

Masateru gave a nod to his Kissaki bodyguards, ducked through the door, and stepped down onto the narrow staircase beyond. One of his bodyguards pushed Saneh through; both of them were now openly wielding compact machine pistols.

★★★

The now-manic András began organizing his four men. "You two, get out there and stop the bastards from getting in." The gunmen opened the office door and tentatively peered out. The dim hallway lighting was still intact.

"What the fuck are you waiting for?" András's brow furrowed and he reached into his drawer for his Škorpion machine pistol. All his men knew it was his preferred way to deal with disloyal employees.

The two men disappeared into the corridor.

"Lock it and barricade it," he directed the other men.

They pushed a chair in front of the door and leaned the coffee table against it. "What about the girl?" one of them asked, indicating Kalista, still bleeding on the couch.

"They can have her. She's worth nothing to us now." He turned his attention to his computer, attempting to delete a number of folders. "Come on, you son of a bitch." The computer froze as he repeatedly stabbed at the keyboard with one finger.

An AK chattered in the corridor, followed by a deep boom. The overpressure rattled the door.

"Fuck it!" András picked up his submachine gun and fired a burst into the computer. It hissed and sparked. Then he kicked it off the desk. "Smash it and let's get the hell out of here."

One of the guards stomped on the box, splitting it in half. He used the butt of his AK to smash the hard drive as András left through the doorway that Masateru had used.

A massive explosion blasted open the office door, throwing furniture across the room and knocking both guards to the ground. Two black-armored operatives charged in through the smoking hole in the wall, weapons ready.

"Target down," Mirza reported as he shot a guard in the face.

An AK roared in the confines of the room and Pavel was knocked sideways as he pivoted to engage his target. Bishop punched in through the doorway and fired his MP7 on full automatic. It hissed like an enraged taipan and the second guard fell backward, his chest riddled with bullets.

"MAN DOWN!" yelled Bishop.

"I'm OK, I'm OK." Pavel was kneeling propped against the wall. A round had hit him in the abdomen but had not penetrated his state-of-the-art armor.

"Saneh's not here," said Bishop, attending to Kalista on the couch. "Neither is András or Masateru." He spotted the open side door and stood. "You guys look after the girl. I'm going after them."

"Wait!" Mirza yelled, but it was too late.

Bishop had already darted through the door.

CHAPTER 31

A round cracked past Bishop's head as he charged through the open door. He tripped down the stairs, found his feet, and hugged the center of the spiral staircase as bullets sparked off the stone.

Ahead of him, András let loose another burst from the Škorpion. He turned and continued down as fast as his stocky frame could take him, fumbling with the weapon's magazine as he ran.

Bishop fired a burst in return, taking three stairs at a time as he chased his prey. By the third twist in the staircase he caught up and shoved András in the back, sending him stumbling forward. The mafia boss tripped headfirst, landing with a sickening crunch, his head twisted sideways. Bishop shot him in the back of the head and continued downward.

The stairs finished a few more flights down at yet another heavy wooden door. Bishop's lungs were heaving as he turned the handle. It was unlocked.

"Mirza, can you hear me?" he transmitted over his radio.

He heard nothing in reply. The thick walls were blocking the signal.

The sound of squealing tires could be heard beyond the door.

"Fuck it." He swung the door open.

A Mercedes SUV's tires spun as the driver revved the engine. Bishop recognized Masateru in the passenger window and he snapped up his submachine gun, the trigger half-pressed. He paused, catching a glimpse of Saneh sitting next to the gangster. The G-Wagen rocketed out of the garage, narrowly missing the automated castle gates as they swung open.

"Fuck!"

He looked around the converted stable, desperately searching for a key cabinet. He found it on the floor next to a beautiful silver Maserati. It had taken the Japanese precious time to rip it off the wall and smash it open. Fortunately they'd not had the foresight to take the rest of the keys. Bishop grabbed a set from the floor and fumbled for the remote button. The lights of the Maserati flashed twice. He had found a ride.

The V8 roared to life and Bishop punched the sports tourer through the single vehicle entrance to the garage. He gunned the engine, spinning the GranTurismo's wheels on the smooth cobblestones. It slid sideways and bounced off a minibus with a crunch.

"Whoops."

He backed off the gas and corrected the oversteer, easing through the castle gates just before they swung shut.

"Aleks, Kurtz. Can you hear me?"

"Yes, loud and clear," Kurtz replied over the comms link.

Bishop hit the gravel of the estate's driveway and accelerated after the taillights disappearing into the darkness. "I'm in the sports car leaving the castle now. Did you see the four-wheel drive?"

"*Ja*, Mirza said to hold fire. He said Saneh was probably in it."

"Correct, she's in the backseat. I'm in pursuit. Is Mitch on station?"

Bishop fought to keep the high-performance vehicle on the narrow track as he spoke into his headset. He jabbed at buttons and pulled the control stalks, searching for the lights. Finally he found them and the vehicle's powerful high beams lit up the road.

"Bishop, this is Mitch, I'm thirty seconds out from your location."

"Roger, there's a Mercedes four-wheel drive ahead of me. I need you to track it till I catch up."

Bishop glanced down at the speedometer. The illuminated gauge was nosing 110 miles an hour. The Yakuza must be hammering it, he thought.

"I'm on it." The chopper roared overhead.

Bishop kept the accelerator to the floor. Trees flashed past in the beams of the headlights. He crested a small rise and the Maserati left the ground before slamming down onto its suspension. He fought for control, barely managing to keep it on the road.

The road straightened and up ahead he caught a glimpse of the set of taillights turning left.

"Bishop, you're about to hit the security checkpoint. I've got multiple armed hostiles; it looks like they're chaining the gate."

Bishop kept his speed up, closing rapidly. High above him a stream of tracer fire leaped out of the sky.

"Tangos down, your G-Wagen's gone left. Taking care of the gates next. Better slow down, old man."

"Negative, we'll lose them."

The car was racing toward the gate at breakneck speed.

Two hundred meters.

One fifty.

One hundred. "Hurry up, Mitch!"

"Coming round."

Fifty meters.

The helicopter unleashed a volley of flaming rockets.

Bishop slammed the brakes and the car skidded along the road.

The rockets streaked over the top of the Maserati and slammed into the heavy wrought iron gate, blowing it off its hinges.

Fragments cracked the windshield as Bishop continued through the smoldering wreckage and veered left onto the main road. He opened up the big V8, aiming the sharklike grille at the taillights. "Could you make it any closer?"

"Missed by an inch, missed by a mile," replied Mitch.

"If that was an inch, you're overcompensating."

On the open road the sports car ate up the distance quickly and it did not take long for Bishop to be on the tail of the SUV.

"You want me to disable them?" Mitch asked from the Mi-17 tailing the vehicles.

"Hit them with the spotlight first." Bishop was keeping the Maserati just behind the G-Wagen.

The beam of light shot out of the sky, engulfing the vehicle. It swerved slightly as the driver was caught by surprise.

"If I PIT them they're going to flip," said Bishop, referring to the Pursuit Intervention Technique of nudging a car sideways. "At this speed it'll kill them all."

A submachine gun appeared from a side window of the Merc. Bishop swerved as it spat rounds at him. One of them punched through the windshield inches from his head. "Motherfuckers! Give them a warning, Mitch!" He backed off his pursuit, letting them pull away.

The floodlight disappeared, plunging the black four-wheel drive into darkness. Then a glowing line of tracer lanced out, striking the asphalt in front of it.

The G-Wagen ignored the blast and kept barreling down the road.

"I'll ramp this up a little, Bish." A streak of flame appeared from the darkness and a rocket slammed into the forest ahead of the cars. A ball of flame turned night into day as the cars flashed past it.

"They're not stopping."

"Things just got worse: cop cars ahead."

Bishop could just make out the flashing blue lights closing rapidly. "Once we pass them, stop the Merc."

"Roger!"

At the speed they were traveling it was seconds before the police cars sped by, responding to the priority call from the castle.

Another burst of tracer streaked from the sky and rounds slammed into the G-Wagen's hood. At nearly eight thousand rpm, the German-built engine disintegrated, pistons tearing the block apart. The drive shaft seized and the gearbox exploded. The driver slammed on the brakes and the ABS brought the mortally wounded vehicle to a shuddering halt.

Bishop braked sharply, stopping his own car fifty meters short. He killed the headlights and leaped out with his MP7 held ready. The Mi-17 could be heard overhead, its spotlight illuminating the stricken SUV.

The driver was still in his seat when Bishop shot him through the window. The man's brains sprayed across Masateru, who dived out of his door. The man in the backseat was already out. He fired a burst from his MP9 from the back corner of the car.

Bishop angled away from the Mercedes to get a clear shot, searching for Saneh. The Yakuza gunman fired another burst of 9mm and made a run for it. Illuminated by the helicopter's spotlight, it was an easy shot. Bishop fired twice and the man spun sideways, hitting the ground with a grunt. On the other side of the vehicle Masateru sprinted into the darkness.

"Mitch, we've got one hostile heading into the forest. He's the priority target."

"Roger." The spotlight shifted to the side of the road.

The thud of the chopper's blades and the pinging of the cooling remains of the Mercedes' engine were the only sounds in the early-morning air.

Bishop activated the flashlight attached to his MP7 as he approached the G-Wagen. He confirmed the driver was dead, then checked the backseat. Saneh was there, curled in a ball, her hands bound and mouth taped. He freed her hands quickly, then gently pulled the tape from her lips.

"Told you that four o'clock gym session was a bad idea," Saneh said icily.

"I thought I'd lost you." Bishop threw his arms around her.

She pushed him away. "You going to start listening to me anytime soon? You pretty much blew this entire mission."

"Not even a thank-you for the rescue?"

The look Saneh gave him told the entire story: She was fuming.

"Bishop, this is Mirza, you OK?" The voice came through over the radio.

"Yeah, mate, I'm good. I'm with Saneh. We're on the main road out of the facility."

"Roger, we're traveling in a white minibus. Picked up Aleks and Kurtz already and are on our way to you now. Local law enforcement just passed us heading toward the castle. We'll be in your location in five. Mirza out."

There was a moan from the ditch by the side of the road. Bishop handed Saneh a pistol from his vest and they investigated.

The wounded Yakuza gunman shielded his eyes with one hand as Bishop illuminated him. "He's in bad shape."

The man's pants and jacket were drenched in blood.

Bishop checked him over for weapons. "He's taken a round to the thigh and one to the shoulder. Punched through his soft armor."

Saneh tore the medical kit from Bishop's rig, used the shears to cut away the wounded man's suit jacket, and removed his soft armor. "None of them look life-threatening." She started working on the wounds.

"Bishop, this is Mitch, no sign of your mate. I can't track him through the trees."

"Ack . . . I'm going to look for him." He glanced up the road at the approaching headlights. "I've got a few minutes."

"No." Saneh grabbed him by the arm. "We've got to get out of here, before the police come back looking to see what happened."

"This guy's just a bodyguard. Masateru's the one we want and he's hiding somewhere out there." Bishop pointed to the forest. "We get that fucker, we can blow all of this wide open."

"We need to go; we can't take the risk."

Mitch's voice came through on the radio. "Guys, I'm going to put down on the road. We need to evac ASAP."

"Fuck!" Bishop looked out into the woods, the individual trees becoming visible as dawn approached. "Yeah, OK, let's get the hell out of here."

As the Mi-17 descended onto the road, a white minibus pulled up. Aleks and Kurtz were the first to alight. They were still carrying their long rifles and with their ghillie suits they looked like a pair of swamp monsters. Kurtz had his rifle slung and was carrying the young woman that Masateru had sliced. He gave Bishop a solemn nod and waited for the helicopter to land before carrying the girl up through the clamshell doors, followed by Aleks. Mirza got out next, leading the rest of the girls on board from the van. The rest of the CAT, Kruger, Miklos, and Pavel, were the last out. They helped carry the wounded Yakuza bodyguard.

A few hundred meters up the road a police car sped toward the helicopter, its lights flashing angrily.

The Mi-17 strained under the extra weight. It rolled forward, beating its blades in a furious attempt to detach itself from the earth. With a lurch it jumped into the air and started climbing. By the time the Hungarian police arrived at the abandoned vehicles the chopper was nose down and heading for the Ukrainian border at more than 140 miles an hour.

★★★

"Who do you work for?" Bishop questioned the wounded Yakuza as they flew toward the border. They were crammed in the back of the Mi-17, not the best location for interrogation, especially with an audience of young women.

The heavyset gangster gave him a blank look. Bishop wanted to punch him in the face, but he refrained. He did not want to scare the girls any more than they already had been.

"Can I talk to him?" Kurtz had left the wounded woman—Kalista—in Saneh's care. The German's face was still covered in camouflage cream but he had taken off the ghillie suit.

Bishop glanced across to where Saneh was dressing Kalista's wound. The former Iranian spy had used butterfly strips to secure the flap of flesh hanging from her face. The younger sister, Karla, had her arms wrapped around the girl.

"I can't see why not, just don't be too rough. We'll save that for later." Bishop sat to the side and Kurtz took his position in front of their captive.

The German leaned in close to the man's face and spoke softly. "You think you're the tough man, *ja*? Selling young girls to dirty old men."

The Japanese criminal stared into his face.

"If you tell me who you work for I won't have to kill you."

The man smirked. "You can't kill me, policeman, I know your rules."

"Rules?" Kurtz laughed. "Do you really think I follow rules?" He gripped the man's bandaged leg, applying pressure to the gun-shot wound.

The gangster gasped in pain, then spat on the floor. "Fuck off, pig."

"Now you're beginning to piss me off." Kurtz sighed. "Tell me what you know and I might think about letting you live."

"Forget it, Kurtz, he won't talk," said Bishop. "These guys have a code. They'll die before they rat on their mates."

"What would you know about our ways?" the man snapped. "You're all *gaijin* scum, just like these whores."

Kurtz grabbed the front of the thug's shirt and jerked him out of his seat. He dragged the wounded prisoner down the center of the helicopter, between the girls. Reaching the back of the chopper he punched the button that activated the clamshell doors. They swung open with a hiss and the wind whipped into the aircraft.

No one could hear what Kurtz said to the prisoner; he held him by the front of his shirt, their faces inches apart.

The Yakuza thug glanced over his shoulder at the ground racing by underneath. He turned back and said something in a panic, his face a mask of terror. Then he disappeared, dropped from the back of the helicopter.

Kurtz hit the button for the doors and they closed with a snap, returning the cabin to a more tolerable level of noise. Then he walked between the two lines of stunned teenagers and sat back down next to Bishop. They stared at him in shock.

"Mori-Kai," Kurtz said flatly. "Does that mean anything to you?"

CHAPTER 32

ABANDONED AIR BASE, UKRAINE

"Good work, team." Vance's voice emanated from a laptop perched on a pile of equipment cases.

The PRIMAL operatives were back in the Ukrainian Air Force hangar. They had dropped the girls at a nearby Red Cross clinic before returning to their staging base and packing their gear. Work complete, they were now enjoying a well-earned beer.

He continued. "Yeah, it went to shit but that's what contingency plans are for. Key thing is, we took apart the Hungarian side of the operation. I'll hand you over to Chua for the latest intel before we make our next move."

Chen Chua's face replaced Vance's on the laptop screen. "The intel you pulled off the castle has turned up a few solid leads. First, we've started following up on the Arab *sheikh*. It's a pity Bishop lost his sunglasses so we don't have a picture of him. Shedir's a common name but Tariq's confident he can track him down based on his travel movements."

PRIMAL's benefactor, Tariq Ahmed, was the CEO of a multi-billion-dollar logistics empire. The former Emirates police officer-turned-businessman maintained his connections with the Abu Dhabi Special Branch and ran his own network of agents. If anyone could track down the Arab flesh peddler, it was him.

"The critical piece of new information is the name Kurtz extracted. The Mori-Kai were an ancient Japanese clan based in

Himeji. While my research hasn't dug up anything recent, I'm convinced we're on the right track. Additionally, the computer hack Bishop installed turned up a number of links between the Hungarian crime syndicate and mainland Japan."

"The guys at the castle were absolutely Yakuza but they didn't look like your average white-collar variety," Bishop said as he took a swig from his beer. "The bodyguards were switched on, definitely ex-military. They rolled with submachine guns and covert armor."

"I agree. It's just a shame the one you grabbed managed to kill himself," Chua said.

Bishop nodded; he hadn't told Chua and Vance exactly what happened. The helicopter incident was something he needed to discuss with Kurtz.

"If there are no more questions, I'm going to hand you back to Vance." Chua finished and the camera feed swapped to the PRIMAL director.

"OK, team, that's the intel. Now for the good stuff. We're gonna follow these leads and start pulling apart this network. Aleks, you and Kurtz are going to set up surveillance on the girls at the Red Cross facility. If these guys are as serious as we think they are, they're going to find them pretty damn quick. We need to be ready if they do."

Aleks and Kurtz nodded in unison.

"Mirza, you and your boys are heading across to the UAE. Once Tariq finds Shedir I want you to shake him down and get what you can out of him. When that's done, I'll hold you in place as a commander's reserve. I got the log team to book you in at Atlantis. Take the opportunity to get a bit of R and R until you get back to the island."

"Appreciated, sir," said Mirza.

High fives were exchanged between Pavel and Miklos. Kruger also looked happy.

"That leaves Bishop and Saneh . . . no rest for the wicked. You two are heading to Japan. You'll hook up with Chua's cop in Tokyo and see where this Mori-Kai angle leads."

"Do we have anything more to go on?" Bishop asked.

"Negative, that's why you're heading over there. We've got jack shit on this so far. We need you guys in-country to start gathering info. Chua and his team will work around the clock to turn it into actionable intel. We'll deploy additional assets when doors need kicking. Anyone else got questions? Nope? Now get out there and kick some ass."

The video link dropped and the screen went blank.

Bishop stood up. "All right, team, let's get the last of this gear loaded and get the hell out of here. Good luck with your missions."

They split up and Mitch and the CAT went back to stripping the weapon modules off the Mi-17 and packing them onto cargo pallets. The weaponry would go back to the island on a Lascar Logistics flight and Yuri, their arms dealer, would arrange to return the leased helicopter.

Bishop strolled over to where Aleks and Kurtz were loading equipment into their new car, an Audi A6 sedan. Their original V8-powered Audi and its load of weapons had been destroyed, a remotely activated incendiary device covering their tracks.

"New car OK?" Bishop asked.

"*Da*," Aleks replied. "Not as fast as the other one, but Yuri made sure it has everything we need."

"You got time for a quick chat?" Bishop directed Kurtz across to an empty corner of the hangar. "I was wondering if there was anything you wanted to tell me?"

"What do you mean?"

"I mean is there something that happened in Hungary that you think I should know about?"

Kurtz stared at him for a few seconds. "You mean with the girl."

Bishop nodded.

"What else could we do? We had to try and save her."

"We're talking about Aurelia, yeah? Your contact inside the kidnap gang?"

"Yes, they captured her. Aleks and I stormed the manor. We were too late; they killed her." Kurtz could not hide the pained look on his face. "We found Kalista half-dead; we had to take her with us."

"How did she end up at the castle?"

"I'm not sure. We left her in our safe house with instructions to stay put. But she must have wandered out onto the street and got picked up by the police."

Bishop considered the information. "You could have compromised this entire operation."

Kurtz remained silent.

"But I know why you did it and I probably would have done the same. Let's just make sure it doesn't happen again, OK?"

Kurtz nodded solemnly. "You're not going to tell Vance?"

"No, I don't think that's necessary. But I do want to talk about the Jap in the helo."

"There's not much to say. I extracted the information we needed and then disposed of him."

"We needed to bring that guy back here and run him through a full debriefing."

"What more do you think he would have given us? He led us to this Mori-Kai. Then he ceased to be useful."

"That's not your decision to make!"

"This is true and for that I apologize. It won't happen again." Kurtz locked eyes with Bishop. "Now, if there's nothing else, Aleks and I need to start our mission. The girls at the clinic are vulnerable."

"Remember, we're all a team here, Kurtz. We fight together, we support each other. That's what we do."

"Maybe something you should remember as well, Aden. Now I have to go." With that Kurtz turned and left Bishop to contemplate his words.

Bishop wandered back over to where Saneh was packing communications equipment.

"What was that all about?" she asked as he sat down on a crate.

"Nothing, just the guy on the helo."

"The jumper?"

"Yeah."

"Go easy on Kurtz, Aden. He's like you in more ways than one."

"What's that supposed to mean?"

"You know exactly what it means; he wants to save everyone. He's all heart and not enough brains."

"Yeah, that's what I'm afraid of."

"Aleks will look after him, just like Mirza and I have to look after you."

"That's right, is it? You and Mirza draw straws to see who's got to babysit me, hey?"

Saneh snapped shut the lid of a Pelican case. "Something like that. Now let's move or we're going to miss our flight."

CHAPTER 33

CASTLE LORAN

"We think was Special Force raid, no marks of attackers, many bullets, many bodies." The Hungarian police officer's English was terrible. It was, however, markedly better than his French, and Interpol Capitaine Rémi Marcen did not speak Hungarian.

"Yes, very good, thank you." He turned away from the man. "Fucking moron." The local police were about as effective at reading a crime site as his twelve-year-old daughter.

Marcen had arrived just after midday after flying in directly from Lyon. He had left within an hour of receiving the call, then had hired a car in Budapest and driven three hours to get to the castle.

The local police had been kind enough to lay out the bodies of the dead inside the courtyard and he had positively identified András and a few of his men. There were a dozen other people in custody, mostly the hotel staff but also two of András's clients. The clients had been handed over to one of Rémi's men, who spirited them away in his car. By now they would be on their way to the airport and back to their homes.

His phone buzzed; he flipped it open, checked the screen, and dropped it back into his pocket.

"I'm going now," he told the senior Hungarian policeman.

"So soon?" The man grinned, not bothering to hide his contempt for the Frenchman.

Rémi turned, climbed into his rental car, and drove off down the gravel driveway. He passed the bullet-riddled remains of a four-wheel drive that had crashed into the ditch that ringed the castle, then continued across the open field and down into the forest that surrounded it. He drove slowly with the windows down until he spotted a thin black tie in a tree. He stopped the car and beeped the horn twice. There was a rustling in the bushes and a disheveled-looking Masateru appeared.

"So, we finally meet," the Yakuza lieutenant said once he was in the car.

"I wish it were on better terms." Rémi shook his hand, then continued driving down the road.

"Did you go up to the castle?"

"Yes."

"Is anyone alive?"

"Only two of your clients; they're with my men now. András and his thugs are all dead."

"What about the girls?"

"They're gone, just like you said. The local cops have no idea what happened, thick as shit."

They slowed as they drove through the mangled gates at the estate guardhouse. The car shuddered as it drove over the pockmarked asphalt. A pair of local policemen waved them through.

"The men who did this are professionals, not a rival gang. It had to be state-sponsored," said Masateru when they were out on the highway and heading back toward Budapest.

"I concur. András and his men were directly targeted by a well-trained and highly effective force."

"They wore all black, with helmets," added the Japanese gangster. "Like Navy SEALs."

"It wouldn't be American. I would know about it."

"Even if it was the CIA?"

"Since when has the CIA been interested in the sex trade? Why would they target András?"

"Perhaps András had other business, something he'd hidden from us."

"Then why would they take the girls? Was there anything at the castle that could link András to you?"

"No, but they took one of my men."

"Shit, will he talk?"

"No, never. He'd die rather than betray us."

"Let's hope you're right, otherwise these people could be coming after you."

"Not if we find them first."

"You've got a plan."

Masateru nodded. "I've arranged for more of my men to arrive in Budapest. You will provide them with weapons and have your people find the girls. The *oyabun* still wants the blonde, and I have a feeling that Mr. Nigel Martin will not be far away."

"I'll put a call out. It won't take my people long to find the girls."

CHAPTER 34

SVALYAVA, UKRAINE

"I think I see a trend developing with us," Kurtz said over his radio. He was sitting in their new car, watching the street.

"What are you talking about?" asked Aleks from the apartment they had rented as a safe house.

"A trend, you know when something happens over and over."

"Ah, like when the target uses the same route to work every morning."

"*Ja*, just like that. Except the trend I'm talking about is related to us always getting picked for surveillance jobs. Always watching and waiting."

"We didn't just watch when we went after Aurelia. We killed bad guys."

"Yes, but we weren't supposed to."

"What about the castle, then?"

"Again, watching and waiting. The only reason it went hot is because Bishop messed up. It's as if Vance says, 'Hey, we've got a job that needs two people to sit around watching something for weeks. I know, let's give it to Aleks and Kurtz.'"

"Comrade, the mission is in Eastern Europe."

"So?"

"So, we speak five local languages between us."

"Good point."

Aleks laughed. Kurtz always complained about the surveillance jobs. "You're just nervous about seeing the girls again. Pull yourself together. I'll meet you in the hospital."

"I'm not nervous," Kurtz mumbled under his breath as he completed a check of his zones. Seeing nothing out of the ordinary, he opened the car door and stepped out onto the street.

They were on the outskirts of Svalyava, a reasonable-size Ukrainian town not far from the airbase PRIMAL had used to launch operations into Hungary. Its only hospital was small, run by the local branch of the Red Cross. A charitable facility, it had welcomed the rescued girls, conducting medical checks and providing second-hand clothing. Kalista had required significant medical treatment and had to stay, watched over by her sister Karla. The rest of the girls had been bused to a Red Cross center in Kiev for identification and return to their families.

Kurtz strolled toward the hospital, stopping at a newsstand to purchase an English paper and a selection of women's magazines. He tucked them under his arm as he crossed the street, narrowly avoiding being crushed by a school bus packed with children. Safely on the other side he entered the foyer of the hospital and took a seat in the waiting area.

A minute later, Aleks entered, walked through the foyer, and turned left into one of the wards. Kurtz got up and followed him.

The floors were spotless linoleum and squeaked under Kurtz's boots as he walked. He caught up as Aleks stopped next to one of the patient rooms.

"You OK?" Aleks asked.

"Yes, I'm good. Why wouldn't I be?"

"No reason." Aleks knocked gently on the door and pushed it open. "Ladies first."

Kurtz gave him a friendly punch as he stepped into the room.

Karla smiled warmly from where she was sitting next to the hospital bed. She wore a tracksuit, her long blonde hair up in a ponytail. "Please, take a seat." She stood and directed him to a chair.

Kalista lay in the bed, her face heavily bandaged. Her eyes were closed and she looked to be deep in sleep.

Kurtz moved to sit down, then thought better of it. "I bought you these." He passed Karla the magazines he had bought. "I thought you might like something to read."

"Thank you very much." Karla placed the magazines on a side table. "It's Kurtz, isn't it?"

"Yes, that's right, and Aleks."

Aleks gave her a nod from the doorway.

"You are police, yes? Kalista told me how you saved her. Thank you so much. She would have died if it wasn't for you."

"How is she doing?"

"They just gave her more of the pain medicine. She should be sleeping for a few hours."

"Do you want us to go?"

"No, she won't wake up."

"She going to be OK?"

"Yes." Karla nodded. "She will have scars but she'll be OK."

"That's good." He looked down at his boots. "We won't stay long. We just wanted to let you know we're in the area."

"Thank you." She looked up at him with crystal-blue eyes. "After what Kalista told me about the police taking her to the castle, it is hard to know who we can trust."

Kurtz gave her a phone. "If anything happens, you can call. My number is programmed into the phone already."

Karla took the phone.

"You see anything suspicious and you call us right away, *da*?" Aleks added from the doorway.

"Do you think people are still after us?"

"I think we got them all but we don't want to take any chances."

Aleks nodded in support. "We just wanted you to know that help is close by if you need it. Now I think we should be going. You look like you need some rest as well." He smiled and then left the room.

As Kurtz made to leave, Karla spoke up. "Kurtz," she came after him. "Kalista told me everything. How you rescued her from the manor, how you stayed up all night." She wrapped her arms around his tall frame. "Thank you so much." She looked up with tears in her eyes. "I nearly got her killed, and you're the only reason she's alive."

Kurtz stood awkwardly as she hugged him. After a moment he wrapped his arms around her. "It's OK. It's my job." He smiled. "Now we need to get her well and back to your family."

Aleks stuck his head back around the door and gave a nod. Kurtz broke the hug. "If there is anything you need, just call, OK?"

Karla wiped the tears from her eyes and nodded.

As Kurtz strode out of the room, he wiped a tear from his eye. "Shut up, Aleks, I don't want to hear it."

Behind him his partner smiled.

They left separately. Kurtz headed back down the road to the car, while Aleks crossed the street, heading back to the apartment.

Both of them missed the nondescript sedan parked across the road from the hospital. The single occupant waited until the two PRIMAL operatives were out of view, then made a phone call.

CHAPTER 35

LYON, FRANCE

Rémi was breathing hard as he leaned into the Fourvière hill. His morning run was a ritual he performed every day. It cleared his head and helped hold back the inevitable belly that came with middle age.

By the time he reached the top of the steep rise his legs were burning almost as much as his lungs. He stood in front of the ancient cathedral fighting for breath as he looked out over the city. Lyon's landscape was a sea of terra-cotta roofs and quaint white-faced buildings. Despite the encroachment of modern development, it still felt like part of the Roman Empire. This was one of Rémi's favorite spots in the city, a bit of serenity in his otherwise hectic life.

The phone in his pocket buzzed. He pulled it out and checked the text message on the screen. It was good news. Rémi dialed a number and lifted the phone to his ear.

"It's me. They've located the blonde girl. The others have already been returned to their homes."

Masateru paused for a moment on the other end of the line. "Good, as long as I get the blonde the *oyabun* will be happy. The sooner I get back to Japan the better."

"She's at a clinic in the Ukraine, small town called Svalyava across the border."

"Well done."

"Have your extra men arrived?"

"Yes, they're ready. Your people delivered the weapons last night."

"You should know, there are two men with the girls. A tall blond and a big brute with a beard."

"Let me guess, they're claiming to be Interpol officers?"

"That's what they told the clinic."

"And naturally your people still have no idea who they really are . . ."

"Not yet, but we're working on it. All the more reason for you to get back to Japan as soon as possible. Once you get the blonde you should leave this to me. I'll find out who they are. It may take a week or so."

"You forget yourself, Rémi. If I wanted your advice I would ask for it."

"My apologies, Masateru. It's just—"

"Enough. Your role is to find me a replacement source of women. Every day that passes is lost revenue. Demand still exists; you will find the supply."

"I'm looking at a number of organizations—"

"I don't want excuses, I want results. Stop providing results and you will be replaced." The Yakuza lieutenant hung up.

Rémi jammed the phone back in his pocket. All the stress his run had melted away came flooding back. Masateru was becoming too demanding. Rémi's biggest challenge now was finding a way to extricate himself from their business relationship. Unlike regular criminals, the Yakuza could not be intimidated. Nor did Rémi's reach extend to Japan. Wearily, he turned and started jogging down the hill, wishing he had never agreed to work for Masateru.

✫✫✫

Four thousand miles away another man was gasping for breath, this time in a poorly ventilated basement.

Shedir was secured to a chair, his head tipped back, a wet towel covering his face. Mirza stood above him with a bucket of water. Kruger and Miklos were holding the chair back on an angle. Pavel was ready with the next bucket.

"I don't think you understand the gravity of this situation, my friend." The man speaking was an immaculately dressed Arab, Tariq Ahmed. With his neatly trimmed beard and fitted Savile Row suit, PRIMAL's financial benefactor would have looked at home in one of the finest fashion houses of Europe; however, he remained, at times, a field operative. In particular, he liked to keep a close hand on affairs in his home country. "You've gotten yourself into a particularly undesirable situation. You see, I happen to be a firm advocate of women's rights and I tend to look poorly on men who treat them like merchandise."

"Listen, my brother, I have done nothing—"

A nod from Tariq and the wet towel was whipped over the man's face. Mirza sent a stream of water pouring over it, silencing him. A second or so and the flow stopped. The captive spluttered and coughed as the drowning reflex kicked in. Waterboarding was only one of a number of interrogation methods available to Tariq, but it was still favored due to its lack of physical trauma. The only wounds it left were psychological.

"I am not your brother, Shedir Sajwani. No brother of mine would peddle in the flesh of innocent children. You are a dog. In fact, more worthless than any dog. You are like the dirt that occasionally sticks to my shoe. Do you agree?"

"Yes—yes . . ." he sobbed.

"Tell me everything you know and perhaps I will let you live."

Shedir coughed again. "I don't know anything more, I promise. The Hungarian, András, he would arrange the auctions. I would go, bid on the girls, and if I won they would be delivered to my clients. That is all, I promise. I know nothing of the Japanese. I had never seen them before, I swear by the prophet."

"I think you're lying," said Tariq.

Mirza dropped the wet towel over his face again.

"No, no, I swear I'm telling the truth. I swear." The Arab sex trafficker's hysterical voice was muffled under the towel. The room filled with the acrid smell of urine.

Tariq signaled for Mirza to remove the towel. When it was off he leaned in close. "I want you to give me the names of all of your clients, every single one. If I find out you have left any out, you are going to experience discomfort far beyond a wet face. Do you understand?"

The terrified Arab nodded vigorously and Tariq signaled for the CAT operatives to right his chair. They sat him upright and released his hands.

Tariq brought another chair over and sat down, crossing his legs elegantly. He looked relaxed and comfortable as he opened a leather-bound notebook. "Before we start, is there anything you would like? Perhaps a glass of water?" He gave the man a wry smile.

Shedir shook his head.

"Very well, let us begin."

CHAPTER 36

PRIMAL HQ, LASCAR ISLAND

"So what have we got, guys?" Vance arrived in the Bunker conference room and dropped into a chair at the head of the table. The other occupants of the room included Chen Chua and one of his analysts. Sixteen hours had passed since Bishop and his team had left the hangar in Ukraine, a long time in the world of espionage.

"We'll start with what we got out of Hungary. Flash has been working on intel from the castle," said Chua.

"Morning, Vance," said Paul "Flash" Gordon, Chua's signals intelligence analyst. A former member of the National Security Agency, he specialized in tearing apart communications networks and exploiting electronic devices.

"Morning, Flash. You get out on the blacktop yesterday?"

Both he and Vance had a collection of old-school motorcycles in the hangar that they tinkered with in their downtime, racing on the island's airstrip when they could get the bikes to work.

"Yeah, gave the Vincent a run."

"How'd she pull up?"

"Bit rough. I can't get that new carburetor to idle smoothly."

"Might come good. Give it some time."

"True. Worst case, I'll get Mitch to have a look at it."

"You want to ride it, not be flung into orbit!"

Flash laughed as he activated his tablet and got down to the business at hand. "Like Chua said, I've been working the exploitation piece from the castle in Hungary. The good news is Bishop's Trojan gave us full access to their network. The bad news is, it looks like the data has been cleaned."

"What does that mean?" Vance asked.

"It means that someone has been through it with a fine-tooth comb and removed every trace of our Japanese friends."

"Or it was never there in the first place," Vance added. "These guys seem to have pretty tight OPSEC."

"True. So right now, apart from the names Bishop identified and the Yakuza link Kurtz dug up, the only other real useful piece of info was the phone Mirza grabbed."

"That the one András had?"

"Yeah, it looks as if he changed it regularly. No stored numbers, wiped his recent calls; like you said, these guys run pretty tight OPSEC. However, I still managed to pull a couple of numbers from it. One was to the local cops; the other was a number I traced back to France. To be more precise, Lyon."

"Lyon? Why does that ring a bell?" Vance asked.

"It's the HQ of Interpol."

"No shit, so we think that András had a link back to Interpol?"

"Yep. The number is now inactive and it seems to have been bought under an alias; however, we're still crunching data and should get a solid lead soon."

"Keep on it. If some corrupt Interpol clown is neck deep in this, I want to know about it. That it?"

Flash nodded. "I'll get back to it and let you both know as soon as we get something more concrete."

"Roger, and we'll get out on the bikes sometime soon."

"For sure." Flash ambled out through the conference room's door.

"Anything from the boys in the Ukraine?" Vance asked Chua.

"Negative. Aleks and Kurtz haven't had anything to report. No sign of any suspect behavior in Svalyava."

"Well, there was always the chance the Yakuza would get away. The guys from the castle have probably hightailed it back to Japan. What about the Abu Dhabi lead?"

"Interrogation report came in a few hours ago. Tariq wrung a few names out of him but nothing else."

"Just names?"

"Clients. We'll develop a plan for each one and put the authorities onto them. If additional action is required, I will bring them to you for sign-off."

"And Shedir himself?"

"He could have identified Tariq, so he had an accident. It would seem that alcohol and swimming pools don't mix."

"A bit embarrassing for a Muslim to be drunk, isn't it?" asked Vance.

"It must be," Chua agreed. "The police are reporting it as a heart condition."

"So where does that leave us now? Just Flash's work on that phone?"

"That and Japan itself. Bishop and Saneh are due on the ground in the next few hours."

"And their contact?"

"Ivan's report is positive, it's just . . ."

"What? You don't trust his guy?"

"I'd like to say yes, but it's too early to tell and we're fast-tracking the process. He's checking all the boxes but I can't hang my hat on this one without more time developing him."

"Your gut feeling?"

"You know me, I don't run on feelings. But the facts are in his favor. He's divorced, middle-aged, lost a family member to a stray Yakuza bullet, and seems genuinely interested in making a difference."

"So you're happy for Bishop to make contact when he arrives in Japan? Because if you're not, we can wait."

Chua studied his tablet for a few seconds. "It's all good. Let's make it happen."

CHAPTER 37

NARITA INTERNATIONAL AIRPORT, TOKYO, JAPAN

Bishop left immigration with his backpack slung over one shoulder and joined the crowds of travelers moving in and out of Narita International Airport, one of the world's busiest air terminals.

A few minutes later he was sitting in a taxi as it weaved through the dense Tokyo traffic. He checked his phone, the latest iPRIMAL model. He pressed his thumb against the touch screen and it unlocked the device. Without his biometric imprint it was just a normal smartphone. Even if someone hacked it they would not reveal its capability. He checked his message log, no new intel updates. There was a message from Saneh. She had traveled separately and was waiting at the hotel for him.

During the flight from Europe he had read through the intel package from the Bunker. He agreed with Chua's assessment that the Japanese police officer Baiko looked like a perfect PRIMAL source. Ivan had recommended him; the former KGB spy and PRIMAL's lead Blade was rarely off on his assessment of a man's character.

The taxi driver pulled over to the curb and Bishop glanced out the window. A huge gray fortress of a building filled the skyline, the National Police Agency headquarters.

"Brian Wilson to see Inspector Baiko," Bishop said as he approached the reception desk. He left his details with the female police officer and took a seat in the waiting area. He picked up a magazine and started flicking through the bright pictures. He paused on a photo of two Japanese women dressed in fluorescent colors with their faces painted to look like cartoon characters. He did not understand Japanese taste.

"Mr. Wilson?"

Bishop looked up. Baiko looked nothing like a disgruntled policeman. He had strong angular features, a short neat haircut, and a set of broad shoulders that filled his suit jacket.

Bishop stood and grasped the outstretched hand. "Inspector Hajime Baiko?"

"This is correct. Can I please see your identification?"

Bishop pulled his fake FBI contractor pass from his pocket and handed it over.

The Japanese officer handed it back to him with a nod. "We will head upstairs to my office."

Bishop followed him through the security gates and into the elevator. They said nothing as they climbed up fourteen floors.

"Welcome to the organized crime section," Baiko said as the doors opened. He led the way into a large open-plan office space. They stopped at a small kitchenette. "Would you like a coffee?"

"Sounds great, thanks."

Baiko poured two black coffees from a percolator as Bishop surveyed the room. A line of enclosed offices and an open-plan area filled with cubicles covered the entire floor. Room for about thirty or forty people if it was full. Currently it was occupied by half a dozen officers. None paid any attention to his presence.

"This way." Baiko handed him a hot mug and led him across to one of the individual offices. He offered Bishop a chair and took his place behind a sleek white desk. The office was immaculate. Bishop noted the complete absence of plaques or other career memorabilia. He dropped his backpack on the floor and took a seat.

"Your friend from the embassy said you are looking into the sex-trafficking industry," Baiko said matter of factly. His English was accented but near fluent.

"Yes, the FBI's asked me to track down a lead they uncovered in Europe."

"They don't do their own work anymore?"

"The Bureau often uses contractors to chase up leads. If this turns out to be solid, they'll deploy a full team to work with you on the case."

"But until then it is just you?"

"Yep, just me."

"Interesting . . . and the lead?"

"Not much I'm afraid. Only two words to be precise. Mori-Kai." Bishop watched Baiko's face for any sign of recognition.

The police officer smirked. "Mori-Kai? Are you sure?"

"Absolutely."

"The Mori-Kai was one of Japan's deadliest and most ruthless families."

"Really? What else do you know?"

Baiko chuckled. "I know that now, they no longer exist. You've flown halfway around the world to chase ghosts, Mr. Wilson. The Mori-Kai family has been dead for hundreds of years."

"We think they might be back, or at least someone is using their name. Possibly an element of the Yakuza."

Baiko drank from his coffee, contemplating Bishop's words. Then he placed the mug back on the desk. "This is possible. I did hear a rumor a while back of a new underground Yakuza element in the Osaka region. Perhaps this is your Mori-Kai."

"The guys we're looking for have been running an international kidnapping syndicate. Collecting women in Eastern Europe and shipping them out to clients across the world. We think they're running the show out of Japan."

"It is not like the Yakuza to spread their criminal activity internationally. Business, yes, but kidnapping? Very unlikely."

"One of their bosses called himself Masateru. Does that help?"

"This is a very common name. Do you have a photo?"

Bishop unzipped his backpack and pulled out a printed photo. It was a shot the team had taken of the Japanese man Kurtz had pushed from the helicopter.

"I don't have one of Masateru, but this is one of his thugs. We arrested him in Europe. He was trying to move twelve teenage girls out of the country."

"Can you e-mail that to me?" Baiko pushed his card across the table and then logged in to his desktop.

"Sure." Bishop used his iPRIMAL to send a digital version of the photo from an anonymous Gmail account.

A few seconds later the Japanese policeman was running the image through his databases.

"No matches," he said after about thirty seconds of searching. "That is very unusual. I ran it against all of our databases. Even if he wasn't listed on the criminal system he should appear on our immigration database. It is almost as if he doesn't exist."

"Could someone have scrubbed him from the system?"

"That is possible. The Yakuza have people in most levels of

government. Usually they would not bother with such a small matter. They own plenty of judges, so why hide?"

"So this guy's definitely well connected?"

"Maybe, but it is also possible that he is not Japanese. Perhaps he is Korean."

Bishop shook his head. "No, he's Japanese all right. I just need to find out where he's from."

"If your man is using the name Mori-Kai then he is most likely from the Osaka-Kobe area. If they exist, then that is where they will be, and only one organization will know about them."

"Who's that?"

"The Yamaguchi-gumi."

"Yakuza?"

"The biggest. They are the ones that can tell you more."

"Don't you have a police contact I can speak to first?"

Baiko laughed and shook his head. "No, Mr. Wilson, if what you are looking for exists, you can't rely on the police here to help you."

"Even in the organized crime department?"

"Especially here. The Yakuza have people in every level of government. They are part of our life. We either learn to live with it or we end up dead."

Bishop thought he spotted the slightest frustration on the policeman's face, and then it was gone.

"Can you hook me up with the Yamaguchi?"

"I will mention it to the right people and they will know you are coming. If you catch the train to Kobe tomorrow they will find you."

"Is that dangerous?"

"Of course, but the Yakuza will always give you a warning before killing you. Show respect for their ways and they will extend you that courtesy."

"What if they're the ones behind the Mori-Kai?"

"That is unlikely. The Yamaguchi are involved in many things, but selling women into slavery is not one of them. Strip clubs and prostitution are more their style. They tend to value honor more than profits." Baiko got up from his chair and gestured for the door. "Now if you will excuse me, I have a meeting that I must attend. We must leave now if I am to see you out."

CHAPTER 38

THE PENINSULA TOKYO HOTEL, TOKYO

"Room 1407, Mr. Wilson." The concierge handed him a cardboard slip with his room pass in it. "Your lady friend has already checked in."

"Thanks." Bishop took the pass and made for the elevators.

"You also have a package."

"Ah, yes, of course." Bishop turned back to the counter, where the concierge had deposited a tough-looking Pelican case.

He rode the elevator up to the fourteenth floor as he mulled over the information that Baiko had given him. He had already purchased two tickets for the bullet train to Kobe. The plan to meet the Yamaguchi was sketchy but it was all they had. He would run it past Saneh and see what she thought.

He reached room 1407, knocked on the door, and swiped himself in. The bathroom door was shut, the shower running. He dropped his bag in the corner, taking no notice of the sweeping city views through the floor-to-ceiling windows. He placed the heavy Pelican case on the bed and swept his iPRIMAL over it. The device synced and the case's lock opened with a snap.

Inside was a block of foam. He removed it, revealing three pistols, complete with suppressors, holsters, and loaded magazines.

"It's amazing what you can get sent by FedEx nowadays," Saneh said as she walked out wrapped in a robe.

"Only if you know the right people." Bishop closed the box and sat down in a chair; like many things in Japan, it was compact and functional. He gave Saneh a quick update on his meeting with Baiko.

"Sounds like a long shot," she said as she lay back on the double bed.

"That's what I was thinking. We could just cut it away and spend a few days in Tokyo waiting to see what Chua and the team come up with, then head back to Hong Kong and jump a Lascar flight over to the island."

Saneh raised one of her perfectly sculpted eyebrows. "Really? Aden Bishop wants to give up on a tenuous lead and wait for better intelligence? Avoid running into what could by all accounts be a trap?"

Bishop laughed. "OK, not when you put it like that."

"You're getting a little wiser in your old age, Aden." Saneh got up off the bed and padded across the carpet to where he was sitting. She bent down and kissed him gently on the forehead, letting her robe fall open. He caught a glimpse of her breasts and reached out to wrap his arms around her.

She pushed him away. "That's all you're getting, stud. I still haven't forgiven you for that stunt in the castle." Saneh strolled back into the bathroom. "Some room service might improve my mood. The sashimi salad looks amazing."

"So what do you want to do tomorrow?" Bishop asked as he flipped through the menu.

"Kobe."

"I thought you said . . . ?"

"I did, but that doesn't mean I don't want to follow up on the lead."

"Women," Bishop sighed as he picked up the hotel phone.

CHAPTER 39

STEAK MATSUSAKA RESTAURANT, OSAKA

"Welcome to our humble establishment, Superintendent Supervisor." The owner bowed his head low.

"My table?" asked Yoshiharu Tanaka, director of the regional police bureau.

"This way, sir." The elderly restaurateur led the way through the dimly lit dining room to the private booths. Despite its humble entrance and dingy interior, Steak Matsusaka was a highly sought-after dining experience. The owner pulled back a curtain and gestured for the police chief to enter.

"Bring me sake." The policeman removed his shoes and suit jacket and sat at the low table.

A moment later one of the thin wooden panels on the wall behind him slid to one side. A well-built man in a smart suit stepped through the gap, gave the room a once-over, and stood back outside.

The next person to pass through the doorway was a middle-aged gentleman dressed in a dark-gray business suit, white shirt, and bright tie. He had a gray moustache and long salt-and-pepper hair that almost touched his shoulders.

Superintendent Tanaka jumped to his feet with a confused look on his face as he recognized the man. Then he connected the dots and bowed deeply. "*Oyabun*, it is a pleasure to finally meet you."

"No, the pleasure is mine, Yoshiharu. Please." The *oyabun* responded with a dip of his head and gestured to the low table.

They sat and a waiter appeared with a pot of sake and two earthen cups.

The *oyabun* removed his jacket and handed it to the waiter. "The sake here is very good."

Tanaka picked up the sake flask and filled the cups. They downed it at the same time. "You're right, it is excellent." He dabbed his mouth with a napkin. "Your taste in sake is as good as your selection of women."

The *oyabun* laughed. "Something that you have been taking full advantage of."

"You said . . ."

"I did and nothing has changed. The women are still available whenever you want them. The Mori-Kai looks after its friends."

The policeman bowed his head low. "An honor, *oyabun*."

The *oyabun* reached into his jacket pocket, pulled out a thick wad of cash, and placed it on the table. "We look after our brothers."

"It is too much, *oyabun*."

He scowled. "You dare insult me?"

"No, *oyabun*." The money disappeared into Tanaka's jacket. He quickly lowered his hands to hide their tremor. Even the region's most powerful law enforcer had fears, and the man sitting opposite was not one he ever wanted to displease.

"That is a small gesture, only the beginning."

"I have a gift for the Mori-Kai in return. Information on the man whose picture you sent me."

"He's in Japan?" Gray eyebrows shot up in surprise.

"Yes." The policeman took two pieces of paper from his pocket and unfolded them. He pushed them across the table. "This man arrived at Narita this morning. The woman as well."

The *oyabun* studied the photo intently. It had been captured by a digital camera on an immigration clerk's desk. He recognized the man, a thirty-something *gaijin* with dark eyes and a mop of brown hair. It was the same man who had infiltrated the operation in Hungary.

"He arrived on a flight from Hong Kong; the girl came separately. His immigration details say he is a security consultant from Philadelphia. The name on his passport is Brian Wilson."

"And the girl?" The *oyabun* studied her photo. She was beautiful. High cheekbones, almond-shaped eyes, and a mane of long black hair. She would be a worthy addition to his stable.

"She claims to be a fashion blogger from Turkey. I don't have any more information on her. Wilson said he was working for the FBI. He met with an investigator at police headquarters in Tokyo, the anti-Yakuza section."

"FBI? But at the airport he said he was a security consultant."

"He apparently said he was contracting for the FBI, but when I made further inquiries I could not verify this. It may be a cover."

The *oyabun* nodded, deep in thought. "Good work. Do you know what this Mr. Wilson discussed with the anti-Yakuza section?"

Tanaka shook his head. "No, but my people indicated he was coming this way. I think he wants to talk with the Yamaguchi-gumi."

"You have done well, Yoshiharu."

"Do you want me to have them found and arrested?"

The *oyabun* shook his head. "No. I will have my people take care of it."

"I would prefer that it didn't happen in my district."

"I understand. I will have my men deal with them before they arrive." He clinked his sake cup against the warm pot and a few seconds later a waiter appeared. "For now let us enjoy our food; then perhaps we could partake in some other delicacies."

CHAPTER 40

TOKYO TO KOBE

Saneh and Bishop boarded the bullet train to Shin-Kobe at 0715. At precisely 0720 it pulled away from the station, on time. They relaxed into the plush seats of green class and watched the scenery race past at an increasingly rapid pace. It didn't take long for the gentle motion of the train to lull Bishop into sleep.

"Aden, wake up." The urgency in Saneh's voice immediately snapped him out of his slumber.

"What is it?"

"We're being watched."

"What? By who?"

"The two big guys sitting up in the front. They just got on at Osaka and they've walked past us a couple of times now."

Bishop sat up a little taller and sneaked a glimpse. The men both sported short, military-style haircuts and looked like bruisers.

"I swear they were casing us when they passed," whispered Saneh. "What do you want to do?"

Bishop glanced at his watch. They still had twenty minutes to go before they hit Kobe.

"Just keep an eye on them. If they try anything we'll be ready." Bishop unzipped his backpack at his feet. He slid his hand in and touched the grip of the pistol, reassuring himself it was still there. Saneh did the same with her overnight bag.

"They're coming back," said Saneh.

The two men had started down the aisle toward them. They strode with military bearing and were obviously well built underneath their bulky jackets.

"We're out of here!" Bishop took Saneh's hand and led her down the aisle, then hit the button that opened the doors to the next carriage. They opened with a hiss; Bishop sent her through the airlock, then followed, glancing over his shoulder as he moved ahead. The men following had their hands under their jackets, only a few seconds behind.

As the first door closed, Bishop drew his suppressed pistol from his backpack and fired a round into the latching mechanism, destroying it. He slid the gun under his jacket.

The two assailants were trapped on the other side, helplessly pushing the door button. They glared at Bishop as he turned and followed Saneh through the airlock's second door and into the next carriage.

"We're running out of train," said Saneh as they moved through the carriage.

"Damn, there are more of them."

At the other end, another pair of Japanese heavies were making their way up the aisle.

Bishop looked back; the two men behind them were trying to force the door open. It wouldn't hold them for long.

"I'll deal with them." He pushed past Saneh. "Keep an eye on the guys behind us."

The two men in front of them looked more like traditional Yakuza. They wore their trademark dark suits, tattoos peeking out from the collar and cuff.

"Bishop, they're through." There was panic in Saneh's voice.

He pushed deeper into the carriage, focusing on the newer threat as he pulled his pistol from his jacket. The passengers on the train looked at him in shock.

As soon as he saw the black pistol, the stocky Yakuza directly in front of Bishop lifted his hands. "Friend, friend!" he yelled. Bishop couldn't help but notice one of his little fingers was missing.

"What the fuck?" Bishop lowered the pistol as the solidly built gangster stepped past, knocking him into a row of seats. He landed on the lap of an elderly woman.

The second Yakuza followed the first and both men strode past Saneh, directly into the path of the military-looking guys, who had now broken through the jammed door. The stocky, fingerless Yakuza barreled straight into them. The other, a thin whippet of a man, pulled a small club from inside his jacket and rained blows down on the stunned pair. Having gained the initiative, they turned and ran. "There's more, go, go, go!"

Saneh was already sprinting toward the next carriage door. She punched the release button and Bishop joined her.

"We can't go any farther." Saneh was punching the release button on the next door. It wouldn't open. They had reached the last car.

"Shit." Bishop turned around as their Yakuza allies reached them, frantically searching for a way out.

The roar of a submachine gun filled the confined space of the train. Bullets slammed into the plastic and glass, sending shards flying through the air. One of the military-looking thugs had pulled an MP9 machine pistol from his jacket.

The thin Yakuza convulsed as bullets tore into him. He stumbled and fell forward. Screams filled the train.

Bishop and Saneh pressed themselves up against the walls.

Their stocky guardian dropped to one knee and raised a stainless-steel revolver. It boomed, sending a high-velocity slug down the aisle. He rolled sideways as a burst of automatic fire narrowly missed him.

"Who are you?" Bishop demanded as he returned fire with his suppressed Beretta.

"Yamaguchi-gumi," the barrel-chested man growled as he fired another two rounds from his revolver.

"And those guys?" Saneh asked, pulling her own pistol from the overnight bag slung over her shoulder.

"Mori-Kai dogs."

"Bingo," muttered Bishop under his breath. "How many?"

"Four, maybe more."

Another torrent of bullets slammed into the rear of the carriage.

"If we stay here we're dead." Saneh checked that her suppressed PX4 had a round in the chamber.

The burly gangster nodded. "We need to attack." He thumbed out the cylinder of his revolver, dropped six shells, and reloaded, one round at a time. "I will lead."

"No, wait—" Bishop started.

The Yamaguchi had already stepped out into the aisle, firing his six-shooter like an old-West gunslinger.

"Here we go." Bishop followed him, the PX4 held ready. Saneh tucked in behind, aiming over his shoulder.

Their two .45 pistols snapped as they spat rounds past the Yakuza man's shoulders, the PRIMAL operatives drawing on hundreds of hours of training. The old-school gangster seemed to have had no such training; he simply fired one-handed as he ran.

The first two Mori-Kai gunmen were hit by Bishop's and Saneh's rounds. One had the top of his head taken off with a wet slap, throwing him backward. His partner staggered as a volley of .45 rounds slammed into him, finally toppling when a bullet hit his face.

"They're wearing armor, aim for the head," Bishop yelled.

"Reloading." Saneh knelt in a vacated row of seats.

Their Yamaguchi juggernaut powered on until he was struck in the shoulder. He grunted and staggered, tripping on a bag left in the aisle.

Bishop stepped past and over him, his PX4 drilling another of their attackers through the skull. He went to fire at their final assailant when his pistol jammed, an empty cartridge wedging itself in the slide.

The remaining Mori-Kai operative fired his machine pistol. The burst ripped past Bishop's head as he knelt and racked the slide of the PX4. He shook out the offending shell, released the slide, and squeezed the trigger. Nothing happened. He stared directly into the muzzle of the MP9 machine pistol. "Fuck."

A weapon belched flame with an ear-splitting boom. Bishop flinched. The MP9-wielding Mori-Kai was thrown backward as a .357 magnum slug smashed into his chest.

"The old ones never fail." The Yamaguchi grimaced, lowering the six-shooter, his left hand grasping his shoulder. The weapon fell out of his hand and hit the floor with a solid clunk. Saneh stepped forward and finished the Mori-Kai with a bullet to the face.

Bishop picked the revolver off the floor and stood up. The pistol had polished walnut grips and a stainless finish, a Colt Python. He handed it to the Yakuza man, who took it with his left hand.

"Thanks, buddy. Name's Brian. And you are?"

"Kenta."

"You OK?" The shoulder of Kenta's suit jacket was wet with blood and his right arm hung limp.

"It's just a scratch."

The wound was serious and the pain would have been considerable but Kenta showed no outward signs of discomfort.

Terrified faces appeared from behind the seats on both sides of the carriage. The passengers looked around in horror at the bodies littering the train. Kenta spoke in a deep voice, addressing them in Japanese. There was a pause and they stood up and started clapping.

"What's that all about?" Bishop asked, taking a bandage from his backpack.

"I told them we were special agents and we just defeated an attempt to hijack the train."

"I can see why they'd be happy about that. How about you sit down and let us bandage that shoulder."

Kenta holstered his revolver and slumped into a seat. Saneh took the bandage from Bishop. "My name's Sarah. Let me take a look at that."

"It's OK."

"Actually, you could do with a few stitches." The bullet had cut through Kenta's shoulder at an angle, opening up a deep gash. Saneh helped him remove the suit jacket and gave him a compress to hold against the wound, slowing the bleeding.

"The *oyabun* sent me to bring you to him," Kenta grunted.

"We would be more than happy to meet him," Bishop replied.

"Good, we get off at the next station."

The train started to slow and Bishop dropped into the empty seat opposite the Yamaguchi man. He glanced at his watch; they were only a minute or two away from Kobe. He took Saneh's pistol and stuffed it into his backpack with the rest of their weapons and ammunition. For a second he considered leaving it on the train but he knew it was unlikely that armed police would have had time to establish a cordon. Plus, he did not want to be caught without a weapon if the Mori-Kai made another attempt on their lives.

CHAPTER 41

KOBE

Bishop's fears were allayed when they alighted from the bullet train at Shin-Kobe station. He had been on the money; the police had not yet arrived.

"Follow me." Kenta led them through the station to the parking lot, where a pair of black Mercedes waited. Another dark-suited Yamaguchi opened the doors and they climbed in. Kenta got into the car behind them.

As the convoy sped out of the parking lot, the sound of police sirens filled the air.

"This isn't good," said Bishop as a police car blocked the exit.

The first Yakuza sedan screeched to a halt mere inches from its bumper. The driver of the Mercedes honked his horn and wound down his window, yelling angrily.

The police car gave an almost apologetic wail of its siren and backed out of the entrance, leaving a gap.

"Pretty bloody clear who's running the show," murmured Bishop.

"I'm not sure this was a good idea," responded Saneh.

"This was your idea."

The cars raced across the city of Kobe, running red lights and forcing other cars off the road. It was midday and the traffic in Japan's fifth-largest city was flowing freely. The black sedans blasted past a speed trap, continuing to demonstrate seeming immunity from the police, up to and including the most major traffic laws. None of the officers showed the slightest interest in pulling over the Yakuza vehicles.

"Excuse me." Bishop reached forward and tapped the man in the passenger seat on the shoulder. "Where are you taking us?"

The man looked at him blankly and then spoke to the driver in Japanese.

"We take to *oyabun*," the driver explained in halting English. "Great honor."

"Where is that?"

"Great honor," the man repeated.

Bishop leaned back. "Great honor," he murmured, shaking his head.

"I think we're there," said Saneh.

They slowed as they approached a high stone wall topped with razor wire on the outskirts of the city. The cars turned through a pair of heavy steel gates and onto a gravel driveway. CCTV cameras stared down at them from almost every vantage point. A blue uniformed guard armed with a radio manned the entrance.

Despite the high security, the compound radiated a sense of serenity. The noise and pollution of the city were replaced with the idealized landscape of an immaculate Japanese garden. Perfectly manicured lawns and bonsai trees surrounded a number of ponds teeming with water lilies and multicolored koi.

The cars drove up a small rise and came to a halt in front of a wide stone staircase. A blue-uniformed Yakuza servant opened the car door while another offered them a tray filled with hot towels. Bishop waved him away but Saneh used the opportunity to clean the gunpowder residue from her hands.

"Now that's impressive." Bishop gave a low whistle as he took in the mansion that loomed above them.

The base of the two-story building was built of solid rock; the stairs led up to a ground floor clad in heavy black wooden panels. Perched above it were a series of layered tiled roofs and a smaller second floor. Ornate carvings at the corner of each roof gave the whole building a majestic feel. It looked like something out of a movie about seventeenth-century Japan. Bishop half-expected black-clad ninjas to leap off the roof and do battle with an army of samurai.

"It's stunning," Saneh whispered.

"Edo period if I'm not mistaken," said Bishop. He was an architecture buff, and the simple lines of the era's buildings appealed to him. "It must have been in the family for hundreds of years. Talking about old, where's that Kenta character disappeared to?" They had not seen him since the station.

"This way." A servant waved them up the stairs to the entrance.

Both of the PRIMAL operatives noticed the thick, steel-lined door and the additional CCTV cameras; security was just as tight inside the mansion.

The uniformed servant led them to a waiting area. Like the rest of the building it had obviously been constructed by master artisans. A hardwood wall had a large logo engraved into it, a bold black diamond, the same that adorned all of the servants' uniforms. Beside the emblem hung full-size portraits of the previous masters of the manor.

"You will wait here." He waved Saneh toward a low wooden bench. Bishop went to sit but the servant stopped him. "No, woman wait. You come to *oyabun* now."

Saneh looked at Bishop. He shrugged his shoulders.

A side door slid open and a heavily tattooed Yamaguchi-gumi dressed in a short-sleeved shirt and black pants gestured for Bishop to enter.

The room was as traditional as the rest of the building. On the polished wooden floor covered in bamboo mats sat a low table surrounded by cushions. The walls were paper screens emblazoned with martial scenes depicting samurai engaged in combat. A number of windows faced out over the gardens. Bishop noted the refraction caused by the bulletproof glass.

"Please, come in." A deep voice emanated from the other side of the room, where a man was gazing out one of the windows.

Bishop kicked off his shoes and padded softly to the low table. Behind him the tattooed Yakuza closed the door and stood off to the side.

The man at the window crossed the floor at a slow place, the pad of his feet matched with the tap of a walking stick.

"*Oyabun.*" Bishop dipped his head in a polite bow.

The head of Japan's most influential Yakuza clan nodded slightly.

Bishop put his age at early seventies. A once-powerful frame hunched over with old age, evidence of hard labor as a boy. His hair was snow white, as were his eyebrows. Intelligent brown eyes held Bishop's own gaze.

"Please, sit." The Yamaguchi-gumi boss lowered himself deftly onto a low chair at the end of the table.

Bishop followed his example, adjusting himself to find a comfortable position at the low table. Another blue-uniformed servant appeared with a pot of coffee and cups.

"Kenta tells me you saved his life."

The servant poured two cups and then backed away from the table, his head bowed.

"The other way around, I'm afraid. Sorry about the loss of your man."

The *oyabun* dipped his head in acknowledgment as he lifted his cup and gestured for Bishop to do the same. "I understand you have traveled from America to find men . . . 'trafficking in women' is the phrase, I believe?"

"That's correct. I'm looking for criminals dealing in human slavery. Yakuza to be precise." Bishop sipped, wondering how much the Yakuza boss actually knew.

"Have you been to Japan before, Mr. Wilson?" The old man's gaze never wavered.

"A few times, just holidays and the like." He was a little surprised at the use of his cover name. It was unlikely that Baiko had passed the information. It was more probable that the Yamaguchi had people in immigration.

"So you know a little of the Yakuza?"

"Only what I have read as a part of this investigation, and what's in the papers."

"And what picture did they paint?"

"To be completely honest, not a good one. Typical criminal activities are extortion, illegal gambling, muggings, kidnappings, theft, prostitution, blackmail . . . The list is long and not particularly flattering."

The *oyabun* placed his cup of coffee back on the low table. "It is true, that at one time or another, we have been involved in such things. But they do not embody what it is to be 'true' Yakuza. The Yamaguchi-gumi follow a strict code, the *ninkyodo*."

"*Ninkyodo*?"

"It is the path of fighting the strong and protecting the weak. We are not petty criminals. We are businessmen and humanitarians who belong to an exclusive brotherhood."

"Humanitarians?" Bishop almost snickered.

"Your media does not report everything, Mr. Wilson. When the tsunami struck Fukushima it was the Yamaguchi-gumi who moved first. While the government was bogged down in bureaucracy and corruption, it was we who first brought aid to the people of Japan."

"Indeed. And yet there are elements of the Yakuza who clearly pay no heed to your rules. Hence, my coming here."

A frown creased the forehead of the *oyabun* and anger flashed in his brown eyes. "They are not true Yakuza. They are dogs who have stolen the name of the honorable and sullied it with immoral crimes and drugs."

"Dogs like the Mori-Kai?"

"Yes, they may well be the worst."

"What do you know about them?"

"What little they reveal. My men have had some minor encounters."

"So you're sure they exist?"

The Yamaguchi *oyabun* nodded his head as a servant scurried forward to replenish his coffee. "Yes, our investigations have been limited but I can confirm the rumors are true."

"What sort of rumors?"

"An underground Yakuza that holds no respect for our traditions. A small syndicate that is well connected, heavily armed, and trading in Western flesh. They display ruthlessness that overshadows even the most hard-line of the Yamaguchi-gumi."

"And this poses a threat to your organization?"

"It is the responsibility of the Yamaguchi-gumi to oversee Yakuza activities, but the Mori-Kai play by their own rules. This is unacceptable." The *oyabun* stared intently while he sipped his coffee.

Bishop nodded. "It would seem that we have a common enemy. I need to investigate the Mori-Kai, locate their headquarters and key personnel, identify their criminal ventures, and report back to my superiors."

The *oyabun* laughed. "And then what?"

"The FBI can then work with your authorities to put an end to them."

"What makes you think you can succeed where the Yamaguchi-gumi have not?"

"We have our ways. I have already shut down the Mori-Kai's operations in Europe."

"I had not heard of this." The *oyabun* gave him a strange look. "You are aware that they will be stronger here in Japan. They have killed a number of my men. Escaped my spies . . ."

"They didn't seem to bother Kenta."

"That is because he is different, old Yakuza. A powerful *kyodai* in an army of *shatei*." The old man drank from his coffee.

"Yes, Kenta is strong, but the little brothers have eyes," said Bishop translating the Yakuza term. "They can help."

The *oyabun*'s eyebrows raised in surprise at the Westerner's comprehension of the Yakuza ranks. "And if what you say is true, you have teeth. Perhaps a partnership could take advantage of these strengths."

"What do you suggest?"

The *oyabun* raised his voice and rattled off a number of commands in Japanese. He turned back to Bishop. "My Kobe *waka-gashira* will provide you with everything you need. Eyes and ears, cars, a base of operations."

The tattooed man standing by the door bowed and walked to the table. He was slightly built but still managed to strike an imposing figure. The sleeves of his business shirt were rolled up to the elbow, revealing intricate tattoos that covered his forearms. His head was closely shaved and tinted glasses covered his eyes.

"Agent Wilson, I would like you to meet "Saemonsaburou Takahiro.""

The man bowed as Bishop climbed to his feet and shook his hand.

The *oyabun* issued a directive to the man in rapid-fire Japanese, then rose to his feet. "It has been a pleasure, Mr. Wilson. The *wakagashira* will get you anything you need." He turned and walked stiffly toward a door on the other side of the room.

"Hang on, what do you want from us?" Bishop asked.

The *oyabun* continued walking. "That is simple. I want you to help us destroy the Mori-Kai."

With that, the *oyabun* disappeared through the sliding door.

"So just you and me, hey?" Bishop said to Takahiro.

The Yakuza lieutenant nodded.

"How's your English?"

"My English is passable."

"That's good news. The bad news is, I'm not even going to try to pronounce your name. How about I just call you Hero?"

Takahiro stared at him through tinted lenses. "If that is what you want to call me, then that is what you can call me. Now follow." He led Bishop back to the waiting area.

"What's going on?" Saneh asked.

"This is Hero, our new liaison; he wants us to follow him."

"Hero?" Saneh asked.

"Trust me, you don't want to try his full name, wheelbarrow something or other."

Saneh rolled her eyes and followed them through another doorway and down a flight of stairs.

"This place has some pretty heavy-duty security," Bishop commented.

"We are not strangers to violence, Mr. Wilson."

"Please, call me Brian."

"Very well, Brian. Five years ago our *oyabun* was killed in a raid by rival Yakuza. Changes were made to the building to ensure it does not happen again."

They traversed a stone-lined corridor and emerged in a garage filled with black Mercedes sedans. Kenta was leaning against one of the vehicles, a cigarette in his hand. He was wearing a leather motorcycle jacket. He showed no sign of his bullet wound.

"I have many things that I must attend to. Kenta will look after you and if there is anything you need he will provide it. He will accompany you at all times."

"That's a nice gesture but we don't really need a babysitter," said Bishop.

"Does your lady friend speak Japanese?" Takahiro asked bluntly.

"No," Bishop replied.

"Then Kenta will prove very useful. If you are worried about your protection, he was once the *Tokko Tai-Cho.* He will keep you safe." Bishop made to object but Hero stopped him. "This is not negotiable. Now if you will excuse me, I will leave you in Kenta's care." With that, he turned and disappeared back down the corridor.

Bishop waited until he was out of sight, then turned to Kenta. "Wow, he's an intense guy."

"He is the most favored of the *waka-gashira* and destined to one day be chairman," Kenta replied. "How was your meeting with the *oyabun*?"

"He seemed genuine enough. I get the feeling he doesn't quite trust me yet."

"It is not every day we have an FBI agent ask to work with us. One who carries a silenced pistol and wants to destroy our enemies . . ."

"True, it's an unusual situation, but the Mori-Kai is not your average gang."

Kenta nodded. "The *oyabun* is wiser than you think, Mr. Wilson. You should know it is a great honor that you were able to see him. It is an even greater honor that he ordered one of the *waka-gashira* to provide you with help."

"There's more than one *waka-gashira*?" Saneh jumped in on the conversation.

Kenta laughed. "Yes, there are a great many."

"Tell me, Kenta, what is the *Tokko Tai-Cho*?" Bishop asked, pronouncing it "Tokyo Thai Show."

"An old title I used to have. Those days are gone now." Kenta dropped his cigarette on the ground and stomped on it with a black leather shoe. "So what car would you like?"

"Any of them." Bishop made a mental note to Google Kenta's old title later.

Kenta nodded.

Saneh had crossed the garage and was inspecting a Kawasaki Ninja. "Does it have to be a car?" She stroked the tank of the black sports bike.

"It is all at your disposal, except for the other one." Kenta gestured to a vintage Kawasaki cruiser parked next to the Ninja. "That one is mine."

Saneh sat on the Ninja motorcycle. "What do you say, Agent Wilson? It's fast, unobtrusive, and we can cover multiple locations."

"Knock your socks off, kiddo. I've got something a little more comfortable in mind." Bishop walked to the back of the garage, where he had spotted another vehicle. "The *oyabun* said anything, right?"

"That is correct."

Bishop patted the hood of a late-model Nissan GT-R. "Then let's get the keys for this bad boy."

✯✯✯

The residence sat on a hill that overlooked the city of Himeji. It was a fusion of modern technology and Japanese culture. The glass-and-concrete structure had sweeping views; the stone garden and interiors were a tasteful merging of minimalist Japanese art and landscape design.

The boss of the Mori-Kai lay in a robe on a low settee, oblivious to the picturesque surroundings. His eyes were closed, his face emotionless as a masseuse worked on his bare feet. A glass of Yamazaki whiskey sat on a table next to him along with a half-empty bottle.

"My apologies, *oyabun*." Ryu entered the room and gave a deep bow. The commander of the Mori-Kai's militant Kissaki was tall and lean with angular features, his head completely bald, shaved clean with a razor. Like the men who had attacked Bishop on the bullet train, he normally wore practical clothing: cargo pants with a bulky jacket to hide weaponry. Today, however, he wore a formal dark suit. In one hand he carried a full-length samurai sword, in the other, a shorter version.

"What do you want?" The *oyabun* did not open his eyes.

"You wanted to be informed of the mission to kill the *gaijin*."

"Yes." His eyes snapped open.

"They failed. Yamaguchi men were there and killed the team."

"The Yamaguchi-gumi killed three of the Kissaki?"

"Yes, *oyabun*," the man bowed his head. "I offer my own life as an apology for our failure." He presented the handle of the sword to his master.

The *oyabun* remained on the lounge. "Do not be a fool. The lives of my best men will not be squandered on obsolete traditions.

It is bad enough that three of you died at the hands of those Yakuza dinosaurs."

"As you wish, *oyabun*. I will have the rest of the men ready. We will exact revenge for our loss."

The Yakuza boss closed his eyes and returned to a relaxed state. "Not yet. Masateru will soon return, then we will strike a far more devastating blow on the Yamaguchi-gumi. Continue to gather information. Find the Westerners and do not lose them. They remain our priority."

"Yes, *oyabun*."

"Have you informed Masateru of your failure?"

"No, he's still in the air and I have been unable to reach him."

"But he is aware of the Englishman's presence here in Japan? That he is with the girl and is claiming to be an American FBI operative?"

"Yes, *oyabun*, I spoke to him before he left Kiev."

"Very well. That is all."

Ryu turned on his heel and made to exit the room.

"One more thing."

"Yes, *oyabun*."

"Get rid of those swords. We no longer use blades, we use bullets."

"Yes, *oyabun*."

"Also, did the shipment of weapons arrive?"

"Yes, *oyabun*."

"Excellent, have your team start training the others. I have a feeling we will need more foot soldiers in the coming weeks."

CHAPTER 42

SVALYAVA, UKRAINE

"Something's not right." Aleks was sitting with Kurtz in the Audi. It was late afternoon and they were conducting a handover of responsibilities. Kurtz had been watching the hospital for the last eight hours.

"Yes, this is shit coffee." The German was drinking from a take-out cup. He gave it an angry look but continued sipping from it.

"No, not the coffee." Aleks pointed to the car's windshield. "The guy over there, he's been hanging around too long." The middle-aged man was standing opposite the medical clinic with a newspaper under his arm.

"He has been there for a while." Kurtz activated his iPRIMAL. "Let's check him out." His fingers danced over the screen. "No electronic emissions except for a phone. I can't isolate the number."

"He's definitely watching the hospital."

Kurtz was still looking at his interface. "Nothing out of the ordinary here."

"He's looking at us."

Kurtz looked up from the screen. "I think we need to talk to him."

"Too late, he's moving."

Their target stepped out onto the street as a white sedan slowed in front of him. He glanced once more in their direction and jumped in the vehicle.

"We should follow him," said Kurtz.

"You sure?" Aleks started the Audi.

"Yes, quickly, they're getting away."

Aleks pulled the Audi away from the curb and onto the road. The white car was pulling away from them and he accelerated to catch up. They passed through the small town center and into a residential area.

"Not too close." Kurtz dialed a number on his iPRIMAL and made an encrypted call. "Bunker, this is Kurtz. Can you run a check on the following plate number?"

"Roger, send."

The white car continued down the road at a leisurely pace. Aleks matched its speed, staying a few hundred meters behind.

"I read bravo, sierra, three, four, seven, whiskey, romeo."

The watch officer in PRIMAL HQ repeated the numbers and told Kurtz to wait.

Aleks continued to follow the car.

"Kurtz, this is Bunker. Ukrainian road registry has nothing outstanding on those plates. They are privately registered."

"Acknowledged, thanks. Out."

"Nothing?" Aleks asked.

"*Ja*, nothing."

"So what do we do now?"

"Keep following them." Kurtz reached over to the backseat, lifted a blanket, and pulled out an MP7. Both men were already wearing low-profile body armor and pistols under their jackets.

"Turning left."

"Close up," Kurtz said as he cocked his submachine gun and checked the magazine.

The white car turned into an alley between two fenced-off industrial compounds and disappeared from view. Aleks steered the Audi after it a moment later. The wheels skidded as they hit the gravel single-lane track.

"We're going to lose them."

The car was already turning another corner farther down the road. Aleks accelerated to catch up. As they rounded the corner into an open area he slammed on the brakes.

The white car was stopped fifty feet in front of them in what looked like a builder's lot. Piles of bricks, steel, and other debris offered plenty of places to hide. The car's doors were open. It was empty.

"Back up, back up!" yelled Kurtz.

It was too late.

Gunfire slammed into the Audi. Both men lay low behind the dash as bullets ripped through the windows. Aleks floored the car in reverse and its wheels spun. There was a huge bang and the engine died under the hail of bullets.

Aleks had his pistol out and was leaning sideways across the center console to stay below the windows. Bullets continued to rip through the windows and thud into the doors.

"At least we know the Kevlar works," Aleks yelled as more rounds thudded into the reinforced doors. Unable to procure another fully armored vehicle at short notice, Yuri had ensured their sedan had sufficient modifications to increase survivability.

Kurtz pulled the glove compartment open and handed a set of thermal-imaging goggles to Aleks. He pulled his own pair on over his face.

"You get smarter every day: It's light outside, comrade space cadet."

More bullets slammed into the car as Kurtz reached into the center console and retrieved an ignition device. Four leads ran out of the bottom of it into the dash. He flicked the safety off. "Not for long it isn't. You ready?"

Aleks smiled. "*Da.*"

Kurtz crunched the clacker, which sent an electric pulse to the four smoke grenades cable-tied under the car. Tiny detonators snapped each of the ties and they dropped onto the road, handles flying off.

Within a matter of seconds thick smoke had obscured the vehicle and the surrounding area.

"Let's go." Kurtz activated his goggles and pushed open his door, diving out onto the ground with his MP7. Aleks replicated the move with his pistol.

A hail of gunfire slammed into their car as their attackers fired blindly. The rapidly expanding cloud of smoke had engulfed them.

The thermal goggles' view cut through the smoke, the hot weapons of their targets glowing red in the cool evening air.

Kurtz took a prone firing position and shot one of the heat signatures as it stood from behind a pile of bricks. A man screamed and fell to the ground. Kurtz rolled sideways from the car and popped up behind a wall, the sight of his MP7 superimposed into his thermal goggles as he scanned for targets.

On the other side of the car Aleks had crawled in behind an abandoned pile of scrap metal. An old refrigerator gave him some cover.

"You see anyone?" Kurtz communicated through his iPRIMAL.

"Negative, they're laying cat."

"Laying what?"

"Laying cat. Bishop says it all the time. You know, laying cat to make sure they're not seen."

"You mean lying doggo?"

"*Da*, that's the one." Through the smoke Aleks caught a glimpse of three heat signatures moving back as a tactical unit, covering each other as they withdrew. "There, toward their car."

Aleks fired his pistol at one of the shapes; there was a cry and the man stumbled, hitting the ground. A burst of return fire sent bullets hissing through the smoke around him.

Kurtz took aim as one of the men grabbed his wounded partner and started to drag him. The other man fired his submachine gun blindly in an attempt to cover them. Kurtz fired a long burst into the wounded man and his rescuer. Their bodies convulsed as the 4.7mm rounds cut through them.

Aiming toward the sound of gunfire, the other man let rip another wild burst. Kurtz ignored the bullets, adjusted his aim, and fired a double tap. The target dropped like a puppet with its strings cut.

The two PRIMAL operatives waited as the smoke slowly cleared. Seconds passed, then minutes. No one else appeared.

"I think that's it," Kurtz said. "Check it out. I'll cover you."

As Aleks moved forward, Kurtz's pocket began to vibrate. He pulled out his iPRIMAL and checked it. Nothing. He checked his other cell phone, a local phone. He had two missed calls; both of them were from the phone he had given Karla. "The hospital!"

Aleks knew what his partner meant immediately and he ran straight to the white car. The keys were not in the ignition.

He inspected the men they had killed, stripping their pockets and using his iPRIMAL to capture images of their faces. The gunmen all looked Japanese.

Kurtz did the same with the first man he had shot behind the bricks. "Got the keys!" The driver had been the only European out of the group. "You get the rest of the gear," he said as he started the white sedan and backed it up to their shot-up Audi. They transferred their bags to the new vehicle, including what they had taken from the dead bodies. Aleks dropped a thermite grenade on the driver's seat of the Audi and they sped off. The four-thousand-degree detonation would burn it to the ground, covering their tracks.

"It was a diversion," said Kurtz.

"More Japs."

"Yes, all except the driver we followed. Did you see how they moved?"

"Well trained, ex-military."

They slid sideways out of the alley and sped back onto the main road. Kurtz thumped the horn as he narrowly avoided a car coming the other way. He pushed the little sedan to its limits, the engine screaming.

"*Scheisse!*" He thumped the steering wheel with the palm of his hand. "How could I be so stupid?"

"We," Aleks reminded him. "We both fell for it."

Kurtz sent the car careening through the town, his hand constantly on the horn. They screeched to a halt directly in front of the medical center. Kurtz sprinted through the front door. His boots rang on the polished floor as he stormed past the nurse's station. Ignoring the duty nurse's cry he pushed open the door to the girl's room.

Kalista was sitting up in bed, tears streaming down her bandaged face, mobile phone clutched in her hand.

Kurtz punched the wall in frustration.

They were too late.

CHAPTER 43

"He took Karla." Kalista managed to get her words out between sobs. "He, he's going to kill my sister."

Kurtz sat down and held her hand. "No, he's not. He's not going to hurt her. He won't have enough time to hurt her because I'm going to get her back."

That seemed to calm her a little.

"What did he look like?"

"He, he, he was the one who cut me." She burst into tears again.

The Yakuza boss, the one Bishop had described. That made sense, Kurtz thought; after escaping the battle with Bishop, he had stayed in Ukraine and requested reinforcements.

"You'll find her, won't you?" cried Kalista. "You found us last time. You can do it again."

"I'll find her, and I'll arrest the man who cut you. If you think of anything that might help, you call, OK?"

She nodded, holding the cell phone he had provided earlier. "I will." She forced a smile.

"Who are you?" a voice asked from the doorway. Kurtz looked up to see a policeman and a nurse. The officer had his hand on his pistol and was watching him warily.

"Interpol." The PRIMAL operative took his forged credentials from his pocket and held it at arm's length. "We've been protecting the girls."

The policeman relaxed as he examined the identification card.

"There's a lot of you in town," the officer commented. "The nurse said an Interpol agent left with the other girl. I think he was Japanese."

"I can't tell you what this is about. Security reasons," Kurtz explained. "But I need you to put a protection detail on this girl's door. Her life may be in danger."

"No," the nurse said, pushing past them both. "Her life *is* in danger if you don't leave her alone. I'm going to have to ask you both to leave." She activated the buzzer on the bed stand and adjusted the IV bags feeding into Kalista's arm.

Kurtz looked into the bright-blue eyes of the teenager and gripped her hand tight. "I'll bring her back to you if it's the last thing I do. I promise."

She squeezed his hand in response and then closed her eyes, succumbing to exhaustion and the warmth of the increased pain medication.

Kurtz strode out of the room, leaving both the nurse and the police officer in his wake.

He found Aleks talking to another police officer at the front of the hospital. Kurtz threw him the keys. "Come, we need to go; you drive."

Aleks excused himself and followed Kurtz.

"Where are we going?" he asked as he started the engine.

"Get us out of town and I'll see if we can track her. Karla's been kidnapped by the Yakuza. They need to get her out of the country and they'll do that via an airport. Where's the gear from the tangos at the yard?"

"In the bag behind your seat."

Kurtz reached behind and pulled out a black plastic bag. He fished out two phones, unclipped their backs, and popped out the sim cards. One at a time he stuck the cards into his iPRIMAL and ran an exploitation app. When both cards had been exploited, he sent the data to the Bunker.

A minute later the phone rang. "Kurtz, it's Chua. We're running the numbers off the two phones you picked up."

"Aleks and I ran into some trouble. The Yakuza have Karla again."

"How? When? Are you both all right?"

"*Ja,* we're OK. They led us into an ambush, and while we were occupied they kidnapped the girl." He could hear Chua's fingers dancing over the keyboard in the background.

"Flash has worked his magic and he's got one of the associated numbers heading north on the E50. It's our only lead."

"That's got to be him. He'll be heading to Kiev International." Kurtz nodded to Aleks, who punched the airport into their GPS navigator.

"Agreed. He'll get her out on a private jet. I'm loading the phone's ID into your interface; you can track him via that."

"We'll get her back as soon as we can."

"No, we've got an opportunity to track these assholes back to the source. You will follow but do not make contact," PRIMAL's chief of intelligence ordered. "Bishop and Saneh will pick her up at the other end once we know the destination."

"No! We can't afford to lose her again."

"Listen to me, Kurtz. She's going to be fine. We'll pick her up at the other end. This is our best chance to take down the guys abducting young women all over Europe and selling them into slavery. This is bigger than just one girl."

"How can you be so sure?"

"Look, first sign of danger we'll pull her straight out. You continue to monitor and if you see anything suspect on the trip to Kiev, we'll reevaluate."

Kurtz clenched his fist and sighed. "OK."

"Check back in an hour and I'll let you know what else we got out of those numbers."

"*Ja*, one hour."

"Bunker out."

Kurtz sat in silence, watching the road in front of the car. The sky had started to fade and he could make out the faint glow of the headlights on the asphalt. It was a golden color, reminding him of Karla's hair.

"So, we follow to Kiev?" Aleks asked.

Kurtz activated the tracking app on his iPRIMAL. "Yes, we're going to stay on their tail. No contact." He turned to his partner. "They want to use her as a lead."

Aleks nodded in silent acknowledgment of his partner's pain.

CHAPTER 44

SVALYAVA TO KIEV

Two hours later the little white sedan sped through the darkness along the single-lane road that ran east across Ukraine. Kurtz and Aleks paid no attention to the forests and towns that flashed past in the moonlight. They were fixed on the tasks at hand.

Kurtz studied his iPRIMAL intently, watching the pulsing icon that indicated the location of the suspect phone. Aleks's eyes stayed on the winding road as they traveled at breakneck speed.

Kurtz glanced at the speedometer. "Can we go faster?"

They took a bend at high speed and the wheels of the cheap sedan squealed in protest. Red taillights appeared in front as they came out of the corner. Aleks threw the little car into the oncoming lane and they narrowly avoided impact with a truck. The harsh glare of headlights filled the car as an oncoming vehicle raced toward them.

"Fuck!" Aleks muttered and he flicked the car sideways, narrowly missing the oncoming car and the side of the truck. "Don't you think we're going fast enough?"

"*Ja.*" Kurtz let out his breath. "They're only a few kilometers ahead."

"We'll catch them in the next hour. Nothing is going to happen to her while they're on the road."

Kurtz's eyes had returned to his iPRIMAL. "They've stopped up ahead."

Aleks slowed their speed slightly. "We don't want to shoot past him, he might recognize the car."

The German gave him a stern look.

"Fine." Aleks accelerated again. "But if we both end up dead and in hell, I'm not going to talk to you again."

✭✭✭

A few miles ahead a dark sedan was parked by the side of the road. Masateru opened the door and pulled Karla out. "If I take the handcuffs off, you will behave, yes?"

She sniffed, nodding.

"I will let you go to the bathroom but if you try to run I will go back to the hospital and cut off your sister's hands." He took the tanto knife from his jacket and flicked it open.

She burst into tears, her hopes of escape dashed. The Yakuza lieutenant waited for the sobbing to subside, then took a key from his jacket and removed the cuffs.

"Go, here." Masateru used his knife to point at the ditch beside the road.

Karla rubbed her wrists, squatted over the dirt, and relieved herself. When she was finished Masateru directed her back into the car. They set off along the highway, Karla continuing to cry into her sleeve.

"These will make you feel better." Masateru reached into his jacket and took out a pill bottle. He shook two large tablets into his hand and held them out.

Karla eyed them suspiciously.

"They won't hurt you. If I wanted you dead it would have already happened."

She took the pills and put them in her mouth. He tossed a bottle of water into her lap.

She put the plastic to her parched lips and downed the sedatives.

"You will find that if you behave things will not be so bad."

"Being raped is not so bad?" She managed a teary laugh. "Have you tried it?"

"You will find that most of your clients will treat you very well. We will not let anyone hurt a beauty like you. You might even start to enjoy it."

Karla tossed the water bottle back to him and looked away.

Masateru lowered his voice. "What I'm telling you now may save your life. And your sister's. Listen carefully. You need to forget about your old life. This is your future now. Embrace it and you will lead a life of luxury and pleasure, just like our other girls. You will have everything you want: fancy clothes, fine food, even money to send to your sister. She will benefit from your service. She will be able to go to university. She will also have a good life."

Karla looked at him through glazed eyes.

"Fight it," he said, "and your life will end being gang-raped in a cheap hotel. Or maybe a businessman will pay a premium to cut your throat and fuck your corpse. Your sister will also bear the consequences of your actions. The choice is yours." Masateru turned his attention to the driver. "How much farther?" he asked.

"Only a few more hours to Kiev."

"Have you heard from any of the others?"

The driver shook his head.

Masateru checked his phone again; it had been hours since he had lost contact with his team. Not one of them would answer their phones and there was no doubt in his mind that they were dead or captured. He sighed and turned off his phone, almost out of power. The sooner he got out of this depressing country, the better.

⭐⭐⭐

"Can you see them?" Kurtz asked over the radio as he scanned the airport's private hangars with his binoculars. From his vantage point on the other side of the runway, he had hoped to get a clear view of the aircraft the Yakuza were using.

"*Nyet*, it's like they've disappeared." Aleks was positioned out in front of the private terminal in the car.

"Fuck!" Kurtz could see all the hangars but not one aircraft. It was possible the private jet was behind a hangar or inside. "I have to move."

As he lowered his binoculars, his iPRIMAL buzzed in his pocket. He pulled it out and checked the alerts. Their target phone was active again. On the digital map the hit was exactly where he was looking. The time of the signal intercept was only seconds ago.

"Aleks, you get that?"

"Can you see them?"

"Negative. It might be behind one of the hangars. You need to get eyes on."

"Got it, I'm moving now."

As Kurtz ran along the fence line looking for a better position, a sleek white business jet nosed out from the hangars and turned onto the airport apron. He skidded to a halt and pulled the iPRIMAL from his pocket. Lifting it up to his face, he let the camera sensor capture the scene. It took a few seconds for the augmented reality mapping to load, but when it did he could see a marker hovering over the location of the phone intercept. It was almost on top of the jet that was taxiing. He grabbed the binoculars.

"They've got a private jet. It's white, currently moving away from me on the taxiway. I can't make out the tail number."

✮✮✮

"I'm on it." In front of the terminal, Aleks was out of the car and running between the security posts that denied vehicle access. Once he was on the other side he found alternate transport.

"Sorry, comrade." He yanked the airport attendant from his seat on a golf cart and deposited him on the sidewalk. Taking his place he accelerated the cart to its top speed of fifteen miles an hour and aimed it toward the aircraft hangars. He waved his Interpol badge at the security guards manning the checkpoint and zoomed through. With security guards running behind him, he rounded the hangar sheds. A few hundred feet away the white business jet was taxiing down a feeder lane toward the start of the runway. He snapped a photo with his iPRIMAL as it swung onto the main strip and accelerated sharply. A few seconds later it was airborne.

"Did you get the tail number?" Kurtz's voice came through his earpiece.

"Yeah, brother. I got it."

CHAPTER 45

PRIMAL HQ, LASCAR ISLAND

"Sneaky fuckers," said Vance.

"You're telling me they've got someone in the anti-people-smuggling department of Interpol?" said Chua. "That's not just bold, it's brilliant."

They were sitting around Flash Gordon's workstation, four wide-screen monitors mounted in a row, giving them a massive amount of screen real estate in which to conduct their work.

Vance put on his reading glasses and squinted at the screen. "So who are they? What are the links from Interpol back to mainland Japan?"

"Their COMSEC is extremely tight," Flash explained. "They change handsets regularly and keep it brief. Those phones Aleks and Kurtz picked up broke out their network in Europe but if they are talking with Japan it must be on another clean handset or by some other means."

"And what about this Masateru guy who seemed to be running things at the castle?"

"Still no leads." Flash shook his head. "Even the trail from Bishop's computer hack didn't give us anything specific. It led to some commercial servers in Japan, but no addresses or identities. Their online profile is nonexistent." A spiderweb of lines connected icons representing phones, computers, people, and locations on the screen. Flash manipulated the model with his mouse and it spun like an LSD-fueled laser show. "In Europe, everything we've got comes back to this guy." A central icon flashed red within the web.

"And that's the Interpol guy?" Vance asked.

"Yep. Capitaine Rémi Marcen. One of their lead agents in the people-smuggling department. Works out of the headquarters in Lyon."

The man's photo appeared onscreen, a long, thin face with piercing brown eyes.

"Capitaine, eh?" Vance said. "Arrogant-looking motherfucker."

"He has to be their main man on the sourcing end," Chua added. "He's got access to all the gangs. All he has to do is bring in some low-end crim, put him through the wringer, and then release him. Before you know it, he's talking to the animals that steal girls out of their beds."

"And making a tidy bit of cash on the side," said Vance.

"He's the go-to guy, that's for sure," said Flash. "Call chains from him reach out all over Europe." He pointed to the different networks sprawling out over a map on one of the other screens.

"So this Capitaine is the linchpin. He needs to go," stated Vance. "Work up a target pack and let's get it up to Tariq." PRIMAL's benefactor was always consulted when they were considering kidnapping or assassinating a high-profile individual. He acted as a sounding board for Chua and Vance, helping separate the executive decisions from the guys deep in the weeds.

"Use Kurtz and Aleks?" Chua asked.

"Yeah. If we didn't give this to them, Kurtz would mutiny, and he'd take that crazy Russian with him."

"It's either them or Mirza's team in the Middle East. They're due out in the next few hours but we could redirect them from their next tasking."

"No, let's use Tweedledum and Tweedledee. They've got a stake in this game, and after the last couple of days they need to chalk up a win. That reminds me, did we get a fix on that aircraft tail number they sent in?"

Flash pressed a few keys and a map displayed on one of the screens. "Yeah, we're tracking her across China at the moment." A small airplane icon appeared on the map tracking east. "Set to touch down in Kobe in about six hours."

"Good, let's get Aleks and Kurtz briefed on the Interpol job and a target pack up to Tariq." Vance turned to face Chua. "Have you briefed Saneh and Bishop on Karla and her ETA?"

"I've sent them the intel," Chua said. "They should be checking in soon. Their hookup with the Yamaguchis certainly helped out. They've got vehicles and additional surveillance at their disposal."

"Baiko set that up, yeah?"

"That's correct. Having someone inside the police is going to be critical to this mission."

"Then that hunch of yours has turned out pretty well."

"It's a bit early but it would seem so."

"Getting more like Bishop every week." Vance grinned.

Chua frowned. "Unlikely. Unless I start chasing random women and getting myself ambushed every five minutes."

CHAPTER 46

YAMAGUCHI-GUMI SAFE HOUSE, KOBE

"Not a bad pad," said Bishop as he came up from the basement of the unused nightclub.

"Perfect hideout," agreed Saneh from the bar, where she sat with her laptop.

Kenta had taken them to the safe house, located on the outskirts of a commercial sector in Kobe. Nestled in a back alley, it was discreet, allowing them to come and go without drawing attention. The building itself was tall and narrow. Four stories with a drive-in basement, perfect for hiding their vehicles.

Bishop rummaged through a box behind the bar. "Gotta be something decent to eat in here," he said as he discarded packets of dried squid and seaweed. Giving up, he turned to Saneh. "You know Kenta's going to be a while . . ." Their Yakuza liaison had taken the car to get supplies. Bishop slid in next to Saneh and put his arm around her waist.

"You've got a one-track mind." Saneh looked back at her computer screen anxiously. "When was the last time you checked the messages from the Bunker?"

"This morning. Why?"

"This just came through. Aleks and Kurtz lost Karla."

Bishop's arm dropped back to his side. "Lost her? What the hell, how did—"

"Shut up and listen." Saneh scanned the rest of the message. "Your Yakuza pal Masateru lured them away from the hospital into an ambush. Then he grabbed Karla from the hospital and got himself onto a private jet out of Kiev."

"Are our boys OK?" Bishop peered over her shoulder.

"No injuries, just pride; they've been retasked to pick up a loose end in France."

"Kurtz has got to be going out of his mind."

"The job's been passed to us now. We've got less than three hours to set up surveillance on Kobe Airport before they land."

The rattle of the roller door in the basement filled the building.

Saneh shut the laptop and headed upstairs to the building's offices. "You help Kenta. I'll talk to Chua and get confirmatory orders."

Bishop watched her as she climbed the open staircase, his gaze fixed on the way her cargo pants fitted around her backside.

"That's not helping," Saneh commented without looking back at him.

"OK, I'm on it."

He met the stocky Yakuza at the top of the stairs from the basement and relieved him of one of his packages. "Hey, mate, you've got to watch that shoulder."

Kenta grunted dismissively and placed his package on the bar. Bishop did the same.

"I hope your rooms are acceptable," said Kenta.

They were staying in the upstairs offices, converted into bedrooms with tatami floor mats.

"The place is perfect—somewhere to park the car and plenty of room," Bishop replied.

"The *oyabun* has delayed its destruction so we can use it. Once we are finished it will become apartments."

"Another move toward legitimacy," Bishop joked. "Pass on our thanks to the *oyabun*. He's a very generous man."

"*Toran to seba mazu ataeyo.*"

"What does that mean?"

"If you want, then first you must help. We need you to destroy our enemies. So of course the Yamaguchi will help you to do so."

"We'll need your help now," said Bishop. "Saneh's upstairs talking to our people. They've tracked Mori-Kai operatives and a kidnapped girl from Eastern Europe. They're flying into Kobe as we speak."

"They are bringing in girls?" Kenta's impassive features took on a concerned look.

"We think it's just one. A very pretty young girl from Croatia. They're flying in by private jet."

"If they are using their own plane they will land at Kobe Airport."

"That's the intel we have as well."

"Touchdown in three hours," Saneh said from the top of the stairs, her laptop tucked under her arm.

"That is not a lot of time," said Kenta.

"No it's not," agreed Bishop.

"You will need some of the things I have got you." Kenta picked up one of the packages and gave it to Saneh. "This should fit you."

She tore open the brown-paper package and pulled out a full-length black leather biker suit and a pair of boots. "My god, they're amazing." She grinned.

Kenta shrugged. "It's too dangerous to ride around Kobe without leathers."

"Now it's going to be every red-blooded male who's in danger of crashing," Bishop said. "I hope you don't expect me to wear that getup."

"No. It wouldn't fit you," Kenta replied, deadpan.

Saneh put down her leathers and opened her laptop on the bar. "First things first. Let's talk about the targets." On the screen appeared an image of Karla's face. "This is the only photo we have. We think she'll be escorted by a high-ranking Mori-Kai named Masateru."

"He looks like a Japanese Elvis," Bishop added.

"All we know is he's involved in coordinating their kidnap operations in Europe. This next slide is where they're going to land." The screen changed to a map of the Kobe Airport complex.

"Kenta, you know the lay of the land. Where's the best spot to pick these two up?"

"It is easy. Here and here." Kenta pointed to either end of the bridge that provided the only access to the island airport. "I have also brought radios so we will be able to spread out."

"Good thinking, mate," said Bishop as Kenta handed out the covert radios, complete with wireless earpieces and microphones. "That's going to make things a lot easier."

Kenta smiled and nodded.

Saneh zoomed in on the digital map. "So we wait for them up here and then we tail them, yes?"

"*Hai, dozo.* That is a good plan." Kenta nodded. "Then once we find them we kill the Mori-Kai."

"Well, maybe not straight away," said Bishop.

Kenta looked at him blankly.

"First we get the intel, then we do the killing," clarified Bishop.

"Ah, yes, very good. First intel, then killing."

"Never thought I'd hear you say that, Agent Wilson." Saneh smiled sweetly. "Someone's finally growing up."

CHAPTER 47

KOBE TO HIMEJI

The business jet touched down at Kobe Airport at 1600 hours. As it taxied across the tarmac to the private terminal, Masateru finished his drink and turned to Karla. "Welcome to Japan, your new home."

The striking blonde glared back at him over her glass of champagne. Despite her anger she looked comfortable wrapped in the expensive leather chair.

The aircraft came to a smooth halt and the flight attendant opened the doors. Warm air carried the damp smell of the ocean into the cabin.

Masateru slicked his hair back with a comb and donned his jacket. He waited for Karla to finish her own preparations, then directed her to the exit. At the top of the stairs he gave her a moment to take in the scenery, her eyes wide with wonder. The airport was on its own island, just off the coast of Kobe. The cries of seagulls filled the air; it was nothing like the quiet European village she had grown up in.

"Get in the car." Masateru gestured toward the black Lexus sedan.

A sturdy Japanese man wearing a long jacket and sporting a crewcut stood at the open door.

"*Oss,*" he said in greeting, bowing slightly. Masateru nodded in return. Hideaki was among his most trusted Kissaki, recruited from the same Special Forces unit as Ryu.

"Where are we going?" Karla asked. "Why the guard?"

"Not everyone here is our friend, my dear. We're going into the city. Then you will meet your new master."

Masateru waited until Hideaki had put Karla in the car. "Where is Ryu? Why isn't he here?"

"The *oyabun* has tasked him to find the *gaijin*."

"And?"

"The *oyabun* wishes to brief you himself."

Masateru scowled as he climbed into the Lexus. Although Ryu was the Kissaki commander, the former Japanese soldier worked for Masateru, not the *oyabun*. It was Masateru who had thought of the idea to recruit former Special Forces; it was he who had formed the Kissaki. The *oyabun* only provided the funds that made it possible.

Inside the car, he passed Karla a blindfold. She looked at him with angry eyes and then slowly tied it around her head. He issued a command in Japanese and they drove off the tarmac through a set of security gates and onto the causeway that separated the man-made island from the docklands.

☆☆☆

"A black sedan, Lexus I think," Kenta transmitted over the radio. He had parked his motorcycle in the parking lot opposite the main terminal. From the far side it offered an uninterrupted view of the airport's facilities. He was using a long-lens camera to watch the jet land and had caught a glimpse of the blonde when she paused at the top of the stairs. "The girl is definitely in the car. She arrived with a man. I think I know him."

"Bad hair, bad suit?" Bishop transmitted.

"*Hai*, I have taken some photos. They're leaving now."

"I've got them." Saneh waited for the car to hit the halfway point on the causeway before gunning her Kawasaki Ninja and slipping into the traffic behind it.

"Don't get so close," Bishop warned as the car passed by the shabby-looking warehouses of the docklands.

"I know what I'm doing."

"Of course you do," Bishop said to himself as the black sedan raced past his parked GT-R. A second later Saneh flashed by on her bike. "Women," he sighed. "They can't be told."

"No, but they can remember to take their thumb off the transmit button."

Bishop laughed as he pulled the GT-R away from the curb. "Maybe I wanted you to hear."

"Then you're more special than I thought."

Kenta's voice filled the airways. "Are you sure you're not married?"

"The downside of working together for so long." Saneh now tailed the Lexus by half a dozen car lengths. Kenta followed another hundred feet behind, with Bishop bringing up the rear in the GT-R.

"They're turning onto the highway," said Saneh.

"Left or right?" asked Kenta.

"Left."

"They're heading to Himeji," said Kenta.

"What's in Himeji?" asked Bishop.

"It is the traditional home of the Mori-Kai."

"That was over a thousand years ago, right?"

"In Japan, traditions take more than a thousand years to die."

The Lexus accelerated along the sweeping highway ramp that joined with the Hanshin Expressway. The high-rises of Kobe's commercial district flashed past as they traveled along the coast.

Behind them Saneh was focused, crouching low in the saddle and weaving the superbike between the traffic. "They're pushing it hard."

"You want to hand over?" asked Bishop over the growl of the GT-R. "I'm doing fine. Kenta, where are you?"

Silence on the airwaves.

"What the hell happened to Kenta?" Saneh wove the bike between two slow-moving trucks.

"Nice move! I'm not sure. He was here a second ago."

"Damn it, I guess it's up to us then."

Saneh continued to tail the Lexus as it powered down the highway, scarcely able to absorb the scenery as it flashed past. High-rises, warehouses, tunnels, forests, and apartment complexes blended into a blur of color as she focused on tailing the car without being spotted.

Behind her, Bishop concentrated on keeping her in sight, ready to take over the tail if Saneh thought she might be compromised.

Fifteen minutes later Saneh lost sight of the car as it rounded a corner. She accelerated the bike to close the gap and rocketed past an exit. The Lexus was nowhere to be seen. "Damn, I've lost them."

"You're kidding me. Where the hell could they have gone?"

"The exit, take the exit!"

Bishop was in the outside lane as he came round the bend, overtaking a bus filled with children. He slammed on the brakes and sent the GT-R sliding sideways across four lanes. The tires shrieked as he angled toward the exit ramp.

"Fuck, fuck, fuck!" The exit barrier loomed in Bishop's window. He took his foot off the brake and punched the accelerator. The GT-R roared, regained its footing, and blasted down the ramp. "Where to now?"

"I don't know. I'm trying to find a way off this thing." Saneh remained on the highway looking for an exit.

"We're going to lose them." Bishop stopped at the lights at the bottom of the ramp. He couldn't see the car in either direction. He slammed his palms into the steering wheel in frustration.

"I'm off, a couple of blocks ahead," reported Saneh, her voice distorted. The little UHF radios were almost out of range.

"Screw it, I'm going left." Bishop turned the GT-R toward the docklands.

"I'm doing the same," Saneh announced.

"Keep coming, I've got them. They're heading into Himeji's docklands." Kenta's voice came through over the radio.

"Where the hell have you been?" Bishop asked.

"I took a shortcut to get ahead of them," he responded calmly. "You and she raced off and I couldn't reach you on the radio."

There was a pause.

"They've stopped," said Kenta. "They've gone into a warehouse in the *Shirahama-cho* Usazakiminami block."

Bishop glanced up at a street sign, the characters meaning nothing to him. He activated the car's in-dash GPS; the Japanese characters confused him even more. "I'm somewhere in the docks area, heading toward the water, not sure what happened to Sarah."

"I'm right behind you."

Bishop looked into his rearview mirror. There she was, clad from head to toe in skintight leathers and wearing a full-faced helmet. She gave him a nod.

"No need for you to come closer," Kenta said. "I know where they've stopped and they do not know that we know. We should try to keep it that way."

"Good idea. Can you get extra men to help?" Bishop pulled the GT-R into a shopping complex parking lot. Saneh brought her bike in next to him.

"Yes, I have already called for more men."

"Good, we're parked in a 100-yen shop three blocks from the highway exit."

"I know it. I'll meet you there once my people arrive."

The door to the GT-R opened and Saneh lowered herself into the passenger seat. She dumped her motorcycle helmet on the floor and adjusted her hair. Bishop couldn't help but smile as she struggled to bend her legs in the tight leather.

"Shut the hell up," she snapped.

"I didn't say anything."

"You were going to. I know I messed up the follow."

"All good. Kenta seems to have it all in hand."

"I missed the last conversation. What's the plan?"

"Just as we discussed, Kenta's going to bring in more men. Then we can bang in, grab the girl, and nail Masateru."

"No, we need to get intel on these guys. You said it yourself."

"We'll get intel off the target."

"I think it's too early to show our hand. We've got the advantage now; the Mori-Kai don't know we're here."

"What do you think we should do?"

"We wait and watch, follow any vehicles coming or going. Once we have a second location we hit the warehouse."

"What if we lose her?"

"That's a risk. But if we grab her now we definitely won't find the next level up in the chain. If the Mori-Kai are all they've been made out to be, this shitty warehouse will be just one link in a chain of facilities."

"OK, fine, we wait. But I'm not happy about it."

"When are you ever happy about my decisions?"

"When they're right."

CHAPTER 48

HIMEJI DOCKLANDS

"Where are we?" Karla demanded as they pulled up outside a gray, concrete-walled warehouse. A heavy steel door blocked their way.

"I want to show you something," said Masateru.

"I can't see anything with this on." She gestured to the blindfold.

"You will soon enough."

The driver made a phone call and a few seconds later the gate slid open. They drove into a large garage and parked next to a pair of white windowless vans.

Hideaki helped Karla out and led her alongside Masateru to where a suit-wearing Yakuza waited. The facility manager bowed, a look of uncertainty on his face.

"What brings you here, *waka-gashira*?" the man asked in Japanese.

"I have the *oyabun*'s new bitch. She needs to be shown how it will be if she doesn't behave."

The other man laughed. "Then come this way." He led them through another door into what could have passed as a cocktail lounge.

The floor was traditional polished wood, the walls decorated in a tasteful crane motif. Luxurious leather couches lined one of the walls and a small bar graced the wall opposite it. A handful of men were lounging on the couches and sitting at the bar. They all stood and bowed as Masateru entered.

"Take off her blindfold," he ordered Hideaki.

Karla squinted in the light of the waiting area. Her eyes darted around, painfully aware she was the only woman in a room full of gangsters. "What is this place?" she asked.

"This is where you will end up if you do not follow every command you are given. Now come."

Masateru led her down a poorly lit corridor with metal doors running off either side. He stopped in front of one of the rooms and gestured for Karla to join him. He slid back the heavy bolt on the door and pushed it open.

Inside it looked to be a prison cell, complete with a bare stainless toilet and a mattress on the floor covered in blankets.

There was a moan from the pile of blankets and Karla recoiled in horror as a young blonde girl appeared from under the covers.

Her once pretty features were sunken and drawn, her skin pale. The dull gray eyes widened as they focused on Karla and she gave a desperate look. "Help me," she mouthed.

Masateru slammed the door and slid the bolt home.

"Why is she here?" Karla looked up at him, her eyes filled with tears. "What did she do?"

"You're not that naive. She services the needs of our clients." Masateru kept walking down the corridor until he got to another room. "This facility is for some of our more, shall we say, creative guests." He pushed open the door and waved Karla inside.

"Oh my god."

Metal grates covered the floor, the smell of antiseptic lingered in the air. Chains hung from the roof, supporting a heavy leather harness. In the corner were a variety of strange chairs, mechanical contraptions, and benches with built-in restraints. A stainless-steel bench against the back wall was covered in wicked-looking surgical tools, whips, and vaguely phallic devices.

"Get me out of here," Karla screamed, pushing toward the door.

Masateru calmly grabbed her hair and forced her across to the table.

"NO, NO, NO, NO!" she screamed as he picked up a solid steel rod and held it in front of her face.

"This is what's going to happen if you don't comply with every direction we give you. You'll be brought here, locked in a cell, and fucked with something like this every day until you die. Is that what you want?"

Karla was crying hysterically.

"Do as you're told and you will never see this place again. Plus I'll guarantee your sister will be safe. You wouldn't want something like this to happen to her, would you?"

She shook her head and Masateru released her. She stumbled out the door and he followed her back into the corridor.

"This is not your life, my little angel." Masateru stroked her hair as they walked back to the waiting area. "Your destiny is one of privilege and comfort."

"You're pigs," she sobbed. "How can you do this?"

"Because it is our right. These women are cattle and we will do with them as we wish. You should be thankful that you are more valuable."

Masateru ushered her back to the waiting area, where Hideaki was sharing sake with the other gangsters.

"Would you drink with us, *waka-gashira*?" the facility manager asked in Japanese.

"What's the occasion?"

"To fallen brothers."

Masateru nodded and lifted a glass.

"The Yamaguchi will pay now that you have returned."

"What have the Yamaguchi done?" Masateru asked after he downed the liquor.

The other man looked surprised. "You don't know? The Yamaguchi ambushed three of our men on the Shinkansen."

"Kissaki?" Masateru asked.

"Yes. All dead."

Masateru drew a deep breath, his usually calm exterior dissolving. "Hideaki, you did not inform me of this."

His bodyguard bowed his head. "Like I said, *waka-gashira*, the *oyabun* wanted to speak to you first. He has plans."

Masateru threw the sake glass against the wall. It shattered in an explosion of glass shards. "You forget who you fucking work for?"

"No, *waka-gashira*." Hideaki dipped his head in deference.

"The Kissaki work for me and only for me." He slapped Hideaki with an open hand, sending the man reeling. He lifted his arm to strike him again and the facility manager grabbed him.

Masateru's knife appeared out of nowhere, a flashing blur of steel. Blood sprayed into the air as the blade sliced through the bridge of the manager's nose. He screamed in agony, clutching his face. The other men in the room stood still, in horror.

Masateru pulled out a handkerchief and wiped the blade clean. "Put the girl in the car. We're leaving."

CHAPTER 49

"Our people are in place." Kenta had joined Saneh and Bishop in the GT-R parked in front of the 100-yen store.

"How many?" Bishop asked.

"Five. They will take turns watching. If anyone leaves they will follow," Kenta explained from the backseat.

"That should be enough," said Bishop. "Now we wait and see who comes and goes. That right, Sarah?"

"Correct." Saneh had the Yamaguchi's camera and was looking at the photos he had taken at the airport. She paused on a shot that showed Masateru's face. "Kenta, what did you say his real name was?"

"If he is the man I think he is, then his name is Hinata. He was expelled for dealing in heroin."

"Well, he goes by Masateru now," Saneh said. "He's a real piece of work. I watched him slice a girl's face like he was peeling an orange."

"He never fit in with the Yamaguchi-gumi."

"If you find out anything else . . ."

"I will tell you immediately." Kenta nodded as he opened a take-out food container. The odor of teriyaki filled the car.

"That smells good," said Bishop, looking over his shoulder.

"Would you like some?" He handed a container full of fried vegetables and rice toward him.

"No, it's OK."

"There is plenty, I have enough for us all."

"I'll try some." Saneh took the container from him. "Do you have any chopsticks?"

"*Hai.*" He passed a disposable pair across.

Saneh handled the chopsticks with a deftness that surprised Bishop. "You're pretty good at that."

"I love Asian food," she responded between mouthfuls.

"That much is evident," Bishop smirked.

"Do you want some?"

"Hey, Kenta, you got a fork?" Bishop asked.

"No. I'm sorry."

"It's cool."

"You can't use chopsticks?" Saneh asked.

"I can use them; it's more of a phobia."

"You're afraid of chopsticks?"

"Let's just say we don't get along."

Saneh laughed between mouthfuls. "Did you have a bad experience with a particularly slippery piece of tofu?"

"Firstly, I don't eat tofu. It makes men grow tits. Secondly, having a chopstick stuck up your nose is quite a traumatic experience for a young child."

Saneh looked at him with her mouth open. "You're joking, right?"

"Do I ever joke?"

Saneh laughed. "The question is, do you ever stop?"

"You are both very funny!" Kenta said, cracking the first broad smile that Bishop had seen from him. "Very entertaining, like American TV."

Bishop chuckled. "It gets worse, trust me."

Saneh punched him in the shoulder and gave the container

back to Kenta. "So tell us about yourself. When did you start with the Yamaguchi?"

"There is not much to tell. When I was fifteen the Yamaguchi-gumi took me in. I have been with them ever since."

"What makes a fifteen-year-old boy join the Yakuza?"

"I didn't have a choice. My brother was a foot soldier. When he died I replaced him."

"That must have been traumatic." Saneh had noticed the scars on his face and hands.

Kenta ate another mouthful before continuing. "Worse things could have happened to me. I always wanted to join the police but I would have ended up a Yakuza puppet. My duty would have been corrupted. This is better, I think."

A blast of noise from Kenta's radio interrupted Saneh. High-speed Japanese emitted from the speaker as though from a verbal machine gun.

Kenta replied, giving a series of equally rapid orders.

"What's going on?" Bishop asked.

"The Lexus is leaving the compound; the girl is in it," Kenta translated.

"Do we need to follow?" asked Bishop.

"My people will tail them," Kenta replied.

"We should leave it to the locals, Brian," said Saneh. "They'll draw less attention."

"Yeah, OK," agreed Bishop.

Kenta gathered the food into the takeout bag. "We should be ready to move. Can you let me out?"

Saneh exited and flicked her seat forward, allowing Kenta to extricate himself from the back of the sports car.

"Once my men have found the next location, we will go. I will lead."

★★★

"Where to?" Masateru's driver asked.

"The Apartments."

The Lexus left the secure parking lot of the warehouse and turned onto the main road north to Himeji city.

Masateru turned to Karla. "We're going to your new home."

She turned away, staring out the window.

They drove in silence for a few minutes before the driver spoke again. "*Waka-gashira*, I think we are being followed."

The Yakuza lieutenant swiveled in his seat to look out the back window. "Which car?"

"The black Nissan."

"Who are they? Police?"

"No. I think they are Yakuza."

"How the hell did they find us?"

"What do you want me to do?"

"When I say go, I want you to accelerate and take the next left turn. Don't slow down for the corner. As soon as we are around it, stop. Hideaki and I will take care of this problem."

The Kissaki in the front passenger seat nodded and pulled his MP9 machine pistol from under his jacket. He opened the glove compartment and drew out an identical weapon, handing it back to his boss. Both men checked that their weapons were loaded and unfolded the stocks.

"What's happening?" Karla stared at the weapons.

"Just stay in the car," Masateru said in English before switching back to Japanese. "NOW!"

The driver jammed his foot down on the accelerator and the

Lexus leaped forward. The tires squealed as he threw the car around the next left turn.

"Stop here!" Masateru yelled after the turn, and their car screeched to a halt. Masateru and Hideaki leaped out with their weapons in their shoulders as the Nissan came barreling around the corner in pursuit. They fired automatic bursts into the front of the car, shredding its tires. With a screech it veered onto the pavement and crashed into the side of a building.

A series of single shots were fired from the immobilized Yamaguchi vehicle, a feeble attempt at self-defense. The response was overwhelming. The MP9s spat flame, firing more than fifteen rounds per second. The torrent of bullets smashed holes through the windshield of the sedan and into its occupants.

Masateru's weapon ran dry, the bolt locking open on an empty magazine as he walked toward the shattered car. He pulled open the driver's door. The man at the wheel was dead, missing half his face. His partner in the passenger seat gurgled, struggling to breathe through punctured lungs. An old revolver was still in his limp grip.

Masateru tossed the pistol aside and grabbed hold of the man's shirt. "Who do you work for?"

Bloody froth spilled from the man's mouth as he tried to respond.

"Useless swine." Masateru handed his empty submachine gun to Hideaki. He drew his knife from his jacket and opened it with a deft flick of his wrist. Pulling the man's head back by the hair, he slashed his throat with the blade, severing the windpipe, blood vessels, and tendons. Blood sprayed across Masateru as he cut down to the spine. His victim's arms and legs convulsed, his eyes wide in shock.

Thirty seconds later Masateru was back in the Lexus, severed head in the trunk, and they resumed their journey.

Karla stared at him in horror as he used a handkerchief to wipe the blood from his face.

"Who . . . who were those men?" she asked quietly.

"Other Yakuza. Yamaguchi."

Karla's hand shook as she touched the window where one of the stray Yamaguchi bullets had hit the armored glass. "They shot at us."

"They wanted to kill us. They wanted you."

"Me? Why?"

"Because you are worth a great deal of money as a slave. They want to sell you to a rich, fat Arab for a million dollars. A rich Arab who wants to rape beautiful, young, blonde infidel women." He let the words sink in before continuing. "But you do not need to fear this, because I will never let them take you. You belong to the *oyabun* and soon you will realize that serving him comes with great benefits."

Masateru handed Karla another two pills.

She swallowed them and waited for their numbing effect. For a moment her thoughts wandered back to her sister and her home village. A single tear ran down her cheek and she consoled herself with the hope that at least her sister would be able to lead a normal life.

CHAPTER 50

"Oh shit, I'm sorry, Kenta." Bishop could see by the amount of blood sprayed throughout the inside of the Nissan that the Yakuza men were dead, not to mention the fact that one of them was missing his head.

"They paid the penalty for their mistakes," the Yamaguchi enforcer said, his face betraying no emotion.

"These guys were using fully automatic weapons, judging by how this windshield is all shot to shit." Bishop picked up an expended shell. "Nine-millimeter submachine guns. Same as on the train."

The downshifting of a high-performance motorcycle engine announced Saneh as she brought her bike alongside them, killed the engine, and lifted her visor. "What happened?"

"Compromised and executed," said Bishop. "Now we've lost the girl and the lead."

"We can still watch the compound. They'll come and go—"

"Enough watching!" Bishop cut her off. "We hit the warehouse now and we hit them hard. Then we break down one of these assholes and put him through the wringer. I'll make him sing like a motherfucking canary."

"Brian, I don't think that's the right thing to do. We—"

"I'm calling the shots now. Kenta, how many men do you have left?"

"Three and myself."

"That's all? What about Hero and all that talk of anything we needed?"

"This is all we will get until we have proven our worth. It will be enough; we will kill these Mori-Kai."

"OK, it'll have to do."

In the distance a police siren wailed.

"We need to leave now," said Kenta. "My people are still watching the warehouse. We will meet them and then attack."

"Sounds good; we'll follow you." Bishop was already getting in his car.

Kenta donned his helmet and jumped on his cruiser. He roared up the street with Saneh and Bishop following.

A few minutes later Bishop followed the two bikes into a warehouse. He glanced in his rearview mirror as two Yakuza gangsters closed the doors behind him.

The building was about the size of a tennis court. The holes in the roof and garbage piled in one corner were evidence that it had been abandoned. At the far end were two Yamaguchi Mercedes. Kenta was standing close to them with Saneh and one of his men. Bishop grabbed his backpack from the trunk of his car.

"We are very close to the Mori-Kai," said Kenta as Bishop joined them. The gangster drew a rough diagram with his finger on the dusty trunk of the Mercedes.

"Good choice," said Bishop as he watched Kenta carefully mark out a map of the building.

The two Yamaguchi henchmen who had slid the doors shut joined the group. They were dressed in the dark suits and white shirts that seemed to be the uniform of traditional Yakuza.

Bishop shook his head. "Some tailor's making a killing off you guys."

Kenta looked at him blankly.

"Never mind. Go on."

"It is a big concrete warehouse. There are heavy steel doors at the back where the Lexus drove in. I think it is a place to keep cars."

"A garage?" Saneh asked.

"Yes, a garage, but that is not the best way in. At the other end of the building there is a wire fence and a door. Without explosives it is the only way in."

"Great work, Kenta, you've done well. Any ideas how many are inside?"

Kenta shook his head. "Hard to say. I think at least six, maybe more."

"Damn, pretty sure you guys aren't packing CQB rigs."

"I don't understand." Kenta looked confused.

"I meant, what firepower have we got?"

"I have my revolver, these two have pistols, and he has a shotgun."

"That's a bit light," Saneh pointed out.

"It'll be fine," Bishop said as he unzipped his backpack and pulled out the PX4 9mm subcompact and two magazines. "You used one of these before, Kenta?"

"Like a Makarov." He nodded.

"Kind of." Bishop handed him the weapon. "That old hand cannon of yours is shit-hot but I thought you might like a few more bullets. Run it as a backup if you want."

Kenta took the weapon. The lightweight polymer pistol with its thirteen-round magazine looked like a toy in his tattooed fist.

"Thank you."

Saneh gave him a quick rundown on the controls while Bishop quickly checked their other two handguns.

"So, how we going to do this?" Saneh asked once they were ready.

Bishop tapped the trunk, where Kenta had drawn a map in the dust. Everyone gathered around. "It will be simple, yeah. We drive through this fence in the Mercs. Shoot all the bad guys and free any women they might have captive. Somewhere along the way we'll want to grab a prisoner. The higher up, the better."

"What do we do with the girls?" Saneh asked.

Kenta replied, "I'll call our friends in the police. They will take the women."

Bishop nodded. "And if the police do their investigations properly this should lead to other locations." He made a mental note to ring Baiko. "It's a good plan. Let's go kill some Mori-Kai." He cocked his pistol, securing it in a paddle holster on his hip. The four Yakuza followed suit before getting into the two Mercedes.

Saneh grabbed Bishop's arm as he made to jump into one of the front passenger seats. "Look, cowboy, we're not running armor or long arms and we have no idea what's in that building. These MK guys are playing for keeps, so take it easy, OK?"

Bishop gave her a hard look and then nodded. "We'll let the Yamaguchi boys do the heavy lifting. But if it goes sideways don't expect me to sit back and do nothing."

CHAPTER 51

MORI-KAI HOLDING FACILITY, HIMEJI
DOCKLANDS

"Hold on!" grunted Kenta as the Mercedes bounced over the curb and smashed into the security gate. The automated sliding mechanism sheared off and it buckled, jumping out of its track as it wrapped around the front of the car.

The Mercedes crunched into the side of the building as Kenta slammed his foot on the brakes.

Bishop jumped out of the car, lifted his pistol, and fired a shot at the CCTV camera positioned over the door. He missed. Before he could fire again, Saneh blew it off the wall.

"Getting shaky, old man."

"Nice shooting, Tex."

The four Yakuza made for the door and stacked up on either side of it, weapons ready. Their actions reassured Bishop. The gangsters seemed to have experience in room clearance; either that, or they had watched too many action movies.

One of the men reached for the door and tugged on it. It was locked. He did what any inexperienced soldier would do, tried to kick it in. The steel-framed door didn't move an inch. He grunted in pain and limped to one side. Another of the Yakuza lined up to repeat the performance.

"STOP!" Bishop holstered his pistol and wrenched the Remington 870 from the hands of one of the Yakuza. He pumped the action, raised the weapon, and fired it directly into the door handle.

The blast tore the locking mechanism completely apart and the door bounced open a few inches. Bishop pumped the shotgun, blasting two rounds in through the gap.

He leaped back to the side as automatic fire slammed into the door from the inside, flinging it open. One of the Yamaguchis aimed his pistol in through the gap and fired. A bullet punched through his forearm, shattering the bone and knocking the handgun to the ground. More rounds snapped through the doorway.

Bishop grabbed him, dragging him away from the fusillade of fire. He handed the shotgun back and drew his pistol.

"Saneh, cover me." He moved up close to the open door.

"Covering." Saneh came in behind Bishop.

He moved swiftly across the doorway, his pistol transferred to his left hand. He caught a glimpse of a target and fired twice. Once he reached the other side he returned the gun to his master hand and fired again.

Bishop made eye contact with Saneh and moved through the doorway into the room. Shots from a pistol rang out and Bishop fired toward the muzzle flash. Someone grunted and fell to the floor.

Saneh was right behind him. She pumped a shot into another figure already facedown on the carpet. "You said they'd do the heavy work."

"Did you see those guys? They'd all be dead by now. CHECK!"

"Covering," Saneh responded as she scanned the two doors leading from the room. Bishop ripped the magazine from his pistol and slapped in a fresh one.

"On gun," he announced as he raised the pistol.

"Off gun," Saneh responded.

Kenta and two uninjured men moved into the room behind the PRIMAL pair. "Where to now?"

"Now we clear every room," replied Bishop.

"We will lead. You have done enough." Kenta moved forward with his revolver holstered, PX4 in hand. He opened the far door and flinched as a bullet sizzled past his head. He fired three rounds back down the corridor. The shotgun-wielding Yakuza joined him, blasting the corridor with buckshot. Both of them ran through the door, jogging down the corridor.

"This is not going to end well." Bishop stripped the MP9 submachine gun off one of the dead Mori-Kai, pulling a fresh magazine from under the dead man's jacket.

Saneh grabbed the third Yamaguchi and oriented him toward the remaining exit. "You watch this door." He looked at her blankly so she pointed at her eyes and then the door. He nodded.

"Sarah, get in here!" Bishop was in the corridor, submachine gun in his shoulder. Kenta and his offsider had already passed through the next door. Shots rang out and the air filled with the stench of cordite.

As Saneh moved down the corridor she looked in through a door window at a pretty blonde Caucasian chained to a bed. She was wearing lingerie. "You're kidding me," she muttered.

"It's a damn holding facility," Bishop said as he checked the other rooms. "There's six girls here. They're all chained."

"It gets worse." Saneh was peering in at the torture cell, replete with the tools of bondage and pain.

"Motherfuckers," Bishop spat.

More gunfire sounded from deeper in the facility and Bishop started jogging toward it. "That doesn't sound good. We'll come back for the girls."

He pushed open the door at the end of the corridor. A few feet in front of it the shotgun-wielding Yamaguchi lay facedown in a spreading pool of blood. Halfway across the waiting room a Mori-Kai gangster was lying on his back, his torso savaged by buckshot.

Another one was dead in front of a bar, his face blown away. More gunfire sounded from a doorway at the end of the room.

Bishop stopped to check the Yamaguchi for a pulse.

Saneh kept moving and poked her head around the door into the garage area.

"Kenta!" she exclaimed.

The Yamaguchi heavy was crouched behind an overturned workbench. Bullets gouged the concrete around him and slammed into the steel-plated bench top.

"How many?" Bishop joined Saneh at the doorway.

Kenta held up three fingers and then pulled out his Colt Python revolver, firing over the bench with a pistol in each hand.

A submachine gun chattered in response, spraying the area with bullets.

"We're outmatched." Saneh fired two rounds in the direction of the vans parked in the garage.

"That's what the Russians thought in Stalingrad."

"You want to wait for winter to kill them?" Saneh fired another two rounds.

Bishop grabbed a bottle of 150-proof whiskey and a book of matches from the bar. "No, I'm going to improvise with this." He pulled a tie from the neck of one of the men Kenta had killed and wrapped it around the neck of the bottle. Then he grabbed the shotgun and handed it to Saneh. "I'll need you to hit the bottle once I've thrown it. I'm borrowing this straight from Uncle Molotov's guide to revolutionary warfare."

"We've only one round," she said, checking the tubular magazine under the barrel. "You're a better shot. You should do it."

"Tell that to the camera you nailed. Plus I've got a better throwing arm." Bishop lit the tie. "Kenta, cover us!" he yelled. "On two."

"One."

Kenta's pistols barked as he emptied them over the bench. "Two."

Bishop stepped out from the doorway and lobbed the bottle into the air. It sailed high up above the vans.

Saneh raised the shotgun and fired.

The bottle exploded, spraying flaming liquid across the garage.

Bishop took advantage of the homemade distraction and sprinted through the doorway into the garage. He fired a long burst from the looted submachine gun as he ran toward the vans. One of the Mori-Kai died with a bullet through the head as he beat at the burning alcohol on his jacket.

Saneh dropped the empty shotgun and followed Bishop into the fight. She moved to the opposite side of the vehicles, her pistol held ready. The barrel of a machine pistol appeared at the rear of a van and she fired, forcing the Mori-Kai back. She punched two more .45-caliber rounds through the side window and the back of the van. There was a grunt, followed by the clatter of a weapon hitting the ground.

The remaining gunman had been under the bottle when it exploded. The burning liquid ignited his polyester suit, turning him into a blazing fireball, screaming and rolling across the floor, beating at his clothes. Kenta silenced him with two bullets to the chest.

"We've got a live one here." Saneh was standing over the man she had shot through the van, her pistol pointed directly at his face. He was clutching his arm. "He's the last."

Bishop aimed his submachine gun at the wounded man, then lowered it. "Good work. Kenta, get him on his feet. We'll take him to the torture cell."

The three of them escorted their captive back down the corridor. Bishop opened a metal door and Kenta dumped the Mori-Kai on the metal grated floor. The injured man grunted in agony as he landed.

"Saneh, can you use Kenta's mate to sort out the wounded and the girls?"

"Why? Because it's a woman's job?"

"Really, you want to do this now?"

She fixed him with a stare and disappeared down the corridor.

Bishop took a plastic chair from the corner and placed it in the middle of the room. Then he lifted the man off the floor and dropped him onto the chair.

"Kenta, I want you to repeat everything I say in Japanese and then translate his response back to me, OK? We don't have long, so this needs to work smoothly."

Kenta shook his head. "It does not matter. He will not talk."

"Why do you say that?"

"Because he is Yakuza."

"I thought you said the Mori-Kai were not true Yakuza."

The Mori-Kai watched them from the chair. His arm was bleeding but his face remained impassive, eyes devoid of emotion.

"I did, but even if he is not true Yakuza he will not talk. Even the lowest dog in Japan has honor."

The gangster in the chair spat on the floor and started speaking Japanese.

"What's he saying?"

"He wants to know why I am working for you. He wants to know why the Yamaguchi are slaves to *gaijin*."

"Tell him we are working together to stop scum like him trading in flesh. Then ask him where they took the girl, the blonde."

Kenta translated.

The wounded man laughed and then spat directly into Bishop's face.

Kenta's tattooed fist plowed into his nose, spraying blood across the floor.

The prisoner continued to laugh as blood ran from his nose. He looked up at Kenta with defiant eyes and spat out a single Japanese phrase, "*Teme okubyōmono.*"

Kenta strode across to the stainless-steel bench and grabbed one of the dildos used by the Mori-Kai clients to defile young women. It was heavy and black, as long as a man's forearm.

"No, Kenta—" Bishop tried to intervene.

Kenta shrugged him off and swung the dildo like a baton, smashing it into the prisoner's face. The tool became a blur of black rubber as he flailed the man, each blow making a sickening, wet thud. Within seconds their captive had fallen sideways out of the chair, head slamming onto the metal floor. Blood flowed from his face as he tried feebly to protect himself from the bludgeoning sex implement.

The muscle-bound Yamaguchi was grunting but showed no sign of tiring. His victim's face was now a bloodied mess, eyes swollen shut, nose destroyed beyond recognition.

Bishop didn't try to stop him. Kenta had lost five of his friends in the last twelve hours, seen the putrid condition of the Mori-Kai slaves, and now his rage was spewing out of him, engulfing everything it touched.

Even after he had beaten the man into unconsciousness Kenta continued to bludgeon away, the blows slowing as fatigue set in. Finally he stopped, chest heaving, and dropped the bloodied club on the floor next to the battered body.

"I'm sorry." Kenta walked back into the corridor.

Bishop shrugged. "Like you said, he wouldn't have talked."

CHAPTER 52

MORI-KAI APARTMENTS, HIMEJI

"All of them? They took all of them? How long until you get here?" Masateru waited for the response from the other end of the phone, then threw it across the room.

He ran a hand through his hair, adjusted his suit, and gazed out the windows of the apartment. Built on the side of a hill on the outskirts of Himeji, it commanded an uninterrupted view of the low city skyline. A company contracted by the Mori-Kai had recently completed the six-level luxury accommodation. A second building was under development in the adjoining block, a testament to their expansion.

Known as "The Apartments," the complex was an unobtrusive fortress, home of the Kissaki and the *oyabun*'s finest women, a living arrangement that Masateru took full advantage of. A door led from his own apartment to a lounge and bar shared with the apartments of the girls. It served as an entertainment area for him and his men.

A firm knock heralded Ryu's arrival. Masateru opened the door and fixed the leader of the Mori-Kai's paramilitary warriors with a hard stare.

"It seems the Kissaki become soft when I am away."

Ryu looked down at the carpet. "My apologies, *waka-gashira*."

"What happened this time?"

"The Yamaguchi-gumi attacked, with two *gaijin*. Our men killed some of them but there were too many. They took all the girls, killed four Mori-Kai, and put one in a coma."

Masateru walked away and returned to the view, looking out over the city.

Ryu continued, "The police were there. They've claimed it a great victory against organized crime."

"Corrupt dogs, they couldn't find our operations if we set up shop inside their buildings." Masateru absentmindedly took the tanto knife from inside his jacket, extended it, and spun it in his palm. "We've taken serious casualties, Ryu. The disaster in Europe, the Yamaguchi on the train, and now this."

"You think they're all related?"

"A week ago no one knew we existed. Now we've been raided by Special Forces in Europe, investigated by the FBI, and attacked by the Yamaguchi. There's no doubt in my mind that these events are all related. And there's one man involved in it all."

"The FBI agent."

"Yes, if that's what he really is. He and his whore have cost us dearly."

"We need to find them and kill them."

Masateru pondered the idea as he watched the evening traffic. The city lights were starting to turn on. Soon the view would be transformed from a picturesque landscape to a hectic light show.

"I suspect that the *gaijin* are part of a larger organization. What we need to do is separate them from their new friends. We need to hit the Yamaguchi hard and teach them a lesson."

"And at the same time flush out the foreigners."

Masateru turned back to Ryu. "Precisely. Without their local support we'll be able to deal with them on our own terms. Then we'll find out who they actually work for. We will need to select our target carefully."

"Yes, *waka-gashira*. After they killed my men on the train I have been developing a suitable target for retribution. One that will strike fear into the Yamaguchi-gumi."

"Who?"

"Your counterpart."

Masateru's lip curled up in a half smile. "Very good, develop a plan. Once it is ready we will brief the *oyabun*. He will want to strike swiftly."

"As you wish." Ryu paused. "You should also be aware that the *oyabun* requested an increase in training for the gangs."

"And?"

"And I thought it would be prudent to comply, considering it aligned with the guidance you provided."

"You have acted accordingly?"

"Yes, we have commenced training of another sixty men."

Masateru nodded. "My army grows stronger. That will be all, Ryu. Finish your planning."

"Yes, *waka-gashira*." Ryu dipped his head and left the room.

Masateru recovered his phone from the other side of the room and dialed his boss, anticipating his fury.

"Welcome home, *waka-gashira*."

"Thank you, *oyabun*." Masateru was surprised at the relaxed tone.

"I trust you have the girl?"

"Yes, she is in good health."

"A shame the same cannot be said for her sister."

"An unfortunate circumstance."

"Indeed, and not the only one to have been bestowed upon us."

Masateru paused, unsure of what to say next.

"The attack at the dockland stables," probed the *oyabun*. "How bad was it?"

"Our men are dead; the girls are gone."

"The press is reporting that the raid was conducted by the police following a tip-off from the Yamaguchi-gumi. Is there any truth to that?"

"There was a Yamaguchi element involved."

"I trust that you are putting together a suitable response?"

"We already have a target in mind. Once it is fully prepared I will call for your approval."

"There is no need; use your judgment. I want action taken immediately."

"It will be done."

"The man from the castle, the British mercenary. Is he involved? Superintendent Tanaka believes he and his female companion were planning to meet with the Yamaguchi."

"We can safely assume that they are now working together. I'm not sure if he is in fact British. He's using a US passport and claiming to work for the FBI."

"Whatever he is, my chief concern is his influence over the Yamaguchi. Should I be worried about this sudden show of teeth? Can I expect a repeat of what happened in Europe?"

"No, the Yamaguchi are as weak as ever. They stumbled on one of our locations with the help of the foreigners, that is all. It will not happen again. Our security measures have already been enhanced and there was nothing linking the docklands facility to our other locations."

"What about our European operations? The Frenchman, has he found a new provider?"

"Not yet, but he will. He would not dare to fail us."

"He had better not." The authoritative tone of the *oyabun* softened. "Masateru, I am concerned we do not have enough men."

"Our numbers are more than adequate. But if we decide we need additional Kissaki, Ryu has already identified more candidates among the Tokushu Sakusen Gun," said Masateru, referring to the Japanese Special Forces Group.

"Good. In your absence I ordered Ryu to begin training the gangs."

Yes, as Ryu already told me, thought Masateru. He smiled to himself and said, "A wise decision, *oyabun*."

"We will need their loyalty once we strike back at the Yamaguchi. Ensure your attack is decisive and report to me once it is done."

"Yes, *oyabun*."

The call disconnected.

Masateru stared out over the lights of the city for a few seconds, contemplating the *oyabun*'s words. He walked through the doorway that led into the adjoining lounge.

The room was spacious and had the same view as his own. There was a well-stocked bar, leather settees, and a pool table. The smell of cigarettes lingered in the air—the *oyabun* would not let his women smoke but there was no such rule for the Kissaki. They drank here often, not allowed to touch but reveling in the company of the *oyabun*'s harem.

He stopped at the bar and took a cold bottle of champagne from the refrigerator. With two glasses and the bottle in hand he walked into the hall that led to the individual apartments of the *oyabun*'s harem. He stopped at one of the doors and knocked.

There was no response.

He punched an override code into the security lock and pushed open the door.

The luxurious apartment was strewn with women's clothes and shoes. Hundreds of thousands of dollars of glamorous dresses were thrown across the king-size bed. Shoes were piled up on the floor. Handbags, scarves, hats, and other items were hanging on chairs and tossed on a dresser. Cupboards and drawers hung open, revealing even more clothing.

Masateru smiled as he surveyed the mess. A noise from the bathroom caught his ear. A woman hummed a tune as she splashed.

He knocked softly on the door.

"Who is it?"

"It's Masateru. May I come in?"

"Do I have a choice?"

Masateru laughed as he pushed open the door. "No, I guess you don't."

Karla was neck-deep in the spa bath, her naked body hidden underneath a blanket of bubbles.

"What do you want?" She did nothing to hide the venom in her voice.

"I just wanted to make sure you had settled in. I see that you have been trying on the clothes." Masateru placed the glasses on the marbled side of the spa and popped the champagne cork.

"Yes."

"I'm sorry about today. I did not want to expose you to such danger." He poured the alcohol and handed her a glass.

"No, thank you." She glared at him suspiciously. "I know why you are really here."

Masateru gave her a wounded look. "I think you have me wrong. My job is to keep you safe, not to take advantage of you."

She eyed him suspiciously. "Those men today, they were really trying to take me?"

"Yes, of course. You're a very valuable commodity in Japan. If you behave you will find there are great rewards." Masateru sipped his champagne.

"You mean if I sleep with your boss and his friends?"

"I could always take you back to the stables if that is what you would prefer."

Karla shook her head.

Masateru raised his glass. "Then make sure you behave." He got up to leave the bathroom. "You never know, you might even be able to send some money to your family."

He left Karla crying in the bath next to the bottle of champagne.

CHAPTER 53

YAMAGUCHI-GUMI SAFE HOUSE, KOBE

"The girls are all safe?" Bishop was sitting at the bar in their temporary safe house, his local cell phone held to his ear.

"Yes," replied Baiko. "There were six of them, all in very bad shape. Addicted to heroin, heavy bruising, and evidence of violent sexual assault. They ranged in age from sixteen to nineteen."

"Fucking scumbags."

"That isn't the worst of it," the police investigator continued. "Two of them had been subjected to an operation to return them to virginity."

"You're kidding me."

"No, they sew the—"

"That's enough, I get the gist of it."

"The worst thing is, this doesn't end with the one facility."

"I'm sure it doesn't. Did forensics find any leads? Phones, computers, client lists?"

"No, no records at all. One of the girls told us she'd been there for three months, though. She said there were other women."

"What happened to them?"

"She didn't know. They took them away and they never came back."

"Sold?"

"Or worse." Baiko paused. "One of the girls described a beautiful

248

blonde girl who came in today. She positively ID'd the photo you sent me."

"I think she was there for about half an hour before they took her to another location."

"I'm sorry to hear that."

"It's OK, we'll find her. Did you get any information on the other photo I sent you?"

"Yes and no. One of my team recognized him as a low-level Yamaguchi from a few years back, but there is no information in our databases. Like the others he seems to have been removed."

"All right, keep your ear to the ground. And be careful. The Mori-Kai seem to have friends in high places."

"I will let you know what I hear."

"Thanks, Baiko, I appreciate everything you've done for us."

"No, thank you. If you hadn't done something about those girls they would have eventually been murdered. Good luck."

The policeman terminated the call and Bishop returned his phone to his pocket. He climbed the stairs up to the offices that were serving as their accommodation.

"Saneh, you set up?"

"Yes, connecting now," she said as he stood behind her. She had set up the laptop on a desk next to her bedroll. Kenta had provided her with a wireless Internet dongle and she was using it to connect to the Bunker. The link was secure, encrypted to military standards at both ends.

On the screen a program similar to Skype was attempting to link to one of PRIMAL's remote servers. A rapidly lengthening blue bar indicated its progress.

"Just a few seconds . . ." Saneh adjusted the volume as she waited. "And we're up. Bunker, this is Saneh, how do I read?"

Vance's big bald head appeared on screen. "Got you loud and clear, Missy; how you guys doing over there?"

"We're doing fine. Ran into a bit of trouble but nothing we couldn't deal with."

"What sort of trouble? Not the type where Bishop levels an entire block, I hope."

"No, nothing like that," Saneh continued. "We tailed Karla and Masateru from the airport. They stopped in at one of their warehouses, where they kept kidnapped women. At that point we were forced to intervene."

Vance's brow furrowed. "So, Karla . . . I gather she's not with you now?"

"Ah, negative," interjected Bishop. "She got away with Masateru. We rescued six other girls and took down the Mori-Kai—"

"Saneh, didn't I tell you to keep him the hell out of trouble? You're supposed to be doing recon, not starting a war with the Mori-Kai."

"It wasn't just his idea, Vance. We both decided it was the only option after one of the Yamaguchi surveillance teams was compromised."

"Did you at least grab some useful intel?"

"Our Yamaguchi liaison got some photos of Masateru, thinks he's a former Yamaguchi member, excommunicated for dealing drugs," said Bishop. "They've got no recent leads."

"Anything else?"

"We bagged a Mori-Kai gangbanger but he wouldn't talk. The girls were handed over to the cops. Apart from weapons the site was pretty clean."

"So we've got nothing?"

"Pretty much. The cops ran a fine-tooth comb over the joint

and came up cold. The Mori-Kai have things locked down pretty damn tight."

"Well, that's awesome—not only do we have jack shit, but a bunch of tooled-up, sake-swigging, psycho Yakuza are now fully aware of your presence in-country."

"It's not that bad, Vance. We've won serious face with the Yamaguchi. With their help we'll find these bastards fast."

"That's if the Mori-Kai don't put a hit on us first," Saneh added. "Vance, I think the recon phase is over. We're going to need some extra hardware. We're up against automatic weapons, body armor, and god knows what else. We need a full loadout."

"I'll get Mitch on it."

"What about reinforcements?" Bishop asked. "Are Aleks and Kurtz done yet in Europe? Mirza and his team?"

"I can't get you anyone yet. Mirza and his guys are about to deploy on another op in Myanmar. Aleks and Kurtz are tying up some loose ends with our Interpol cop. Once that's done they'll RV with you."

"Kurtz is going to lose his shit when he hears we don't have Karla."

"Yep, I'll leave that in your hands."

"The joys of being a team leader."

"The weight of command, bud."

The throb of the twin exhausts on Kenta's bike shook the building as he arrived in the basement garage.

"Nice-sounding pipes," nodded Vance. "Looks like you've got company."

"Yeah that's Kenta, our Yamaguchi liaison," said Bishop. "He was off checking in with his people so we'll need to find out what's going on. Will check back in as soon as we get anything concrete."

"Well, stay out of trouble and keep us in the loop. If we're going to wrap up these fuckers we need intel."

"Roger," replied Bishop.

Saneh nodded and shut the laptop, and they made for the staircase.

"You didn't need to cover for me like that," said Bishop.

"You might have forgotten that we're supposed to be a team, but I haven't."

Bishop shook his head as he followed her down the stairs. She was pushing him further and further away and he wasn't happy about it.

Kenta met them at the bar. He was still dressed in his leather jacket. His helmet was under one arm, a backpack hung over his shoulder. A broad smile was painted across his normally impassive features.

"Brian, Sarah, I have very good news."

"We're not in trouble?" Saneh asked.

"No," Kenta shook his head. "The *oyabun* is very impressed."

"Even though we got three more of his men killed?"

"You inflicted a great defeat on our enemy. The loss of foot soldiers is acceptable. Now the *oyabun* wants to do more." Kenta hefted the backpack off his shoulder and unloaded half a dozen boxes of ammunition.

"What does that mean?" Bishop asked as he checked one of the boxes. "Better weapons? More intel? Good work, by the way, these are top-quality slugs." And more than enough to top up their .45 pistols as well as the 9mm MP9 submachine guns they had looted from dead Mori-Kai.

"Thank you. Yes, we are all to meet with the *waka-gashira* to discuss how best to apply his people to defeating the Mori-Kai and finding the girl."

"That's good news, Kenta," Saneh said as she took one of her spare magazines out and thumbed rounds into it as they talked. "How is Hero?"

"The *waka-gashira* follows the *oyabun*'s orders, but I know he too is very worried about the Mori-Kai."

"Damn straight he should be worried," said Bishop. "But we can help even the odds. I should have some more men and equipment arriving in the next few days."

"Anything that can help will be greatly appreciated."

"So your boss Hero wants to work closer with us? It's going to be good to have the full extent of the Yamaguchi's resources behind us." Bishop followed Saneh's lead and started reloading his own weapons.

"The Yamaguchi is not as powerful as you seem to think, Brian. The subelements have become richer and more powerful but the *oyabun* has been forced to relinquish power. He no longer commands his own army of foot soldiers. He must pander to the subclans for additional support."

"That also means you are vulnerable, yes," said Saneh. "If the Mori-Kai can weaken the head, then the clans can be targeted individually or even bought off."

"Yes, that is why the *waka-gashira* wants you to come to the meeting early tomorrow."

"How early is early?" Bishop asked.

"First thing in the morning. The *waka-gashira* has called an emergency meeting at the Hotel La Suite. You have been invited. It is a great honor."

"You've done well, Kenta. We're very grateful," said Saneh. "Now if you will excuse me, gentlemen, I am going to get some sleep." Saneh left the two men standing at the bar.

There was a long pause before Bishop broke the silence. "I bet you've never met a woman like her before."

"Most Japanese women are more, how you say? Submissive?"

Bishop reached behind the bar and pulled out a bottle of clear liquid. "Drink?"

"Yes."

The PRIMAL operative splashed the liquid into two glasses and handed one to the Yakuza criminal that had become his comrade. "I've never met another woman like her. She drives me insane, but on the other hand she's damned good at her job."

"She is most impressive."

Bishop lifted his glass. "To impressive women."

"Yes, impressive women." Kenta downed the drink in one gulp and proceeded to splash another round into the glass.

Bishop held out his own glass. "I've been wanting to ask you. What did you do to lose your finger?"

He shrugged his powerful shoulders. "I was young and foolish. I cannot remember the exact details, but now it is a badge of honor, like your nose." He downed his sake.

"What the hell's wrong with it?" Bishop rubbed his fingers along the crooked bridge of his nose. It had been broken on more than one occasion, but still . . .

"Nothing, it is very honorable." Kenta splashed another shot of sake into his glass. "More?"

"Negative, big man. I'm going to get some sleep. Gotta look my best for tomorrow's big meeting."

CHAPTER 54

DOWNTOWN KOBE

Except for the early risers, shopkeepers, and cleaners, the streets of Kobe were deserted. Without any traffic, the black Mercedes sedan cruised freely through the outskirts of the city. Neon reflections flashed on its armored glass as it drove toward the business district and the Yamaguchi-gumi's morning rendezvous at the Hotel La Suite.

It was a journey that the *waka-gashira* Takahiro took every Sunday to meet with his subordinates. The second-in-command of Japan's largest Yakuza clan oversaw every aspect of Yamaguchi activities throughout the country. Today's meeting was even more important, and consequently earlier than usual. The threat from the Mori-Kai had forced him to request the presence of all of the underbosses.

"Drive faster, we're running late." Takahiro adjusted his tinted glasses and glanced at the expensive watch that adorned his heavily tattooed wrist.

"Yes, *waka-gashira*," his driver replied.

"Is the problem at the construction site resolved?" The Yamaguchi lieutenant turned to the man sitting next to him.

"It will be. The Koreans have agreed to an increase of five percent." The assistant was dressed in the same dark suit and white shirt as his boss.

"Five percent?" he exclaimed. "The dogs are leeching us dry."

"The strike was costing us ten million yen per day."

Takahiro took a pack of cigarettes from his jacket. He extracted one of the slim menthol smokes with a flick of his wrist.

"How much cheaper are they than Japanese labor?" He lit the cigarette with a gold Dunhill lighter.

"Half the price."

"But also half the quality." He stared out the solid laminated glass window as smoke filled the cabin. "What happened to the old days when we could kill the ringleaders and force them back to work?"

The driver adjusted the air-conditioning in an attempt to clear the sickly sweet smoke.

The assistant coughed. "The Korean gangs have grown stronger, *waka-gashira*. We could force them but it would take all of our strength. The Koreans would fight back and there would be a war. It would engulf Kobe."

Takahiro did not notice the black SUV at the intersection facing them. "We have become nothing more than weak businessmen. We are even relying on foreigners to help deal with this new Mori-Kai threat."

The black SUV leaped forward and sped at them. It had a heavy metal bull bar, unusual for the streets of Kobe.

"Look out!" Takahiro yelled.

The powerful vehicle hit the front of the Mercedes, throwing it sideways with a crash and screech of tires. It slammed into the side of a building, knocking the *waka-gashira* forward into the back of the driver's chair. He blacked out momentarily from the force of the blow. When he came to, his assistant was already opening the car door.

"Stay inside!" Takahiro yelled.

Gunshots rang out and bullets thudded into the car's armor. The assistant fell backward onto the door, his face blown apart. Takahiro scrambled across the seats, kicked the dead man's body out of the way, and grabbed the heavy door. He slammed it shut as a black-clad figure appeared at the rear of the vehicle.

"Lock the fucking doors, get us out of here."

The driver quickly hit the central locking and dropped the heavy Mercedes into reverse. There was a crunch and Takahiro spun around to see a second black four-wheel drive wedging them against the building. Another burst of machine gun fire thudded into the armored rear window, damaging the laminated polycarbonate but leaving it intact.

The driver floored the accelerator, causing the rear wheels to spin. "We can't move; they've trapped us!" He spoke rapidly, panicked. "They're going to kill us, they're going to kill us!"

"Calm down, you fool." The *waka-gashira* pulled his cell phone from his jacket, dialed a number, and waited for it to connect. "Our people will be here before they can get in."

★★★

On the other side of town, Bishop, Saneh, and Kenta were in the GT-R on their way to the meeting. This time Saneh was wedged in the backseat. Kenta was driving, giving them a rundown on the Yamaguchi-gumi's history in the city as he sped through the quiet early-morning streets.

"We have been a part of Japan for over seventy years," Kenta explained.

"I read that it all started in the chaos after World War Two," said Bishop.

"That is correct. The Yakuza is much older but the official Yama-guchi-gumi formed after the war."

"In the debris of war the rats grow fat on death," Bishop quipped.

Kenta laughed. "We do not shy away from what we are, Agent Wilson. To lose touch with the past would also lose all that has been learned. You might be unaware but we also helped rebuild Japan's cities, even the ones destroyed by your nuclear weapons."

"Hey, you guys started it when you bombed Pearl Harbor, buddy," said Bishop.

"You're a little ray of sunshine this morning, aren't you?" Saneh added from the backseat. "Too much sake—" She was interrupted by the sound of Kenta's phone.

"Please excuse me." He picked it up, listened for a few seconds, then fired a torrent of Japanese down the line. A moment later he had the information he wanted. The phone was tossed onto Bishop's lap.

"*Chikushou!*" he swore. The GT-R's quad exhaust roared as he punched the accelerator to the floor, sending the car screaming down the highway.

"Bad news?" said Bishop.

"Hero has been ambushed."

"Fucking Mori-Kai!" Bishop checked the looted MP9 he had in his backpack. "How far? Is he still alive?"

"Other side of the city, maybe five minutes. His car is armored and he is still alive." Kenta drove the nimble GT-R like a madman, weaving in between early-morning commuters, overtaking them as he gained speed.

"He should be OK in an armored Merc. Those things are built like a safe," said Bishop.

Saneh had a concerned look on her face. "Not if they know what they're doing. What will happen if they kill him?"

Kenta honked the horn, blasting through a red light. "It would not be good. He is the only one who is keeping the clans together."

★★★

"How long now?" Masateru asked from where he was sitting in the back of one of the SUVs.

"Three minutes, *oyabun*," Hideaki replied from the front seat.

"What the fuck is taking so long?"

"I will find out."

"No, stay where you are," Masateru barked. He wound down the window and called out to Ryu. "Hurry the fuck up!"

"It's locked, windows armored," Ryu answered through his balaclava. "We're going to need to breach." The Kissaki commander was dressed in the same tactical gear as the rest of his men. Head to toe in black. A nylon-covered ballistic chest plate laden with pouches adorned his front. He had a pistol on his hip and a submachine gun in his hands.

"You've got three minutes. Deal with it."

Ryu ran from the vehicle back to where his men were guarding the Yamaguchi Mercedes. One of their three SUVs was positioned behind it, wedging it against a wall. Two of his men were guarding the doors, making sure their target did not try to make a run for it. Another two were covering the street and a third pair was guarding the intersection behind Masateru's vehicle. His second-in-command was removing the breaching equipment from the back of his vehicle.

Ryu glanced at his watch. This was taking longer than he had planned. He stormed over to his man. "Hurry up and get him out of the damn car!"

"Yes, sir," the man responded sharply. He pulled a pair of goggles down over his eyes, picked up the bulky circular rescue saw, and yanked the pull start.

The saw snarled as he gunned the trigger, its diamond blade hissing like an angry snake. He jogged it across to the captured Mercedes and, under Ryu's watchful eye, placed the saw against the glass of the rear passenger window. The blade shrieked as it bit into the armored laminate, steadily cutting through it. The stench of burnt plastic filled the air.

Inside, Takahiro sat quietly, his hands on his knees, unarmed. His assistant's pistol now lay outside the vehicle along with his corpse. The driver was of no use either. The young man was sweating, his face pale, hands clapped over his ears to keep out the noise of the saw.

The *waka-gashira* looked across at the saw cutting its way through the glass with an ear-wrenching screech. By the blade's progress he judged it would be through in a couple of minutes.

★★★

"He's somewhere along here." Kenta eased off the accelerator and they scanned the road ahead. There were mid-rise buildings on each side of the street, plenty of overwatch positions for a Mori-Kai shooter.

"Up ahead!" As Bishop spoke the windshield of the GT-R cracked, a bullet hitting the glass. "Shit!"

Kenta braked hard, sliding the car sideways, as bullets slammed into the bodywork.

"Out, out, out!" Bishop had his door open before they came to a halt. In a heartbeat he was crouched behind the hood of the Nissan, laying down covering fire from his MP9 submachine gun.

Gunfire echoed down the concrete canyon as rounds ricocheted off the road and rang on the metal of the GT-R. The stricken Mercedes, surrounded by Kissaki and black SUVs, stood only a hundred feet away.

Kenta was out a second after Bishop. He grabbed Saneh by the arm and hauled her from the backseat like a sports bag.

"Everyone OK?" Bishop asked between bursts. All three were taking cover behind the GT-R.

"I'm good." Saneh had her own looted submachine gun out and was firing from the rear of the car.

"OK," Kenta grunted.

"We've got at least six hostiles around the black SUVs," Bishop said. "Looks like they're cutting their way into the Merc."

"Takahiro!" Kenta yelled as he sprinted forward, firing his PX4 on the move.

"You gotta be kidding me." Bishop fired a burst from his weapon to cover the lumbering Yamaguchi.

Bullets sparked off the sidewalk as Kenta ran. He reached a mailbox and crouched behind it. The squat red cube offered minimal protection from the Kissaki's fire.

"Looks like Wyatt Earp's found the only cover between us and them," said Bishop.

"I wouldn't call that cover," responded Saneh as rounds smashed into the soft metal of the mailbox.

The roar of an engine drew their attention. Another black Mercedes swerved around them and sped toward the Mori-Kai. Bullets slammed into it and it careened across the street, crashing into a light pole a mere fifty feet from the black SUVs. The car doors swung open and three Yamaguchi heavies came out, pistols blazing. Automatic gunfire cut down the first two Yamaguchi. They crumpled to the road as rounds tore through their expensive suits.

"NO!" Kenta reloaded with a fresh magazine and fired his pistol from behind the mailbox.

"Don't you fucking move!" Bishop screamed at him. "Cover

me," he said to Saneh and dashed across the road toward the crashed Mercedes.

Saneh fired a series of short bursts at the black-clad Mori-Kai, forcing them to duck behind their vehicles.

Bishop reached the bullet-riddled Mercedes, which, unlike the *waka-gashira*'s vehicle, was not armored. He crouched where a lone Yamaguchi was cowering. As he suspected, the man was in shock, never having seen a real gunfight before. Bishop looked inside one of the open doors. The metallic smell of fresh blood filled his nose. A moan sounded from the front seat, the driver still alive, at least for now.

The loud shriek of an industrial cutting tool drew his attention. From his new position he could see one of the black-clad Kissaki finish cutting in through the back window of Takahiro's armored car.

Bishop took careful aim, snapped off a single shot at the saw operator, and scored a hit on the man's legs. The Mori-Kai toppled over the saw, crashing to the ground. Bishop was forced to take cover as an onslaught of fire returned in his direction.

The sound of gunshots was replaced by the roar of engines. Bishop stuck his head up and could see the Mori-Kai had moved an SUV next to Takahiro's car, blocking the view. Too late, he thought. They were probably pulling Hero from the limo and loading him in the SUV. The other balaclava-wearing gunmen stepped up their fire, covering each other as they embarked in their own vehicles.

Sensing they were out of time, Kenta advanced, firing his 9mm one-handed at the black four-wheel drives. As soon as the breech locked open on an empty magazine, he drew his revolver with the other hand and continued firing.

Bishop and Saneh also increased their volume of fire. A gunman was shot in the back as he attempted to get into the back of one of the SUVs. He collapsed into the vehicle as the door swung open.

Bishop's eyes locked with the passenger sitting in the backseat.

The look on Masateru's face expressed his own recognition of Bishop. He punched his submachine gun out and fired as he accelerated away.

Rounds zipped past Bishop's head as Masateru's vehicle roared off down the street. The other two trucks sped after it, disappearing around the corner with a screech of tires.

Kenta was looking into Takahiro's Mercedes. "He's gone, but the driver is still alive." The wailing of sirens could be heard in the distance.

Bishop joined him and inspected the damage. "You deal with the ambulance," he told Kenta. "You've got two more guys alive in the other Merc."

A deep rumble announced the GT-R as it pulled up next to them, Saneh at the wheel. The car was looking the worse for wear, peppered with bullet holes. The windshield was shattered, the engine was running roughly, and fluids leaked onto the road.

"Do what you can for the wounded," Bishop told Kenta and jumped into the Nissan. "We're going after them."

He slammed the door shut as Saneh punched the accelerator, pushing him back in his seat. She took the first corner sideways, balancing the throttle in a controlled slide.

"Holy shit," said Bishop. "Why haven't you been driving the whole time?"

Saneh floored the accelerator in pursuit of the last SUV disappearing around another corner. "Because you're a misogynist control freak."

CHAPTER 55

"Why are you slowing down?" Bishop asked as they rounded another corner in their pursuit of the black SUVs.

"I'm not," Saneh snapped as she struggled to hold the damaged GT-R on the road. "We're losing power. They must have hit something vital."

The GT-R was still moving fast but it wasn't accelerating with its usual vigor. The engine sounded as if something was trying to escape from under the hood.

"Get us closer and I'll shoot out the tires." Bishop used the butt of his pistol to bash out the remains of his window.

Saneh slid the Nissan around another corner. Despite its failing engine the sports car had made considerable ground on the rearmost SUV, now only fifty feet in front of them.

"Gun!" warned Bishop as the tailgate of the SUV opened to reveal one of the Mori-Kai gunmen sitting in the rear compartment. His MP9 spat lead as Saneh wrenched the GT-R to one side, narrowly missing the hail of bullets.

Bishop fired rapid shots from his pistol, but his aim was off as the GT-R swerved back. Saneh managed to wring a few more horses out of the mortally wounded engine and brought the GT-R almost alongside the SUV.

"Garbage truck!" Bishop warned as they raced up behind the

slower traffic. He fired two more shots as the municipal vehicle loomed in front of them.

"Garbage truck, Saneh."

"I see it."

"We're going to fucking hit it."

"I'm on it." At the last second she wrenched the steering wheel, sending the GT-R up onto the sidewalk on the outside of the truck, putting it between them and their target.

Bullets rang on the metal sides of the truck as the Mori-Kai fired.

Saneh downshifted and revved what remained of the engine. They roared off the sidewalk and back onto the road, narrowly missing a bus shelter, the maneuver putting them slightly in front of the SUV.

A loud bang came from under the hood. "That's it, she's done," Saneh yelled over the clatter of gunfire. Bullets riddled their hood as she flung the stricken sports car to the left, hitting the back right corner of the SUV. The impact shunted the rear end of the vehicle sideways, sending it into a tail slide. The driver panicked and slammed on the brakes.

In the GT-R airbags exploded and they slid sideways, the Nissan's low center of gravity keeping it on the asphalt.

The taller four-wheel drive was a different matter. The impact pushed it one way, while the driver jerked the steering wheel opposite while braking. Tires screeched and smoke filled the air as the SUV slid sideways, throwing the gunman from the open tailgate. As it slid, the rear tires hit the curb and the truck flipped. It rolled sideways down the street, throwing debris in all directions for three full revolutions before it came to rest on its roof.

"That's not exactly how I saw it happening," said Saneh as she pushed the airbag from her and took off her seat belt.

"Pretty shit-hot nonetheless," Bishop grinned.

They got out of their ruined car and ran across to the SUV. Bishop checked the front. "They're dead. No seat belts."

Saneh checked on the third body that had been flung from the vehicle. "This one's also dead." He lay in a crumpled heap at the base of a light pole, his head ninety degrees to his body.

Bishop peered in the open tailgate. "No one else in back. They must have Hero in one of the other vehicles."

They looked around as the early-morning traffic built up around the accident site. There was no sign of the other two SUVs.

"Fuck!" Bishop kicked the door of the truck. "He'll be dead within the hour. That *Miami Vice* asshole was in the truck with him."

"You mean Masateru? You sure?"

"Yep, looked the slippery motherfucker right in the eye."

Sirens could be heard approaching.

Saneh turned and headed back to the GT-R to grab their bags. "C'mon, Aden, let's get the hell out of here."

Bishop grabbed his backpack from her and stormed down a side alley. "This is a seriously fucked-up situation now."

"I know," she said, following. "Targeting the *waka-gashira* is a game changer. What do you think the Yamaguchi will do?"

"What can they do? The Mori-Kai are way beyond Yakuza thugs; that shit they just pulled has special ops written all over it."

"One thing's for sure: We're going to need more firepower. We'll have to lay low until Aleks and Kurtz arrive with our weapons delivery."

Bishop dialed a number as they walked. "Kenta, it's Wilson . . . No, they got away. We need a pickup."

CHAPTER 56

MORI-KAI CASINO CONSTRUCTION SITE, HIMEJI

The two SUVs were waved through the security checkpoint at the front of the construction site. They continued along a rutted access track and down a concrete ramp into the partially completed parking area of the future casino. The complex was one of the Mori-Kai's more ambitious projects: an exclusive hotel and casino, designed to cater to even the most depraved desires of their clients.

"What happened to the other vehicle?" Masateru asked Ryu after they had parked.

"They crashed with the car that was following us."

"How many men?"

"Three."

"A small price to pay for such a successful operation. Make sure the others are rewarded: cash and women."

Ryu nodded and issued a set of orders to his men.

Hideaki dragged their prisoner from the SUV into a storage room. His hands and feet were bound, head covered by a black hood. The room was empty except for a solitary chair. An equipment hoist was bolted to the concrete roof.

"Put him on the chair." Masateru lit a cigarette as he watched them drag Japan's second-most-powerful Yakuza gangster across the floor like a carcass. "Oh, how the mighty have fallen," he whispered.

Hideaki pushed Takahiro into the chair. Then, with a nod from Masateru, he ripped the hood off.

The Yamaguchi lieutenant's hawklike eyes darted around the bare room. A startled expression appeared on his face as he locked eyes with Masateru.

"Hinata, you piece of shit!"

Masateru slapped the immobilized Yamaguchi as hard as he could. "My name is Masateru," he hissed in his former boss's ear.

Takahiro threw back his head and laughed. "I heard you were trying to be a big man now. Got a few thugs with guns and suddenly you think you're somebody? You're still the same weaselly piece of horseshit we exiled for selling heroin."

The Mori-Kai gangster flicked his tanto blade out from his jacket and spun it in the palm of his hand. "Horseshit?" He slashed the blade across the prisoner's face; it bit deep into his cheek, opening up a gash an inch wide. "Who's the fucking horseshit now?"

Blood poured from the wound. Takahiro flinched but did not utter a word.

"You're obsolete, with your tattoos and your self-righteous code. The world is changing and the Yamaguchi are being left behind. Look around you. My men are armed with machine guns, not clubs and knives."

"Your men are trained monkeys," said Takahiro between gritted teeth, the blood from his cheek soaking into his white shirt. "Let's see how well they fare against real Yakuza."

Masateru wiped his knife clean with a handkerchief, closed it with a flick of his wrist, and dropped it into the pocket of his pants. "Real Yakuza? Is that what you think you are? The Mori-Kai are the only real Yakuza. The Yamaguchi are nothing but fat businessmen and relics like you. You have forgotten what it truly is to be Yakuza.

I mean, who ever heard of the Yakuza cooperating with the police or, worse, the American FBI?"

Takahiro sat upright in his chair and matched the Mori-Kai lieutenant's piercing stare. "You cannot change what you are, Hinata. You had no honor when you were expelled and you have none now." He spat a mouthful of blood onto the concrete. "We should have put you down like the rabid dog you are."

"String him up." Masateru pulled out a thin cigarette and lit it.

Hideaki grabbed the hook that hung from the equipment hoist. The pulley system clattered as he pulled it down and looped it through the bindings on Takahiro's legs.

"Your death will be swift if you tell me where the FBI agents are staying." Masateru puffed at his cigarette.

"Go fuck yourself, dog."

"I thought as much." He gave a nod.

Hideaki pulled on the chains and the pulley screeched, lifting Takahiro off the ground. He reached up and repeated the process until their prisoner was hanging upside down with his face at head height.

"Strip his shirt." Masateru dropped his cigarette and took off his jacket, handing it to one of his men.

Hideaki used a knife to cut the Yamaguchi lieutenant's shirt from him, revealing a torso and back completely covered in tattoos. Dragons intertwined with flowers, koi, and other intricate works of Japanese art.

"What beautiful work . . . So sad for it to be lost." Masateru rolled up his sleeves.

"You don't scare me, Hinata. I will tell you nothing."

"Oh, I don't need you to talk, old friend." He took the knife from his pocket and flicked it open again. The sinister blade glinted under the harsh fluorescent lights. "I just need you to deliver a message."

☆☆☆

"What's this?" Baiko asked as a member of his team dropped a file on his desk. The veteran policeman had just sat down and was stirring a sugar into his coffee.

"Initial incident report from the shootout in Kobe."

"What shootout in Kobe?"

"You haven't seen the news?"

"Not yet; did something big go down?"

"I guess you could call it big. Somebody shot up a Yamaguchi-gumi car, killed half a dozen of their men, then split across town. Word on the street is they got Saemonsaburou Takahiro."

"As in the Yamaguchi *waka-gashira*?"

"That's the rumor. Unconfirmed."

"Do we know who made the hit?"

"No. Not yet. In my opinion it has to be the Koreans. We're talking full-auto weapons here. A step up from the usual Yakuza operations."

"You could be right. The Koreans are becoming more active in Kobe. Is there anything else interesting in this?" He waved at the report.

"Not really. It's not very comprehensive. Those Kobe police are second-rate Neanderthals." The officer started to walk back to his own desk. Halfway he stopped and turned. "There was one other thing. There was a mention in the report of a witness describing two Caucasians fighting alongside the Yamaguchi."

"That's odd." Baiko opened the file.

"Not unheard of. Perhaps they were Russian mafia."

"Perhaps." It took Baiko a few minutes to read through the document. His colleague was right: It said very little of the incident. He got the impression that the Kobe police knew a lot more than they were letting on.

The link to the Caucasians was particularly interesting. It had to be Agent Wilson. That meant that in less than forty-eight hours he had been involved in three significant incidents in the area. That did not seem like normal FBI behavior, even if he was just a contracted agent.

Baiko opened his computer and looked up the contact details for the US Embassy in Tokyo. He could not remember the name of the liaison officer who had initially vouched for Agent Wilson but found the embassy FBI number in the police directory. Using his private cell phone, he punched in the number, determined to get to the bottom of exactly who Agent Wilson was.

CHAPTER 57

LASCAR ISLAND

Mitch Freeman hefted the forty-pound gas can above his head, held it high with outstretched arms, and started the climb up the jungle track. Thigh muscles burned, lungs heaved, but he powered on, step after step. A hundred meters later the track leveled out. He dumped the can in the soft mud, crouched low, and leaped into the air, arms outstretched.

The branch flexed under his weight as he caught it. He pulled his chest up, counting out the reps. "One, two, three, four, five . . ."

Twenty-five reps later he was finished and the gas can was back above his head as he navigated the track. One hundred meters ahead came another clearing. This time a heavy sledgehammer and an old truck tire lay waiting.

He pounded the thick rubber, the muscles in his shoulders burning as he slammed it down, over and over again. Then the gas can went back in the air and he was off again.

The track led down the ridge into a creek line. He plunged in and the water rose up to his chest, bringing instant relief from the oppressive humidity of the tropical island.

He carried the gas can down the creek until he reached a lagoon, where the water quickly rose to neck height. After crossing, he roared, threw the heavy container up onto the bank, and climbed out of the water.

Muscle-bound, with a shaggy beard and a mop of hair, PRIMAL's resident scientist resembled an island castaway.

"How ya feeling, champ?" Vance was lying in a hammock strung between two palm trees a short distance from the lagoon.

"'Bout as shagged as those palm trees, mate," Mitch replied, collapsing into the sand.

"What are you talking about?" Vance adjusted his Hawaiian shirt–clad frame and the palms creaked ominously, bowing under his weight.

Mitch smiled and helped himself to a bottle of water from a cooler beside the hammock. "So what brings you out here?" he asked as he regained his breath.

"Same thing as you, little bit of fresh air."

"Gets pretty musty in that bunker of yours, hey? Maybe you should join me out here next session."

"I'm too old for that cross-shit training, Mitch. How 'bout we rack up some metal and fit in a squat session tomorrow? That is, if your little circuit hasn't got you all worn out."

"You're on." Mitch laughed as he crushed the bottle and tossed it in the cooler. "So, how's the team tracking?"

"Good, Aleks and Kurtz are finishing up and Mirza's team is about to head to Myanmar."

"And now you get time for some R&R?" Mitch climbed back to his feet and made an attempt to brush some of the sand from his wet cargo pants. "You going to head over to Thailand again? Maybe catch up with that lady friend of yours? All work and no play makes Vance a dull boy."

Vance laughed as he swung his legs out of the hammock. "Not this time around. Maybe when the teams wrap up. I just wanted to check that there were no problems with getting the gear into Japan. The team's going to need it. Things are starting to get messy."

Mitch glanced at his watch. "It should hit the docks first thing tomorrow morning. Kurtz is going to pick it up."

"I don't want to know how you're going to get over a thousand pounds of ordnance through customs."

Mitch picked up his gas can and emptied it of the water it contained. "I've got my ways, old man. You know, sleight of hand and all that jazz."

They walked down to the beach, where Vance had parked his ATV next to Mitch's.

"Years of living and working in shitholes across the globe didn't prepare me for this life," Vance said as he looked over the crystal-blue waters of the Pacific.

"Not bad, mate, that's for sure." Mitch tossed the gas can onto the cargo rack of his quad bike. "Race you back. Bet you twenty bob I win." Mitch pressed the ignition button of his customized ride. The 1,000cc engine roared to life.

"You serious? God knows what you've done to that thing. Probably goes like a jackrabbit on meth."

"Come on, Vance, everyone knows you and Flash are the biker heads. There's no way yours is stock."

Vance grinned as he climbed into his ATV, barely fitting inside the roll cage. He turned over the engine and it gave an angry snarl. "OK, you're on. Let's see if we can beat Saneh's record." With that he sent the buggy ripping across the sand.

Mitch gunned his quad bike after him, whooping like a rodeo bull rider.

CHAPTER 58

RESIDENCE OF THE YAMAGUCHI-GUMI OYABUN, KOBE

"The *oyabun* will see you now." The house servant bowed low, indicating that Bishop and Saneh should move through the door. This time the *oyabun* had invited Saneh to join the meeting, a direct response to her involvement in operations against the Mori-Kai.

The room where the *oyabun* was waiting was much smaller than the one where he had first met Bishop. About the same size as a family living room, it was decorated in the traditional Japanese style, polished wooden floors with tatami mats around a low table. The *oyabun* was sitting cross-legged on one of the mats, a tray of cookies and a pot of coffee on the table.

"Agent Wilson and Agent Scott, thank you for coming at such short notice. Please take a seat." He looked more hunched over than usual, his brown eyes tired.

"We could hardly refuse after you have been so supportive of our mission." Bishop sat down at the table, Saneh at his side. A servant offered them both a tray with hot towels while another poured coffee.

The two PRIMAL operatives freshened up and returned the towels to the blue-shirted attendant, who moved to the back of the room and waited.

Bishop took a cookie and spoke as he dipped it in his coffee. "We're sorry about the loss of *waka-gashira* Takahiro. Have you heard anything else?"

The *oyabun* snapped his fingers and the servant left the room. "No, my people are scouring the city but they have found no trace of him." There was a hint of sadness in the old man's voice. "That is part of the reason I wanted you to come. Your efforts to save Saemonsaburou Takahiro were commendable, and for that we will forever be in your debt."

"We are deeply ashamed that we could not save him." Bishop bowed his head.

"That is foolish talk. You were outnumbered by men with superior firepower. It is a credit to your skill as warriors that you were able to kill three of them. If it wasn't for you, the Yamaguchi-gumi would have lost all respect in this town." The *oyabun* dipped his head at Saneh, acknowledging her.

"Thank you, *oyabun*," said Saneh. "With your men helping I am sure we will soon find the *waka-gashira*."

"We may, but then again we may not. The threat posed by the Mori-Kai is far greater than we anticipated. My concern now is that by aiding you the Yamaguchi-gumi has made an enemy that we are not equipped to fight."

Bishop finished his cookie and put his coffee down. "Yes, *oyabun*, but working together—"

"You do not understand, Agent Wilson. Takahiro had arranged a meeting of the subclans. He was attempting to bring them together against the Mori-Kai, but his abduction has struck fear into their hearts. They will not pledge men and money to battle an enemy that terrifies them."

"That's exactly what the Mori-Kai want. They want the Yamaguchi to splinter."

"Then they have succeeded."

"And you are simply going to bury your head in the sand and ignore the threat?"

"There was no threat until you arrived, Agent Wilson," the *oyabun* said sternly.

"When we arrived you were happy for us to fight the Mori-Kai. Working together, we've had some success. They capture your *waka-gashira*, and now you want to ignore them?"

The elderly Yamaguchi boss's hands started shaking.

"With all respect, *oyabun*, surely it's better to deal with a threat than live in blissful ignorance," said Saneh. "We mean no disrespect. You're in a difficult position and have suffered a terrible loss. But surely there is something we can do?"

The *oyabun*'s expression did not change. "I will leave the Mori-Kai to their own devices and when the time is right I will offer them terms for a peaceful existence—"

"That is foolish at best," interrupted Saneh. "These people are evil and will stop at nothing to expand their empire. They're already moving in on your—"

"Agent Scott, that's enough," Bishop said. "*Oyabun*, please excuse my partner. The events of the last few days have been very stressful. Perhaps it would be better if we resumed this conversation at a later date."

The *oyabun* made to speak when there was a knock on the door. "Enter!" he yelled.

The door slid open and Kenta came in, carrying what looked to be a tall framed painting wrapped in brown paper. He gave Bishop and Saneh a nod as he placed the picture against the wall in front of the *oyabun*, bowing low. "*Oss.*"

"What is it?" the *oyabun* asked in Japanese.

"I don't know, *oyabun*," Kenta responded in English, "but I did not think you would want to wait. The delivery boy said it was a gift from the Mori-Kai."

"Unwrap it."

Bishop watched Kenta tear off the brown paper. The first thing he noticed was the elaborate gold frame. As the wrapping was removed it became apparent that the artwork inside looked strange and dull, almost like it was printed on parchment. It was a similar design to the tattoos on Kenta's arms.

Bishop looked at the *oyabun*; the old man's face had turned deathly white and for the first time he saw genuine fear in his eyes. Then he realized what the Mori-Kai gift was. The golden frame held the tattooed skin stripped from Takahiro's corpse. It was a message, one designed to strike terror and warn against further action.

The *oyabun* held on to the sides of the low table to stop his hands shaking. "How can we fight this?" he croaked. "How can we fight men who have no honor?"

"We will kill them all, *oyabun*!" Kenta shouted angrily.

"I'm with Kenta," said Bishop. "Give us his support and use of your facilities. I have more men arriving very soon with heavier weapons. Together we will hold the Mori-Kai to account."

"I cannot be seen to support you. I cannot risk an all-out war with these madmen."

Now Bishop smiled. "Then let us wage the war for you. It's what we do best."

CHAPTER 59

HIMEJI

"That's Himeji castle." Masateru spoke to Karla through her headset, pointing out the ancient structure as the helicopter banked lazily over the city.

Karla's face was glued to the plexiglass window of the Bell 429; she had never been in a helicopter before. The ancient castle with its white walls and ornate silver roofing looked like something from a fairy tale.

"Is that where we are going?"

"No," laughed Masateru. "The *oyabun* is a powerful man but even he doesn't live in a national treasure. They call it Shirasagi-jo, the white heron castle. People think it looks like a bird."

"Your city is very beautiful," Karla said, her depression momentarily forgotten.

"Tonight it pales in comparison to you."

Karla was dressed in a simple yet chic black Chanel dress. It ran from midthigh to her neck, hugging her curves and accenting her ample breasts. The other women in the harem had helped her prepare her hair and makeup. Gone was the fresh-faced teenager, replaced by an elegant woman.

The chopper circled their destination, giving Karla a bird's-eye view of the Mori-Kai *oyabun*'s residence. It was nestled on the side of one of the hills that overlooked the city of Himeji, a sweeping estate of concrete and glass surrounded by traditional Japanese gardens.

They swooped over the roof, flared, and touched down on it with a bump. A house servant opened the helicopter door for Karla and helped her out.

Her high heels clicked on the concrete as she followed the servant across the helipad. Masateru walked beside them, then led the way down a flight of marble stairs into the house.

"The *oyabun* is in his office," said the servant in Japanese.

Masateru gestured for Karla to follow and led her downstairs through a sitting room to the closed polished wooden doors of the *oyabun*'s study. He knocked gently.

"Come in."

Masateru opened the door and gestured for Karla to enter.

The *oyabun* was sitting at his desk working on a laptop. His back faced a sweeping view of the city. It was dusk, and the lights of Himeji had only just started to sparkle.

Karla waited tentatively just inside the door. The *oyabun* looked nothing like she had expected. He had shoulder-length graying hair and a moustache, his eyes calculating but not cruel.

"Come forward, girl," he said as he closed his computer. His English was perfect.

Karla tapped across the hardwood floors and stood on the intricate Persian rug in front of his desk.

"Shoes off," he snapped.

She removed the six-inch heels.

"And the dress."

The flush of color that ran to her face was hidden by her makeup but she felt no less embarrassed as she dropped the dress onto the floor, revealing lacy black underwear.

"Now turn slowly." The *oyabun*'s eyes ran up and down her body. There was nothing sexual about his gaze. It was clinical, like the inspection of a racehorse by an astute buyer.

Karla turned slowly, trying hard not to burst into tears as she felt her body being violated by his eyes. Her hands trembled but she kept them pinned to her side.

"Very good. You may go now." The *oyabun* returned his attention back to his laptop.

Masateru gave her a slight nod and gestured for her to leave the room.

She gathered the dress and shoes and made her escape. The house servant guided her from the door.

★★★

The Mori-Kai lieutenant lowered himself onto the low settee and poured himself a tumbler of Yamazaki whiskey from the bottle on the side table. His pack of cigarettes remained in his jacket; smoking was not permitted in the residence.

"She is very beautiful," the *oyabun* said in Japanese, not taking his eyes from his computer screen. "You have done well, *waka-gashira*. A welcome addition to my stable. One that will bring us great rewards."

"Thank you, *oyabun*."

"You have performed well in the last few days. My sources tell me that the Yamaguchi subclans will not dare to fight us after what you did to Takahiro."

"Everything is in accordance with your plans, *oyabun*."

"Yes, but these foreigners still concern me. Especially that one man."

"Our former-SAS, arms-dealing FBI agent."

"What information have you uncovered on him? My contacts indicate he is no more FBI than you or I," the *oyabun* added.

"He and his whore remain elusive. They attacked us during the kidnapping but failed to stop the Kissaki. Then they disappeared, back under the protection of the Yamaguchi, no doubt."

"They are proving most difficult for you to destroy. I believe they have been hired by the Yamaguchi to target us."

"Perhaps, but here in Japan they are only two. Inconsequential in our wider strategy. The trouble they caused in Europe will be repaired. The Frenchman will find us new resources. The damage here in Japan has been slight."

"That is no guarantee for the future. What is to prevent more of them from arriving to join the fight?"

Masateru nodded respectfully. "I understand your concern. But if they think to challenge us, they will be disappointed. They cannot hope to match our firepower."

"There is another shipment of weapons due soon, yes?"

"In the next few days. The Kissaki have already started training the Koreans and the Chinese. With the next shipment we will be able to double our forces."

"Very good, and what have you done about the risk to our facilities?"

"I have increased security, extra Kissaki and some of our more trusted friends. Two shipments of women have arrived from the Philippines. We have put them in a new holding area. The Yamaguchi and their *gaijin* attack dogs will not be aware of this."

"Filipino trash does not make us money, Masateru. How long until the Frenchman finds us more Caucasians?"

"He's located a suitable network. I am expecting a report any day."

The *oyabun* shut his laptop and rose from his desk. "Despite minor setbacks our business plans are still on track." He walked across to the settee and sat opposite Masateru, who poured him a drink.

The head of the Mori-Kai raised his glass. "Loyalty, reward, and power."

Masateru repeated the toast and the two men drank.

"I have decided to reward you for your work."

"That is not required."

"The girl, the blonde. I have seen you look at her. Tonight she will warm your bed."

"The gift is too much. She's a virgin—"

"Very well, if you do not wish—"

"No, *oyabun*, I would not dishonor you by refusing such a gift."

The head of the Mori-Kai laughed. "No, I am sure you wouldn't. Go, enjoy yourself."

CHAPTER 60

LYON, FRANCE

Rémi was eating his lunch on a park bench, watching the swans glide elegantly through the blue waters of the lake at the center of Parc de la Tête d'Or. It was a favorite lunch spot in Lyon. He came here at least once a week during the warmer months. The calmness of the setting helped clear his mind.

A vibration from his cell phone interrupted a mouthful of baguette. He fished it from his pocket and checked the screen.

Have you identified a new florist who can get us lilies?

Rémi laughed. The Japanese were sticklers for security. They used code words and veiled speech even when he assured them no one was monitoring his phone. He changed it every month and passed them the new number via a coded system in an Internet chat room.

Yes, have identified new supplier. My contact is meeting with them today to check quality and quantity.

The new source of girls was a Romanian crime syndicate that Rémi had been investigating for arms smuggling. It had been easy for one of his local contacts to organize a meeting. When it came to making money, everyone was an opportunist.

Very good. Once quality confirmed we will send funds for first shipment.

Excellent, Rémi thought. He had started to worry that he would have to dip into his savings to make the repayments on his wife's Range Rover. When combined with the fees for his daughter's horse-riding and ballet lessons, his Interpol salary did not go far.

He finished his lunch, threw the paper bag in a trash can, and started the short walk back around the lake to the office.

A hundred meters down the track he spotted a tall blond runner coming toward him. An avid runner himself, he admired the man's stride; he was clearly an athlete.

The man was only a few meters in front of Rémi when he stumbled on the edge of the track. He lost his footing and collided with the policeman, knocking the two of them to the ground.

"I'm so sorry," said the runner in English accented with German.

"Watch where you're going, you fool!" Rémi clutched his arm where the man had hit him.

"Are you OK?" The German was up and offered Rémi a hand. "I was so focused on beating my time I wasn't paying attention."

"Just leave me alone." Rémi got back up onto his feet and staggered. Suddenly he felt overwhelmed by the urge to vomit. His world started to spin and he toppled forward.

"You should sit down, you've taken a nasty knock," said the German, grabbing him by the arm before he hit the ground.

"I . . . I . . . ah . . ."

Rémi collapsed against the runner.

"Where am I?" Rémi awoke with a start as Aleks injected an antidote to the sedative Kurtz had punched into his arm.

"You're somewhere where no one is going to hear you no matter how loud you yell," the German runner said from the corner of the room.

Rémi turned his head from side to side. He could see rough stone walls all around him. A bare lightbulb hung from the ceiling. He was lying down, strapped to a bench. The air was heavy with the musty smell of hay and cow manure.

"Do you know who I am? You idiots have abducted a policeman."

"Oh, we know who you are, Capitaine Rémi Marcen," said Kurtz. "The question is, do you know who *we* are?"

The Frenchman struggled against his restraints.

"No, I didn't think so." Kurtz dragged a chair across to the bench. "Tilt him up a bit."

Aleks lifted the bench up, sliding a brick underneath it.

"Now we can have a nice little chat, yes?"

"Fuck you." Rémi spat in Kurtz's face, then screamed in agony as the German drove a kitchen knife into his thigh.

"Manners, Rémi. Manners will stop you from dying a very painful death." He flicked the knife with his finger.

In response, the policeman screamed.

"Now, let's start again. I'm going to ask you some questions and you're going to answer them politely, OK?"

"Yes," Rémi managed through clenched teeth.

"Very good." Kurtz plucked the knife from his leg. "Who is your contact in Japan?"

"My what? Japan? I don't know what you're talking about."

Kurtz gave him a long, hard stare. "I didn't want it to be like this. But if you don't want to tell me what you know then I'm going to have to treat you very badly. Aleks, if you please."

Aleks kicked the brick out from under the bench, and suddenly their prisoner was lying horizontal again. He used a pair of medical shears to separate the side of the Frenchman's pants leg.

Rémi turned his head, his eyes wide with fear. "What, what are you doing?"

Kurtz stood above him, kitchen knife in hand. "Nothing to worry about. Just preparing you for a little ad hoc surgery. I'm very experienced in these things. I probably could have been a surgeon if it wasn't for the hand tremors."

Aleks cut the other leg's seam and then the belt and waistband. He grabbed what remained of the pants and tore them off. Then the shears went to work on the underpants.

Kurtz retrieved something from the wooden bench. "You will appreciate the irony of this." Kurtz stood next to Rémi's head so the now terrified policeman could see what he was doing. He held up the cook's knife and a phallic-looking cut of beefsteak. "The blade is Wüsthof." He smiled. "Good German steel." He cut cleanly through the meat, effortlessly slicing the fibers of the muscle. "And I'm going to use it to cut off your cock."

"MASATERU! Masateru, he's the only one I've ever talked to. He handles all the shipments and payments. I just find the gangs who supply the girls. That's it. That's all." Rémi's face was white; beads of sweat had appeared on his brow.

"How do you talk to this Masateru?"

"Phone! He makes me change my number every month."

Kurtz took the Frenchman's phone from the pile of his things they had placed on a workbench. He checked the calls and then the messages.

"These texts, are they from him?"

"Yes!"

"Good." Kurtz pulled the sim card from the phone, took his iPRIMAL from his pocket, and inserted it in the purpose-designed slot. He uploaded the data from the card and sent it to the Bunker.

"They're going to kill me now," the Frenchman wept.

"No, they're not," Kurtz said quietly as he took his pistol from his jacket. "Because I am."

Twenty minutes later, the old farmstead was burning furiously. The Frenchman's body and the last of their equipment would be reduced to ash or bare steel by the time anyone responded to the blaze. By then the PRIMAL duo would be out of the country and heading for Japan.

CHAPTER 61

MORI-KAI CASINO CONSTRUCTION SITE, HIMEJI

Hideaki drove the Lexus down the ramp into the underground parking lot and pulled in next to a line of black SUVs. The car had barely come to a halt when Masateru climbed out, speaking rapidly into one of his phones. Twenty seconds later the call was over. He dropped the phone in his pocket and pulled out another. He stripped the sim card out and ground it into the concrete with the heel of his Italian shoes. Then he threw the phone against the wall, smashing it to pieces.

"Is everything all right, *waka-gashira*?" his bodyguard asked as they walked across the parking lot to where Ryu was supervising the unloading of a truck.

"No, it's fucking not," Masateru snapped as they joined the Kissaki commander.

"*Oss*," Ryu greeted him in the traditional way.

"I just got a call from France."

"Rémi?' Ryu asked. "Has he confirmed the quality of the product?"

"Not exactly . . . he's dead."

"What? How?"

"Our man doesn't know." Masateru referred to the Kissaki that they had left in Europe to keep an eye on the Frenchman. "He disappeared. Police found his remains in a burned-out farmhouse near Lyon."

"The *oyabun* will be furious," said Ryu. "To make matters worse we still don't know who we're up against."

"We'll find out soon enough. Do we have enough weapons yet?" He gestured toward the wooden crates the men had been unloading.

"For the peasants, yes. But my men need more specialized equipment."

"Yes, the additional list you gave me. It has been arranged. Expect delivery in the next twenty-four hours."

"Once it arrives we will be ready."

"Even the gangs?"

"Yes, the training has progressed well. Would you like to see them?"

"Please. A favorable report on our capabilities may temper the *oyabun*'s rage." Ryu guided them toward his SUV. "We started with the basics; now they've moved on to fire and movement in pairs." Ryu climbed into the driver's seat. Masateru and Hideaki got into the back. They drove up the ramp and out into the muddy construction yard, where they weaved between heavy equipment.

"Are they going to be capable of dealing with the foreign mercenaries?" Masateru asked.

"More than capable. Those two that attacked us at the ambush site were skilled but not well armed."

"It was easy for us to get weapons; no doubt it will be easy for them."

"True, but they are not the Kissaki."

"Yet they have still managed to kill a handful of your men."

Ryu accepted his boss's rebuke silently as he drove them up a dirt track at the rear of the construction yard. At the top of the steep rise they pulled over.

"This way."

He led Masateru and Hideaki along a footpath that weaved through the thick vegetation, stopping at a high vantage point looking down over a large, open-cut quarry. "Be careful, it's a very long drop." Ryu gestured toward the men in the quarry below. "We've been training them here for a few days. They have improved significantly."

"Not the rabble we last saw," added Hideaki.

Down in the quarry half a dozen Korean and Chinese gang members crouched behind cars, barrels, and other debris. They fired AK assault rifles at targets, covering each other as they dashed forward to gain ground. Their fire was synchronized, one man shooting as another tore a magazine from his vest and reloaded. Black-clad Kissaki moved among them, providing instruction, yelling at those who did not move fast enough.

"Are they using silenced weapons?" Masateru asked, noting the lack of gunfire.

"No, airsoft guns. They operate the same as the real thing, just fire BBs instead of bullets."

"Very good, no chance that the Koreans will turn on your men and steal the weapons."

"My men can take care of themselves. This is more about conserving ammunition and not drawing attention to what we're doing. Once they become competent we'll move them on to live rounds."

They watched the training for another five minutes before Masateru spoke again. "You've done well, Ryu. They will be effective against our enemies."

"Thank you, *waka-gashira*." The former military officer paused for a few seconds. "I have been thinking . . . If we could ambush the foreigners we could easily defeat them."

"I have come to the same conclusion." Masateru took his cigarettes from his jacket.

"We just need something to lure them out of the shadows and into our trap."

"Every trap requires bait."

"We need to find something they want."

Masateru lit one of the slim cigarettes and smiled as his thoughts strayed to his night with Karla. "We already have exactly that."

CHAPTER 62

KOBE DOCKS

Cargo container LASU4588993 shuddered as the unloading arms lifted it effortlessly off the deck of the container ship. A scanner built into the gantry read its radio frequency tag, giving the operator instructions on its destination.

It was marked HIGH PRIORITY, meaning it would be immediately loaded onto one of the waiting container trucks and freighted direct to its destination.

Giant pulleys sang as the container descended toward the next truck in the lineup. The six-wheeled Nissan accepted the twenty-foot container with the slightest dip of its suspension. It drove the length of the wharf and turned into a vehicle park, joining a line of other trucks. The driver slowed to the directed five-kilometer-an-hour speed limit as he passed through a sensor gateway. A green arrow flashed, directing him out of the queue and into a dedicated inspection bay.

The driver parked the truck in the designated area, jumped out of the cabin, and joined a customs officer in his lead-lined control booth. An X-ray machine had scanned the truck, displaying its contents on a screen.

"There's something wrong here," said the officer in Japanese. The screen showed a cold-storage container full of boxes of fish.

"What's the problem?" the driver asked.

"The refrigeration unit doesn't look right, it's not working." He left his inspection box, climbed up onto the back of the container, and inspected it with a light. "It isn't working at all."

"Sometimes they don't need it," said the driver, eager to be on his way.

"The manifest says the load is fresh salmon from Australia. It has priority because it needs to be delivered within twenty-four hours."

"It will be if you let me go. If it's broken it's not my problem."

"Open it up."

"Fine." The driver stomped his way to the rear of the truck and cut the security tags with a pair of pliers. "You need to sign though. I'm not losing my bonus because you wanted it open."

"Just let me inspect it quickly. Then you can go."

The driver cracked the handles and swung the reefer doors open. He recoiled back as an overwhelming stench of fish hit him. The stacked foam boxes completely filled the container.

"OK, OK, close it up." The inspector screwed his face up in disgust. "I'll print you off an inspection form and then you can go. The customer can have his rotten fish."

"I don't care if it's rotten, I just need to make sure it gets there on time." The driver resealed the container.

"Someone's going to be very unhappy . . ." The inspection officer handed over the paperwork.

"Not my problem," the driver replied as he climbed back into the truck.

Three hours later the container finally reached its destination, a warehouse on the outskirts of Osaka. The driver checked the address against the invoice and backed the truck into the compound's parking lot. It was a simple drop-and-go, no signature required.

The Nissan was designed to offload containers without the use of a crane. The driver activated the hydraulic system and the deck that held the container slid rearward. It tipped slightly, extending toward the ground. With a snort of thick smoke the truck shuddered out from under the container, which slid off the tilt tray and onto the ground with a thud. The driver jumped out of the cab, checked there was no damage, and returned the tray to its transit position. A minute later he was on the highway, heading back to the port.

The container sat in the parking lot for another five hours before a taxi pulled up outside the warehouse. A tall, lanky backpacker paid the fare, then wandered into the compound.

The tourist wore a scruffy-looking fleece jacket, jeans, and a baseball cap, his angular features unshaven. Closer inspection revealed he looked to be in his late twenties, older than the average backpacker.

He wandered around the container, checked the serial number, and took out his cell phone. He activated an application and punched in a code.

With a hiss the back of the container hinged upward, broken cooling unit and all. Inside the container, shielded from X-rays by high-tech panels, was a white Toyota van. There was a whir of gears and the nose of the van slid forward on a moving floor until the front doors were clear of the container. The backpacker reached under the front wheel arch, removed the keys, and climbed into the cabin. He drove out into the parking lot, the container closing behind him.

The van's GPS was already programmed with a route and he activated it, noting that it was in English. As he followed the directions he snapped his smartphone into the cradle and initiated a secure call.

"Bunker, this is Kurtz, checking in."

"Kurtz, this is Bunker. Can we confirm you have married up with your equipment and are now en route to pick up Aleks?" a crisp military voice asked over the speaker.

"Confirmed, container is now ready for pickup. Please pass on my thanks to Mitch."

"Roger, good luck."

Kurtz terminated the call and checked the GPS again, making sure he was still on the correct road. He yawned, still jet-lagged. The flight from Paris passed through eight time zones and he had not slept well.

He drove for ten minutes into the bustling city before stopping the van in a loading zone in front of a train station. It was only a few minutes before an imposing, bearded figure approached.

The passenger door opened and Aleks jumped in. "Hello, Kurtz, been a while." They had traveled to Japan separately, a standard security precaution.

"Are you a retard? It's been eighteen hours." Kurtz pulled the van away from the curb and into the traffic.

"I was making a joke!"

"Well, your jokes stink."

"Not as much as this van." Aleks sniffed the air. "Did you steal it from a fishmonger?"

Kurtz laughed.

"See, my jokes are good."

Kurtz shook his head. He glanced at the GPS and then at the heavily congested traffic in front of them. "It says two hours until destination. At this rate we'll be lucky to get there in three."

CHAPTER 63

YAMAGUCHI-GUMI SAFE HOUSE, KOBE

"I've installed CCTV cameras at the front and the rear." Bishop dumped a cardboard box on the bar. "They're IR, so we've got coverage by day and night."

They had decided to enhance the security of the safe house. The kidnap and subsequent murder of the Yamaguchi *waka-gashira* had revealed an enemy more sophisticated than they had anticipated.

"I've picked up all the feeds." Saneh had set up a laptop and a wireless router on the bar. It was synced with the cameras Bishop had installed. "We can run watch from here."

"Do you think that's a good idea?"

"What do you mean?"

"You want to have the nighttime sentry location behind a bar and you want Kenta, a semi-alcoholic gangster, to pull watch?" He raised an eyebrow. "Just saying, that's all."

"That's a valid point. I'll move it over by the couches."

Bishop's iPRIMAL buzzed in his pocket and he checked it. The onscreen map showed that Aleks and Kurtz were close. Kenta's icon was farther to the west, where he was meeting with one of his sources. Bishop had loaded an application onto his phone so they could track his movements and communicate securely. "Aleks and Kurtz are a couple of minutes away. I'm going to go downstairs and let them in."

"OK." Saneh didn't look up from the laptop.

Bishop climbed down the stairs and into the basement of the club. Saneh's bike and the replacement for the GT-R, an ordinary-looking Toyota sedan, were parked against the back wall.

He watched the symbol denoting Kurtz and Aleks's location getting closer to the safe house. It slowed and turned into the ramp that led down to the basement parking. Bishop activated the roller door and the white van entered and parked next to the other vehicles.

"Hey, boys, how the hell are you?"

"Boss, it is so good to see you." Aleks grasped Bishop in a bear hug and lifted him clean off the ground. "I hear you have been having too much fun without me."

"I'm sure you two have been having plenty of fun." Bishop grunted as he dropped back to the floor.

"Kurtz! What's up?" He extended his hand.

Kurtz shook it awkwardly. "I'm fine, Aden. I was wondering about Karla. Vance said you would be—"

Bishop was already heading to the back of the van to check the contents. "Mate, I'll brief you in a few. Let's see what Mitch has sent us."

"I have the invoice." Aleks handed him a piece of paper. "A lot of hardware on that list. Full CAT assault rigs for each of us, armor-piercing ammunition, surveillance gear."

Bishop scanned the list, nodding approvingly. "We're not just dealing with thugs here, boys. The Mori-Kai are rolling with submachine guns and body armor."

"Former Special Forces, like the men that ambushed us in the Ukraine?" asked Kurtz as he helped unload the van.

"Yep. The team we ran into breached an armored Merc in under four minutes. They're well trained and well equipped."

"But they're in trouble, now we're here," said Aleks.

"Yep, we're going to hunt the bastards down. Find Karla and dismantle their entire operation." Bishop checked a trunk marked with his name.

Kurtz stopped what he was doing. "Did you say *find* Karla? I thought you knew where she is."

"Things didn't go exactly to plan."

Kurtz's jaw clenched and his blue eyes narrowed. "What happened?"

"We followed them from the airport to another location. Karla and Masateru managed to slip out of the Yamaguchi cordon before we could bang in."

"Where is she now?"

"We're working on that. Chua's team is crunching the data from the phone you pulled off Rémi. Once we locate Masateru, we'll have Karla."

"I told you we should have picked her up in the Ukraine," Kurtz muttered to Aleks.

"That wouldn't have helped anyone," said Bishop. "We needed her to lead us to the Mori-Kai."

"Except now we're no closer and she could be dead."

"This is bigger than one girl; think of all the other lives—"

"No, fuck the big picture, Aden," Kurtz cut him off. "How many people have to die for your stupid missions? You got Jess killed, now Karla; who's next after that, Saneh?"

"That's enough." Bishop's voice was low. "You need to pull your head in."

"Pull my head in?" Kurtz repeated, his face turning crimson. "You kill another innocent woman and you want me to pull my head in." He stepped toward Bishop with his fists clenched.

"That's enough." Aleks grabbed him by the arm. "We're all comrades here."

"He's not my comrade," Kurtz spat. "He's a self-absorbed fool."

"You really want a piece of me?" Bishop squared off into a fighting stance. "Is that it?"

"ENOUGH!" Saneh's voice echoed around the parking lot. "I leave you alone for two minutes and suddenly you're acting like schoolboys." She stepped off the stairs and strode across to the back of the van. "Aleks, can you help Kurtz take your personal gear upstairs? Bishop, a word please."

"No problem." Aleks grabbed a trunk. "Come on, Kurtz."

Kurtz reluctantly broke eye contact with Bishop. "Hello, Saneh," he said meekly as he removed his own gear from the van and carried it toward the stairs.

"Good to have you both here." She gave them a smile.

Once they were alone Saneh turned to Bishop. "What the hell was that all about?"

"Kurtz, he's obsessed with the girl. He's a fucking liability. I want him off this job."

"You can understand why he's upset."

"Yeah, that Hungarian woman he was sweet on. He got too attached, she ended up dead, and now he's playing protector to another helpless damsel he knows nothing about."

"Look," said Saneh, "he and Aleks are a lot closer to this than you or I. Yes, it's about Aurelia. But they've also rescued this girl and her sister twice now."

"That's not the point. The point is, I can't trust him. He wants to run off and rescue every damsel in distress. I need operators who are calm and levelheaded, not loose cannons."

"Loose cannons? That's a bit rich coming from you, don't you think? Kurtz is usually the most levelheaded person I know; maybe he just needs you to cut him some slack."

The concern in Saneh's voice dampened some of Bishop's anger. "Maybe you're right," he conceded.

"I know I'm right. What he needs now is for you to be a leader. Aleks will look after him. You need to focus on the mission, and part of that is recovering the girl."

Bishop grunted, grabbed Saneh's kit bag from the van, and lugged it up the stairs.

Saneh shook her head as she followed him.

CHAPTER 64

LOVE ANGEL CLUB, DOWNTOWN KOBE

Kenta walked under the gaudy neon signs and up the red-carpeted stairs of the Love Angel Club. A bouncer dressed in a shiny polyester suit eyeballed him cautiously as he entered the dimly lit nightspot. He took a seat at the bar, caught the attention of the bartender, and ordered a whiskey.

"Your man is in the corner," the Yamaguchi informant whispered as he sloshed the golden liquid into a heavy glass tumbler.

Kenta turned around and surveyed the poky establishment as he drank. The hostess bar was one of many in Kobe that serviced the city's frustrated business elite. Bored with their wives and stressed by the intensity of their work, they came here to drink and meet girls.

The man his informant had identified was a regular; he was sitting in the corner with two of his friends. All three were dressed in expensive suits. Ties had been discarded, shirt collars opened, and now the executives were drinking and smoking. Kenta was surprised they did not have girls with them. He checked his watch: probably a little early for that.

He picked up his glass, walked over to the table next to the men, and lowered himself into one of the chairs. "Hey, bartender! Bring me the bottle," he yelled.

A waitress scurried across to him with a bottle of whiskey and an ice bucket.

"You're very pretty," said Kenta. "Would you like to sit with me?"

The girl shook her head as she placed the bottle and ice on the table and retreated back to the bar.

Kenta laughed. "See, even the help doesn't want to be with me. What hope do I have with my wife?"

The executives at the next table could not help but overhear the comment. "Maybe you need to drink more," one of them joked.

"Fuck you," said Kenta.

The other table went deathly quiet.

"Maybe you're right." Kenta filled his glass to the brim, tipped back his head, and threw the potent liquor down his throat.

The three executives burst into nervous laughter.

"Perhaps if I drink with you I'll have more luck." Kenta dragged his chair over to the group and thumped his bottle down on the table.

The man who had spoken thrust out a hand. "My name is Takeshi."

Kenta shook his hand. "Kenta."

The other men at the table introduced themselves and Kenta passed his bottle around.

"So you're having problems with your wife?" asked Takeshi as he dropped a handful of ice in his glass.

"She's fat and lazy, loves her food more than my cock."

They all laughed and nodded in understanding. Before long the four men had ordered another bottle, swapping tales of debauchery as they drowned their frustration in eighteen-year-old whiskey.

Half an hour later, one of them took his leave. He shook Kenta's hand and wished him luck. His colleague departed ten minutes later, leaving Takeshi and Kenta drinking on their own.

"We should get some girls," said Kenta. The bar was now full and heavily made-up women had started mingling with prospective clients.

"Feel free," said Takeshi.

"You're not interested? Don't tell me you prefer boys."

"No, I just don't like trashy Japanese moles."

"Then you're shit out of luck in Kobe," laughed Kenta.

Takeshi leaned in close. "If you're not short on cash you can fuck the highest-quality *gaijin* girls."

Kenta's eyebrows shot up. "White girls? Blondes?"

"Anything you want." Takeshi grinned, showed him his phone, and flicked through photos of women. They ranged in age from early teens through to midtwenties. All of them were Caucasian, scantily clad, and had the glazed look of a drug addict.

"Very nice." Kenta pretended to be impressed as he fought the urge to drive his fist into the man's face. "How do you get girls like this?"

"Like I said, it's very expensive. The people I use bring them to my apartment. Then I can do whatever I want to them."

"Whatever you want?" Kenta took another sip from his whiskey.

"Yes, all of those things you would like to do to your wife but can't."

Kenta raised his eyebrows. "They let you beat them?"

"That's the best part, they have no choice. They have to do everything you want."

"So they are slaves?"

Takeshi smiled. "That's exactly what they are. Slaves you can rent."

"If they are *gaijin* how do you tell them what to do? I have a hard enough time trying to get my wife to do things, and we speak the same language."

"Most of them speak English." Takeshi tipped back his head and drained his glass. "I'm afraid I have to go now, my friend. Let me take care of the check and maybe we can drink again soon. Unlike you, I'm not married, so I'm here most nights." He stood up, a little unsteady, and scooped up his jacket from the back of his chair.

"I'd like that," Kenta said as they shook hands.

Takeshi swayed as he walked across to the bar and handed the barman his credit card.

"I need to see ID," the bartender insisted.

The executive tossed his wallet onto the bar. "Call me a cab as well." Once he signed the receipt he gave Kenta a wave and set off down the stairs to the street.

The Yamaguchi enforcer sat quietly by himself for a few minutes before leaving the table. On his way out the bartender passed him a slip of paper; he stuffed it in his pocket and walked outside to hail his own cab.

CHAPTER 65

YAMAGUCHI-GUMI SAFE HOUSE

"Mate, you got a minute?" Bishop walked over to Kurtz, who was sitting by himself in the corner working on his body armor. It was late and the team was checking through their gear before turning in.

"*Ja.*" Kurtz continued to attach pouches to his armor.

"I was pretty harsh on you before and I want to apologize."

Kurtz looked up at Bishop with his piercing blue eyes. "Apology accepted," he grunted as he returned to his pouches.

"We're going to get Karla back. I promise you that."

"We'll see."

"We good?"

Kurtz nodded. "We're good, Aden. Let's focus on the mission."

"I'm glad. You know we can't succeed without you."

Bishop returned to where Saneh was sitting.

"How did that go?" she asked as she cleaned her Tavor assault rifle.

"How do you think it went?" Bishop fired back.

Saneh shook her head. "It's like working with children," she said under her breath as she returned to oiling the bolt of the weapon.

A pinging noise emitted from the security laptop, and she glanced at the screen. Motion sensors had detected someone walking down the narrow street that led to the safe house. As the man got closer she zoomed in the camera. A yellow square highlighted their Yamaguchi partner's face as the recognition software identified him. "Kenta's back."

"I'll let him in." Bishop met the stocky Yakuza at the front door. "Hey, how did it go?"

"Good. Has the rest of your team arrived?"

"Yeah they have." Bishop sniffed as Kenta passed him in the corridor, reeking of alcohol and cigarette smoke.

"Kenta, have you been drinking?" Bishop grabbed him by the shoulder.

"*Hai*, I spent four hours in a girlie bar; of course I was drinking."

"Are you drunk?"

Kenta started laughing. "Half a bottle of whiskey doesn't get me drunk. I do have the name and address of one of the Mori-Kai's clients though." He handed over the scrap of paper and continued into the main clubroom.

Bishop slapped him on the shoulder, walking beside him. "Good work. This could be the break we're looking for."

As they entered into the clubroom the rest of the team looked up from what they were doing.

"Kenta, let me introduce you to Aleks and Kurtz."

"Hello." The Yamaguchi gangster bowed his head in greeting.

Aleks got up from where he was sitting on his trunk and shook hands. The Russian was a full head taller and just as broad. Kurtz followed suit.

"I see you came very well prepared." Kenta stood in awe of the amount of hardware lying on the floor. Open equipment boxes revealed more weapons, armor, and combat gear than he had ever seen in one location before.

"We have equipment for you as well," Kurtz said. "Plenty of weapons for everyone."

"I think we may even have a rocket launcher somewhere," added Aleks. "If you're into that sort of thing."

"Are they joking?" Kenta asked Saneh.

"Nope, deadly serious." She smiled. "Gentlemen, do we have a KRISS? I think it might suit Kenta's fighting style."

"I have one here." Aleks opened one of the equipment trunks and pulled out the chunky submachine gun, offering it to Kenta. "You like it, it's yours."

Kenta took the weapon and weighed it in his hands. It was heavy and solid, more like his revolver than the lightweight pistol Bishop had given him. "I think we are going to get along very well." He grinned.

Bishop folded his arms across his chest. "Just like that, you're going to throw away the pistol I gave you?" he joked.

"No, Agent Wilson, I like the gun you gave me. It's just . . ." He looked down at the KRISS. "This feels more like a man's weapon."

They all laughed.

"Listen, Kenta, since you're working so closely with us, I think we can drop the bullshit. Our real names aren't Brian and Sarah. They're Bishop and Saneh."

"Ah, you travel under different names. That is not so unusual. The Yamaguchi do that from time to time."

"Yeah, well, you're part of the team now."

"It is a great honor, Bishop. So, can I ask you if you are really FBI? These guns, they are very high tech, even for policemen."

"Let's just say we come from a special unit."

Kenta nodded. "Well, policemen or not, now we have the information and the gear. I think it is time we start killing Mori-Kai."

Bishop held up the piece of paper that Kenta had given him. "So talk us through what happened at the girlie bar. Who is this guy and how do we get to him?"

"There is not much to tell. My informant told me he had a regular who bragged about raping Western women. Slaves, he called them. His name was Takeshi, I met him at the bar, we drank, he talked, and now I have his address." Kenta sat down on a spare weapons trunk.

"And he uses the Mori-Kai services?" asked Saneh.

"I am unaware of anyone else offering these services."

"Do you think he would know where they keep the girls?" Saneh continued.

"No, he said the girls are brought to him. It is the same with the girls that work with my people. Our drivers take them to their clients. This would be no different."

"Except the girls have been kidnapped and are being held against their will," said Saneh. "A fairly significant point of difference." She finished with the bolt and slid it back into the weapon's body. "So we've got, one: a guy who uses the girls; two: his home address; and three: the bar he drinks at."

"This is correct. We also know he speaks English."

Bishop went to speak but Saneh continued. "I say we get our people to work up a target pack on the residence and we plan a little break-and-enter op. Then have our boy put a call out for girls, leave them cold at the door, and follow them home."

"Sounds like a good plan to me," said Bishop.

Kurtz and Aleks nodded in agreement.

"It's a good start. We can add the detail once we have more information on the building," concluded Saneh as she finished assembling her Tavor. "In the meantime, I'm going to get some sleep." She put the weapon back in her trunk and headed up the stairs. "Don't stay up late, boys." She turned around and pointed at Kenta. "And no more drinking!"

Kenta gave Bishop a questioning look.

"Hey, you're on your own, champ. I wouldn't mess with her and my recommendation is that you don't either." Bishop started packing his own gear.

Aleks got up from his trunk and walked over to Kenta. "If you want, I can show you how to use the KRISS. Maybe later we can go through some basic drills."

"I would be grateful," said Kenta.

"Then when everyone else is gone we can have a quick nightcap. I have some excellent vodka in my trunk." Aleks gave a wink.

Kenta grinned. "Just one, though. I wouldn't want to upset the boss." Both men laughed.

★★★

"Can you see?" Aleks asked as he tapped on the mirrored lens that covered Kenta's eyes. They were both wearing the sophisticated battle helmets and assault armor that PRIMAL operatives wore on high-threat missions. He'd been training Kenta for most of the day, and now they were inside a Yamaguchi-gumi warehouse down by the Kobe docks, preparing for live firing at night.

"It is very dark," said Kenta as he turned his head left and right. "But that is not unusual, considering you turned the lights off." His voice sounded muffled and metallic.

"Wait a second, comrade." Aleks reached under the jawline of the armored faceplate and pressed a small button.

Inside the helmet the central processor activated and Kenta's previously black lenses instantly turned into a sharp green image. "This is unbelievable!" He lifted his hand up in front of his face. He could make out intricate detail as the state-of-the-art sensors built into the helmet projected the image inside his visor.

"It gets better," Aleks's voice came through clearly on the integrated communications system. He pressed another button and toggled from infrared into fused mode.

Kenta exhaled sharply as a thermal image was layered over the green. Now he could make out the heat signature of his instructor. "Unbelievable," he said again.

"Now activate the laser on your gun like I showed you."

Kenta toggled the rubber switch with his thumb and the laser appeared. "So I just put the dot on the target and pull the trigger?"

"Yes."

"I didn't know things like this even existed."

"Most people don't. Remember that the button under the laser is your radio switch. If you press it you transmit and your comrades can hear, just like I am now."

Kenta nodded and pressed the button. "Very useful; you don't have to take your hands off the gun. I like that!"

"*Da.*"

"But I'm not sure about this body armor. It feels too light. Wouldn't the bullets go straight through?" He thumped his fist against his black, nylon-covered exoskeleton.

Aleks had fitted Kenta out with an older set of his carbon-nanotube armor. It was not as light as his latest set but it still only weighed a few pounds.

"No bullet will get through." Aleks slipped out a fighting knife and poked the chest plate with it. "But if you get hit it can still hurt like being kicked by a fucking elephant."

"I will take your word for it." Kenta's laser was dashing round the walls of the warehouse like a schizophrenic firefly. "So, can we shoot now?"

"Do you think it's clear outside?"

"Ever since they opened the new terminal no one comes here. We'll be fine."

Aleks grabbed a bag filled with plastic bottles and followed Kenta through a side door.

The wharf was completely empty. The long concrete structure had grass growing in the cracks and rubbish scattered across it.

Kenta and Aleks walked to the water's edge. There was no exterior lighting and no moon, but despite the darkness they could both see perfectly through their helmets. The city lights in the distance provided enough ambient light for the helmet's sensors.

Aleks tossed the bottles into the water. "OK, like we practiced."

Kenta took a magazine from one of his pouches, inserted it into the submachine gun, and jerked the cocking handle rearward. He activated the laser and lined it up on one of the floating bottles. The KRISS spat slugs through the suppressor, hammering into the plastic. He fired long bursts from the hip, quickly emptying the thirty-round magazine.

"You're pretty good at this." Only one target remained unscathed.

"I'm looking forward to showing it to my Mori-Kai friends," Kenta said as he reloaded. "Last time they had an advantage. The next time they will not be so lucky."

"They'll get what they deserve. Now hurry up and finish or we'll miss the mission briefing."

Kenta ripped off another long burst that shredded the last bottle. Slowly it sank to the depths of Kobe harbor.

★★★

"So that's the plan." Bishop was standing in front of a 3-D building schematic being projected onto the wall of the clubhouse. "Does anyone have any questions?"

Aleks and Kurtz looked at each other and then the Russian put his hand in the air. "Excuse me if I missed this, but what exactly are Kurtz and I doing during all this?"

"Just about to get to that. This job's small: Saneh, Kenta, and I will handle it. You two have a far more important role." He clicked the remote in his hand and the building plan was replaced with a photo of the Yamaguchi-gumi *oyabun*. "Analysis of the Mori-Kai's intent and previous modus operandi leads me to the conclusion that this man, Kenta's boss, is likely to be the next target of the Mori-Kai's assassination squad."

Kurtz rolled his eyes. "More babysitting."

"Yes, but only until we locate the next Mori-Kai location. Then we're going to need all our firepower in one place."

"When do you want us to leave?" Aleks asked.

"As soon as you can. Take the van. I'm going to check in with HQ now to see what other intel they may have picked up. I'll pass on anything new as soon as I get it. The rest of us will roll in an hour."

"OK, boss," said Aleks. "But you have to promise you won't run off and start a gunfight without us. Right, Kurtz?"

The German sat quietly, staring intently at the photo of the *oyabun*, his hand resting on the stock of his Tavor. "Something like that."

CHAPTER 66

MORI-KAI CASINO CONSTRUCTION SITE, HIMEJI

The Nissan sedan drove in through the gates of the construction site, followed by a medium-size Toyota van. The guard at the gate was expecting them. He waved them through as he lifted his radio to report their arrival.

The vehicles' headlights swept across heavy machinery and piles of building materials as they bounced their way across the heavily rutted construction yard. The newly built casino rose up above them like a sinister fortress as they approached.

Another guard, armed with a glowing traffic wand, waved them down a ramp and into the well-lit interior of an underground garage, where Masateru was waiting with Ryu, Hideaki, and two more of his black-clad Kissaki.

Xinhai, the head of one of Kobe's most powerful Triad gangs, stepped out of his vehicle and surveyed the parking garage with a snakelike intensity. He was an intimidating character, his face, bald head, and arms covered in Chinese tattoos designed to hide the deep burns caused by an attempt on his life. The molten skin was a testament to his resilience in a world where leadership shifted like the winds.

"Welcome to our humble project, Xinhai." Masateru bowed his head. His visitor was the head of nearly five hundred Chinese criminals, a man even the Yakuza treated with caution.

"Congratulations, you have built a parking lot. I do hope that there is more to this meeting." The Triad boss nodded to one of his companions, who walked across to the van and slid open the side door. No fewer than ten Triad heavies climbed out.

"Oh, I think you will find it's worth your while. Come with me." Masateru gestured to the elevator. "Unfortunately some of your men must remain here."

Ten of them, five Mori-Kai and five Triad, took the elevator up to the ground floor of the casino.

"What is this?" Xinhai asked as they stood in the concrete shell of the reception area.

"This will be a casino, the first owned by the Mori-Kai. It will be fully integrated into our other operations."

"Impressive, but what does this have to do with us?"

"We have an offer to make you."

"And what is that?"

"Exclusive rights to run the gambling here."

"And why would you offer this? Couldn't you use your own people?"

"We're focused on other enterprises. It would be more efficient to let your people run the casino and have our people supply the girls."

"And the cut?"

"Half and half."

Xinhai laughed. "Forty-sixty."

"I'm already working with the Koreans; it would be just as easy to make an arrangement with them."

"Koreans will fuck it up." Xinhai spat on the ground. He looked around the half-built reception area, visualizing the completed casino. "You do know that I have sworn my loyalty to the Yamaguchi *oyabun*?"

"Yes."

"Well, do you think I have no honor?"

"No, I—"

"Then why do you ask me to break my oath? Do you think my loyalty is so easily bought? I know you are at war with the Yamaguchi, yet you invite me here like we are brothers."

Masateru swept his hand through his slick hair and glanced nervously at Ryu. If the former Special Forces operator was nervous, he was not showing it. His chiseled features, like his eyes, remained impassive. He looked poised and lethal.

"Even a dog has a master," Xinhai continued. "Until that master is dead he will not entertain a new master."

"I understand."

"However, the terms that you offer are most desirable. We would be foolish not to consider them."

"I understand that there is the matter of your allegiance with the Yamaguchi, but you should know that they are weakened by the loss of the most powerful of the *waka-gashira*. Without him the *oyabun* is helpless; he will soon lose control of the subclans."

A wicked smile split the Chinese man's tattooed features. "That was you? Is it true that you sent Takahiro's skin to him in a frame?"

"He screamed like a woman when he died."

Xinhai laughed, a low, wicked sound. "He always thought too highly of himself. They say a man must know his place. Now his is probably hanging on his master's wall."

Masateru smiled, then gestured the Triad leader and his men back to the elevator. "I can assure you, this issue of your loyalty to the Yamaguchi *oyabun* will be resolved shortly. Once the necessary changes have been made I will arrange another meeting."

"I look forward to it."

They returned to the parking lot, where the rest of the Triads were waiting. They piled back into their van as Xinhai climbed into the Nissan. Before the sedan drove away, he wound down the window. "Masateru, my people tell me that the Yamaguchi have plans of their own. Tomorrow their *oyabun* is meeting with his most trusted lieutenants. If I was a betting man, and I am, then I would put my money on an offering of peace."

Masateru nodded, then shrugged. "There will be no peace."

The two vehicles disappeared up the ramp. Masateru took out his phone and dialed his *oyabun*. "The Triad will support us once the Yamaguchi *oyabun* is dead. Until then they refuse to work with us."

"Understandable."

"He also revealed that the Yamaguchi are holding a clan meeting tomorrow."

"And what is the meeting for?"

"Apparently they want to make peace."

The Mori-Kai *oyabun* laughed. "Unfortunately not everyone can get what they want. It is time to put our new foot soldiers to work. Put a price on the old man's head. That should motivate them."

"Ryu will coordinate the raid."

"Yes, but let the Koreans do the fighting."

"As you wish, *oyabun*." Masateru ended the call and turned to Ryu. "Use the Koreans and hit them when the lieutenants have gathered. If the old man is killed the reward will be double."

The Kissaki commander nodded. "It will be done."

"Kill every Yamaguchi piece of shit you come across, Ryu. Leave no one alive. I don't care if they're gardeners or cooks. Everyone must die."

CHAPTER 67

YAMAGUCHI-GUMI SAFE HOUSE, KOBE

"What have you got for me?" Bishop was sitting in front of a laptop at a desk in one of the offices. He had dialed into the Bunker for an intel update; it had been almost forty-eight hours since Kurtz and Aleks had ripped the data from the Interpol agent's phone.

"Not a lot, I'm afraid." Flash's face filled the screen. "My team's been working around the clock on the Interpol phone as well as the castle data but all we have is a general link to the Himeji region. There were other numbers on the phone but only one in Japan."

"Any other details for the Himeji number?"

"No longer active. Someone knew that the Frenchman's handset was burnt so they got rid of it."

"Account data?"

Flash shook his head. "Nothing useful. Even the Trojan horse you implanted has been a dead end."

"Shit, I was kind of hoping it would lead us right to the bad guys."

"Afraid not. All I got was a general location. Sorry."

"All good, we've got a HUMINT lead we're following up tonight. If that pans out we should at least know where these guys are keeping the girls."

"Sounds promising. If you get anything else for me just fire it through."

"Will do, thanks again."

"Good luck tonight. Flash out."

Bishop sat at the desk for a moment, pondering Flash's information. The Mori-Kai were running tight security procedures. If tonight did not work out there was a chance they would never find Karla. Worse still, the Mori-Kai might even decide she was too much of a liability and dispose of her. He pushed the thoughts from his head, closed the laptop, and glanced at his watch. According to Kenta, by now Takeshi would be shit-faced in his dingy little bar. It was time to get the mission rolling.

★★★

DOWNTOWN KOBE

"I've been meaning to ask," said Saneh to Kenta. "Do you have any family?" She was sitting in the back of the Toyota sedan with Bishop while Kenta drove them to the target building.

"Only the Yamaguchi."

"Then why is it that you have respect for women when so many Japanese men do not?"

"My father taught me that everyone deserves two things in life: respect and justice."

"A noble notion," said Bishop. "Were your ancestors samurai?"

"No," Kenta chuckled. "Farmers."

"An even nobler profession."

Kenta pulled the car over to the side of the road. They were in a well-to-do area of the city. Large blocks of luxury condominiums nestled together around parks and shopping areas.

"That's the address." Kenta pointed out one of the buildings.

"Yep, recognize it from the target pack." Bishop checked his watch; it was two in the morning. "Let's go to the drop-off point."

Kenta drove into the alleyway behind the condo. It was deserted. "You good with this, Kenta? Your part's pretty important."

"Yes, I know what I have to do."

Bishop and Saneh ducked out of the back of the sedan and walked quickly across to the fire exit. Chua's analysis had confirmed that only the entrance and the underground car park were covered by security cameras.

They were dressed completely in black, wearing Nomex hoods rolled up on their heads, climbing harnesses, covert radios, and windproof jackets to ward off the cold night air. Bishop was carrying a battered climbing backpack.

Saneh used a thin piece of metal to card the lock; it opened with a click and Bishop moved inside. She followed and they jogged up the stairs.

"No sign of our man," Kenta's voice came through their earpieces. "The security guard just finished his rounds." He was watching the front of the building from the Toyota.

"We'll be ready to go in a few minutes," Saneh replied, short of breath. They continued up, both breathing heavily by the time they had covered all twenty flights of stairs.

They exited the stairwell onto the rooftop and out into the crisp night air. Saneh pulled a rope from Bishop's pack, passed it around a heavy air-conditioning unit, and handed it to Bishop. He took the rope and tied it into a carabiner. Then he took two rope bags out and tied those ropes into the carabiner. He finished off the system by zip-tying a tiny remote detonator to each of the anchor lines.

"Taxi has arrived," Kenta transmitted as a cab stopped at the curb near the entrance to the building.

"Not going to be as late a night as I thought," replied Bishop. "We're good to go."

Kenta watched the target from inside the Toyota.

A man paid the cabdriver and lurched up the steps to the lobby of the building fumbling in his jacket for his keys.

"He's been drinking," Kenta transmitted.

"No shit," Bishop said as he checked his rope and peered over the edge. "Can you confirm it's our boy?"

"Yes, it's him," reported Kenta.

"Roger." Bishop adjusted the anchor line to ensure they would drop cleanly down the middle of the building. He snapped his descender onto the line and fastened the rope bag to his leg. Saneh did the same and they checked each other's equipment.

"You look good in black." Bishop pulled his balaclava down over his face.

"Mind on the job, Aden . . ." She tried unsuccessfully to hide her grin behind her Nomex hood.

"We're moving now," Bishop transmitted as they backed up to the edge of the building, controlling their ropes as they slid through the descenders attached to the front of their harnesses. "You ready?" he asked Saneh.

She nodded and dropped off the building.

"Ladies first, I guess," Bishop murmured as he dropped after her.

"One." He counted off the floors to himself as they bounded past each apartment's balcony.

"Two." He passed Saneh.

"Three.

"Four.

"Five." Bishop pulled down on the descender, bringing him to a halt. Saneh slid down silently next to him.

They hung fifteen floors up, perched next to their target balcony. Bishop reached down to the rope bag on his leg and gathered a length of rope, looping it over his descender and locking it off.

"Wait here," he whispered.

"Wait here?" repeated Saneh. "Where on earth would I go?"

Bishop let go of the rope, spun upside down, and shuffled himself across to peer into the target apartment. Takeshi lay passed out on his bed, fully clothed with the lights on.

"All clear." He spun back upright and pulled the loop of rope, restarting his descent. He dropped over the balcony lip and touched down gently. Saneh followed his move a few seconds later. They took off their rope bags and unclipped their descenders, leaving them on the balcony. Bishop drew his suppressed pistol from his backpack.

Saneh checked the sliding door; it was unlocked. Bishop followed her in and they moved toward the bedroom.

"Clearly a bachelor." Saneh wrinkled her nose in disgust as she surveyed the squalid state of the apartment. There were piles of clothing on the floor and empty bottles of alcohol on every horizontal surface.

Bishop strode past her, straight into the bedroom. "Wake up!"

Takeshi moaned and rolled over, opening his eyes. "*Kono yaro—*"

"English, motherfucker!" Bishop slapped him with a gloved hand.

The executive's words dropped off as he focused on the black-clad, balaclava-wearing intruders who stood in front of him. Fear spread across his plump features. "I've paid what I owe!"

"We're not here for money, Takeshi. We want to know everything you know about the Mori-Kai."

"All I know? If you're not them, then who are you?" His alcohol-muddled brain struggled to comprehend the situation.

"If you tell us everything you know, then we are friends. If you don't, then, well, we'll make you regret you ever heard of the Mori-Kai."

The businessman shook his head. "If I tell you anything they will kill me."

"No." Bishop's voice was low. "If you tell us everything they might kill you. They might find out our information came from you, they might be able to find you, or then again they might not be in a position to do anything to you. There is lots of uncertainty when it comes to the Mori-Kai and you." Bishop raised his pistol.

The man's eyes grew wider as he focused on the muzzle of the suppressor.

"The situation here is far more certain than any Mori-Kai threat," Bishop continued. "If you don't tell me what I want to know I'm going to take you out to your balcony, give you one last look at the lights of Kobe, and then help you over the rail. From this high up you will make a lovely smear on the street. Just another high-powered executive who burned out."

The businessman wiped the sweat from his forehead with a sleeve of his shirt. His beady eyes darted back and forth between the two balaclava-wearing PRIMAL operatives. "OK, what do you want to know?"

"We can start with what you know about their prostitution ring."

"I only use them for white whores, young virgins."

Bishop slapped him, drawing blood from his mouth. Tears poured from the corners of his piglike eyes.

"Please don't kill me. That's all I know. I send a message, I order girls, and they bring them here. That's it."

"How do you pay?"

"Cash, always cash."

"How long does it take them to get here from when you order?"

"Not long."

"What the fuck sort of answer is that? Give me a time frame. Is it less than an hour?"

"Yes, yes, about an hour."

"About an hour or less than an hour? Make up your fucking mind, Takeshi, I'm losing my patience here."

"Less than an hour, less! Maybe forty-five minutes."

Bishop looked at Saneh and nodded. The Mori-Kai facilities had to be close. He turned back to Takeshi. "I want you to take out your phone and order a girl to be here within the hour."

Saneh took his jacket from the floor, pulled out his BlackBerry, and tossed it on the bed.

Bishop continued. "If you try to call the police, if you try to let them know we are here, if you do anything other than send your order, I'm going to shoot you in the head."

Takeshi nodded and picked up the BlackBerry. He wrote a short message and sent it.

Bishop grabbed the phone and inspected it. He copied the e-mail address into his iPRIMAL and sent it off to the Bunker; another lead to keep Flash busy.

A beep signaled a reply message and Bishop showed Takeshi.

"It is done," the businessman said. "She will be here soon."

"How does it usually happen?"

"They buzz, I let them in. They escort her up and then they wait outside. I pay when I am finished with her."

"Good, now I want you to sit there and shut your mouth." Bishop made himself comfortable in a chair, his pistol aimed at Takeshi's face.

Saneh moved into the living room and radioed Kenta. Once she had updated him she quickly searched the apartment. At the bar she poured a tumbler of scotch, adding a vial of horse tranquilizer into the drink. In the bathroom cabinet she found a stash of pills, everything from amphetamines to Valium. She returned to the bedroom, scattered the pills on the floor, and gave Takeshi the glass of whisky. Their prisoner refused to drink until the suppressed barrel of Bishop's pistol was pressed against his skull. A minute later he was passed out on the bed again.

"He's going to wake up with a nasty headache," said Saneh as they retreated to the balcony. They closed the glass door, strapped on their rope bags, hooked back into their ropes, and waited.

Down below Kenta had left the car, wearing a black bomber jacket and a cap. The clothing was emblazoned with the logo of a local security company. He carried one of the long D-cell Maglites popular with night watchmen. The gangster was waiting in a dark spot between two streetlights, hidden from view.

"I think this might be our delivery," Bishop reported twenty minutes later as he peered over the balcony. Saneh was sitting in one of the balcony's chairs.

A long, silver Lexus sedan stopped in front of the building. The passenger door opened and a man in a dark suit walked up to the entrance and pressed a button.

The intercom inside the apartment buzzed.

"Yep, that's our guys," confirmed Bishop. "Kenta, you're up."

"OK."

The guy at the front door buzzed again and again. He waited for a while, then walked back to the Lexus and got in.

At the same time Kenta strolled down the road in his security outfit. "I can confirm there's a girl in the back," he transmitted. He approached the vehicle and tapped on the front passenger window.

"Hello, can I help you?" he asked as the window wound down.

"Do you work in the building?" the dark-suited passenger asked.

"No, I just walk the grounds."

"Then you can't help me." The Mori-Kai gangster raised the tinted glass.

Kenta tapped his Maglite against the window and it lowered again.

The man pulled back his jacket to reveal the butt of a pistol. "Look, old man, I don't want any trouble. You need to keep your nose out of our business."

"That's fine but you need to move your business along," Kenta replied. As he gestured with the flashlight it slipped out of his hand and bounced into the gutter.

The passenger rolled his eyes. "We're going anyway. Hurry up and get your light saber."

The driver laughed at the joke and started the engine.

Kenta dropped to a knee and reached into the gutter. He pretended to fumble the flashlight as he unclipped a false magnet base and transferred it to the underside of the car.

"Hurry the fuck up, Granddad." The passenger had lit a cigarette and dropped the ash out of the window. It landed in Kenta's hair.

Kenta slowly got to his feet and proudly showed the Maglite to the men. "I got it."

"Great work, Skywalker," laughed the passenger as the Lexus pulled away from the curb, the window rising.

Kenta watched the limousine disappear before heading back to his car. "The tracker is attached," he transmitted.

"Good job, mate. See you on the ground." Bishop turned to Saneh with a grin. "Race you down!" Bishop pushed off from the balcony and hissed away into the darkness.

"Child," sighed Saneh as she descended after him.

Aided by nearly fifty extra pounds, Bishop hit the ground first, touching down lightly. A split second later Saneh was next to him. They ran the lines through their equipment and started stashing them in Bishop's backpack. He activated an app in his phone and the two micro-detonators he had attached earlier cut the lines on the roof with a snap. The weight of the ropes pulled the anchor lines clear of the roof and they landed on the sidewalk with a thud. Kenta pulled the Toyota alongside; they bundled their gear into the trunk and jumped into the back of the car.

As they drove away, Bishop activated the tracking application on his phone. The flashing icon of the tracker came up straight away. "Good job, people, we are up and running. Very soon we're going to know exactly where the Mori-Kai are holding their most prized possessions."

CHAPTER 68

RESIDENCE OF THE YAMAGUCHI-GUMI OYABUN, KOBE

"And once again we find ourselves watching and waiting." Kurtz slumped back in his chair. "This is pointless . . . the Yamaguchi have better security than half the government agencies I've worked with."

Aleks grunted and fumbled with a pair of chopsticks as he tried to eat a soba noodle salad for breakfast. The pair were sitting in the security room of the *oyabun*'s residence with two of the uniformed Yamaguchi security guards. Located deep within the mansion, the room's sophisticated security system controlled all of the access doors and monitored the CCTV cameras.

"Did you see the photos in the foyer?" Kurtz continued. "Every one of those guys has been assassinated. None of the *oyabun* die of old age—that's why their security is so high." He gestured to the rack of Mossberg shotguns on the wall. "Us being here is a waste of time. We should be out helping find Karla."

"Could be worse," Aleks said between mouthfuls.

"How? I doubt there is really a threat. Bishop just wanted me out of the way."

A noodle slipped through Aleks's chopsticks and back into the bowl. "Sweet mother Russia! How do these people not starve to death?" He lifted the bowl up to his face and used the sticks to shovel the noodles into his mouth.

"That's right, Aleks, you focus on the important things."

"What? I'm sorry, did my eating interrupt your whine? Perhaps you would like some cheese with that."

Kurtz gave his partner a withering look, then burst out laughing. "You are such a clown."

"Look, another Mercedes." Aleks nodded toward the monitor covering the front gate. "These guys love them."

"That's because they're German engineering. All the best things are German."

Aleks rolled his eyes and continued with his meal.

"That's the fifth one this morning. They must be having a meeting of their leaders."

"Or they're all members of the same car club." Aleks scraped the last of the noodles into his mouth and placed the bowl down on the table.

"Yes, a car club whose members are Japanese businessmen that hang out with heavily tattooed, fingerless thugs."

They watched the screens as the cars stopped in front of the stairs and the blue-shirted servants scrambled to get in place. They bowed low as the Yakuza leaders, all in suits, walked up the stairs and gathered in the foyer.

Kurtz turned to one of the Yamaguchi security guards, who was absentmindedly looking at the screens. "Where is the *oyabun*?"

The man stared at him blankly.

"The *OYABUN*," he said slowly.

"*Hai, oyabun.*" The man hit a button and the view on one of the screens changed to an image of the kitchens, where the *oyabun* was overseeing the preparation of the food trays.

"The *Führer* is more obsessed with food than you are," said Kurtz.

"Huh?" Aleks looked up at the screen. The cooks were preparing a feast for the arriving guests.

"Never mind. Here comes another car." On a different screen the compound's metal gates slowly swung open as another black Mercedes drove in. One of the two Yamaguchi guards manning the gate leaned forward to confirm the identity of the passenger. He was greeted by the muzzle of a pistol. A distant crack was heard and the man collapsed.

Kurtz leaped out of his chair. "Shots fired! Front gate."

Aleks joined him, reaching for body armor and assault rifles.

"Comms check." Aleks donned an earpiece and opened a channel on the iPRIMAL.

"Loud and clear."

Automatic fire sounded from the front of the building, followed by pistol shots. On screen the Mercedes had been joined by a large delivery van. Heavily armed gunmen were spilling from both vehicles.

"At least twenty of the *Schweine*," said Kurtz. "They're wearing armor, carrying automatic weapons."

The two security guards were screaming at each other in Japanese. One of them grabbed a shotgun off the rack and bolted out the door.

"Where the fuck is he going?" asked Kurtz.

"To join the fight." Aleks pointed at the screen. It showed the guard running toward the foyer.

The other guard armed himself with a shotgun and stared at the two PRIMAL operatives, clearly looking for direction.

"*Oyabun!*" Kurtz pointed at the screen that showed the kitchen. "Protect the *oyabun*."

The man nodded and dashed out the door.

More gunshots sounded from the front of the building where the drivers and servants had been waiting.

"What's the plan, comrade?"

"The *oyabun* is safe in the kitchen for now. We need to stop these *Schweine* from killing all of the clan leaders."

The PRIMAL operatives ran down the corridor that led to the foyer. Sporadic gunfire could be heard. A shotgun boomed; the security guard was in the fight.

Bullets ripped through the air as they burst into the waiting area. The traditional Japanese building materials of paper and wood were offering little resistance to the full-metal-jacket rounds used by the attackers.

Half a dozen of the Yamaguchi-gumi clan leaders were standing in the waiting room, their pistols drawn. One of the house servants was with them.

"GET DOWN!" Kurtz screamed at them over the sound of gunfire.

The servant dropped to the floor as a round slapped into one of the tattooed lieutenants. He toppled over, blood gurgling from his severed throat. The other men immediately lay down.

"Does anyone speak English?" Kurtz yelled.

"Yes I do," the servant replied.

"Get these men to the kitchen," Kurtz ordered. "They need to protect the *oyabun*."

The young man nodded and relayed the order. The Yamaguchi lieutenants filed back down the corridor as intermittent gunfire continued outside.

Aleks checked the Aimpoint sight on his suppressed Tavor. "Let's do this."

Kurtz kicked open the front door and was greeted by an AK-wielding maniac. The Korean screamed with rage, firing his gun blindly from the hip. Kurtz double-tapped him in the face, blowing his brains across the landing.

Bullets snapped through the doorway, forcing Kurtz to lunge to the side.

A pair of gunmen charged up the stairs until they collapsed in a hail of bullets, Aleks rapid-firing his Tavor as he cut them down. He peeked out the door, surveying the carnage.

The bodies of Yamaguchi servants, drivers, and guards littered the driveway between bullet-riddled limousines. The remainder of the attackers were spread out, hunting down the last few Yamaguchi men outside before assaulting the main building.

"Kurtz, can you cover me?" At the bottom of the stairs a Yamaguchi guard was trying desperately to crawl into the house. He had been shot in both legs, leaving a smear of blood on the driveway.

Kurtz ejected a magazine from his Tavor, slapped in a fresh one, and released the working parts, all in one smooth motion. "Covering." He leaned out from the front door and started firing bursts at the intruders.

Aleks charged down the stairs and had almost reached the wounded man when a volley of rounds slammed into the Yamaguchi guard's body, spraying him in blood.

Bullets ricocheted off the stairs as Aleks dashed back inside. Attackers closed in after him, covering each other as they advanced on the new threat.

Kurtz emptied his magazine and knelt behind the door as he pulled out a D-cell battery–size smoke grenade. "Too many out there," he said, rolling the grenade down the stairs.

Aleks was crouched on the other side of the doorway, catching his breath. "*Da*, we need to get back to the *oyabun* and defend from the kitchen."

"Go!" Kurtz fired another burst at the attackers as billows of smoke filled the entrance. Silhouettes appeared from the haze, the Koreans screaming fiercely as they charged.

Aleks took his cue and peeled back into the corridor that led toward the kitchen. He propped on one knee and aimed at the front door. "Covering!"

Kurtz sprinted back as bullets slammed into the door and attackers burst into the foyer, firing their submachine guns.

Aleks fired automatic bursts, cutting down the first wave. More figures emerged from the smoke, replacing their fallen comrades.

"ON ME!" Kurtz yelled as he retreated down the corridor toward the kitchen.

Aleks walked backward as he engaged targets. The rifle ran dry and he let it drop, drawing his pistol, then continued to shoot at the charging attackers. He felt Kurtz's elbow pressing against his shoulder and they edged backward.

They moved instinctively as a pair, killing another two of their assailants before they reached the kitchen. As they pushed through the swinging steel doors, a bullet smashed into Aleks's back. He grunted and snapped his pistol around to face the threat.

The smoking revolver was held in the shaking hand of the Yamaguchi-gumi clan leader.

"I'm on your side, fuckhead," Aleks snapped, pushing the revolver down with a gloved hand and entering the industrial-size kitchen.

The gray-haired leader of Japan's largest criminal syndicate was leaning on his cane with a defiant look on his face. Two of his chefs, both wearing aprons, and four of his clan leaders were all that was left of his entourage. They were armed with an assortment of kitchen knives and pistols.

Kurtz fired a burst into the corridor and joined them. "That's the *oyabun*."

"I know." Aleks holstered his pistol and changed the magazine on his Tavor.

"We need to get him out of here."

"*Da*, I know that too." He started shoving an industrial stainless-steel refrigerator across the floor to block the entrance. Kurtz grabbed the front of the appliance and they slid it screeching in front of the door.

Rounds thudded into the refrigerator. A Korean attempted to climb over the barrier until Aleks shoved his Tavor against the man's skull and blew off the top of his head.

"Is that a way out?" Kurtz asked a Yamaguchi crouching beside a door at the other end of the kitchen.

The man shook his head. "Enemy. Too many!"

Sporadic gunfire could be heard approaching from the corridor.

"What about in here?" Kurtz opened a door that led to stairs heading downward.

"That is the wine cellar," a voice spoke out in clear English. The house servant that had led the clan leaders to safety appeared from behind an upturned bench. He was clutching a meat cleaver.

"Is there anything else down there?"

A few of the Yamaguchi bosses gave blank looks. The servant looked down the stairs. "The underground parking lot is near but does not connect to the cellar."

Kurtz nodded to Aleks. "You check it out." He pointed to the rest of them. "Help me barricade this door."

As the others focused on the defenses Aleks inspected the wine cellar. It was cool, refrigerated to preserve the rows of wine and sake stacked on the oak shelving. He shoved crates of wine aside and knocked on the walls. He inspected the far wall, tapping it with his pistol. Loosening his armor, he twisted it to get to one of the back pouches. The demolition charge contained less than two pounds of explosives, about half what he would use for an exterior wall. He tore the adhesive coat from the back, stuck it to the smooth concrete, and pulled out the arming pin.

"Hurry up!" Kurtz's voice urged through the transmitter in his ear.

"Almost done." Aleks stacked a few crates of wine in front of his demolition charge and armed the charge using his iPRIMAL. "Five seconds."

"Four." Aleks ran up the stairs and slammed the cellar door shut. "Three." He crouched to one side of the door. "Two. Eyes and ears! One."

The slab detonated with an almighty explosion, blasting the cellar door open in a spray of broken glass and wine. A haze filled the kitchen and the entire building shook.

Aleks gave it a few seconds to settle, then inspected the damage. The explosives had shattered every single bottle of wine. The floor of the cellar was ankle deep in liquid, the earthy smell of red wine and the metallic taint of sake blending in a pungent assault on the nose. But the rear wall had also been breached, a jagged three-foot hole blown through the cinder blocks.

"We're through!" Aleks yelled. Through the dust he could see cars in the underground garage as he ducked through the hole.

"OK, let's go." Kurtz directed the *oyabun* and his entourage down into the cellar. The old man hobbled along, aided with his stick.

"This is going to take all day." Kurtz aimed his rifle up the cellar stairs as the Yamaguchi ducked through the hole in the wall. "Aleks, you've got about a minute before they realize we're getting away," he transmitted over his radio, then fired a burst through one of the barricades toward the sound of voices. The SLAP ammunition punched through the fridge, resulting in panicked Korean cursing.

In the garage, the English-speaking servant ran to the key cabinet and grabbed the keys to the two black Mercedes parked in the garage.

"Start your car, and follow my lead," Aleks ordered the lieutenants as they emerged from the breach.

The servant translated, handed them a key, and they piled into one of the black saloons. The *oyabun* emerged from the hole in the wall with Kurtz and he bundled him into the other Mercedes with Aleks and the servant.

"Go! Go!" Kurtz had the window down and was covering the breached wall.

"Two seconds." Aleks tore open the car's fuse panel and wrenched out a handful of wiring.

"What are you doing idiot, drive!"

A Korean's head appeared at the hole in the wall and Kurtz fired, slotting the man through the face.

Aleks shrugged as he dropped the car into gear and punched the accelerator to the floor. "Airbag sensors. We will smash out of here, *da*?"

The Mercedes S63 roared up the ramp and onto the pebble driveway. A gunman appeared in front of them. He was too slow in reacting and they smashed into him. His face thudded on the windshield as he was catapulted over the car. Aleks accelerated, holding the steering wheel steady as they slammed into the back gates, smashing them open. He glanced at the mirror, confirming the other car was behind them, then wrenched the steering wheel, sending them sliding onto the streets of Kobe. A few hundred meters up the road he slowed, allowing the other Yamaguchi car to take the lead.

"Good job." Kurtz slapped his hand against the dashboard. "You got us out of there in one piece." A beeping noise in his earpiece alerted him to a new message on his iPRIMAL. He pulled it out and inspected the screen.

"What is it?" Aleks asked as he concentrated on keeping up with the other speeding Mercedes.

"It's Bishop—they've got a lead on Karla's location."

"And?"

"And we're going in."

"When?"

"Tonight."

Aleks thumped the steering wheel. "This is good." The adrenaline was still pumping through his body. "See what happens when you bitch about always watching and waiting. Every time you do it something big goes down."

"Maybe I should bitch more often."

A cough from the backseat reminded them of the presence of the *oyabun*, forgotten in the heat of the moment.

Aleks looked into his rearview mirror. "*Oyabun*, are you OK?"

"I owe both of you my life. This will not be forgotten," said the Yamaguchi-gumi leader.

"Just doing our job," replied Aleks. "We have just one small favor to ask."

"Speak."

"Once we have you secure in a new location, can we borrow this car?"

CHAPTER 69

CONSTRUCTION SITE ADJACENT TO THE
MORI-KAI APARTMENTS, HIMEJI

"That's the plan, team. Nice and simple, in and out." Bishop sat on an upturned crate. It was 1830 hours and around him, in a semicircle, were Saneh, Kenta, Aleks, and Kurtz.

"We sure on the location?" asked Kurtz. Like Aleks he was still wearing his rig from the defense of the *oyabun*'s residence. After dropping off the Yamaguchi boss at a secret location on the outskirts of Kobe, they had driven directly to Himeji to take part in the mission. The rest of the team was wearing the same: heavy-duty pants and lightweight jackets worn over concealable chest plates. Their weapons consisted of suppressed Tavor assault rifles and pistols; Kenta toted his KRISS.

"I'm ninety-nine percent sure we've got it right. The tracker Kenta planted on the Lexus lines up with our communications analysis on the Interpol handset. Kenta's men have also reported a number of similar vehicles coming and going."

"What about the e-mail address Takeshi used?" Saneh asked. "Did Flash get back to us?"

"Yes, but he's not sure he'll be able to hack it. The whole server's running through a number of ghost IP addresses, very sophisticated setup. Kenta's tracker is the best we've got."

The location the tracker had revealed was a new block of apartments that overlooked Himeji. Some of Kenta's most trusted men had been watching it since the morning. Now, Kenta and the PRIMAL team had assembled in the basement of a similar building that was under construction in an adjoining block. It was halfway to completion, a large crane set up beside it with building materials stacked around its base. The work crew had left in the midafternoon, eager to escape early before the weekend.

"So the intel is good, but the plan is hardly simple," continued Kurtz.

"Your job is critical. If you've got any doubts you need to voice them now."

Kurtz shrugged. "No, it will not be a problem. But I would prefer to be in the assault."

"Look, you've got the most experience with this sort of thing. But we could probably swap you with Aleks if he's OK with it."

Kurtz looked across at his partner and shook his head. "It's fine the way it is."

"I have a question." Aleks extended his hand in the air as if he were at school.

Bishop smiled. "Yeah, Aleks, what is it?"

"This plan is a little crazy. I like that, we keep the surprise. But how do we know the place is not crawling with hostiles? Should we not hit it in full assault gear?"

"We've had the place under obs since this morning and we've seen nothing to suggest they're using this for anything more than accommodation for the women. The only security is at the front door. That's why we're running light. It also gives us more flexibility. If we have to scoot you're not going to get far looking like Darth Vader."

"If you've had it under observation all day, have you seen the girl?" Kurtz asked.

"Negative. All movement in and out was by vehicle. Windows were tinted but thermal signatures indicated the passengers were mostly female."

"Do we have a cordon?"

"As I've briefed, Kenta's guys will be out there. They'll attempt to delay any outside response until we're ready to extract."

The team sat in silence for a few seconds.

"No more questions?" Bishop asked. "Saneh?"

She shook her head. "Plan sounds good."

"Kenta, anything from you?

"Not a question, Bishop. More of a statement."

"Shoot."

The stocky gangster rose from the bags of cement he was sitting on. "A statement of thanks. Your people saved the *oyabun* today." He nodded toward Kurtz and Aleks. "Without their swift action the Yamaguchi-gumi would have been dealt a blow from which we would not have recovered. This is not a debt we will ever forget."

Bishop nodded in agreement. "Great work, guys." He stood up, adjusting his equipment. "Now, if there's no more to add, let's get this show on the road."

★★★

The sun was setting as Kurtz scaled the narrow ladder that ran up the side of the crane, and by the time he reached the cabin light was fading fast. He picked the lock easily and gained access. A scan of the controls identified a numeric security keypad that locked out the joysticks that controlled the eighty-foot boom and the hook.

"Bunker, this is Kurtz, I need technical advice," Kurtz communicated through his iPRIMAL.

There was a pause for a few seconds before the watchkeeper replied. "Roger, I'm putting you through now."

A few more seconds passed.

"Kurtz, let me guess, you need an override code?" one of the geeks asked, expecting the call.

"Yes."

"OK, send make and model."

"It's a Dasion QTZ sixty-three." Kurtz could hear fingers typing.

"I have a code."

"Send."

"Four-four-eight-five."

Kurtz punched the number into the numeric pad. A hum filled the cabin and the control panel lit up.

"Thanks, Bunker, Kurtz out."

He moved one of the joysticks. There was a whir and the cabin turned slightly. He nudged the other joystick and the hook in front of him dropped a few feet.

"How are things tracking up there, mate?" Bishop asked over the iPRIMAL.

"The crane is operational. I'm lowering the hook now."

"No dramas; I'll guide you on."

Twenty feet below Kurtz, on the recently laid sixth floor of the apartment, the rest of the team had emptied a metal Dumpster.

Bishop stood in the center of the bin and grabbed the big hook as it was lowered. "Hold it there. Aleks, pass me the cables."

The bearded Russian climbed in and handed Bishop the first of the four cables attached to each corner. Bishop looped them over the hook as he received them and closed the metal gate once all of them were secure. "Take up the slack, Kurtz."

The hook rose by a foot, pulling the cables tight. "Hold it there. OK, team, all aboard."

Kenta and Saneh joined them inside the cramped space.

"Tell me again what was wrong with the front door?" she asked.

"Heavy security and no element of surprise." Bishop checked the cables once more. "Everyone comfortable?"

No one responded.

"I'll take that as a yes, then. Kurtz, take us up."

The Dumpster rose five feet into the air before Kurtz sent it sliding along the boom, out over the hillside in front of the building.

They hung in midair for a moment, then he started to turn the crane.

"I don't think this is the best way to do this." Aleks was crouched low, peering over the edge of the bin.

Bishop was standing up watching the target building; exterior floodlights illuminated it in the darkness. "Kurtz, I think you need to raise us a little if we're going to make the roof."

The bin rose by a few feet as they gained speed. It swung in an arc toward the adjacent building.

"Up, Kurtz, UP!" Bishop yelled as the building loomed.

"I am."

"Faster, we're going to hit."

"OK, OK!"

"Fuck, too late." Bishop ducked into the Dumpster just before it smashed through the plate-glass windows of the top floor.

CHAPTER 70

"Everyone all right?" Bishop asked.

"I'm good," Aleks responded cheerfully.

"As am I," said Kenta.

"What in god's name happened?" Saneh asked.

An alarm started wailing as Bishop shook shards of glass from his hair. "Kurtz misjudged the distance."

"The controls jammed. I've got no elevation," Kurtz transmitted.

They had landed in what looked to be an entertaining area. The Dumpster had smashed through the floor-to-ceiling windows, shoving a number of tasteful leather sofas out of the way, and was lodged with a third of it still hanging out over a six-story drop. The impact had severed its front two cables.

"Everybody out, this thing isn't stable," said Bishop.

As Kenta jumped out, the Dumpster gave a groan and slid a few inches backward.

"Everybody out, NOW!" Bishop dived over the side as a door burst open. A submachine gun barked and rounds slammed into the Dumpster, the thick steel ringing like a bell.

Kenta let rip with a long burst, punching holes through the wall above the door and showering the shooter with plasterboard. The suppressed weapon was barely audible compared to the enemy's submachine gun.

Bishop followed up with rapid-fire shots from his Tavor, splintering the doorframe as the gunman took cover. "Go, go, go!" he screamed.

The Dumpster slid again as Aleks dived over the side and rolled for cover.

The Kissaki operative fired another burst, then withdrew back into a corridor. Rounds slammed into the Dumpster, forcing Saneh down behind the heavy steel walls. There was a groan as the bin edged farther backward, scraping along the floor.

"Anyone got a bead on this guy?" Bishop yelled.

The Mori-Kai gunman remained far back in the corridor with a clear line of fire direct to the Dumpster, but none of the PRIMAL team could hit him.

"No," Aleks responded.

More rounds slammed into the Dumpster as it slid, the heavy chains attached to the crane dragging it through the broken windows.

"Aleks, Kenta, shut this fucker down."

"I'm on it." Aleks fired a burst into the doorway as he moved toward it. With his left hand he pulled a stun grenade from his rig and yanked out the pin using the thumb of his master hand. He fired his weapon as he tossed the grenade through the doorway.

The explosion shook the walls; bottles fell from the bar and smashed onto the floor. The gunfire from the Mori-Kai guard stopped.

There was a scraping noise as the heavy bin teetered on the edge of the apartment. Saneh swung a leg out and Bishop grabbed her as the Dumpster slid out from underneath her and flipped downward into the darkness below.

"That was close," Saneh said as she looked outside. The bin was hanging sideways from the remaining two of its cables.

"What happened?" Kurtz asked over the radio.

"The bin made a rather dramatic exit," said Saneh. "Everyone's OK."

"*Scheisse*. Well, I have a backup extraction plan."

"What's that?" asked Bishop.

"Just get to the roof when you're done and I'll be ready."

"Roger." Bishop was already planning the next move. The room they had landed in had two doors leading off it, and an entrance area where the elevator and fire exit were located. "Aleks, I want you and Kenta to cover the entrance. That's the most likely approach for reinforcements. Saneh and I are going to clear the doors to the left and right. Keep an eye out for more shooters."

"Got it."

Saneh peered into the corridor she was covering. It led into a long hallway lined with doors. The Mori-Kai gunman lay sprawled in a pool of blood. Bishop moved past her, inspecting the doors.

"More holding cells." He tapped his knuckles against heavy steel. "We'd need some serious bang to crack this. They've got breach-resistant hinging and electronic locks."

"Yeah, it looks a little more upmarket than that last one." Saneh walked past Bishop and down the corridor. There were three doors on either side, all of them exactly the same.

"A gilded cage is still a cage." Bishop used his knife to pry the keypad from the wall. Behind it was a power cable, the line running to the locking mechanism, and a network cable. He pulled out the network cable, checked the plug, and fished in his backpack for a mobile data modem. He plugged the network cable into the modem's port, synced it with his iPRIMAL, then opened a communications line to PRIMAL HQ. "Bunker, this is Bishop, I need a security crack on a data link."

One of the techs responded immediately. "Got the feed. Give me five minutes to crack it."

Bishop left the modem in place and led Saneh back into the original room. "It's going to take a few minutes. We should check out what's behind door two."

The door was deadlocked. Bishop aimed his Tavor at it and shot the locking mechanism clean out. The door swung open when he kicked it.

"Wow, ritzy," he said as he stepped into the luxurious apartment. A quick check of the bedroom, sitting area, and huge bathroom confirmed they were empty. "Clear!"

Saneh inspected the rooms. "King-size bed, plush carpets, massive Jacuzzi in the bathroom, expensive yet somewhat tasteless art, and an amazing view. Someone important lives here."

"I concur; let's toss it for intel." Bishop opened the door of the walk-in wardrobe and started rifling through drawers. "Whoever this guy is, he sure loves a shiny suit." He checked between all the clothes on the racks.

"Masateru wears bad suits and there's certainly enough hair product in here to maintain that slick look he favors," Saneh reported from the bathroom.

"You're probably right." Bishop felt around the floor of the closet for a safe. "Find anything interesting?"

"Negative."

"I've got nothing either; these guys are OPSEC tight." Bishop's iPRIMAL vibrated and he checked the message. "Let's go back to the corridor. We just got access to one of those cells."

As they walked back out, Bishop halted.

"What's wrong?" Saneh asked.

"Nothing, I just think it would be rude to drop in and not leave a gift."

"No, that's a bad idea . . . you could end up hurting someone innocent."

"Who in this building is going to be innocent?"

"Emergency services."

"Good point." He took a CS gas grenade, pulled out the pin, and wedged it inside a drawer of a beautiful antique Japanese dresser. "That won't hurt anyone but it will send a pretty clear message when he checks to see if we stole his panties."

Saneh shook her head.

"Bishop, this is Bunker, I've got control of all security systems." PRIMAL HQ's transmission came over their earpieces.

"Excellent, can we get a heads-up?" Bishop asked as they moved back into the corridor with the locked rooms.

"I've got what looks to be a barracks facility at the rear of the building," the technician reported. "CCTV coverage is minimal but apart from the first guy you took down it looks like the occupants aren't home."

"What about the other floors?"

"All empty, except for a security detail on the third floor. Four heavily armed SF types coming up the stairwell. Looks like they were in the basement—there's a fleet of vehicles down there, a security office, and a gym."

"Roger. Aleks, have you and Kenta got that stairwell covered?" Bishop asked.

"Yes, boss."

"Bunker, what can you tell me about the apartments in this corridor?"

"There are six apartments in total but no cameras inside. The security design indicates they are some sort of detention facility. I don't think you'll find hostiles in there," the PRIMAL HQ technician advised. "You should have full access now."

"Good work, keep us posted on the hostiles on the stairs." Bishop nodded to Saneh. "You take the three on the right; I'll take the three on the left." He gently pushed open the first door and moved into the room slowly. "Hello, anyone here?"

There was no reply.

The apartment was almost as plush as Masateru's, although smaller. He moved through the bedroom and heard a faint whimper from the bathroom.

"Hello, I'm not here to hurt you. I'm with the police. I'm here to take you home." He turned the handle of the bathroom door and pushed it open. He took a deep breath and slowly stuck his head around the door, keeping his weapon out of sight.

A blonde girl was cowering next to the toilet wearing cotton pajamas. Black streaks of makeup had run down her cheeks; her eyes were glazed and her hands shaking. She was every bit as beautiful as he remembered Karla to be, with long hair, a delicate oval face, and crystal-blue eyes.

"Hello, I'm with the police. I'm here to take you home."

She flinched as gunfire sounded from the rear of the building. An intense firefight followed for a few seconds, then nothing.

"We got the drop: threat neutralized," Aleks reported.

Bishop focused on the young woman. "That's nothing to be afraid of; we're here to help." It took him a few minutes to coax her out of the bathroom and into the bedroom to get changed. When they stepped out into the corridor Saneh was waiting with two more women. "You done?" she asked.

"No, can you check my last two? I need to call someone."

"Fine." Saneh made for the two remaining apartments.

Bishop walked out to the main room with the smashed windows to make a call on his local cell phone.

"Agent Wilson," said Inspector Baiko. "I am glad you called."

"Why is that?"

"Because I just received a call from the Hyogo Prefecture police asking me why I had a team of my men and community workers in their backyard." The police officer had been tipped off by Bishop to be prepared to receive any rescued sex slaves.

"I've got the address, at least four Western girls, all without papers." Bishop gave him the location of the apartment block and Baiko put him on hold for a few seconds.

"They're on their way. I wouldn't recommend you being in location when my men arrive. Questions will be asked that you cannot answer."

"This is from a source in the Yamaguchi. The FBI would never sanction active operations in Japan."

"Of course, Agent Wilson, of course." The police investigator hung up and Bishop moved back into the corridor.

"Five girls, no Karla." Saneh had them all huddled together. "She was here but the girls said she left with Masateru in a helicopter."

"Where to?"

"They don't know. Girls have been taken before but they've never come back."

"Fuck, they're always one step ahead."

"We're regaining the initiative. This is going to hurt them."

"You're right. Let's get the girls out of here."

They led the way to where Kenta and Aleks waited in the stairwell. The dead Mori-Kai had already been dragged into a janitor's closet, but the smears of blood and shell casings remained as evidence of the earlier gunfight. The girls stared at their deceased captors with wide eyes.

"Karla?" Aleks asked.

Saneh shook her head.

"Bunker, how are we looking?" Bishop asked.

"All clear, no hostiles in the building."

"Roger, switch to passive monitoring. Thanks for your help."

"Not a problem." PRIMAL HQ deactivated the comms link.

"Kenta, can you have your guys come in and babysit the girls until the police arrive?"

"Yes, my men are already outside. I will go down and let them in."

"Saneh, can you sort that out and meet the rest of us on the roof?" She nodded.

"Make it quick, the cops are on their way."

Bishop and Aleks started up the stairs for the roof. "Kurtz, how's our extraction plan going?"

"Nearly ready. Did you find Karla?"

They burst out of the emergency exit onto the flat roof of the apartment block. "Extraction, Kurtz; focus on your fucking job."

"Give me a moment."

Bishop could see the boom of the crane over the building site. In the ambient light being thrown across the hills from the city he could make out a figure climbing the ladder to the control box. Flashing blue and red lights caught his attention and he leaned over the edge of the building. No fewer than four police cars had pulled up outside and officers ran from the vehicles to the building.

"Kurtz, you need to hurry the hell up."

"Keep your pants on, I'm moving as fast as I can." The long boom started to swing gracefully through the air.

"Bishop, we have police in pursuit. We need that evac ASAP," Saneh said over the comms, breathing heavily as she ran up the stairs.

The boom slowed over them and there was a whir as the hook lowered. "You got to be shitting me," Bishop said as he grasped the four webbing straps attached to the hook. Each strap had a cara-biner attached to the end of it. "Where did you find this gear?" Bishop gave one of the lines a sharp pull; it looked strong.

"They use them on the worksite for safety," said Kurtz. "Japanese standards are almost as high as German. They'll hold."

"They'd better." Bishop hooked the carabiner through the loop on the back of Aleks's armor, and checked it. The Russian returned the favor.

Saneh burst through the door onto the roof with Kenta in hot pursuit. Aleks and Bishop were ready. They hooked in the last two lines, gave them a few seconds to tighten their leg straps, which had been worn loose during the assault, and then Bishop radioed Kurtz.

"Lift off, fast as you can!"

The crane hummed, ripping them off the ground as it rotated. All four were pressed tightly together as they swung through the air.

"I don't like this," Kenta whispered.

"What's wrong, comrade?" Aleks bellowed. "This is fun!"

"I can't feel my . . . my manhood," Kenta grunted.

All four of them laughed as they sailed through the air.

CHAPTER 71

RESIDENCE OF THE MORI-KAI OYABUN, HIMEJI

The Lexus LS600 flew up the mountain, its heavily armored chassis rolling on its suspension as it sped around the sweeping corners.

"My eyes are *still* stinging!" Masateru rubbed his bloodshot eyes with a wet face towel. He punched the headrest in front of him, startling Hideaki, who was driving.

The Mori-Kai lieutenant, along with Hideaki and Ryu, had returned to the apartments as soon as the Tokyo police had left. The local cops had been paid off and allowed them to inspect the site. It had been Masateru who had tripped the CS tear gas canister left in his dresser.

"Careful, Hideaki, you don't want to add our deaths to their accomplishments." Ryu gripped the door with one hand as the car sped around another corner.

Masateru shot him a cold look. "Hideaki will drive as fast as I tell him to."

"Apologies, *waka-gashira*."

Masateru's bloodshot gaze lingered. "Now that we have a whole team of foreigners killing your Kissaki and their hirelings, your plan had better be ready."

"Yes, sir, it is. You just need to place the bait."

"I will do that tonight."

The Lexus pulled up at a security checkpoint and Hideaki confirmed the identity of his two passengers with the armed guards.

They drove through the gate and up the winding driveway through the sprawling estate.

"I'm going to see the *oyabun*; I'll see you after," said Masateru as the car came to a halt. He strode up the concrete steps and into the mansion's foyer. A servant greeted him with a bow. "He will see you in his office."

Masateru threw the man his jacket. "Have that laundered." He stormed through the building to the office and knocked.

"Come in."

He pushed the doors open. The head of the Mori-Kai was sitting on a sofa, a ceramic carafe of sake perched on the table with two matching cups.

"Masateru, come, sit, drink."

The Mori-Kai's second-in-command sat down opposite his master and lifted a cup of cold sake to his lips.

The *oyabun* watched as Masateru downed the cup. "Our minor irritation has become a festering wound." He spoke slowly and deliberately. "The *gaijin* saved the *oyabun* and dealt us a painful blow."

"Our raid against the Yamaguchi-gumi was not without success, even with the presence of the *gaijin*."

"Success! How? The Yamaguchi dog lives."

"Yes, but he has fled Kobe and we killed half of his *wakagashira*. Now that he is in hiding, the Triads will support us."

"And yet he strikes back, a raid into the very heart of our organization. We lost five of our most valuable women."

"That was not the Yamaguchi. The foreigners have reinforcements."

The *oyabun* slammed his fist down on the antique table, almost knocking over the sake. "How is it we know nothing about them? Who are they, Masateru? FBI, CIA? Why hasn't your Interpol source given you a name?"

Masateru refilled his cup and downed it. "My source is dead, killed in a fire."

"You think they killed him?"

"It is likely. But Rémi knew little about us; nothing he could tell them would be of any use."

"They must be dealt with, Masateru. You have built me an army—use it to kill them."

"I already have a plan. We will use the girl Karla to lure them into a trap."

"You think the girl is at the center of their campaign?"

"I believe so."

"Did her family hire these people?"

"Her family are simple peasants, *oyabun*. No, these people are something else. Their assaults on our business did, however, coincide with her recruitment, and they've followed her to Japan. I can't explain it, but it's too much to be a coincidence."

"You have questioned the girl?"

"Yes, in detail. In the Ukraine she was put on board a helicopter with a team of operatives pretending to be Interpol agents. There were at least ten of them. The only ones she remembers clearly are a tall German and a large bearded Russian. These were the two who provided her security at the hospital."

"The ones that your Kissaki tried to ambush but failed?"

"Yes, *oyabun*."

"Germans, Russians, Americans, and yet we have no idea who they work for."

"But we do know what they want and that can be used to our advantage. We will use the girl to lure them to a location of our choosing."

"And then crush them with our army."

"Exactly."

The Mori-Kai leader leaned back on the sofa.

"The plan is ready, *oyabun*. It needs only your word."

"It is given. Destroy the *gaijin*."

Masateru rose from his seat. "It will be done, *oyabun*." He made for the door.

"Masateru."

He stopped. "Yes, *oyabun*?"

"Keep one of them alive. I want to know who hired them. My preference would be the woman."

The Mori-Kai *waka-gashira* nodded and left the room. There was much work to be done.

CHAPTER 72

YAMAGUCHI-GUMI SAFE HOUSE, KOBE

"Way to go, team, you handed the Mori-Kai a damn good ass-kicking in the last twenty-four hours!" Vance's bald head filled the screen of the laptop.

The computer was on an equipment case, the team sitting around it, except for Kenta, who was out checking in with other Yamaguchi.

"Thanks, but it doesn't feel like much of a win," said Bishop. "The Yamaguchi are all but out of the fight and we still haven't found Karla or the head of the Mori-Kai."

"Yeah, well, I think that's about to change. Chua's gonna brief you on the latest intel."

Vance's face was replaced with that of PRIMAL's chief of intelligence.

"Thanks, Vance. Good to see you all, great work so far. I know intel's a bit light, but I think that's about to change with—"

"Just tell us what you've got," Kurtz cut in.

Bishop looked at Kurtz, then Chua, and shrugged.

"OK, I'll get to it." Chua looked a little taken aback. "I had one of my people give Kalista, that's Karla's older sister, a follow-up call a few days ago on behalf of Interpol. She gave us her e-mail address and we've been monitoring it ever since. A little under an hour ago she received mail from her sister."

"So now you know where Karla is, yes?" asked Kurtz.

"No, the IP address was scrambled. We didn't get a location."

"What did she say?" asked Saneh.

"That's the clincher; she asked for Kurtz's number. We think she's going to call him for help."

"Really?" said Bishop. "She's only been in Japan a few days and the super-secret Mori-Kai let her surf the web and fire off some e-mails? And now she's got herself a phone to call Kurtz?"

Chua nodded. "It would seem so."

"It's got to be a trap," Bishop stated. "All just a little too convenient, don't you think?"

"I agree," Vance cut in offscreen. "But even if it's a trap, we may be able to use it to turn up some intel."

"I concur," continued Chua, "we've e-mailed her a European number for Kurtz and routed it through to his iPRIMAL. When the call comes in we're going to use NSA assets to locate the source."

"What if it's a landline?" Saneh asked.

"Then we'll use more conventional means. Either way, we'll find it. Flash has already made all the necessary arrangements."

"And what do I say to her?" Kurtz asked. "Sorry we let you get sold into sex slavery?"

"No, we need you to elicit as much information from her as you can. Get her to describe her situation, how many guards, what her surroundings look like. Anything that might be useful."

Kurtz nodded, torn between hope and sharing Bishop's cynicism.

"Is there any other new intel from your other sources?" Bishop asked.

"No, unfortunately not. These guys are running some of the tightest OPSEC I've seen. Every attempt Flash and the team have made to pull apart their communications network has failed. Every device we've exploited has led to a dead end."

"So we sit and wait for a phone call that may or may not come."

"That's why we call it the waiting game, Bish." Vance's face replaced Chua's on the screen. "You've also got Kenta's boys out scouring the streets, right?"

"Yeah, but that's not going to be effective in tracking down Karla. The MK aren't going to be taking her out shopping anytime soon."

"So Karla calling is probably our best shot all round," said Vance.

Bishop nodded. "It would seem so."

"Yeah, well, I better let you get back to battle prep. You've done some good work, people. Get some rest while you can."

"Thanks, Vance," said Bishop as he ended the call. He turned to the group. "Vance is right. We've got an opportunity here. Yeah, it might be a trap, but we'll play along. And we'll make them regret it. Now, if Karla does call, we need to be able to move fast, so get your gear prepped and then get some sleep." He turned to Kurtz. "Mate, can I have a minute?"

"Sure." He followed Bishop across to a corner of the room.

Saneh and Aleks watched from where they were sitting.

"If this is about the crane, I had no control over that problem," said Kurtz.

"This isn't about the crane; you did a good job getting us out of there. This is about me needing to know you're not going to fuck this up."

Kurtz's face turned crimson. "No, I'm not going to fuck this up. It is our last chance to recover Karla. I would not risk that!"

"This is exactly what I'm talking about, Kurtz. I know how much it hurt to lose Aurelia, OK? And I realize that you feel obligated to save Karla. But you got to get your mind off the goddamn woman and back on the mission. Karla is an objective, she is not the endgame. Taking down the Mori-Kai is."

"We all have our own priorities, Aden."

"Not on my team, we don't. Get with the program or get out." The two men stared at each other.

"Do not screw this up." Bishop left the German standing in the corner and returned to his equipment.

Saneh sat down on the trunk next to him. "Aden, you need to go easier on Kurtz."

"He's an operator, not a child."

"No, he's a man. A man who's faced significant trauma. A man with wounds that need to heal."

"This isn't a rehab clinic. We're a covert team running high-risk ops. He needs to focus on the mission, not the girl."

"You and your missions, Aden. What do they matter if you don't look after your own? You need to stop being a mindless machine and give him a break." Saneh stormed off and disappeared up the stairs.

"Women, comrade," said Aleks with a light pat on Bishop's shoulder. "The ruin of every good man."

"Don't I know it."

CHAPTER 73

MORI-KAI CASINO CONSTRUCTION SITE, HIMEJI

"I take it this will suit your requirements, Ryu?" Masateru stood on the upper level of the partially constructed casino.

Ryu surveyed the construction site. "It has everything we need: isolation, places to conceal our men, and elevated firing positions." The upper levels of the seven-story, crescent-shaped complex were still naked concrete forms piled high with building materials and equipment. A high, chain-link fence surrounded the site, separating it from the surrounding properties, also in various stages of development.

"There are a number of methods they could use to get in," Masateru observed.

"We will position men to cover all of them. We have the numbers. Look, the first of them are here." Ryu pointed to the bus that turned in through the front gate. It drove down the main access road and stopped inside the crescent. "We have already issued them their disguises."

The doors of the bus opened and men dressed in fluorescent vests filed out and clustered around one of the construction foremen, a Kissaki operative.

"And the security cameras are all working?"

"Yes, cameras, motion sensors, the security system is complete. No one will move without us knowing about it."

"Excellent. How long until everyone is in place?"

"Half an hour."

"Then I think it is time we laid the bait."

The two men walked into an elevator. Masateru got out at the second floor, leaving Ryu to continue down to the casino's underground security center.

The lower floors were almost finished; the builders had completed the basic fit-out with walls, doors, and wiring. Electricity and air-conditioning had also been installed. Masateru headed down a bare corridor to where they were keeping Karla.

He nodded to the guard on her door and knocked gently.

★★★

"Come in," Karla said as she stood up from the bed.

Masateru entered the room, one of the first in the casino complex to be completed. Fully carpeted, painted, and furnished, it could have been in any modern hotel.

"How are you feeling?"

"I thought you had forgotten about me." Karla's eyes were glazed, a bottle of sedatives on the bedside table. She wore jeans, midcalf boots, and a cashmere sweater.

"How could I forget you?" Masateru sat on the bed and gestured for her to sit next to him. "It is my responsibility to protect you."

"Is that why I am here?" she asked as she sat.

"Yes." He stroked her hair. "I've identified a rival organization that is trying to take you from me."

"Who?" She looked startled.

"You remember the men you told me about? The Interpol agent Kurtz and his friends."

"Yes, they saved me from the castle."

"Not saved, Karla, kidnapped. They were pretending to be

policemen. Their men were the ones that attacked us when we arrived in Japan."

Karla looked confused.

"These men are actually a powerful crime syndicate that trades weapons, women, and drugs across the world."

"He seemed so nice." She hung her head. "They saved my sister. Without them she would have died."

"That's what they *wanted* you to think. What they really wanted was both of you to sell to their clients."

"And these men are here now, in Japan?"

"Yes, last night they attacked the apartments. They killed two of the girls and took the others."

Tears filled Karla's eyes. "*Killed*? Why would they do that?"

"Clearly, the girls resisted. They didn't want to be taken. I'm telling you, these men aren't who you think." Masateru put his arm around her shoulders and held her tight. "That is why we have moved you here. This is where we are going to make them pay."

Karla pulled away from him. "I already sent the e-mail to Kalista like you asked, and she gave you the phone number. I don't want to do any more. Please."

"You've done very well. I just need you to do one more thing. That's all. I need you to call this man Kurtz and tell him where you are."

"If I do that they will come for me."

"Yes, and I will destroy them. Then there will be no more fighting, and you'll be safe."

She nodded. "OK. I will make the call. But only if you promise that once it is done there will be no more killing. No more blood."

"I promise, once these men are dealt with there will be no more." Masateru pulled a phone from his pocket. "Now listen closely. I'm going to tell you exactly what to say."

CHAPTER 74

YAMAGUCHI-GUMI SAFE HOUSE, KOBE

The sound of a ringtone woke Bishop from a nap. Kurtz's iPRIMAL was ringing and vibrating on the trunk they were using as a coffee table. "Kurtz!" he yelled. "Incoming call, you're up." He glanced at his watch: midmorning.

The lanky German appeared from the direction of the bathrooms, still zipping his pants. "I'm right here."

"What's going on?" Aleks leaped from the other couch with his pistol in hand.

"What's up?" Saneh yelled from the top of the stairs. She was wearing tracksuit pants and a T-shirt but had her Tavor in one hand.

"Everyone quiet! It's the call we've been waiting for," said Bishop.

The phone continued to ring and vibrate. Kurtz watched it move in little circles on the plastic. Finally he picked it up. "Hello."

The voice on the other end of the line was a whisper. "Is this Kurtz?"

Everyone in the room was silent, listening to the call on the speaker that had been set up on the bar.

"Yes it is. Who is this?" Kurtz replied.

"It's Karla."

"Karla? Karla, is that really you?"

"Yes, it's me."

"Where are you? Are you OK?"

"No, I'm not. I need you to help me. I need you to get me out of here."

"All right, let me know where you are."

"Japan, I'm in Japan. I think the city is called Hajami or Hejimi."

"What about the building, what does the building look like?"

"It's a construction site, a new hotel. Only a few of the floors are finished. There are workers everywhere, I found one of their phones."

"OK, Karla, that's good. Very good. Now I need a little more information about your location. Do you have a window?"

"Yes."

"Describe what you see."

"It's a wide-open area filled with trucks and building things. I can see that the hotel curves around like a horseshoe."

"Very good. What else?"

"I don't know." She started to cry. "Just get me out of here. I want to go home," she said between sobs.

"We're going to come for you, I promise."

"I have to go. If they find me with a phone they'll hurt me. I have to go. Help me." She terminated the call.

Everyone sat in silence for a moment watching Kurtz, who looked stunned.

"It was her. No doubt," he said quietly.

"And we're going to get her back, comrade." Aleks grasped him by the shoulder.

Bishop stood up. "OK, team, Chua's going to want to brief us in the next couple of minutes. Saneh, can you give Kenta a call and find out where he is and when he can get back? Aleks, you set up the laptop and open a comms line to the Bunker." He walked across to where Kurtz was sitting on the crate. "You did well, mate. This time we're going to get her back."

Kurtz ran a hand over his face and nodded. "Let's just focus on the mission."

"We're hooked into the Bunker," Aleks announced from behind the laptop.

"Kenta's thirty minutes out," Saneh confirmed as she sat next to Aleks.

"Roger, let's hear what the Bunker's got to say."

They all focused their attention on the screen.

"Hello, guys." Chua's face popped up onscreen. "Hey, great work, Kurtz. You kept her on the line long enough for us to get a fix and you also extracted some good detail that we've used to confirm the location."

"So you know where she is?" Kurtz could not hide the excitement in his voice.

"Yes," Chua responded. "Flash pulled a 100-meter bubble off the satellite and our work on the description narrowed it down to this location west of Himeji." Chua's face was replaced with a satellite image.

Bishop whistled appreciatively; he had no idea how PRIMAL's intel chief managed to access NSA resources.

"It's exactly how Karla describes it," said Chua. "A curved building under construction. It's located in a new development zone, listed as an entertainment complex being built by a large conglomerate. We're doing a deep dive to see if there are any links to the Mori-Kai."

"Is it a hotel or a casino or something?" Saneh asked.

"I did a quick search on the net and I found this."

The map was replaced with a flyer showing a dazzling seven-story, crescent-shaped casino complex.

"It's being plugged as a top-dollar destination that places particular emphasis on being able to satisfy any desire."

"Sick fucks are building their own rape hotel," said Bishop. "Can you imagine what's going to go on in there?"

"Flash is hacking the construction company's server at the moment. I should have a full set of floor plans within the hour," said Chua.

"Good stuff. What about the big question: Is this a trap?" asked Bishop.

"Stress levels in Karla's voice could indicate she was lying or it could simply be a result of her kidnapping."

"Well," said Kurtz, "there's one thing she wasn't lying about. She wants us to get her out."

"No doubt," agreed Bishop. "But that doesn't mean Masateru isn't using her to lure us into a trap. Chua, what about the phone, does it tell us anything?"

"Not really, based off its data it could well be a construction worker's."

"Why are we even discussing this?" Kurtz demanded. "We know where she is. Let's go and get her."

"I'm not going to let us blunder into a trap," Bishop snapped.

"But what if it's not a trap? By the time we make a decision they'll have moved her again."

"He's right," Chua added. "If this isn't a trap and they find out she's made a call, they'll definitely move her."

"Have you run this past Vance?" Bishop asked.

"I'm here, Bish." Vance's face appeared onscreen. He looked haggard, the result of pulling some long shifts. "You've got my approval for a recovery op but I don't want you to take any unnecessary risks. The priority is taking down Mori-Kai and generating more intel, got it?"

"Loud and clear, boss." Bishop gave Kurtz a pointed look.

"Good luck." The screen went dead.

"You heard him, team. We need to come up with a rock-solid plan that mitigates the risk of this being a trap."

"I've got the quadcopter for the recon," said Kurtz, nodding toward the boxes stacked in the corner of the room.

"That's a bloody good start," said Bishop. "Let's take a closer look at this casino. You know what Vance always says . . ."

CHAPTER 75

MORI-KAI CASINO CONSTRUCTION SITE, HIMEJI

"How many men do we now have here?" Masateru asked Ryu as he strode into the casino's security center. His Kissaki commander was using the underground facility as a command post. The hardened, high-tech hub would one day scrutinize gamblers and spy on the hotel rooms, but today it allowed them to observe all the approaches to the casino. Black-clad Kissaki monitored the screens, displaying visuals from the CCTV cameras, and used radios to stay in contact with the gang leaders.

"Ten Kissaki, fifty Koreans, and forty Chinese."

"A formidable force." Masateru smiled and ran his fingers through his hair.

"If we can keep them from killing each other."

"Leave that to me. How have you divided their responsibilities?"

"They're operating in teams of ten. Each team has been given a level or a sector of responsibility."

"And the Kissaki?"

"I have five here with me. The rest are located off-site, our reserve." The radio on Ryu's belt squawked and he raised it to his ear. "The gang bosses are ready for you. They're gathered in the ground-floor dining area along with the weapons you requested."

"Let's go." Masateru led, heading toward the elevator. Ryu and two Kissaki, wearing black body armor and wielding G36 assault rifles, followed close behind.

The restaurant floor was unfurnished. The kitchens were operational but the dining areas were still bare concrete. The Chinese and the Koreans had separated into two groups in the middle of a large open space. The gang leaders eyeballed each other suspiciously, guns held tightly. Both groups favored short hair and heavily tattooed bodies. They had all been issued gray coveralls with high-visibility vests.

Silence filled the room as the occupants became aware of Masateru's presence. He stood watching them for a few seconds before speaking. "On behalf of the *oyabun*, I thank you all for being here."

"So why are we here?" one of the Koreans asked, his face fixed in a permanent scowl.

"Because you have all sworn loyalty to the Mori-Kai and with that comes certain responsibilities."

"You want us to kill someone?" This time it was one of the Triad bosses who spoke. Since the Yamaguchi-gumi *oyabun* had gone into hiding, the Chinese had been quick to switch allegiances.

"That's very astute. It is exactly why you have been brought here. The Yamaguchi-gumi, our exalted brothers, have brought a team of Western mercenaries into Japan to destroy the Mori-Kai." His eyes glanced around the room. "To destroy the brotherhood that you are now a part of."

"I say let them come." A particularly savage-looking Korean stared directly at Masateru with unblinking eyes. "We killed the Yamaguchi dogs; we can easily kill their Western slaves."

Masateru met his gaze. "And you are to be commended for your attack on the Yamaguchi. Although you missed the *oyabun*, it was still a success. But these men are different, they are a formidable enemy, and we must work together to destroy them."

"What's in this for us?" one of the Chinese asked quietly.

"Eternal gratitude," Masateru said. "But if you need additional motivation I will give you a million yen for every Westerner you kill. Other, even more profitable arrangements have also been made with your bosses."

The mention of a reward set tongues wagging and it took a few seconds for the posse of hardened gangsters to return their attention back to the *waka-gashira*.

"If you succeed in destroying our enemies, the benefit for all will be substantial. If you fail, then all loyalties will be questioned. But do not be disheartened. My good friend Ryu has equipment you'll need."

Ryu and his two Kissaki walked through the throng of gangsters toward the plastic cases stacked against a wall. There were ten of them. Ryu selected one. The two men picked it up by its straps and brought it across to Masateru. They placed it on the concrete and unclipped the fasteners.

"The Kissaki have already trained you in these weapons. They are yours to use in killing our enemies." Masateru flipped up the lid. Inside lay a PKM machine gun and a 66mm rocket launcher.

✮✮✮

The quadcopter was a drone. Four tiny electric engines kept it aloft for periods of up to twenty minutes. Plenty of time for it to zip around the construction site and capture every detail with its cameras. High above the construction site it hung in the air, focusing on a pair of workmen. Then with the faintest whir it darted sideways and down to get a better horizontal shot into the bare upper levels.

"Careful, Kurtz, keep that thing out of visual and audible range." Bishop was sitting alongside the German as he piloted the tiny aircraft.

"Pfft. It's so small and silent I could fly it inside and no one would notice." The screen in front of him showed the location of the drone on a Google Earth–style map. Alongside it another screen, split into quarters, displayed each of the feeds from the drone's cameras.

The entire team had relocated to a small house among rice paddies a few miles from the Mori-Kai casino. Kenta had found the house on a real-estate site; it had been on the market for months and the agent had been nice enough to confirm it was currently unoccupied. It had taken Kurtz a few seconds to pick the lock on the double garage and now their borrowed Yamaguchi Mercedes and white PRIMAL van were parked inside. There was an inspection scheduled for the following Monday but by then they would be long gone.

Bishop gave Kurtz a slap on the shoulder and moved across the living room to check on another computer.

Kenta's eyes were fixed on the laptop's screen. "This is amazing. One minute it's blank and now we have a full picture of the casino." A 3-D model of the building site was displayed as the program collected images from the drone's cameras and assembled them into an accurate schematic. It had even started to exploit shots that reached inside to build up the internal floor plan.

"Pretty cool, hey." Bishop checked to see that the model was complete. "A great thing about it is once we've got a full scan we can input it into this machine here." He took a USB stick from the laptop and walked across to the dining room table. Perched on it was what looked like a robotic arm hanging from a frame the size of a microwave oven. Bishop plugged the USB into a small touch screen attached to the side of the device.

"What does it do?" Kenta asked.

"It's a 3-D printer. It makes things." Bishop touched the screen and the little robotic arm sprang to life. A burning smell filled the air as it started building. "I'm going to check on Saneh. I'll be back in a few minutes; by then it should be done."

Saneh was in one of the bedrooms hunched over her laptop, streaming the drone feed from their Wi-Fi network. She was wearing a pair of dark-framed glasses.

"You look good in those." Bishop placed a hand on her shoulder. "How are we looking?"

"Not so good." She shrugged out from under his hand. "The place is crawling with workers."

Bishop dropped his hand to his side and leaned in to see the screen. "It's a big project."

"It is, but the problem is no one's doing any real construction work. They're all smoking, talking, or moving things from one place to another."

The image on Saneh's screen was a still frame taken from the drone feed.

"What about weapons?"

"Kurtz got this a few minutes ago."

The new image was a grainy shot through a missing section of windows on the third floor of the casino. It showed four armed men; one of them was carrying what looked like a PKM machine gun.

"These guys are packing some serious heat."

"Not only that." Saneh brought up a wider image. "I ran an optics detection filter over it." The image showed no less than seven points of reflection. "The casino's CCTV network has been installed; we can safely assume it's up and running."

"They're more than ready for us."

Saneh nodded. "There's no way we can hit this with just five people."

"Even with more Yamaguchi support?"

"These people would massacre the Yamaguchi."

"Yeah, they proved that at the *oyabun*'s house. Let me think about this."

Bishop walked back to where Kenta was watching the 3-D printer. Aleks had joined him from where he had been working in the garage. "It's building the casino," said the Russian.

Kenta nodded. "That's amazing."

Bishop watched the printer's robot arm as it danced across the plastic model. It was constructing level by level, racing back and forth to add minute details.

"How the hell are we going to deal with this?" Bishop said to himself as he watched the building taking shape. Even in its miniature form the casino looked like a formidable objective. Combined with heavily armed guards and a high-tech security system, it would be like assaulting Fort Knox.

"Maybe we could set up some sort of distraction? Even start a fire or hijack an ambulance?" suggested Aleks.

"Whatever we do, we're going to need help."

"I have an idea," Kenta said and the other two looked at him. "Once, when I was much younger, a more powerful gang kidnapped my *waka-gashira*'s girl while I was looking after her. He told me if I did not get her back he would take my life."

"How did you get her back?" Bishop asked.

Kenta sat back from the laptop, stretched, and smiled. "Like you said, with help. I paid the police to do it."

CHAPTER 76

NATIONAL POLICE AGENCY HEADQUARTERS, TOKYO

"Please give me your attention." Baiko stood at the front of a room filled with his colleagues. "The latest information from my source indicates that a Yakuza syndicate in Himeji is using a construction site as a distribution node for weapons."

"Are these the same Yakuza responsible for the attacks on the Yamaguchi-gumi?" asked one of the other members of the Organized Crime Department.

"I think so. All of the incidents around Kobe and Himeji in the last forty-eight hours have been linked to them. We've got reports that they're an obscure clan that call themselves the Mori-Kai."

"What sort of weapons do they have?" another of the team asked.

Baiko fished a USB out of his pocket and handed it to the officer manning the room's computer terminal. He waited for the image to be displayed onscreen. "I'm no expert but that looks to me like some kind of machine gun." Bishop had e-mailed him the picture, taken only a few hours earlier by the quadcopter drone. It clearly showed a man carrying a PKM and two others with AK assault rifles.

The room filled with noise as the task force members started talking among themselves.

"That's a goddamn cannon," said one officer.

"We've never seen anything like this before," added another.

"Let's keep the noise down!" The department head, an overweight, middle-aged police officer wearing a brown suit, rose out
of his chair and stood at the front of the room. "Thank you,
Inspector Baiko, for that latest update. Just so you are all aware, the
commissioner general himself is watching this very closely. He has
given us additional resources to ensure that this emerging Yakuza
threat is dealt with decisively."

Once again the room filled with the buzz of conversation.

"In the last three days we have had a number of successes
thanks to Inspector Baiko and his work. His source is very well
placed and continues to provide him with actionable intelligence.
Because of this I am sending him to Osaka to coordinate with Zero
Company. They will be responding to this latest threat."

Zero Company was the Special Assault Team responsible for
the region. Based out of Osaka's Kansai International Airport, it was
the closest tactical unit to Himeji.

"We need to keep up the good work you've been doing with the
other gangs, in particular the Yamaguchi subclans. Now that they've
lost a big chunk of their leadership we can expect infighting."

"Sir, are we coordinating a response across all regions?" asked
one of the officers.

"No, this is a highly classified operation. The only two elements
approved to know about it are us and Zero Company. If I get wind
that anyone is talking to other units, agencies, or press they'll be
transferred on the spot. Is that clear?"

"Yes, sir," the room responded in unison.

"That is all." He gestured to Baiko to follow as he left the room.
Behind them it once again exploded into a verbal typhoon.

In the hallway the department head continued. "This source of
yours has proven to be very knowledgeable, Baiko. He must be very
well placed in this new gang. What did you say they were called?"

"The Mori-Kai, sir."

"Interesting, not a clan that I'm familiar with."

"They have grown strength from remaining hidden."

"And now they are at war with the Yamaguchi-gumi?"

Baiko nodded. "They've already killed most of their senior leaders. It is only a matter of time before the Yamaguchi are finished and these Mori-Kai turn their guns elsewhere."

"Then we must see to it that they are destroyed. The helicopter will fly you immediately to Osaka, where you will brief the Zero Company commander. He is expecting you before midday."

"Yes, sir." Baiko shook hands with his supervisor and started walking toward his office.

"Oh, and Baiko, be careful. These people always have powerful friends."

★★★

Three hours later Bishop received an update from Baiko. He hung up his phone and walked back into the room. "Heads up, team, the SAT has moved into their holding area."

Kurtz, Kenta, and Saneh checked their screens. Saneh had moved in and set up on the living room table next to Kurtz's UAV control station. Kenta also had a laptop on the table, a digital radio interface allowing him to monitor the police radio frequency. Aleks was the only one not perched behind a laptop; he was busy prepping their equipment.

"Police are moving a cordon in." Kurtz piloted his drone around the perimeter of the casino.

"SAT or general duties?" Bishop asked.

"General duties. They're a long way out, so no danger of the guys inside seeing them just yet."

"Oh, they'll know they're there," said Bishop. "Kenta, we got anything on the police scanners yet?"

"Five cars have been ordered to move to the area and establish a cordon."

"Roger, we can expect the SAT to be rolling in soon."

Everything was going according to plan. Bishop walked across to where Aleks was spray-painting a plastic helmet he had manufactured on the 3-D printer.

"We got everything we need?"

"Close enough. We have blue coveralls, I'm printing two helmets, and I have modified two spare sets of armor. We don't have MP5s, so you just have to use the Tavors." Aleks had laid down two outfits on the ground. The two spare sets of armor had POLICE stenciled on the back. "The only thing we don't have are the visors." Aleks picked up the helmet he was painting. "Oh, and make sure you don't stop a bullet with your head: This is plastic, not Kevlar."

"The overall effect is pretty good, mate. You've done well. Unless we walk right up to one of the SAT guys they're not going to know we're fakes."

"At least the police snipers will not shoot you, *da*." Aleks placed the helmet back on the bench. "Boss, there is something I wanted to ask you."

"What is it?"

"I thought maybe it would be a good idea to take Kurtz with you instead of Saneh." Bishop glanced over to where the German was piloting his drone.

"Why is that?"

"I just think it might be good for him. Make him feel less helpless."

"Did he put you up to this?"

Aleks shook his head.

"You're a good friend, but the reason I can't use Kurtz is because he's so tall. Both you and Kurtz are far too big. Saneh and I are the only ones who can pass for SAT operators."

"I did not think of that."

"If we just wanted to kick the door in and kill everyone, you and Kurtz would be running point. This is more discreet; the idea is to slip in, grab Karla, slot Masateru, and get out before anyone's the wiser."

The mobile phone in Bishop's pocket vibrated and he pulled it out. "I promise I'll look after your buddy. Let's just get through this next phase."

Aleks nodded and returned to spray-painting the helmet.

Bishop read the text message. "Listen up team, the SAT ground force is rolling. ETA ten minutes. Kurtz, let's take that drone a little higher."

"Negative, I'm bingo on power. I'm bringing her home for a battery change."

"Ack . . . All right, well, do a confirmatory pass of the overwatch location on the way back. Saneh, have you got any updates for us?"

She broke her concentration and looked up from her screen. "I think I've narrowed down Karla's location."

Bishop looked over her shoulder. "Show me."

"I overlaid the coordinates that HQ sent us. That gave me a rough idea on the broad area. Then I checked the imagery that Kurtz captured off the UAV. It looks as if only parts of the first three levels of the building are finished. The ground and first floor are going to be the reception, casino, etcetera. That leaves this small part of the second floor—hotel rooms—that appears to be completed. So according to Flash's coordinates, she's probably locked up in this small area here."

"How confident are you that this is the location?"

"About ninety percent."

"Right. With any luck, Masateru will be there as well. Can you map out the best route for us to drop off the van, infiltrate through the fence, and get into her assessed location? And try to avoid as many of the cameras as possible."

"I'll see what I can do."

Bishop looked up from the terminal to see Kurtz making for the back door with a battery pack in hand. At the same time Kenta waved him over. "Bishop, we've got a lot of traffic now. The local police are requesting confirmation that they are to hand over to the SAT."

"What's the tone? Are they happy about it?"

The Yakuza shook his head. "No, they are very unhappy."

"That's because they're as corrupt as politicians. So far so good. Let's just hope this doesn't turn into a turf war."

Kurtz strode back into the house and dropped in behind his terminal. "Quadcopter is recharged."

"Let's go in high; we've got SAT on the ground now and I don't want to risk your bird being spotted," said Bishop as he watched the full-motion video feeds on the screens.

"*Ja.*" Kurtz made some inputs on a keyboard and after a few seconds the computer indicated that the drone was flying at two thousand feet as it transited toward the target area. Kurtz slewed the cameras forward and as the little craft approached, they saw a huge black bus parked one block back from the construction site.

"That's their C2 bus." Bishop pointed at the screen. Beside the command bus, and scattered along key intersections, regular police cars blocked the road.

Closer in they saw a black armored vehicle and half a dozen four-wheel drives clustered around the gate to the construction yard.

"There's a lot of them," said Kurtz.

Black-clad SAT operators were swarming around the locked entrance to the construction site.

Bishop looked around at his team. "OK, is everyone good with the plan?"

They all nodded.

"Kenta, what happens if the SAT doesn't commit?"

"I'm going to use the phone to help change their mind."

"Good. Saneh and I are going to gear up. Aleks, is everything ready?"

"It is all in the van, boss. We just need to grab Kenta's laptop and we're ready to roll."

Bishop took a deep breath. "Let's do this."

CHAPTER 77

MORI-KAI CASINO CONSTRUCTION SITE, HIMEJI

"There are heavily armed police all around us now, *waka-gashira*." Ryu and his team were monitoring both the police radio band and their CCTV network. The initial cordon by the general duties police had been a surprise but not a worry. The deployment of the SAT was another matter altogether.

"That doesn't make any sense. We own the police." Masateru drummed his fingers against the desk he was sitting at. "There's no need for concern," he said, more for himself than anyone else. "But we'll need the police dealt with before the *gaijin* would dare attack. Hideaki, phone." His bodyguard handed him one of a number of cell phones he carried.

Masateru dialed a number and waited for the call to connect. "I need to talk to the boss. There's a problem."

There was a short wait.

"What is the problem?" the *oyabun* asked abruptly.

"The police, they've surrounded the casino."

"That's not possible."

"I am looking at them right now. The place is crawling with them, including a SWAT team."

There was a pause on the other end of the call. "Don't worry, I will have our man deal with it."

"Many thanks." Masateru handed the phone back.

"What about the police?" Ryu asked.

"They'll withdraw. Just make sure none of your animals start something."

As Masateru left the command post with Hideaki in tow he almost ran into two of the Chinese gang leaders. "Why are the police here?" one of them demanded in Japanese.

"They're just leaving," Masateru barked in response.

"Why? We have plenty of firepower—we should fucking kill the dogs and show them who runs this town."

"They already belong to the Mori-Kai. Keep your cock out of your hand and wait until the real enemy appears."

The Triad leader grinned and Masateru and his bodyguard continued down the concrete corridor to the elevator.

They headed to the second floor's section of completed hotel rooms. A Kissaki operator was guarding the door to Karla's room. Masateru turned to Hideaki. "I'm going to get some rest. You are to stay here and not wake me unless it is an emergency."

His bodyguard nodded, "*Hai.*"

Masateru knocked softly on the door.

"Come in."

Karla got up from the bed where she had been sleeping. "What is it?" she asked groggily.

He glanced at the bottle of pills by the bed. "I want you to make sure you are ready to go at any time."

She gave him a confused look. "Is something wrong?"

Masateru reached out and grabbed her by the waist. He slipped an arm around her and pulled her close, savoring the feeling of her breasts against his chest.

She stiffened but began to relax as he held her more tightly.

"Nothing is wrong." He kissed her as he slid his hand up underneath her sweater and unclipped her bra.

★★★

"Sir, the regional director is on the phone." The black-clad Japanese Special Assault Team officer handed his superior a telephone handset.

The phone was part of a complex communications suite inside the SAT mobile command post. The heavily armored black bus was parked in a lot a block from the casino.

"What does he want?"

"I don't know, sir, he asked for you by name."

The commander took the handset. "Hello."

"Inspector Hyuman, it's Superintendent Supervisor Tanaka. I understand you are undertaking an operation in my jurisdiction."

"That is correct, sir. It has been sanctioned by the commissioner general and the head of the Organized Crime Department."

"And yet I know nothing about it."

"That is something for you to discuss with them."

"Listen to me, Inspector, you are compromising a police investigation, and you are to end your mission now. Take your men and return to Osaka."

"With all due respect, sir, I am taking my orders direct from Tokyo for this mission."

"Stand down. I will talk with the commissioner."

"Sir, as I said—"

"Don't do something you will regret, Inspector. Stand your men down immediately." The phone went dead as the director hung up.

The SAT commander handed the telephone back. "Something's not right here."

"What do you mean, sir?"

"Why is the regional director being kept out of the loop?" Hyuman knew Tanaka by reputation; he was a highly influential commander responsible for the entire regional police bureau that included Kobe, Himeji, and Osaka. Although technically the Osaka-based SAT was working within Tanaka's jurisdiction for this operation, it was authorized direct from Tokyo. He pondered the issue for a moment, then turned his attention to the rudimentary map of the casino facility that had been drawn on a whiteboard. "Is the sniper section in place?"

"Yes, sir. We have three pairs covering the entire frontage of the facility."

"Good, what about the assault teams?"

"Team Alpha and Bravo are in place with their vehicles here and here." He indicated two locations on the map.

"What additional intelligence do we have?"

"Technical section is still setting up. Once they are up and running we will be able to scan for all communications in the area."

"Good, I think we might sit tight for the time being and let the senior hierarchy sort out exactly what's going on. If they can't come to a decision we're pulling out."

The door to the command bus opened and Baiko walked up the stairs.

"Maybe you can shed some light on the situation," Hyuman said.

"What do you need to know?" Baiko took up a position next to the door. He had briefed the SAT in Osaka and driven down with the commander.

"How about we start with why the regional director is out of the loop on this. I just got off the phone with him and he's pissed."

"I'm afraid that's well above my pay grade. All I know is the operation was compartmentalized."

"You think the local cops are corrupt?"

"Not for me to say, but the Mori-Kai have a lot of money to throw around."

"Well, so far I've seen nothing to suggest that any of your intel is good. This place looks dead."

"They're in there," Baiko replied. "I can guarantee that."

"Good for them, but as long as the hierarchy can't sort themselves out, my men are going nowhere. We'll sit tight for the next thirty minutes, but if nothing happens I'm going to draw back to the holding area and hand over to the local guys."

☆☆☆

Kenta parked the van in front of the shabby-looking apartment block. Chua had highlighted it in his intelligence package as having excellent observation onto the casino. The quadcopter had identified a number of apartments on the top floor that appeared unoccupied.

"You guys good to go?" asked Bishop as Kenta moved into the back of the van.

Aleks and Kurtz were dressed in their standard rig, heavy-duty cargo pants and long-sleeved shirts. They carried large wheeled equipment bags and had day bags slung over their shoulders. Kenta was wearing a similar outfit and was carrying two heavy-duty Pelican cases. He wore a radio scanner on his belt that was wired to an earpiece.

"We're ready," said Aleks.

"OK, good luck. Saneh and I will stay here until you give us word."

The overwatch team jumped out of the back of the van and carried their equipment across to the building. The entrance was in disrepair, paint peeling from the ceiling, glass filthy, and the electronic security system decrepit.

"That makes life easier," said Kurtz as he pushed open the front door and led the team into the foyer.

They waited patiently for the elevator to arrive. When it did, the doors opened with a noise that sounded like a dying cow.

"You trust this thing?" asked Aleks.

"Get in the elevator, you big baby," said Kurtz. "In Russia this would be five stars."

They entered the elevator and selected the top floor.

"You hearing anything interesting on the scanner, Kenta?" Aleks asked.

"No," the Yamaguchi shook his head. "Nobody wants to make a move."

"Well, that's about to change."

They stepped out of the elevator into a long corridor of doors. Judging by the distance between them, the dwellings were shoebox-size.

They counted the room numbers and halfway along the corridor Kenta banged on a door. As expected, there was no answer. He tried again with the same result.

It took Kurtz a few seconds to pick the lock and they all filed in, dead-bolting the door behind them. It was a tiny, furnished apartment; a single bedroom doubled as a living area and compact bathroom-cum-laundry. It had a futon pressed up against the wall and a small table and two chairs crammed in the corner.

Kurtz frowned as he surveyed the room. His previous recon using the quadcopter had identified the overwatch position as being unoccupied, no furniture. They had entered the wrong apartment.

All three looked at each other. It was obvious someone lived here. Aleks checked the bathroom. "I think the owner must be at work, *da*."

Kenta already had one of his cases open and the loaded KRISS submachine gun in hand. He shrugged. "If he comes home early, I will convince him to help us."

"This will do," Kurtz said. "We'll only be here for an hour." He opened the curtains to reveal the view. From their fifteenth-floor vantage point they had an uninterrupted view of the back of the casino. They could actually see through the entire unfinished structure. He slid open the window but left the insect screen in place.

"Keep the lights off," said Kurtz. "If we keep it dark in here they won't be able to see us." It was just after midday and the sun outside was shining brightly.

Aleks dragged the dining table away from the wall and positioned it a few feet back from the window. He pulled a blanket from the futon and draped it over the wood before positioning two chairs behind the table, facing the windows.

Meanwhile Kurtz opened Kenta's cases and plugged the laptop into the scanner array. Within thirty seconds he had the system set up and Kenta was sitting on one of the empty cases monitoring all of the police channels through his communications headset. The Yamaguchi's KRISS submachine gun lay beside him, loaded and ready for any unwanted visitors.

Aleks opened their gear bags and started assembling the two sniper rifles on the table. Kurtz's Windrunner .408 was ready first, the heavy sniper rifle set on its bipod legs pointing toward the window. With the suppressor screwed on, the long barrel almost touched the flyscreen. It took him a few more seconds to snap his semiautomatic G28 together and place it next to the heavier weapon. Then he set up a tablet computer between the two rifles; on its screen was an overhead view of their position and the casino. Ranges were marked on the image, along with the location of CCTV cameras. On the right-hand side of Kurtz's weapon he set up another tablet, this one showing the location of the quadcopter drone. It was currently sitting behind their previous location, ready to launch on command.

The PRIMAL operatives donned their tactical vests and headsets, and laid their ammunition out on the blanket next to their weapons. Kurtz sat behind his sniper rifle, lifted the scope to his eye, and started scanning the building. Within seconds he had identified potential targets, armed gunmen on almost every level of the building.

"Bishop, this is Kurtz. Overwatch is established. I confirm, overwatch is established," Kurtz broadcast over his iPRIMAL.

"Roger, we are ready," Bishop's voice came through over their communications network. "Kenta, what's happening on the police net?"

"It sounds like the SAT is waiting; there is talk they might pull back."

Kurtz focused on looking through the upper levels of the building and down to the front gate. He could see the armored vehicle and black-clad SAT. "I have observation on the front gate. There's no sign of movement from the police."

"Damn, looks like we might have to encourage them," said Bishop. "OK, let's put the contingency plan in motion."

"No problem." Kenta pulled out the mobile phone Bishop had given him and dialed the police emergency line.

Simultaneously Aleks removed the suppressor from his G28 and leveled his crosshairs on the SAT armored car.

★★★

"Sir," one of the SAT officers got Inspector Hyuman's attention. "The sniper teams have reported men armed with military-style weapons."

"How many?"

"Less than five so far, all inside the casino complex."

Hyuman turned to Baiko. "So, there may be some substance to your intelligence after all. Do you have any more updates from your source?"

Baiko shook his head. "As far as I'm aware they're stockpiling the weapons for their war with the Yamaguchi-gumi. My contact will report if he finds out more."

"Sir," the SAT officer interrupted again. "I've got someone on the line who wants to talk to you from inside the casino. He's been put through from the one-ten number."

"Your man?" the inspector asked Baiko.

The investigator shook his head.

"Put it over the speaker." Hyuman reached out for the man's headset.

"This is the SAT commander, who am I talking to?"

"Names are of no concern, Commander. What is of concern is that you are sticking your nose in where it does not belong. No one needs to get hurt, but your people need to leave now."

"Here's the thing. You're in there with some serious weaponry, weapons I'm not going to allow you to keep. Now I might consider letting you leave if your men place all of their guns in front of the building and walk out with their hands on their heads."

"You and I both know that's not going to happen. This is Yakuza business and you have no place being here. It's in the best interest of your men and your career to leave now."

The line went dead.

Hyuman's mouth hung open for a long moment. "The arrogant fuck!" he growled at last.

Almost on cue, gunshots sounded from the direction of the casino. "Shots fired! Shots fired!" announced one of the officers. "Assault team Alpha is taking fire."

"Anyone injured?"

"Negative, the armored vehicle has been hit by multiple shots."

"Those fucking Yakuza punks are trying to scare us off! Alert the Air Team, bring their notice to move down to two minutes. I want them turning and burning. Give the sniper section authority to engage anyone displaying hostile intent."

"Yes, sir." One of the officers started issuing the orders over the radio.

"And tell Alpha team to push forward. I want to know what's going on in there."

CHAPTER 78

"Situation report," Bishop broadcast.

He and Saneh had left the van and were moving toward the casino's perimeter fence, dressed in their makeshift SAT outfits, complete with black Nomex hoods and fake helmets. Behind the apartment block they had slipped into an irrigation ditch and were making their way between two rice paddies.

"Kenta made the call and we engaged the armored car," Aleks replied.

"Have they taken the bait?" Bishop asked.

"It looks like it," Kurtz said.

Kurtz had launched the drone once Kenta had made the call. The tiny craft was hovering high above the location, its powerful sensors focused on the lead SAT team.

Bishop reached the fence line at the outskirts of the casino and took cover in a ditch. He glanced at the drone feed displayed on his iPRIMAL. The ten-man police section was slowly shuffling forward behind a Komatsu light-armored vehicle. The wedge-shaped vehicle carried four men, including a gunner armed with a light machine gun. Black-clad officers armed with MP5 submachine guns and wielding ballistic shields marched behind the vehicle. They resembled Roman legionnaires advancing into battle.

Saneh slid in next to him. "What the hell are they doing?" She used the cuff of her jumpsuit to wipe the sweat from her face.

"An old technique known as recon by force."

"What? Are they trying to get shot at?"

"Yep, I think that's exactly what the plan is."

★★★

"Alpha team, do you have anything to report?"

"Not yet. Moving forward. No more shots fired." The Alpha team leader spoke into his radio from where he was crouched behind the SAT armored vehicle.

"Acknowledged, proceed with caution."

The armored vehicle started rolling forward again. The team leader and his men walked behind it. Every second man was carrying a heavy ballistic shield. They angled them outward to protect from any potential threat. Inside the phalanx of armor, a dog handler and his attack dog walked alongside the team leader.

The dog barked, pulling on its harness.

Automatic fire shattered the silence and bullets slammed into the armored vehicle. The gunner in the turret responded instinctively, wheeling his weapon toward the threat. The rattle of his M249 added to the chaos as he sent bursts of fire into the casino.

The upper levels of the building exploded into a frenzy of flashes. Gunfire rained down on Alpha team as they hunkered behind the armored vehicle.

"We're taking heavy fire!" screamed the team leader. "We need immediate support."

Rounds smashed into ballistic shields, tearing them from gloved hands. Bullets ricocheted off the armored hull of the Komatsu LAV.

"BACK UP! BACK UP!" the team leader screamed into his mike. The LAV started reversing at a walking pace. Alpha team's officers fired their weapons in the direction of the casino, attempting to disrupt the onslaught. SAT sniper pairs engaged in support as the initial onslaught died down to sporadic gunfire.

A bullet hit one of Alpha's officers in the arm, and he grunted in pain. One of his colleagues grabbed him as another wrenched open one of the heavy side doors of their armored vehicle. The wounded man was bundled inside as the other officers kept up the suppressing fire.

From the fifth level of the casino came a puff of smoke. The 66mm rocket screamed past the armored vehicle and slammed into a container.

"We're taking rocket fire," the team leader yelled. "Sniper section, we need cover."

"We're engaging multiple targets," the sniper section leader confirmed. "Heavy weapons are the priority."

"Alpha, this is the commander." Inspector Hyuman's voice came through over the radios. "I have authorized air assault, ETA eight minutes."

Another rocket screamed down from the upper levels of the casino. This time it hit the sloped hood of the LAV. There was an almighty bang and the rocket's shaped charge blasted a hole straight through the engine block.

"I've lost all mobility," the team leader reported. "We're going to be lucky to be alive eight minutes from now."

★★★

"Bishop, the armored car has been mobility-killed. That team is not going to last long. Request permission to engage hostiles."

"Engagement authorized," Bishop replied. "When you get a chance I need you to take down those cameras in front of us."

Bishop and Saneh were lying in the ditch a few feet short of the fence, waiting for the best opportunity to infiltrate the building site. From their position they could hear the intense gunfight raging on the other side of the casino.

"Acknowledged," Aleks replied.

On the top levels of the casino the Mori-Kai's foot soldiers were unleashing everything they had at the police below. PKM and AK fire rained down on the men hunkered below, punctuated occasionally by the blast from a high-explosive rocket. The gunfight was savage and one-sided. The police dog bolted, running away from the maelstrom of noise and violence. Gangsters fired at the animal, bullets lashing the dirt around it, but it escaped.

Kurtz's first round hit one of the gunners. The Korean was using a spool of cable to prop up his machine gun. The heavy .408 round hit him between the shoulder blades, tearing through his spine like wet paper. He toppled forward and fell seven stories. By the time he had hit the ground, Kurtz had worked the action of his sniper rifle and killed another gunman.

Aleks fired rapidly aimed shots through his lighter G28, blowing CCTV cameras off the side of the building. "All clear," he reported a moment later and continued to monitor the side of the building overlooking Bishop and Saneh's approach. He need not have worried; the Mori-Kai's men were focused on the police on the other side.

"We're on!" Bishop hooked a charge onto the wire fence in front of him.

"Four seconds!" he announced as he slid back into the ditch with Saneh.

The explosion wasn't loud enough to block the sound of the gunfight but it split the chain-link fence from top to bottom.

Kurtz's voice came through his earpiece. "Bishop, police snipers have engaged from the north and we've successfully neutralized any Mori-Kai capable of influencing your approach. The roof is now free of hostile elements. Switching fire to lower levels."

"Roger, how are the cops faring?"

"Another team has pushed up and they're extracting their wounded."

"OK, we're moving now."

Saneh had already sprinted through the fence, making a beeline for the fire exit closest to them. Bishop caught up, slapped a charge on the door, and joined her off to the side.

The blast threw the heavy door into an internal stairwell and Saneh charged in, the Tavor tucked into her shoulder.

"We've made entry," Bishop reported.

Saneh consulted her iPRIMAL to locate Karla's anticipated location on the digital map. "We need to head upstairs."

CHAPTER 79

"Do we know who started this shitstorm?" Ryu was pacing the casino security center like a caged animal.

"No, all of the teams are denying firing the first shot," one of the Kissaki replied.

"Of course they would. Because they know once I find out who it was, they're dead."

"Sir, we've lost three of our cameras covering the rear of the facility," another Kissaki reported. "We've also had a breach of one of the rear fire exits."

"The foreigners or SAT?" Ryu left his own terminal.

"I'll bring up an internal shot from the stairwell."

Ryu stood behind him as the operator displayed the camera feed on his screen. Two figures in SAT uniforms climbed the stairs toward the cameras. A weapon pointed directly at the screen and then it went blank. Ryu took his radio from his hip.

"Echo Two this is Echo Zero, we've got SAT in the central stairwell. Inform the *waka-gashira* and escort him and the girl to the command center via the eastern elevators."

"Echo Zero, this is Echo Two, acknowledged," Hideaki replied from outside of Karla's room.

"Sir!" interrupted the Kissaki who had reported the loss of the cameras. "One of the teams has reported helicopters approaching."

"Warn the gangs; ensure they defend the rooftop."

"And what about us?"

"Be prepared to extract once the *waka-gashira* arrives. I'll alert the reserve team. The mission here is over."

★★★

"They know we're here." Bishop had shot the CCTV camera from its wall mount.

"That was always going to happen," Saneh said curtly. "Keep moving, we need to be on the next floor."

Bishop moved up the staircase. "You've been a real joy to work with this time around."

"Just shut up and keep moving, we're here to do a job."

"Right, recover Kurtz's girlfriend."

"You can be such a callous bastard."

"Job'll do that to you."

They reached the fire exit for the second level. Bishop eased the door open a crack and peered into the corridor. "All clear." The corridor was bare concrete, awaiting the attention of the painters.

"Did you hear that?" Saneh stopped. Over the crackle of automatic fire they could just make out the dull thud of rotor blades.

"Bishop, you've got about twenty seconds until the air assault hits the roof," Kurtz reported.

Saneh consulted her iPRIMAL. "Her room should be about halfway around the corridor."

The hallway followed the horseshoe shape of the building, curving around with rooms branching off on either side. The doorways were empty, the rooms yet to be fitted out.

"Sitrep on air assault?" Bishop asked as he and Saneh moved down the corridor. The sound from the gunfire and helicopters outside was muffled but still audible.

"First birds are hovering over the top level. Snipers have effectively suppressed or killed all hostiles."

"Roger."

"Have you found Karla?" asked Kurtz.

"Negative, moving in on the rooms now."

The burst of fire caught Bishop by surprise. It narrowly missed him, ricocheting off the bare concrete walls. He fired a double tap instinctively as the shooter slipped away.

"Did you see him?" Saneh asked.

"Negative."

Bishop pushed forward, his weapon held ready. Saneh moved slightly behind him and off to one side.

Another burst of fire ricocheted down the corridor. Bishop sprinted forward, catching a glimpse of a black-clad figure. He fired again as the man disappeared around the bend.

"This is where she should be," Saneh announced as they reached a section of completed hotel rooms. One of the doors was open. "Looks like someone left in a hurry."

"Check the room, I'll cover you."

Saneh ducked into the room, reappearing a few seconds later. "Not here . . . definitely occupied by a woman, though. I can still smell the perfume."

"They're moving her." Bishop took off down the corridor.

"Aden, wait!" Saneh chased him.

He charged around the corridor just in time to see two gunmen dressed in black shepherding Karla and Masateru into an elevator. Bishop slid onto one knee, raised his Tavor, and as the red dot of the Aimpoint sight hovered over his target, squeezed the trigger.

The SLAP round took the Kissaki gunman square in the chest, plowed through his soft armor, and dropped him to the ground with a thud.

The second man, Hideaki, fired a burst at the same time. A round slapped into Bishop's armor and he toppled sideways, firing wildly as he dropped, blowing chunks out of the concrete wall.

Before Hideaki could adjust his aim Saneh fired a single shot that punched through the bridge of his nose and spread his brains across the wall.

The elevator doors shut with a thud as Bishop regained his feet. "Fuck. Where does this go?" He leaned against the wall, fighting for breath in the wake of the bullet's impact on his armor.

"I'm not sure, probably down to the parking lot. You OK?"

Bishop ignored the question and started jogging back down the corridor. "We can use the stairs. Head them off on the lower levels."

"No, wait!" Again Saneh was too late; he was already disappearing around the bend.

"SAT has secured the roof," Kurtz broadcast.

Saneh caught up with Bishop at the fire exit door to the staircase. "Aden!" He was already through the door and heading down the stairs.

At the ground-floor exit, Saneh grabbed his arm. "You get Kurtz's last update?" she hissed. "Things are about to get real hot in here and we need to go." She pulled him toward the doorway they had breached on their way in.

"We can still grab her if we get down to the lower levels."

"You listen to me, Aden! We're about to be caught between a police assault and the rest of the Mori-Kai. We've got to exfil now!"

"The plan was to recover the girl."

"Yes, but only if it was low risk. The police have this place locked down tight. If we don't get out now we're going to be in serious trouble."

Bishop knew she was right. "Aleks and Kurtz, we've failed to locate the girl. Extracting now."

"Roger, we have your exfil covered but you need to move fast," Aleks replied. "Also, just so you know, HQ was trying to raise you."

Saneh led them in a sprint out of the building. Rotor blades beat the air as they dashed for the wire fence. Reaching the safety of the ditch, they glanced up at the two helicopters hovering over the casino. Long black ropes hung underneath and lines of men were sliding down them onto the roof.

"Bishop, this is Bunker," Bishop heard over his earpiece. "We've got those floor plans."

"Bit bloody late," Bishop snorted as he lay in the ditch, lungs heaving.

"You're going to want to take a look at them. There's a tunnel that leads from the basement level out eight hundred meters to the east. It links into a warehouse."

"Is it uploaded?" Bishop asked.

"It's on your iPRIMAL."

Bishop pulled the device from his vest and pulled up the mapping screen. A GPS icon showed his location and the tunnel was marked in red. "Saneh, check this out."

"You're kidding me. They've got covert access to the casino?"

"Makes sense. They'll want to be able to move high-profile guests in and out without being seen by police surveillance."

"Obviously that's how they're going to get her out," said Saneh. "That's where we'll find Masateru and his cronies."

"Kurtz, do you have obs on that location?" Bishop asked.

"Negative, it's blocked by the right-hand side of the casino construction."

"UAV?"

"Out of power. I've ditched her near the van."

Bishop checked the map. The distance across to the warehouse was about the same as the distance back to the van; however, they would have to run along a track between paddy fields. They would be exposed to anyone on the upper levels of the casino.

"We're going to move on foot, Kurtz; can you guys make sure no one engages us from the roof?"

"Yes."

"Once we're clear pack up and meet us at the warehouse."

"Acknowledged."

"You think we can get there in time?" Saneh asked.

"Probably not." Bishop started jogging. "But we've at least got to try."

CHAPTER 80

"Rooftop secure, sir." The air assault section leader had his team assembled around the roof fire exit door. "I've got at least ten dead hostiles in my location."

"Sniper section will provide support as you assault downward," the SAT commander responded.

"Do we have any snipers located to the south, in an apartment block?" The team leader examined the body of a Chinese gunman. He had been shot by a heavy-caliber bullet. The round had punched clean through an air-conditioning unit and torn him in half.

"Negative. All our assets are located to the north."

"Acknowledged."

The SAT commander continued. "Ground units are in place. Alpha has been extracted. Bravo is in cutoff. You are to proceed with your clearance down through the floors. Use of gas is authorized."

"Yes, sir." The section leader gave the apartment complex a glance before giving his lead team the thumbs-up. "Mask up, we're using gas."

His men took their gas masks from the pouches on their belts and put them on in pairs, one man covering as the other adjusted his equipment. Once they were ready the section leader gave a nod. A group of his men gathered around the air-conditioning units and shoved gas grenades into the air ducts. The grenades popped, billowing tear gas into the air-conditioning system and down into the casino.

"Go, go, go!" the section leader transmitted.

The lead assaulter threw a gas grenade down the stairwell and his team charged through the door and down the stairs. There was a volley of shots as the team pushed into the gas cloud and engaged the Mori-Kai gunmen. More dull thuds and shots sounded as the team threw more gas and continued clearing through the upper level.

AK assault rifles barked, Mori-Kai gunmen firing blindly at shadows, their eyes streaming with tears and lungs burning. They staggered away, spluttering, as the gray clouds spread.

The black-clad SAT moved through the white cloud like wraiths. Unaffected by the smoke, they pushed forward, ruthlessly cutting down Korean and Chinese gang members with well-aimed shots from their MP5s.

The final group of gunmen on that level consisted of a small group of Triads. The Chinese put up a savage fight, shooting magazine after magazine into the haze as it rolled toward them. The SAT dived to the ground as the bullets zipped through the air, slamming into the freshly constructed walls. Eventually, the weapons fell silent as one by one the Triads succumbed to the gas.

Once the fighting on that level had died down, the section leader moved into the stairwell. "Progress?" he asked his team commander, his voice sounding alien through his gas mask.

"At least ten hostiles dead. Snipers had already killed the rest."

"Any casualties?"

"Only one minor wound so far."

"Very good." He checked his watch. At this rate they should have it all wrapped up in under an hour.

✩✩✩

"They're on level five. Gas has been deployed," one of the Kissaki reported. "Our men are taking heavy casualties." The carnage seen on the CCTV screens was evidence enough that the gangs were woefully equipped to deal with the gas.

"Any *gaijin*?" Ryu asked.

"Nothing, sir. Only SAT."

"Damn it."

"How long until they get to our level?"

"They're averaging a floor every five minutes. But if the gangs break and flee they will be much faster."

"Where the fuck are Masateru and Hideaki?" Ryu scanned the video screens.

"I can't raise them."

"We need to be prepared for the worst, then. Erase the video servers and lock down the door."

The security room had a thick steel door that until now had been left open. It took two of the Kissaki to push it closed.

"Stop!" Masateru appeared in the doorway with Karla behind him. "Let us in."

The Mori-Kai *waka-gashira* was breathing heavily as he collapsed into a chair. "You weren't going to leave without me, were you, Ryu?"

The Kissaki sealed the heavy door with a thud.

"I feared the worst."

"Then why didn't you come looking for me? We were nearly captured by the police. Hideaki was killed."

Karla stood in the corner, her eyes wide with fear.

"I would have secured your release from the police later, *waka-gashira*. But if all the Kissaki were killed or captured it would be much harder for us to recover."

"True, that is exactly what the foreigners would want."

"You think they planned this?"

"Without a doubt," said Masateru.

"Sir," the Kissaki behind the computer interrupted, "the SAT have reached the third level. The Chinese and Koreans are offering little resistance."

"We need to leave now," Ryu said. "Those thugs won't hold much longer. We can always replace them."

"They were always meant to be disposable," Masateru added. "Let's go."

Ryu opened an electrical panel that was bolted to the wall. He flicked a number of switches in a preset order. There was a hum of electric motors and one of the concrete wall panels swung inward, revealing a set of stairs.

Masateru took Karla by the hand and led her down the stairs into a well-lit concrete tunnel. Two electric golf carts were parked bumper to bumper, facing away from the stairs. He and Karla climbed into the passenger seats of the first cart. The remaining four Kissaki loaded computer equipment and weapons into the second cart. Ryu closed the escape door behind them and took the wheel of the first cart. He glanced around to check everyone was ready, then set off down the tunnel.

They drove without speaking, the whine of the electric engines the only sound as they raced through the tunnel. A couple of minutes later they reached the end, where a ramp curved upward, and they followed it until they emerged through an open door into a large warehouse.

Parked under bright lights were four black SUVs manned by the reserve squad of Kissaki, all armed to the teeth.

"Load the rest of the equipment," Ryu ordered his men, nodding toward the second golf cart. "*Waka-gashira*, this way." He guided Masateru and Karla across to the closest vehicle.

★★★

"Is this it?" Saneh asked as they reached the warehouse.

Both were breathing hard and sweating in the midday sun. Moving as fast as they could between the older warehouses and rice paddies, they had taken a good ten minutes to reach it. Their boots and pants were coated in mud from a drainage ditch they'd used to avoid being spotted by a police checkpoint.

Bishop checked the map on his iPRIMAL. "Yeah, this is it. We'll breach here once the others are in position."

He checked the back door. Locked.

Saneh examined the door. "I'll prep the charge," she said, taking off her backpack.

"Aleks and Kurtz, how are you tracking?" Bishop asked over his iPRIMAL.

"This is Kurtz; we've collapsed the overwatch position and loaded the van. Will be on the move in a minute. Have you found Karla?"

"Negative. We've located the warehouse but no sign of the girl or the Mori-Kai. We're going to wait in place until you arrive at the cutoff. Once you're ready Saneh and I will clear the building and you can pick up the squirters."

"We'll be with you soon," Kurtz replied.

"Roger." Bishop turned to Saneh. "I'm going to have a quick scout around the corner and see what we're dealing with."

She nodded as she taped two saline bags to a slab of explosives and placed the charge at the base of the door. "Charge ready," she said, sliding a remote detonator into the slab.

Bishop walked slowly toward the front of the warehouse, seeing no sign of any CCTV or surveillance devices. He peeked around the corner; a huge roller door covered most of the frontage. Still no sign of any security.

A faint noise started from the inside. It grew into a loud rumble, the distinctive sound of a diesel engine. Other engines joined the first and the roller door started slowly clanking.

Bishop sprinted back down the side of the warehouse. "Saneh, hit the charge, they're going!"

"What about the rest of the team?"

"Just fucking hit it."

He rounded the corner as the charge detonated. The pressure wave rolled over him as he slid into the breached doorway, his Tavor held ready. He fired as the first SUV leaped out under the roller door, closely followed by the second and third, his bullets chasing them. A fourth vehicle was waiting with its passenger door open.

Bishop caught the man responsible for opening the roller door in the open. He hit him with a burst; the man's body convulsed and dropped to the ground.

Seeing his comrade fall, the driver of the last vehicle slammed his SUV into reverse. Tires squealed as the truck shot backward toward Bishop. He emptied the rest of his magazine as he leaped out of the way.

Saneh was coming through the doorway as the SUV shot backward. She skidded to a halt and the truck hit her with a thud, knocking her to the ground.

The SUV lurched forward, its wheels spinning on the smooth

concrete as they fought for traction. Bishop pulled the trigger again but the bolt had locked back on an empty magazine. He let the rifle drop on its sling, drew his pistol, and fired at the truck as it accelerated.

The heavy vehicle jolted sideways as a tire deflated, dropping onto a flat rim. The driver failed to compensate and hit the side of the warehouse with a crunch. Wheels smoked again as the truck scraped against the wall, slowly turning toward the exit.

Bishop sprinted after the truck, firing his pistol into the back window. The big V8 diesel roared and the vehicle straightened up and accelerated. With a cry, Bishop launched himself through the air, grabbing the tailgate through the shattered rear window as the SUV rocketed out of the warehouse and swung onto the road. The momentum flung him sideways and he hit the ground with a thud, ripping his Tavor from its sling and sending him sliding across the asphalt on his back.

He groaned as he staggered back to his feet and watched the truck disappear into the distance.

"You OK?" Saneh handed him both his guns.

"Yeah." He gave her a concerned look. "What about you?"

"Just a few bruises. Could have gone a lot worse. If we'd banged in a few minutes earlier it would have been a bloodbath."

"Yeah, we were lucky."

"No, you were stupid."

The white van screamed around the corner and stopped alongside them. The doors opened and Kurtz, Aleks, and Kenta jumped out.

"Where's the girl?" Kurtz asked.

"They moved her," Bishop replied.

"You mean we let them get away," Kurtz snapped.

"Yes, they fucking got away. But we did everything we possibly could to stop them."

Kurtz glared at him.

"We might not have the girl, but we have destroyed the Mori-Kai's army," Kenta stated.

"True, but we still haven't cut off the head," said Bishop.

"And we seem to be no closer than before," Saneh added.

"No, we're close. Those guys in the SUVs are going to lead us right to their boss."

She gave him a skeptical look. "Really, Aden? I don't know if you noticed but they got away."

"Yeah I know." Bishop grinned. "The really shit thing is I left my iPRIMAL in the back of their truck."

"You sneaky son of a bitch." Saneh shook her head in disbelief.

"Boss, we should probably leave." Aleks glanced nervously down the road. "The place is crawling with cops and it won't take them long to find us."

"Aleks is right. Let's mount up, pick up the Mercedes, and get back to the safe house. We need to be ready to finish this."

CHAPTER 81

"Sir, the building has been secured," the air assault section leader reported to the SAT commander over the radio. "We are commencing site exploitation and investigation."

"Excellent work," responded Inspector Hyuman from his mobile headquarters. "How many casualties did you sustain?"

"We've got six wounded. Two serious, three minor gunshot wounds, and one with CS gas exposure."

"Estimated enemy casualties?"

"In excess of thirty and we've detained nearly sixty. They've been secured by Bravo section in the building's restaurant area. We've recovered over a hundred military-grade weapons."

"Any Europeans, in particular a blonde woman?" The commander looked across to where Baiko was sitting.

"No, sir, only Korean and Chinese males. No women identified."

"Very good, continue with site exploitation."

Inspector Hyuman placed down the radio handset and sat next to Baiko. "They didn't find the woman. It seems your source was mistaken."

The veteran investigator nodded. "Perhaps you are right. But he did provide us with the single largest weapons bust in the history of anti-Yakuza operations."

"This is true and we managed to do it without getting anyone killed."

"You mean without any policemen being killed."

"Of course," Hyuman nodded. There was a short silence before the SAT commander spoke again. "There's something I wanted to discuss with you."

"Go on."

"Let's head outside. I need a smoke."

They left the command bus and Hyuman lit up a cigarette. "When we first deployed, I received a phone call from the regional director, Superintendent Supervisor Tanaka."

"What did he want?"

"He told me that if I continued with the operation it would be detrimental to my career."

"That's very interesting."

"And remember, after that when I got a call from the Yakuza heavy? He pretty much said the same thing."

"You think that the superintendent is in the pay of the Yakuza?"

Hyuman took a long drag off his cigarette. "You're the investigator, Baiko. I only kick doors. I just think you should be careful. These people have friends in high places."

"What about your career?"

The SAT commander laughed as he dropped his cigarette on the ground and stomped on it with his boot. "Like you said, my men just conducted the largest anti-Yakuza bust in Japan's history. No one's going to be able to touch us. I just thought you might want to know what you're up against."

"Greatly appreciated." Baiko dipped his head in gratitude.

"Let me know if I can help in any way. Your hard work is what led us to this victory." He reached out and shook Baiko's hand before returning to his command bus.

Baiko contemplated the information as he strolled away from

the command bus. In the distance he could see the Mori-Kai's construction site; the half-completed building looked like something from a war zone. He stared at it for a minute, then dialed a number. "Agent Wilson, I have some information that may be of use."

"Go ahead."

"The SAT commander took a call just prior to it all kicking off. It was from the regional director. He tried to order him to cancel the operation."

There was silence on the other end of the phone, then, "And you think that the Mori-Kai may have influenced that decision?"

"I don't have any evidence to support it, but that's my hunch."

"Can you have one of your people check the director's phone records?"

"Not without a warrant."

"Is that a problem?"

"I have a friend who owes me a favor but . . ."

"If you're worried about losing your job, I can assure you that you'll be looked after should anything happen."

"You didn't find the girl, did you?"

"No." Bishop sounded tired. "No, they've still got her."

The police officer was silent for a few seconds. "I'll see what I can do." He terminated the call and stood looking at the half-built casino in the distance. Then he scrolled through his contacts until he found the number he wanted.

★★★

"Looks like the house of someone pretty damned important." Vance's voice came through Bishop's headphones.

"It's isolated, well defended, and it's got a helipad." Bishop was in the upstairs office at the safe house, using a laptop to communicate with Vance. The rest of the team was downstairs preparing for an assault. "My iPRIMAL led us right to it. This has to be the Mori-Kai's headquarters."

The image on the laptop screen was a Google Earth snapshot taken from the iPRIMAL tracking system. It showed a large estate located at the top of a valley in the hills to the northwest of Himeji. A mansion sat in the middle of well-maintained gardens and was surrounded by a substantial fence that ran around the entire property. A driveway wound its way from a guardbox at the front gate up to the mansion. The imagery was just clear enough to identify a helicopter landing pad on the roof.

"You're probably right, bud, but until I get confirmation from Chua on who owns this thing you're not going anywhere near it."

"Vance, think about it. They tried to trap us and failed spectacularly. If nothing else, they have to fear us now, at least a little. So how long do you really expect them to stay at this location? Not to mention, what if they find my phone? Then we're fucked."

"I'll call you back in ten minutes once I've got the facts," said Vance. "Take the time to prep your gear."

Bishop terminated the call without responding. He pondered his options for a moment, then leaped to his feet. He grabbed the laptop, pulled out the compact projector from under the desk, and took them downstairs.

"Gather around, guys," he said as placed the laptop on the bar. He plugged the projector into an outlet and connected it to the laptop. Once it was powered up he focused it on the dirty white wall.

"Team, this is our new objective." He brought up the image of the residence.

"So what are we waiting for?" asked Kurtz. "Let's go."

"That's the plan, mate. I'm just waiting for Vance to look into who owns the place, then give us the green light. Once that happens we're going to gear up in full assault rig and we're going to finish this once and for all."

His local phone buzzed in his pocket. "Excuse me." He took it out and glanced at the screen. The message was from Baiko.

Toru Nishimuru. Town mayor.

"Kenta, do you know who the mayor of Himeji is?"

The Yamaguchi enforcer scrunched up his face in thought. "I don't know him personally. I think his name is Nishimuru."

"Toru Nishimuru?"

"Yes, that's it, Toru Nishimuru. Why do you ask?"

"Because he called the regional police director earlier. Just before the director tried to call off the SAT assault. So if this mansion overlooking Himeji belongs to Mr. Nishimuru, then we're good. Saneh, can I borrow your phone?"

She took her iPRIMAL out of her pocket and tossed it to him. He caught it and walked to the corner of the room. His thumbprint scan unlocked the device and he activated a link to the Bunker.

"Hello?" One of the PRIMAL staff answered immediately.

"It's Bishop, where's Vance?"

"He's in with Chua. Do you want me to put you through?"

"Yes, please."

Bishop waited as the watchkeeper called the intelligence cell, confirmed that they wanted to speak to him, and then put him through.

"Bishop, you're on speaker," said Vance. "I'm here with Chua. Look, we've run into a bit of a problem."

"Has your problem got anything to do with the owner of that property? I'm guessing it belongs to a Mr. Nishimuru, the mayor of Himeji."

"Yeah, how did you know?"

"He tried to get the regional police director to call off the SAT assault. And right now, I'm pretty sure it isn't a bloody coincidence that's where my phone ended up."

There was silence. Then Vance spoke, "If this is true, then . . ."

"Yeah?"

"The mayor of the goddamn city could be the Mori-Kai *oyabun*."

"This could be another trap, Aden," said Chua. "These guys have pretty tight OPSEC. Why would they suddenly break it?"

"Maybe he freaked out when the cops suddenly jumped his party. How the hell would I know? All I know is we've been given an opportunity here and we need to seize it. I'm requesting permission to conduct a crash-action assault on the objective."

There was silence as the men at the other end of the phone discussed his request. Bishop could tell the speaker phone had been muted.

Vance unmuted the connection. "OK, Bish, permission granted. Chua's going to work up all the intel he can get his hands on."

"Great!"

"Play it safe, bud. Don't go charging into this like the goddamn cavalry. Remember, time spent on recon is seldom wasted."

"Yes, Dad."

"OK, go wrap those bastards up."

Bishop turned to face the team and tossed the phone back to Saneh. "Time now is nineteen forty-five hours," he said. "I want to be out the door no later than twenty-one hundred."

CHAPTER 82

RESIDENCE OF THE MAYOR OF HIMEJI

A cricket chirped as Bishop worked in the moonlight. Despite the cool air he had managed to work up a sweat. His hair was damp and the night vision goggles he was wearing had started to fog.

"That's the last one." Bishop sprinkled a handful of leaf litter over the remote-activated gunfire simulator and picked up his assault rifle.

Saneh was farther down the slope, covering him and keeping watch. In her dark clothing she was almost completely invisible.

"Aleks and Kenta, how are you tracking?" Bishop transmitted.

"Just finishing up now. We'll be a few minutes. Meet you back at the RV," replied Aleks.

"Roger." He turned to Saneh. "All good, let's go."

They moved through the darkness away from the mayor of Himeji's residence, using their multispectral goggles to pick a path through the heavy vegetation. The road they paralleled led from the estate's security checkpoint down to a water treatment plant.

"Kurtz, we're two minutes out."

"Understood," Kurtz replied from their base of operations.

Bishop led Saneh down the narrow track into a small clearing. The white van and the borrowed Yamaguchi Mercedes were parked on the far side. His night vision detected a faint glow from the back of the van.

"You hear that?" Saneh stopped halfway across the clearing.

A faint whirring noise drifted in on the still night air. They looked up and spotted Kurtz's drone approaching from the direction of the estate. It hovered above them before descending slowly, touching down with a bounce on the grass next to them. Bishop removed his night vision goggles, picked up the pizza box–size quadcopter, and carried it over to the van, where Kurtz waited.

"You spot anything?" he asked, passing the aircraft to Kurtz.

"They've started patrolling."

"The men on the gate?"

"No, ones from inside. Four of them every thirty minutes, walking the perimeter."

"Any dogs?"

"No dogs. The guards have submachine guns and night vision." Kurtz put the UAV in its foam-padded box and snapped it shut.

"More of our Special Forces buddies." Bishop helped him lift the case into the back of the van.

Kurtz pointed to a larger container. "I need this one."

They slid it out of the van and onto the ground. The German opened the case and pulled out what looked like a mortar tube.

"How long till Aleks and Kenta get back?" Saneh asked. They had also been placing remote-initiated gunfire simulators.

"They were a couple of hundred meters out when the drone returned. Should be here soon." Kurtz positioned the large tube next to the van, extending a pair of legs to prop it up in the direction of the manor. He flicked a switch on the cell phone–size box attached to the body and a green light flashed twice.

"That thing going to work?" Bishop asked.

"There is no reason it wouldn't," Kurtz replied, checking that his iPRIMAL was synced to the precision-fire support unit.

"Kurtz, this is Aleks and Kenta. Fifty meters out," the Russian's thick accent came in over the team's earpieces.

"Affirmative. The others are already here," Kurtz replied.

The two men appeared from the tree line to the north. Also dressed in black, they were barely visible until they arrived at the parked vehicles.

"How did it go?" Bishop asked.

"No problems, everything is in place," said Aleks.

"Good. Recon and prep phase complete, team. Let's gear up."

From the van they pulled out individual gear bags and started preparing their kit. They each had a set of the CAT assault equipment, carbon-nanotube armor and full-faced helmets with built-in sensors. The black armor was covered in pouches that contained ammunition, medical supplies, explosive charges, and anything else they might need during the assault.

Bishop was the first ready. He double-checked his ammunition, helmet, and weapon before helping Kenta put on his armor. "You know you don't have to do this, mate."

"I don't understand what you mean."

"I mean, this is going to get pretty heavy." He nodded toward the others. "We train for this shit, we've done it before. There's no shame in sitting this one out and RVing with us later."

Kenta snapped his last piece of assault armor in place. "Are you trying to offend me?" He made sure his revolver was firmly secured on his belt. "These Mori-Kai peasants need to be taught a lesson in respect. That is not something I can leave to foreigners."

"Fair enough." Bishop checked that Kenta's radio was on the right frequency to talk to the rest of the team. "You just make sure you listen in and follow Aleks's directions. This isn't going to be a walk in the park."

The Yamaguchi nodded as Bishop lifted the fully enclosed helmet onto his head. In the full CAT armor and helmet Kenta resembled a modern samurai. All that was missing were the razor-sharp swords that were the trademark of the Japanese warriors; in their place he carried his trusty revolver and the high-tech KRISS.

The rest of the team had almost finished preparing their own gear. "You expecting more dogs?" Aleks asked Kurtz.

"It pays to be prepared." Kurtz was fitting his armored forearm sleeve with the built-in Taser.

"Everyone ready?" Bishop asked as the last of the equipment bags were stowed in the van. The team lined up and he gave their weapons and armor a once-over. Aleks was wielding a collapsible-stock Mk48 machine gun. In addition to his weapons, Kenta had on a backpack filled with spare ammunition belts for the Mk48. The others carried their Tavors, Kurtz's sporting a 40mm grenade launcher. All of the guns were suppressed.

"Comms check," Saneh reminded Bishop as he checked her equipment.

"All call signs, this is Bishop, radio check," he broadcast.

"Kurtz, loud and clear."

"Saneh, Lima Charlie."

"Aleks, affirmative."

"Kenta, affirmative."

"OK, then," said Bishop. "Let's roll."

The team moved off in single file, disappearing into the thick vegetation. High above them a half moon cast its light across the hills. Everything was peaceful, for now.

CHAPTER 83

RESIDENCE OF THE MORI-KAI OYABUN, HIMEJI

"None of them got away?" Toru Nishimuru, the Mori-Kai *oyabun* and mayor of Himeji, screamed his question at Ryu and Masateru.

"The SAT used gas and massacred the gangs. The rest were captured. There was nothing we could do," said Masateru.

His Kissaki commander stared at the floor. They neglected to mention that nearly half their Kissaki force was dead or in the hospital.

Nishimuru threw his whiskey glass at the windows of his office. It smashed on the armored glass, shattering into pieces on the bamboo floor. "Fucking police. What do we pay them for?"

"We will be able to replace the weapons and the men," said Masateru.

"Not any time soon! Word will get around that working for the Mori-Kai puts you in prison or a grave."

"Our money is still good. We will raise another army."

A phone beeped. Ryu moved to the corner of the room to check his messages.

"The time to strike was today but somehow the *gaijin* outwitted us. They made you look like a fool!"

Masateru's face turned red. "All is not lost. Our facilities are still running—" He clenched his fists, fighting the urge to draw his knife.

"Apologies for interrupting," Ryu said softly.

"What is it?" Nishimuru took another glass of whiskey from a house servant.

"You wanted an update on the search for the Yamaguchi leader."

"Yes, go on."

"We are still searching."

"What about the foreigners?" Masateru asked, regaining his composure.

"They have disappeared."

"What fucking use is your informant network if you can't find anyone?" The veins on the side of Nishimuru's head bulged. "Double the price on all their heads."

"Yes, *oyabun*." Ryu stepped out of the study, leaving the two men alone.

Masateru waited for the door to shut. "I will find the old Yamaguchi dog and skin him personally so you can mount his hide on your wall."

"I want to know what you are going to do about the *gaijin*." Nishimuru slumped into a settee and downed his whiskey.

Masateru poured his boss another drink. "Until I find them, it might be wise to move you to a more discreet location."

"You want me to run like a scared little girl?" His thick eyebrows furrowed as he glared over his glass. "I will not run."

"It would only be until the threat has passed. Once the Kissaki have destroyed the Yamaguchi and the *gaijin* you will be able to return to the manor."

Nishimuru studied his drink. "But they are unaware of my identity."

"Yes, but there are others who are not."

"Superintendent Supervisor Tanaka. That fool failed us . . . He should be dealt with accordingly."

"I think it might be premature to eliminate him; he may yet prove valuable."

"Perhaps." The *oyabun* placed his drink back on the table. "Send for the helicopter. I will retire to another location until our enemies are dealt with."

As if on cue, the crackle of gunfire penetrated the walls of the mansion. From inside, it sounded as if an army was descending upon them.

"It's the police! Tanaka must have sold us out!" The *oyabun's* eyes were wide with fear.

The door to the study burst open and Ryu stormed in with his G36 in hand. "The guardhouse is under attack. We need to lock down the estate."

"Do it," Masateru ordered. "Have the patrol reinforce the guards at the front gate." He glanced at his watch. "I have already called the helicopter. It should arrive soon."

"Yes, *waka-gashira*."

Masateru turned to the *oyabun*. "If it were the police we would have been warned. This has to be the *gaijin*."

"Good," said the *oyabun*. "Kill them all."

★★★

The steel fasteners on the sewer grate screamed in protest as Kurtz attacked them with a small, battery-powered grinder. Sparks arced off the diamond carbide blade as it cut into the high-tensile steel.

The sound was drowned out by the cacophony of noise coming from farther up the valley. The gunfire simulators were doing their job: Flashing in the darkness, they gave the impression that the guardhouse was under attack by at least a platoon's worth of weapons.

Kurtz ground out the final fastener and the grate dropped off the culvert with a thud. "We're through," he told the group.

Bishop led, sliding into the three-foot-high tunnel on his stomach. He held his weapon in one hand and used his elbows to drag himself forward. His helmet filtered out the rank smell of the water.

He slid out of the tunnel and rose to a knee, scanning the area with his helmet sensors. "All clear." The drainpipe had given them access to the gardens of the Himeji mayor's residence. The lights of the house created a faint glow high up on the hill in front of him, past the sprawling gardens.

One by one the team slid through the drainpipe. Aleks came last, a tight squeeze for the big man. Then they fanned out, pausing for any sign that their infiltration had been compromised.

"Push up into a fire-support position." Bishop directed Aleks with a gloved hand.

The hulking Russian was an intimidating sight in his black full-body armor and helmet. He moved in a crouch, climbing a small rise that led up toward the estate. Kenta followed and the pair disappeared into the shadows. Sixty seconds passed before they reported.

"In position."

"Let's go." Bishop led Kurtz and Saneh up through the gardens. The gunfire simulators petered out, expending the last of their cartridges. It left an eerie stillness as they moved through the stone outcrops, manicured lawns, sculpted shrubbery, pebble paths, and small ponds of the traditional Japanese garden.

"It's beautiful," Saneh's voice came over their integrated helmet communications.

"Some good cover and concealment," Bishop added.

"Tangos heading down hill," Aleks broadcast from his position.

"How many?" Bishop asked as his team went to ground behind a large mound covered in manicured turf.

"Four, heading down toward the gate," Aleks replied. "I've got them."

An assault rifle barked in close vicinity to the team and rounds snapped through the air. Aleks fired a burst from his Mk48, the suppressed machine gun clearly audible in the still night air.

"Kurtz, jam their comms." Bishop crawled forward, looking for a better position.

On the back of his armor Kurtz wore what looked like a radio with a short whip antenna. The electronic attack module was controlled by his forearm-mounted iPRIMAL and could block communications within a three-hundred-meter radius.

"Frequencies jammed. Let's kill these bastards." Kurtz crawled up alongside Bishop.

More automatic bursts could be heard coming from Aleks and Kenta's position. "Aleks has them pinned. We can hit them from the flank," said Bishop.

"Let's do it." Saneh joined them.

The three moved forward in bounds, one at a time, dashing between the perfectly manicured grass mounds and rock features.

Saneh closed in on two of the Kissaki pinned behind a boulder, Aleks's 7.62mm rounds impacting around them in controlled bursts. She lined them up with the infrared laser on her Tavor and cut them down with rapid-fire shots, armor-piercing ammunition tearing through their Kevlar vests.

"Good shooting." Bishop moved in next to her. "Where are the other two?"

"We got at least one," radioed Aleks. "I think the other guy pulled back to the mansion."

The modern, two-story structure was lit up with powerful floodlights. Angled outward, they were designed to reduce the effectiveness of night vision and illuminate any intruders. The PRIMAL team's CAT helmets automatically adjusted for the increase in light, relying on thermal imaging to provide a clear image.

Bishop's orders came through over their comms system. "We're going to keep heading up the left flank. Aleks and Kenta, I want you to run ahead and provide fire support."

"Acknowledged, we are moving now," said Aleks.

Bishop led his team along the edge of the property toward the side of the mansion, sticking to the darkest shadows and avoiding the floodlights. They reached the side of the mansion without incident, staying hidden in the garden. From their position they could see through the ground-floor windows. The second level of the building overlooked their approach. He could detect no movement inside.

"It looks like they've locked down and are waiting for us," Kurtz said.

"We could breach in through the garage," Bishop said, pointing at the driveway that led down to a roller door.

"It looks heavy duty," said Kurtz. "We should target the windows, it'll be quicker."

"All right, I'll pop the distraction, and you hit them with the forty mil. Then Saneh and I will hit the lights."

"Good plan." Kurtz cracked the grenade launcher slung under his Tavor and used his thumb to check he had a round chambered. He aimed the weapon at the floor-to-ceiling windows on the ground floor.

A flash lit up the sky when Bishop remotely detonated the explosives at the back of the estate. Half a second later the sound of the explosion rolled over them. He activated another icon on his iPRIMAL and half a dozen more gunfire simulators started going off in the same area.

Kurtz's 40mm grenade arced through the air and slammed into the windows with a crump.

Bishop and Saneh fired their weapons at the floodlights, plunging their side of the mansion into darkness. Guided by the multispectral sensors in their helmets, they moved swiftly through the garden toward the house.

"Fuck! It didn't breach," Bishop yelled as he got closer. Kurtz's grenade had blasted a fist-size hole through the armored glass, which remained otherwise intact.

A burst of automatic fire from one of the balconies stitched the ground at his feet. "SHOOTERS HIGH, SHOOTERS HIGH!" he screamed as he returned fire, backpedaling into a ditch at the edge of the garden.

Caught in the open, Saneh emptied her magazine in the general direction of the upper floor and ran for the cover of the down ramp to the garage. Rounds slapped into the gravel as she sprinted across it.

There was a thump as another of Kurtz's grenades slammed into the heavy balcony wall protecting the shooters on the upper floor.

"Damn it, I'm pinned." Bishop was lying as low as he could. Bullets thudded into the lip of the ditch, showering him in dirt.

"I've got nothing here." Saneh was standing against the heavy steel roller doors of the garage, hidden from the shooters on the second level. A grenade landed on the ramp with a clunk and rolled toward her.

"GRENADE!" She grabbed it and tossed it up the ramp.

It landed a few yards from Bishop and exploded with an ear-splitting crump, showering him in gravel. "Thanks for that," Bishop said. His helmet had protected his ears and eyes from the blast.

"Sorry."

"Kurtz, we're pinned here. You going to take out those clowns upstairs or should I have a nap?"

"I know, I know, I'm on it." Kurtz fired his last grenade at the second story. It detonated on the balcony but failed to neutralize the shooters. "*Scheisse.*" He fired a burst from his Tavor and dropped back into cover.

"Was that it?" Bishop asked.

"No, I'm solving the problem now." He activated the iPRIMAL on his wrist and tapped at the screen with a gloved finger.

"Do we need to get Aleks to move and suppress?" Bishop asked.

"No." Kurtz hit a button transmitting his iPRIMAL screen to the heads-up display in his helmet.

Back down the hill at their vehicles, the green light on the mortar tube he had left behind changed to red. There was a flash of flame and a rocket shot out of the tube into the sky.

It fired up to five thousand feet in a matter of seconds. Then a pair of wings popped out and it glided silently through the night sky.

Guiding the glide bomb via its nose camera, Kurtz sent it into a dive. It gathered speed, finally detonating two feet above the second-floor balcony. Four pounds of high explosives turned the three Mori-Kai gunmen into vaporized flesh, nylon, and steel.

"Holy shit balls." Bishop hugged the ground as bits of the Mori-Kai landed on him. "Aleks, hit the front of the building with suppressing fire. We're going to breach from our side."

"Acknowledged." Aleks's Mk48 opened up. Rounds ricocheted off the armored glass and blasted chunks out of the concrete.

Kurtz sprinted toward the down ramp to where Saneh was taking cover. "You just going to lie there all day?" he commented as he passed Bishop. Both of them joined Saneh at the garage door.

"What now?" she asked. "Clearly we're not getting in through the windows."

"That armor's too thick for blasters," Bishop said, quoting one of his favorite movies. "Can we breach this?" He rapped his gloved knuckles against the roller door.

"*Ja.*" Kurtz shrugged off his pack and pulled out a roll of cutting charge. He cut the angled explosive into four lengths, tore off the adhesive backing, and stuck them to the door in a rectangular shape. "If there isn't a door, make your own."

They faced away as the explosives detonated, their CAT suits protecting them from the blast. The charge cut a perfect rectangle out of the steel roller door. Saneh pitched a flashbang through the hole, waited for it to detonate, then dived through. A moment later came her transmission:

"All clear. We've gained entry."

CHAPTER 84

"Who are these demons?" breathed the *oyabun*, pointing at his computer screen.

Masateru glanced at the monitor, the CCTV feeds showing a glimpse of their adversary, a grainy shot of two armored men carrying machine guns. With a chill he recognized the black suits and futuristic helmets: the same men who had attacked the castle in Hungary.

The Mori-Kai lieutenant looked out the office window and saw only darkness; most of the floodlights had been destroyed. He flinched as another volley of rounds ricocheted off the armored glass.

"Ryu, report," he spoke into his handheld radio. The handset returned nothing but static. "Useless piece of shit." He flung it across the room, unaware that his communications were being jammed.

"Who the hell are they?" the *oyabun* asked again.

"I don't fucking know!" Masateru snapped. He threw open the doors to the study. There were four Kissaki waiting in the corridor. "You two," he pointed to the closest men. "If anyone tries to get through these doors I want you to kill them. I've sent for the helicopter. Once it arrives take the *oyabun* to the helipad."

"Yes, *waka-gashira*." They moved into the study.

"Give me a gun," Masateru asked one of the others. The Kissaki took a Sig Sauer from his holster and handed it over.

"Where are you going?" the *oyabun* demanded.

"I'm going to get Karla and Ryu. I'll meet you on the rooftop."

★★★

Bishop led his team after Saneh into the underground garage. They passed four parked SUVs, which he recognized as the same bullet-riddled vehicles he had shot outside the warehouse near the casino.

"Aleks, update?"

"Nothing to report. I'm not even scratching the glass," Aleks replied. "I can't see any Mori-Kai, and Kenta hasn't gotten a shot off yet."

Bishop grinned. He could imagine the heavily tattooed Japanese wanting to charge into the battle.

"Move down to the garage, meet up with us on the ground floor."

"OK."

Bishop stopped behind an SUV with a shattered rear window. He reached in and unlatched the rear gate, dropping it down so he could see into the trunk. His iPRIMAL was there, lodged in the corner with the remnants of the rear windshield. He dropped it into a pouch.

"We ready for the lights to go off?" Kurtz was standing next to the building's power board.

"Yeah, I always prefer to do it in the dark."

Saneh rolled her eyes.

Kurtz dropped the master switch with a clunk, plunging the building into darkness. Seconds later the emergency lighting flickered on, bathing the garage in a faint glow. Bishop led them up the stairs and into the foyer.

He swept the dimly lit room. It was empty.

"Where is everyone?" said Saneh. Rooms led off to each side and the stairs continued up to the first floor.

Bishop checked the entrance. The heavy doors were locked. "Whoever built this place knew what they were doing. It's a fortress." He moved to the stairs and was peering up them when automatic gunfire ripped into the foyer from one of the side rooms.

Saneh snapped her Tavor up and returned fire through the wall. Kurtz did the same. More bullets came from the other side and Kurtz collapsed, landing on his back.

"Stay where you are!" Bishop yelled from the stairs.

"I can get to him." Saneh fired her weapon again.

More rounds slapped into the wall a foot above Kurtz's motionless body.

"Kurtz, you OK?" Bishop checked his iPRIMAL. The German's icon was still green, his heart was beating. "Saneh, he's out cold. Can you see how badly he's injured?"

"There isn't any blood."

More gunfire snapped through the foyer. The Mori-Kai in the other room were shooting blindly, firing through the walls and doorway at even the slightest noise.

A long machine-gun burst announced Aleks's arrival up the stairs from the garage. "Move out of the way." Aleks reached Saneh and pushed her gently to one side.

His Mk48 fired again, blowing fist-size chunks out of the wall, momentarily suppressing the Mori-Kai gunfire. Kenta dashed forward and grabbed Kurtz by the loop on the back of his armor, dragging him back into the safety of the stairs. Saneh followed and started inspecting Kurtz for wounds.

Aleks continued firing from the hip, burst after burst from the belt-fed machine gun. Bishop moved in beside him, lobbing a grenade into the next room. There was a muffled explosion and Aleks rushed through the doorway and fired two short bursts. "Two KIA," he reported. "Room clear."

Bishop turned back and movement at the top of the stairs caught his eye. He fired his Tavor instinctively and the black-clad Kissaki stumbled backward, disappearing from view. "Aleks, cover the stairwell. Kenta, you stay with me. Saneh, how's Kurtz?"

"He's still out," reported Saneh. "His helmet took the blow."

"Roger. Look after him and let me know when he comes to." Bishop led Kenta to the other side of the foyer, moving slowly and deliberately, assault rifle in shoulder. The door to the next room was open and a makeshift barricade made out of furniture could be seen at the rear of the room. They moved up on the doorway.

"Just like we practiced," Bishop whispered, then entered smoothly through the doorway.

They found themselves in what looked like a waiting room, but the desk, chairs, and coffee table were piled together in a barricade. The furniture was shot up and splintered. Bishop followed a fresh blood trail to the back of the room where solid double doors barred their way. "Looks like someone important usually works in here."

"The mayor?" Kenta asked.

"That would be my guess."

Kenta reached for the door handle.

"No." Bishop grabbed his wrist. "This calls for some bang."

He stuck the compact breaching charge in the middle of the two doors. They took cover on either side.

The charge blew the doors wide open. In the enclosed space the explosion was deafening but the PRIMAL team's assault suits protected them from the overpressure and flying debris. Kenta rushed forward, firing his KRISS full auto as he charged into the room. The two Kissaki fired at the same time. Their rounds pelted the armored juggernaut while his .45 slugs ripped through the men, sending their weapons clattering to the ground.

"Over there." Kenta pointed to the opposite corner of the room, where a thermal signature was crouched behind a couch. He reloaded his KRISS and dragged the man out from behind the furniture.

Bishop activated the light on his helmet and stood over their captive. The man matched the images they had already pulled on Nishimuru, the mayor of Himeji. He was middle-aged with shoulder-length gray hair and a moustache.

"Who are you?" Nishimuru asked in accented English, shielding his eyes from the bright LEDs on Bishop's helmet.

"I'll ask the fucking questions." Bishop's voice sounded metallic and alien through the vents of his mask.

The *oyabun* started to tremble, the masked figure standing above him clearly like nothing he had ever encountered. "Whatever the Yamaguchi are paying you I will double it, triple it. Name your price."

"You think this is about money?"

"The girl, you want the girl. She's safe, she's upstairs. You can have her, take her."

Kenta spoke to the man in Japanese. The facial expression of the *oyabun* changed as he realized the other helmeted figure was Yakuza. He spat onto the floor and uttered what sounded like a curse.

"What's he saying?" Bishop asked.

Kenta raised his pistol and fired. The bullet hit the Mori-Kai boss in the chest. He remained upright for a moment, a surprised look on his face, then tumbled sideways.

"He called me a dog," Kenta grunted before also collapsing to the floor.

"Shit!" Bishop leaped to his side. "Kenta, mate, talk to me, will ya?" He removed the man's helmet. Kenta's face was pale and waxen; blood trickled from the corner of his mouth.

"Kenta's down, Kenta's down," he broadcast as he removed the

Yamaguchi's chest armor. He used his combat shears to slice through the man's shirt, revealing a barrel chest covered in tattoos. "Shit," he whispered. Kenta had been hit twice: One round had glanced off the armor, leaving a nasty bruise; the second had missed the armor and entered under the armpit, burrowing into his chest cavity. "Guys, I'm gonna need some help here."

✶✶✶

Back in the foyer, Saneh had removed Kurtz's damaged helmet. "You go, Aleks, I'll look after Kurtz and cover the stairs." Aleks didn't need to be told twice. He sprinted off in the direction of the others.

Kurtz's blue eyes snapped open. "What happened?"

"You took a round to the face. Just take it easy for a minute." Saneh had her Tavor aimed up the stairs.

"Where are the others?" Kurtz gave a groan as he got back up to his feet. He picked up and examined his helmet. The polycarbonate reflective face shield had a deep gouge in it.

"They cleared the rest of the floor. Kenta's been hit."

"How bad?" Kurtz tried the helmet on.

"It's bad."

He bashed the side of the helmet with his fist and then tore it off, throwing it to the ground. He cocked his head to one side. "Can you hear that?"

"What?"

He grabbed his Tavor and started up the stairs. "There's a helicopter coming. We've got to clear the rest of the building before they get away."

"No, Kurtz, wait for the—"

An assault rifle barked from the second level. Saneh shook her head and followed him.

CHAPTER 85

"The helicopter is inbound," Ryu said to Masateru. "ETA five minutes."

They were in the master bedroom with Karla and could hear the sound of the incoming rotor blades.

"Are we going somewhere safe?" Karla asked.

Ryu said nothing. The Kissaki commander still wanted to abandon the girl to the *gaijin*.

Masateru nodded. "We'll all take the helicopter to a place no one will find us." He turned to Ryu. "Head downstairs and get the *oyabun* up here."

Ryu shook his head. "He's already dead. They've overrun the ground floor."

The reality of Ryu's words took a few seconds to sink in. *The oyabun was dead.* That meant Masateru was now the head of the Mori-Kai. He had access to the bank accounts, to all facilities still running. He smiled. Perhaps he could salvage success from the ashes of defeat . . .

"How many men do you have left?"

"Just the four in the upstairs living area."

"Tell them to delay the attackers. Then meet us at the helicopter on the roof." Ryu adjusted his helmet, checked the magazine on his G36, and moved cautiously down the corridor into the living room.

Two of his men were waiting for him. The other pair were farther down the corridor.

A grenade detonated with a crump, followed by rapid-fire shots from the direction of the stairs. Ryu pulled a concussion grenade from his vest and gave a signal to his men to advance.

★★★

Kurtz reached the top of the stairwell and paused at the two crumpled bodies. They had borne the brunt of the fragmentation grenade he had lobbed up the stairs. He fired shots into their heads as he moved past.

The stairwell led to a short corridor opening up into a large living room. Kurtz stalked forward and took a peek. During the day it would have had a stunning view of the valley. On the other side another corridor led off to the bedrooms.

"How many hostiles left?" Saneh came up the stairs behind him.

"At least one or two. Let's clear this room, then the next corridor."

"Throw a flashbang, then I'll lead."

The helicopter was clearly audible now, directly above the mansion.

"This is Bishop," came over Saneh's radio. "Kenta's in a bad way. We're going to need that chopper to evac him; sounds like it's landing on the roof."

"Acknowledged, we're on it." Saneh pushed past Kurtz. "On my mark."

As Kurtz went to grab his flashbang, another one skidded across the floor and rolled beside them. "Grenade!" screamed Saneh. She turned and pushed Kurtz back down the stairs.

The blast knocked her off her feet and she tumbled down the staircase, landing in a heap.

"Saneh, Saneh!" Kurtz shook her shoulder, adrenaline forcing him to ignore the disorientation and the ringing in his ears. Helmetless, he'd almost had his eardrums ruptured.

"I'm OK," she moaned.

Kurtz flicked his stun grenade out of the stairwell. It exploded at head height, sending Ryu's two last men reeling. He charged forward, cutting them down at point-blank range, armor-piercing rounds scything through their armor.

Ryu opened fire from the far corridor, his unsuppressed assault rifle deafening in the enclosed space. Kurtz's rifle took a slug and flew out of his hands. He dived sideways into the living room, scrambling behind the furniture, ears still ringing from the concussion grenade and Ryu's gunfire.

Several 5.56mm rounds punched through a leather sofa a few inches from his face. Kurtz drew his pistol and fired back toward the shots.

"So, who are you?" Ryu had pulled back deeper into the corridor. "A mercenary?"

Kurtz rose and moved swiftly to the wall near the doorway. There, he held his pistol against a light switch and pulled the trigger. The .45 round drilled through the plastic fitting, out through the switch on the other side, into the hall. He heard the Kissaki commander scream in agony. His rifle fell to the floor with a clatter.

Kurtz rounded the corner, leading with his handgun. "Mercenaries? No, we're just a bunch of Boy Scouts."

"Wait, you don't—"

Kurtz's bullet penetrated Ryu's face, punched through his brain, and mushroomed in the back of his helmet.

The body hit the ground at the same time as Kurtz's empty pistol magazine. He slid a fresh one home and raced down the next corridor toward the sound of the helicopter, his boots thudding on the hardwood as he ran.

Kurtz skidded to a halt as he entered the master bedroom at the end of the hallway. "Stop!" he yelled.

Masateru had Karla by the arm. The pair was halfway through the glass doors that led to the rooftop helipad. He pulled her in tight as he turned to face the threat.

"Karla?" Kurtz barely recognized the shy young girl from the hospital. The woman in front of him wore vibrant red lipstick, her eyes outlined in black, her svelte body clad in a shimmering evening gown.

"Kurtz!" She recognized his face through the haze of the sedatives.

His pistol didn't waver; it pointed directly at them, looking for a clear shot at the Yakuza boss.

Masateru kept himself behind Karla as he slowly raised his pistol. "I think it would be wise for you to drop your weapon."

The two men stood staring at each other.

Kurtz's finger took up the slack on the trigger.

Masateru shoved Karla forward, stepped to the side, and fired rapidly. Kurtz cried out as he was struck multiple times and fell to his knees, dropping his pistol. The CAT armor had stopped the rounds but the blunt-force trauma had crippled his arm and knocked the wind out of him.

"Fucking *gaijin*." Masateru strode across and kicked Kurtz's pistol away. He stuffed his own weapon in his pants and unfolded his tanto blade. "Do you know what you've cost me?" He grabbed a fistful of Kurtz's hair and tilted back his head, exposing his throat.

The knife came down at the same time Kurtz raised his left forearm. Blade met gauntlet, and the powerful Taser circuit initiated with a snap and a hiss, hurling Masateru across the room.

The Mori-Kai gangster lay on his back with his eyes closed. The stench of burnt hair filled the room.

Kurtz drew a dagger from his vest and climbed to his feet. He lurched forward and plunged the blade down.

Masateru's eyes opened. He grabbed Kurtz's knife hand and rolled sideways, wrenching the blade from the PRIMAL operative's weakened grip. In a flash he was back on his feet, the blade slicing through the air.

Kurtz grunted as the steel sliced through his cheek. The knife flashed again and Kurtz blocked with an armored forearm, at the same time punching Masateru in the face.

The Yakuza lieutenant lost his grip on the knife as Kurtz shoved him to the ground and leaped on top of him. With his face covered in blood, Kurtz bellowed like an enraged bull and unleashed a flurry of punches.

A gunshot cut through his blood lust. He looked up to see Karla holding his pistol.

"Stop! Stop killing each other." Tears flowed down her cheeks from glassy eyes.

"It's OK, Karla. It's going to be OK. I'm here to take you home." Kurtz suddenly realized that, covered in blood, he must resemble something from a horror movie.

"Get off him. Stop it all, now!" Karla had the muzzle pointed at Kurtz.

He got up slowly, stepping back from Masateru. "Karla, put the gun down."

"Just stop! Stop the killing!" she screamed hysterically.

On the floor, Masateru gave a moan and rolled onto his side. Slowly he stood and surveyed the situation, his face a bloody mess. "He's one of them, Karla. The men that tried to kill us. Shoot him."

Her hand wavered, the pistol remained pointed at Kurtz. More tears rolled down her cheeks.

"What are you waiting for? Kill him!"

Karla's hand shook.

"Give it to me. I'll do it." Masateru took two steps toward Karla and his face exploded, blood and gore spraying across the room. His lifeless body toppled to the ground, blood pooling on the polished floorboards.

Saneh stood in the doorway and lowered her Tavor. A waft of smoke drifted up from the end of her suppressor. She let the rifle hang on its sling and pulled off her helmet. "Drop the gun, Karla. It's over."

"You killed him!" Karla screamed. The pistol in her hand shook uncontrollably as she looked back and forth between Masateru's body and Kurtz. "You killed him!"

"Karla, drop the weapon." Saneh took a step toward her.

"You killed him!" Karla tightened her grip on the pistol and pointed it at Saneh. At that moment, Bishop charged into the bedroom, assault rifle at the ready. His decision was instinctive: his mind registered the threat and his trigger finger responded accordingly. The three rapid shots caught Karla in the center of the chest, slamming her backward onto the floor. She managed to fire the pistol but the bullet went over Saneh's head and buried itself in the ceiling.

"No!" Kurtz screamed. Both he and Saneh turned in disbelief as Bishop strode past them, his Tavor still pointed at Karla's body.

"We need to get Kenta to a hospital. NOW!" He continued out the double doors to the rooftop garden. Aleks followed, Kenta slung over his blood-soaked shoulders, unconscious.

They dashed up the stairs to the rooftop helipad, where the helicopter was waiting, rotors still turning. Bishop pulled the door open, his weapon aimed at the face of the pilot. "Do you speak English?"

The pilot nodded, hands raised.

Bishop reached into the pocket of his pants and pulled out a wad of Japanese currency. "There's over five hundred K in here. It's yours if you can fly my colleagues to a hospital in Kobe."

The man looked around, concerned.

"You don't have to worry about Yakuza. They're dead, all of them."

"No problem with me." The pilot took the cash. "I am not Yakuza. You give me money, I take you anywhere."

Aleks gently lowered Kenta into a seat in the back and Bishop returned to the others.

Kurtz was slumped against the wall, blood dripping from his nose and ears, face ashen, staring at Karla's dead body. His blast injuries and the blunt trauma from the gunshots had taken their toll now that the adrenaline was wearing off.

Saneh had removed his upper body armor and was immobilizing a broken arm when Bishop arrived. "You didn't need to kill her, Aden," Saneh snapped as she administered a morphine injection. "We had it under control."

"She might have shot you. Now listen, Kenta's already in the chopper. Does Kurtz need to go to the hospital?"

Her eyes flashed as she fought back emotions and words. She looked at Kurtz. The morphine had kicked in and he was glaring at Bishop with glazed eyes. "He needs a doctor. I'm not sure what internal injuries he has but his armor took multiple hits to his head, chest, and arm. He also took some blast when he wasn't wearing the helmet."

Bishop nodded. "You'll escort Kurtz and Kenta to the hospital. Dump all your kit, both of you, no weapons or armor. I'll take care of it all. Hurry up or we're going to lose Kenta."

By the time they got Kurtz to the helicopter Aleks had wrapped Kenta in a space blanket and administered an IV drip. Kurtz slumped into a nearby seat, Saneh sitting between them.

"I'm going to warn Baiko and get him to ring the local police and authorities," Bishop yelled over the helicopter's engines. "Stick to the FBI contractor thing, he'll take care of the rest." He slid the doors shut and gave the pilot a thumbs-up.

The engines of the Eurocopter screamed as the blades bit into the air and the helicopter lurched off the pad. Bishop and Aleks watched its flashing navigation lights disappear into the darkness.

"Dawn's only an hour away," Bishop told Aleks. "Let's exploit what we can and get all our PRIMAL gear back in the van."

The isolation of the *oyabun*'s residence had meant there were no neighbors to alert the police. They would have time to do a thorough search for anything of intelligence value.

"What about the girl?" Aleks asked.

"We'll leave her here. Baiko can arrange for the body to be returned to her family."

Aleks gave him a concerned look. "You going to be OK?"

"You mean about her?"

Aleks nodded.

"She was a threat to my team. It's as simple as that."

"A hard decision, boss. But I think you did the right thing."

"Doesn't make it any easier."

"True," Aleks agreed. "But the day it becomes easy is the day we become like those we hunt."

"That's what I'm afraid off." Bishop dialed Baiko. He had some explaining to do.

☆☆☆

Baiko sped past the guardhouse up the winding driveway and parked his sedan in front of the mansion, next to a now bullet-ridden black Mercedes. Two police officers were busy inspecting the vehicle.

Bishop was waiting next to the PRIMAL team's white van, parked twenty meters away. Aleks sat inside behind the wheel.

"Agent Wilson." The veteran investigator approached and held out his hand.

"Inspector Baiko." Bishop shook his hand. "Pretty savage gunfight we missed."

Aleks and Bishop had spent the last hour going over the battle scene. They had packed away all their assault equipment and weapons and scoured the manor for anything of intelligence value. The *oyabun's* office had been particularly interesting: They had recovered two laptops and a handful of hard drives stored in a safe. Then they had used two Mori-Kai assault rifles to shoot up their borrowed Yamaguchi Mercedes, changed out of their CAT armor, and waited for Baiko to arrive.

Baiko looked at the battle-scarred manor, then ran his eye over the destroyed Yamaguchi vehicle. "It would certainly seem that way. When did you get here?"

"About an hour ago. I got a tip from one of my sources in the Yamaguchi-gumi. By the time I got here the attack was over."

"So you had nothing to do with this?" Baiko gestured toward the car. Bullet casings lay scattered over the driveway.

"I've had a look around. But like I said, it was all over when I got here. I mean, I passed a few black Mercedes on the way here but that's all I saw of the Yamaguchi."

"So it wasn't you who tipped them off that the mayor of Himeji was the head of the Mori-Kai?" he asked with raised eyebrows.

"I don't know what you're talking about." Bishop winked.

"Did you find the girl you were looking for?"

Any joviality disappeared from Bishop's face. "We did. Or at least we found her body. She must have been killed in the attack."

"I'm sorry to hear that."

Bishop nodded. "So I guess you're going to want to get on with your investigation."

"Yes. You sure you didn't see anything else?"

"No, just the aftermath. The Yamaguchi must have torn through this place like a whirlwind."

"Yes, it would seem that the Mori-Kai severely underestimated the Yamaguchi-gumi."

"To their detriment." Bishop offered Baiko his hand. "Good luck sorting it all out."

CHAPTER 86

KOBE CITY MEDICAL CENTER

"I hate hospitals. They depress the shit out of me." Bishop and Aleks had left the mansion just after dawn, going directly to the Yamaguchi safe house to dump their equipment. So it was almost midday before they arrived at the Kobe City Medical Center.

"I know what you mean. Every time I go to one they always have bad news," Aleks replied.

Bishop spotted Saneh sitting in the emergency department waiting area. She looked weary but still beautiful.

"Any news?" Bishop handed her a backpack with a change of clothes in it.

She took the bag without looking him in the eye. "Kenta came out of surgery an hour ago; he's stable. The bullet lodged within an inch of his heart. They got it out and say he'll make a full recovery."

"Kurtz?"

"He has a fractured arm, broken ribs, and his eardrums are damaged. He's in getting an MRI now. I think he'll be OK."

"Any cops been around?" Bishop noticed the stares the three of them were getting from the hospital staff.

"No."

"Baiko must have warned the local police. You can guarantee that the hospital called them when you rocked up with gunshot wounds."

"I think you speak too soon," Aleks whispered.

Two uniformed police officers entered through the emergency department's sliding doors. They were closely followed by a short-haired Japanese man dressed in a beige suit.

"Baiko. Didn't expect to see you again so soon."

"You've been very busy, Agent Wilson." They shook hands.

"That's not an allegation I can deny."

Baiko pulled Bishop aside. "Any chance we can talk alone?"

"Sure, I could go for a coffee."

They walked down the corridor.

"That story you fed me about the Yamaguchi was cute, but it isn't the truth."

They stopped in front of an automatic beverage-dispensing machine. Bishop selected a coffee in a can.

"Now wait—"

"Don't try and deny it. You've got two of your team in hospital with blast and gunshot injuries. The job on the Mori-Kai mansion was slick, slicker than anything I've seen from the SAT, let alone a bunch of gangsters like the Yamaguchi."

"OK, so we might have given them a little help." He pushed a few coins into the vending machine. "How the hell does this work?"

Baiko punched a button and the can dropped out. "You say you helped just a little?"

"OK, a lot, the FBI has—"

"I know you're not FBI," said Baiko. "I checked with the US Embassy."

"OK, OK," Bishop responded. "Perhaps I work for another government agency."

"No, I don't think you work for any government. You single-handedly destroyed an entire Yakuza clan. That's not the work of an organization run by politicians and bureaucracy. Mr. *Wilson*."

Bishop drank from his can and nodded thoughtfully. He knew this discussion had been coming. "All right, you can drop the Wilson crap. My people call me Bishop. And the Mori-Kai, they're not finished yet."

"OK, then, Mr. Bishop. Let me help you."

"You already have. We couldn't have gotten this far without you."

Baiko stopped and fixed Bishop with an angry stare. "I want to do more. I've achieved more in this last week than during my entire eight years with the Organized Crime Department."

Bishop did not doubt the man's sincerity. "I'm sorry, but you're never going to know who we are. We're happy to keep providing you with resources and intelligence, but that's all."

The policeman nodded. "How do I get in contact with you?"

"Someone will call you and we'll formalize our arrangement." Bishop downed his can of coffee and threw it in a bin. They started walking back toward the emergency ward. "First things first, we need to wrap up what's left of the Mori-Kai. Our people will be working through the intel we pulled off the *oyabun*'s place."

"If there is evidence I will need it for my investigation."

Bishop nodded. "I should have all the details to you within the next few days. I'm guessing there will be some very interesting videos on the hard drives we found in the mayor's safe."

"And what about Superintendent Supervisor Tanaka?"

"Don't worry about him." Bishop pointed the way down the hall. "Right now I need to introduce you to Kenta, our Yamaguchi contact."

The two men arrived back at the waiting room. Saneh had changed into jeans and a pullover. The two police officers were talking with one of the medical staff.

"Kenta's awake but they won't let anyone see him," said Saneh.

"We'll see about that." Baiko joined the discussion with the doctors, pulling out his identification. They spoke briefly in Japanese, then Baiko turned back to Bishop. "You and I can go in and see him."

Saneh picked up her bag. "Aleks and I will go see Kurtz. Meet you in the waiting room."

Baiko and Bishop followed the nurse down the hall to another ward. Kenta was in a room of his own with two dark-suited Yamaguchi standing guard at his door. They admitted the two men with a curt nod to Bishop. Kenta was hooked up to an arsenal of machines. Lines ran out of his arm and his nose, sensors clung to his chest. His eyes were open.

"Bishop, you saved me," he croaked.

"You wouldn't need saving if you didn't charge into every gunfight like an enraged bull." Bishop grasped the man's hand. "You're looking a lot better now."

"Did you find the girl?" Kenta asked.

Bishop looked down, a lump in his throat. "In a way. We took the Mori-Kai leaders down, that's the main thing."

"Who's your policeman friend?" Kenta nodded toward the door, where Baiko stood waiting.

"Nothing slips past you, does it? Baiko's the one who's been helping us." Bishop took a deep breath. "The two of you will be working together to finish the Mori-Kai."

"Working with the FBI is one thing. The Yamaguchi-gumi don't work with cops."

"Kenta, you know I don't work for the FBI. I work for an independent organization that specializes in dealing with people like the Mori-Kai. Baiko is now our representative here in Japan."

"And you're happy to work with Yakuza?" Kenta asked the policeman.

"The Yakuza is your family as the police is mine. Together we can be a formidable force."

"A cop who talks sense." He broke into a weak smile. "I like you already, Baiko."

"Good, now if you will excuse me, gentlemen, I need to check on one of my team members." Bishop made for the door. "Oh, and we'll be in touch soon."

He smiled as he strode down the corridor, the death of Karla pushed from his mind for a few brief moments. Then he saw Aleks and Saneh in the waiting area, concern etched on their faces. "What's up with Kurtz?"

"He's gone!" Saneh said, distraught.

"Gone? What do you mean gone?"

"None of the staff know where he is. He walked out of the hospital and disappeared." She held out an iPRIMAL. "He left this on his bed."

"Aleks, what's going on?"

"I don't know. I think the girl dying was too much. I think he is done with us."

"You pushed him away." Tears ran down Saneh's cheeks. "I told you something like this would happen."

"You've got to keep it together, Saneh. Kurtz is a big boy, he makes his own decisions. We need to finish the mission. There's one last loose end that needs tying up."

Saneh wiped the tears from her face. "What's that?"

"Not what, *who*."

CHAPTER 87

OSAKA

"That's correct, compliments of the new *oyabun*." One of Kenta's men spoke into the phone in Japanese. "Yes, sir, I will inform him . . . Yes, sir, we'll bring her right up." He ended the call and handed the phone to Bishop. "The policeman is confused, wanted to know who the new *oyabun* was."

"Will he accept her?" Bishop asked.

"There is no way he can refuse."

Saneh and Bishop were sitting in the back of a black Mercedes van that the Yamaguchi had picked them up in. Aleks had taken the white PRIMAL van to the airport, having been tasked to return their equipment and arrange extraction.

"Saneh, are you good to go?" Bishop's eyes lingered on her shapely legs.

She was dressed in a tan trench coat. Her hair was down and she wore the makeup of a woman with the intent to impress. Dark red lips, smoky eyes, and accented cheekbones. The coat fell short of her six-inch heels and sheer stockings. The rest was left up to the imagination.

"I'm fine."

"OK, let's get rolling," Bishop ordered the Yamaguchi driver.

The van pulled out onto the street. It was eleven in the evening and the traffic was light.

Bishop placed his hand on her shoulder. "If you lose control or there are any issues I'll be straight in."

Saneh removed his hand and adjusted her earpiece, covering it with her hair. "I've got this, Aden."

"I know but I'll be damned if I'm going to let anything happen to you."

They traveled a short distance and the driver pulled the van into a loading bay in the front of a condominium block.

"You clear on what you need to do?" Bishop asked the Yamaguchi helper.

"*Hai*, I take the girl up to apartment seven on the fifth floor and leave her with the client."

"Correct. I'll be right behind you. If anything happens I'll take care of it." Bishop turned back to Saneh. "Once this is done we're going straight to the airport and then home."

"Let's just get this over and done with."

Kenta's man took her by the arm as they left the van. He punched the number of the apartment into the intercom and the door buzzed. Bishop slipped in after them and made for the fire stairs while Saneh was chaperoned into the elevator.

Saneh did her best to look intimidated and confused as she was shoved through the doorway into the apartment.

"Do you speak English?" Superintendent Supervisor Tanaka asked from where he was sitting in the corner of the room.

"A little." She looked down at the floor.

"Drop the coat."

Saneh did as she was told and dropped the beige garment to the floor, revealing a lingerie-clad body with a hint of muscle beneath the womanly curves.

"Well, well, well, what have we got here?"

Saneh stood timidly, her hands clasped together in front of her panties, breasts straining against the lace fabric of her bra.

The policeman reached out and stroked her hair. "Quite the exotic beauty, aren't you?"

Saneh looked up at him with tears in her eyes.

"Don't cry. You and I are going to have so much fun."

He grabbed her by the hair and dragged her across the room. She whimpered as he flung her onto the bed.

"You OK?" Bishop's voice came through her earpiece.

"Yes," she mumbled.

"What did you say?" Tanaka demanded as he undid his belt.

"Nothing." Saneh turned to face him.

"Listen, you *gaijin* whore. The only thing I want out of your mouth is this." He dropped his pants.

"I wonder what your mother would say if she heard you speak to a woman like that." Saneh dropped the submissive act as quickly as she had dumped the trench coat.

The look of surprise on Tanaka's face was rapidly replaced by rage. "What did you say?"

He stepped forward and his feet caught in his pants, tripping him. He swung a punch as he fought for balance. Saneh ducked and lashed out with a blow of her own. The palm of her hand collided with his nose and a stream of blood jetted out onto the carpet.

Tanaka didn't go down. His police career had started on the street in an era of brutal riots and gang wars. He had been shot, stabbed, and beaten but along the way he had learned to be a survivor. Office work had softened, but not completely blunted his skills.

He staggered sideways, stepping out of his pants as he lashed out with his left fist, driving it into Saneh's midsection. The blow met the resistance of a lean fighter's physique but still knocked the wind out of her.

"Baita ni makoto nashi," he growled as he wiped the blood from his face.

Saneh fought for breath as she struck a fighter's pose.

"I don't know who you think you are—"

The door to the room burst open and Bishop strode in wearing a balaclava.

Tanaka whirled. "Who the fuck are you?"

Bishop marched across the room and floored the police officer with a right cross. Kevlar-lined knuckles connected with the side of the man's head and rendered him unconscious before he hit the carpet.

"What the hell, Aden? I had this under control."

"I wasn't taking the chance." He shrugged off his backpack and took out a nylon wallet. Inside was a compressed air injector that used gold nanoparticles to deliver chemicals through the skin. A puff of air later and Tanaka was dosed up with a mild sedative. "Jesus, you did a number on his nose." Bishop lifted the pantsless police officer up onto the bed.

Saneh opened Tanaka's small overnight bag, which sat at the foot of his bed. "Oh my god," she exclaimed in disgust.

"What is it?" Bishop asked as he removed a video camera from his backpack and set it up on a tripod in the corner of the room.

"Look what's in the case."

The bag was full of sex toys, ranging from dildos and vibrators to handcuffs and surgical implements. There was also a roll of tape, garbage bags, and cable ties.

"This sicko had a big night planned." Bishop glanced at his watch and handed Saneh her coat. "You head downstairs and get our Yamaguchi friend to call the cops. I'll finish up here."

She took the coat and headed for the door.

Bishop placed a half-empty bottle of whiskey in the unconscious man's hand. He made sure it had a good set of finger prints on it then removed the lid. Using a rubber tube, he poured some whiskey directly down Tanaka's throat before placing it on the side table. Next to it he placed a bottle of pills, the same sedative that he had injected into the policeman's blood stream.

"Bishop, the police have been called." Saneh's voice came over his earpiece. "They're on their way."

"I'm just finishing up." Bishop took a portable DVD player from his backpack, flipped open the screen, and placed it on the side table next to the drugs and whiskey. He pressed play and the LCD screen came alive with images of Tanaka raping a young white girl. The video was only one among hundreds that had been found at the Mori-Kai *oyabun*'s residence. "Try to explain that, you sick fuck."

Bishop picked up his backpack and pulled the door shut behind him. A minute later he was out of the building and in the van.

As they accelerated down the road, Bishop ripped off his balaclava and spoke to the Yamaguchi driver. "Private terminal, please. We've got a plane to catch."

CHAPTER 88

PRIMAL HQ, LASCAR ISLAND

The Lascar Logistics business jet touched down on the island with a screech of tires and a slight shudder of the cabin.

"Welcome home, team," Mitch announced over the intercom.

Bishop opened his eyes; he had been snoozing since they left Japan. After the week-long mission he was exhausted.

Saneh gathered her personal gear as the jet turned off the runway and nosed into a massive hangar set against a granite cliff face. While the engines wound down, she opened the front door and walked down the steps without saying a word to Bishop.

The PRIMAL operative heard Vance and Chua welcome her as she exited the aircraft. He stayed in the leather recliner for a few more seconds, then slowly levered himself out of it. Every inch of his body seemed to ache as he recovered his gear bag and walked stiff-legged down the aisle.

"Hey, buddy, how the hell are you?" Vance greeted him at the bottom of stairs wearing a bright-orange Hawaiian shirt and board shorts.

Chua had already left with Saneh in a golf cart.

"What, no wheels for us?" Bishop shook his boss's hand.

"I got the feeling Saneh was in a hurry. C'mon, let's walk and talk."

"You heard anything from Kurtz?" Bishop asked as they walked through the giant sliding doors that led to PRIMAL's underground facility. Inside the cavernous space a number of other aircraft were parked, including a hulking Ilyushin cargo plane and a sleek tilt-rotor.

Vance shook his head. "No, he's dropped off the face of the earth."

"What about his bank accounts, e-mail addresses?"

"Nope, nothing. We'll keep an eye out but if he doesn't want to be found . . ."

"Saneh's right, you know. I let the team down. I should have seen it coming. We didn't even save the girl."

"In the heat of battle we make the best decisions we can. Let me and Chua deal with Kurtz. Don't you start doubting yourself now." Vance stopped and grasped Bishop by the shoulders. They stood in the middle of the hangar, underneath the wing of the highly modified four-engined Ilyushin known as the "Pain Train."

"Listen, Bish, this ain't some piss-weak NGO outfit delivering bags of rice. This is PRIMAL and we crack skulls. If our people can't handle that then they're better off hanging up their boots."

"You're right."

"Course I'm right. Problem is, you Australians wear your heart on your sleeve. Us Americans, we've gotten used to every fucker hating us." He laughed and Bishop smiled. "You should be proud of what your team achieved. You took down a high-level sex slavery operation that no one else could touch. This mission is exactly what PRIMAL is all about, making an example of those who think they're untouchable."

"Let's just hope Kenta and Baiko can finish the job," Bishop said and they continued walking.

"Oh, I think they'll do all right. The media are already reporting the scandal involving the superintendent and the mayor."

"Really?"

"Yeah, they're saying the Yamaguchi took down a rogue group of Yakuza 'terrorists.' We nailed the PSYOPS plan—it worked perfectly. The Yamaguchi now have a reputation for packing some serious muscle. No other Yakuza outfit's gonna touch 'em."

"I can see the headlines now," Bishop mused. "'Yamaguchi-gumi Samurai Defeat Evil for the People of Japan.'"

"Exactly."

"How did the intel team go with the rest of the stuff we pulled off target?"

"It's gold. Not only have they got the locations of all the other Mori-Kai properties but they've got full client lists."

"That's got to be an interesting read . . ."

"This guy Nishimuru, the mayor, had a whole network of ultranationalist sex freaks that used his services. It's a veritable who's-who of traditional Japanese powerbrokers."

"They aren't going to be happy when the videos get out."

"Yep. Chua and his boys are putting together the intel packs for your buddy Baiko to sort out. The cops are planning to do simultaneous arrests of the client list, as well as taking down the remaining Mori-Kai brothels."

"Baiko's a solid guy. With Kenta's help he'll do well."

They reached the back wall of the hangar and entered a large cargo elevator. Vance pressed two buttons labeled THE BUNKER and ACCOMMODATION.

"I know you're tired, bud, but once you get some rest we need to brief you on something."

"Another mission already?"

"Nothing serious. It's a counterintel job. There's a journalist snooping around; she's been making inquiries about things a little too close for comfort."

"How much does she know?"

"Chua will give you the details. She lives in New York. You can take Saneh, make a holiday out of it, maybe head back to Sydney once the job's done."

"I don't think Saneh and I will be holidaying anytime soon."

Vance slapped him on the shoulder. "Yeah, I picked up that vibe. What can I say? Women are fickle, brother."

"What's Mirza up to?"

"He gets back from Myanmar in a few days. He can meet you in New York if you want."

The elevator stopped and the doors opened at the Bunker level. Vance stepped out. "Briefing at eighteen hundred, OK?"

"Got it." The doors closed and Bishop let out a long sigh. Maybe Vance was right; a trip to New York would probably do him some good. He could get out of Saneh's hair for a little while and just hang out with Mirza, maybe catch a Yankees game. After this last sojourn in Japan, keeping tabs on a journalist couldn't be that hard.

The elevator opened and Bishop walked out to the foyer and turned into the corridor that led to their rooms. Two doors down he stopped. The plastic clip that held the nameplate of the room's owner was empty: Someone had removed Kurtz's name.

He remembered the last time a tag had been removed, when his close friend and mentor had been killed. Bishop swallowed, pushing the ball of emotion deep inside, and headed to his own room. He opened the door and dumped his bag in the corner. There was a bottle of whiskey on a desk. He sloshed a healthy slug of it into a glass and dropped onto his sofa.

He drank in silence, staring at the bare wall in front of him. All he could think of were the final moments of Karla's life. He played it over and over in his mind, looking for a way out, a different option, a different outcome. No matter how many times he played it, the same choice had to be made, Saneh or Karla. He downed the last of the scotch, glanced at his watch, and made for the door. He would get down to the indoor shooting facility and put some rounds downrange—that always helped clear his head. Then he'd head up for the mission briefing and get ready to fly to New York. As long as he kept moving, the ghosts of the past would never be able to keep up.